Praise
Wil

"Endlessly entertain...
—*Publishers Weekly*

"Wildly entertaining and comical from the start… The love scenes are hot and sexy, and the chemistry sizzles!"
—*RT Book Reviews*

"Robin Kaye's books are vacations for the soul. Indulge yourself."
—Maureen Child, *USA Today* bestselling author of *To Kiss a King*

"Fast paced and laugh-out-loud funny. Robin Kaye brilliantly uses each of her characters to create a portrait of genuine relationships."
—*Night Owl Romance*

"Riveting and wickedly funny…kept me laughing from beginning to end."
—*Bitten by Love Book Reviews*

"Delightfully fun, witty romance."
—*Booklist*

"Completely satisfying… Robin Kaye creates a delightful read that sticks to the reader far past the last page."
—*Coffee Time Romance*

Also by Robin Kaye

Romeo, Romeo

Too Hot to Handle

Breakfast in Bed

Yours for the Taking

Wild Thing

Call Me Wild

A Little on the Wild Side

WITHDRAWN

ROBIN KAYE

sourcebooks
casablanca

Published by Sourcebooks Casablanca, an imprint of Sourcebooks, Inc.
P.O. Box 4410, Naperville, Illinois 60567-4410
(630) 961-3900
Fax: (630) 961-2168
www.sourcebooks.com

Printed and bound in Canada.
MBP 10 9 8 7 6 5 4 3 2 1

A friend is someone who knows the song in your heart and can sing it back to you when you have forgotten the words.

—Unknown

To Ginger Francis, one of the strongest, most loving, and funniest people I know. Since day one, your presence in my life has been a blessing and a blast. For us, singing, however out of tune, is a requirement; dancing on tabletops is optional.

Chapter 1

BIANCA FERRARI GULPED AIR THROUGH HER MOUTH, trying to stop the rise of bile. She'd been in a lot of uncomfortable positions in her lifetime. As an ex-model, she'd been photographed from every angle known to man, except this one—until now.

She looked up from being violently ill and watched herself on the Jumbotron in Times Square—her long blonde hair in one hand, the other holding the edge of an overfilled garbage can.

Her humiliation was now complete.

Another wave of nausea assaulted her, and she heaved into the can. How the mighty have fallen.

James Ness, her only true friend, gently rubbed her back through her cape. "I don't think pregnancy agrees with you. The only time I've seen you glow was when you were green."

A bottle of Evian and a crisp white handkerchief appeared in her line of sight. Bianca grabbed both, straightened slowly, and pulled the collar of her sweater away from her throat—the slightest pressure was enough to get her gag reflex going. She washed out her mouth and was afraid to drink, fearing it might start the whole puking thing all over again. "It's the smell of chestnuts roasting, pretzels, hot dogs—you name it—and the scent makes me yak."

"So, I take it you won't be cooking the turkey or the pumpkin pie."

"You're right. The only things I've been able to keep down are baked potatoes with sour cream, mushrooms, and cheddar cheese, and Five Guys cheeseburgers—go figure."

"What did the doctor say?"

"The guy in Paris? Not much, other than 'you're pregnant' in broken English. He gave me something to help the morning, noon, and night sickness."

The silver threads in James's dark hair caught the midday light. The glacial blue eyes that had him gracing the covers of full-page Ralph Lauren and Calvin Klein ads during his younger days looked her up and down. "It's not working."

"It did help some, but I ran out. Unfortunately, it's not available in the U.S. Damn FDA. If I wasn't so busy, I'd be on the first plane to Paris."

James took her arm. They crossed the street, and he gave the naked cowboy a once-over.

Bianca rolled her eyes. "He's not even hot, James. I thought you had better taste in men."

"I'm just wondering what the guitar is hiding."

"Probably a roll of quarters or a sweat sock."

The corner of James's lip quirked up, but he didn't smile. "Beggars can't be choosers, my dear. Not everybody can snap their fingers and have a hot man at their beck and call."

"Which is how I ended up puking in the middle of the crossroads of America." She slid her hand over her still flat stomach. "Not that I'm complaining." The sideways glance James shot her made her laugh. "Okay, I'm not complaining much. I'm happy about the baby, but it couldn't have come at a worse time.

It's fashion season, and I feel as if I have a terminal case of the flu."

"It's not terminal, it can't last more than nine months. Have you shared the good news yet with His Honor?"

"Hell, no."

James stopped, and since she had her hand tucked into his arm, she was forced to stop too. He faced her and gave her an I'm-disappointed-in-you look. "What are you waiting for?"

"Hell to freeze over." She tugged on his arm to get him moving. "Come on, James. Trapper was fun and everything, but it was a fling."

"Really? Was he aware of that?"

"Of course he was."

James scooted them by the guys handing out flyers for cheap Broadway tickets. "I don't know of any other man who would fly across the country for a fling, not to mention dropping everything to fly to London for a booty call—not even a booty as nice as yours. A few more months, and you can kiss that skinny ass of yours good-bye—just sayin'."

"For your information, I'm actually losing weight."

James put his arm around her shoulder. "That's not going to last either."

Bianca chose to ignore him, and any thought of her increasing waistline, stretch marks, and spreading hips. "So, Trapper likes to travel." If only to see the inside of her hotel room. "Besides, he had his grandfather's jet at his disposal when he came to New York."

"Bianca, my dear, wake up and smell the coffee—"

She covered her mouth with her hand and swallowed the flood of saliva—a prelude to illness. "Oh please, don't mention the smell of coffee."

"No man likes to travel that much. Give me a break. I saw the way he looked at you. It wasn't merely a fling for the good judge."

"Trapper's the seventy-two-hour man, remember?"

"He can last for seventy-two hours?" James's eyes widened and glittered like a window display at Tiffany's.

The answer to that question was yes, but she'd sooner die than admit it. She was pretty sure Trapper could beat the seventy-two-hour limit, but that wasn't any of James's business. "He said he can't maintain a relationship for over seventy-two hours because he finds it impossible to be nice that long. Apparently, after three days, his inner asshole appears. Although the first time I met him, I saw him in all his ass-holi-ness glory—it didn't even take seventy-two seconds. I don't want to be tied to a man like Trapper—well, not longer than a few days."

James held the door of the office building open. "And yet you ended up doing the nasty for several seventy-two-hour stints."

"Once we came to an understanding, he was quite…" Perfect, edible, smart, funny, insatiable, oddly sweet, thoughtful, wonderful, did she mention incredible? "Satisfying."

"What kind of understanding was that?"

Bianca was so done with this conversation. She smashed her finger on the elevator button repeatedly. "It was a no-strings fling."

"You actually had the conversation?"

She looked into James's eyes and nodded. She must have, though she couldn't recite it word-for-word. It must have come up sometime in between all that earth-shaking, orgasm-inducing, mind-splintering sex. She was almost sure of it.

-~~~-

Trapper Kincaid sat at the bar in Humpin' Hannah's, directly beneath the hanging wagon wheel draped with Christmas lights, and wondered if the purple bra dangling from the cowboy boot was a new addition. He emptied the pitcher of beer into his not-so-iced mug, checked to see where his little sister Karma, the bartender, was, and thanked God she worked the other side of the bar. The last thing he needed was for her to catch him checking out the Facebook page of the owner of Action Models, Bianca Ferrari.

Shit. He stared at his iPhone. Bianca's page was filled with the same Happy Holidays, Merry Christmas, blah, blah, blah. No real information. Nothing to tell him where she was, nothing to tell him that she was okay, not a fucking clue as to what the hell happened.

He clicked on Bianca's profile picture—one that had been taken when they were together in Stanley, Idaho, last summer. The first time he laid eyes on her had planted itself in his memory bank for eternity. She'd stepped out of a limo at one thirty in the morning in the middle of the Sawtooth National Recreation Area. He'd been on the porch of his cabin and held his breath as the pointed toe of one seriously sexy woman's boot hit the hard-packed ground. The boot went to mid-thigh and had a heel that seemed as high and thin as the air over Mount Borah. Long, blonde hair hung past her shoulders, playing peekaboo with a rack that was worthy of a limerick—one he'd been working on ever since. The rest of her body moved her right into goddess territory. The woman was breathtakingly alluring and eerily familiar. He'd seen her before—hundreds, if not thousands, of times—on ads, commercials, and if he wasn't mistaken, the cover of the *Sports Illustrated Swimsuit* issue ten or twelve years before.

Saying Bianca Ferrari was beautiful was like saying the surface of the sun was a little warm. He had been sucked into her atmosphere and scorched.

In less than eighteen hours, he'd watched, wanted, pitied, paddled, and propositioned her. In less than a week, he'd kissed, nibbled, and licked every square inch of her. In less than a month, her body had been branded on his brain like a 1940s pinup enshrined in a mechanic's shop. In less than two months, they'd had multiple seventy-two-hour flings—something unheard of in his past—in three time zones—New York, London, and Milan. In less than three months, he found himself sitting at home, alone, waiting for the phone to ring, and staring at her Facebook page, wondering what had gone wrong.

Except for tonight.

Tonight he waited for his brothers to have a preholiday family meeting. He wished they would hurry the hell up so he could get back to waiting and wondering in the privacy of his own home.

Hunter slid onto the stool beside his. "What's going on with you, Trap? You look worn out and strung tighter than a country singer's Wranglers."

"Nothing. I'm just working too hard—a murder case. You know how it is."

"We have about one murder a year here in Boise,

and you always seem to be the one to try them. Is it a bad one?"

"Aren't they all? The DA is going for first degree. Death penalty cases are always the worst." He was just glad that his family members weren't fans of Court TV. He'd okayed cameras in his courtroom for the news, since there was a lot of public interest in the case. He never thought Court TV would pick it up. If his siblings found out he was turning into a star judge, he'd never live it down. Trapper finished his beer and watched his brother over the rim of his glass. Hunter had the Kincaid look—if you added irritatingly, irrationally, terminally happy to the mix. He'd been that way since he'd married Toni. The same weekend Trapper and Bianca had hooked up for the first of their seventy-two-hour flings. He'd counted wrong. They'd had flings in four time zones, not three. Damn, he had to get a grip. He scrubbed his hand over his week-old beard. He'd never been a fan of barbers or shaving, so he needed both. Most of all, he needed to hear from Bianca.

Hunter waved a hand at Karma, and a minute later, a full mug of IPA slid the length of the bar, stopping before it hit Hunter's hand. "At least you have your annual between Christmas and New Year's fling to look forward to. So, who is the lucky lady, and where are you going?"

Trapper tipped his cowboy hat low over his eyes. "I'm not this year. I'm working through the thirty-first. I'll be off after the New Year though."

"And?"

"And who I'm with and where I decide to go is none of your damn business. You've been hanging around your wife too much—you're starting to sound like a gossipy woman."

Ever since Hunter and Fisher had married the loves of their lives, they suffered from the same disease most couples do—the everyone-should-be-happily-married-like-us syndrome. In Trapper's experience, that lasted until the relationship started going south.

Trapper caught a glimpse of Fisher walking in with their quasi cousin Ben Walsh.

They waved to Karma, motioning for pitchers, before joining Hunter and him at the end of the bar.

Ben checked his watch. "We have about forty-five minutes until the women join us. If you want to get this meeting going, we better head upstairs."

Karma set two pitchers of beer in front of them and pulled her apron off. "I'm ready."

All heads turned toward her.

Fisher stuffed his hands in his pockets. "I thought it would just be us guys."

Trapper had to give the boy props, taking one for the team and all, but he should have known better than to go up against Karma. It was a good thing he was an orthopedist. The bones he might have to set could be his own.

None of them had ever gone up against Karma and come out unscathed. And being scathed by Karma was a freakin' nightmare. He should know—she'd been practicing her skills on him since the day she was born. At least he was smart enough to be afraid of her. Very afraid.

Ben laughed. "Right, Karma. Like we want you involved."

Obviously, Trapper was the brains of the family. He sat back making sure he was well out of Karma's reach as her eyes got that freaky green glow of fury. Damn, this would get ugly if he didn't put a stop to it.

"If you four don't cut the crap right now, I'll call the police and have the lot of you thrown in jail. In case you aren't aware, I have the chief of police on speed dial."

Karma slid under the pass-through and rounded the bar, green eyes glaring, body tense, and itchin' for a fight.

Karma put one hand on her hip. Trapper was sure she was keeping her other arm free to punch with. Damn. This was a disaster in the making. Karma stepped back and speared Hunter, Fisher, and Ben with her psycho, green-eyed glare. "The three of you owe everything to me, and now you want to keep me out of the loop? There's one thing you losers don't understand. Boys, I *am* the loop."

Trapper couldn't help it. He rocked back on the heels of his cowboy boots and laughed.

Karma elbowed him in the stomach, almost knocking the wind out of him.

"Hey? What the hell did I do to deserve that?"

"You're my big brother. You should have stuck up for me."

"They're your big brothers too. And I even offered to call the cops. If I had stuck up for you, you would have been pissed at me for fighting your battles. I learned my lesson after trying to defend your honor when Brian Wayne copped an unwanted feel. If I remember correctly, you sent him to the hospital for a few days, and I ended up in the emergency room getting stitches."

"That wasn't my fault."

"You're the one who cut my eye open. I still have the scar."

Karma turned red when he pointed to it.

Fisher checked his watch. "Okay. If we're doing this, we'd better do it now. I don't know how much longer Gina and Toni will be able to keep Jessie in that spa. She thought their plans were tantamount to Chinese water torture."

Karma didn't bother hiding her shiver. "Jessie's right about that. Why do you think I'm working?" Karma grabbed the pitchers. "Let's get this meeting over with."

———

Karma carried pitchers of beer past the nine-foot stuffed black bear dressed in Boise State garb and climbed the circular metal stairs to the second floor. She gazed at the area with pride. She'd worked damn hard to make Humpin' Hannah's the best bar in Boise, and in her opinion, she'd succeeded.

She passed the pool tables, all of which were in use, and made sure all the signs for beer and liquor were lit and the framed Boise State jerseys hanging from the exposed brick were straight. Since the bar was downstairs and cocktail servers worked the second floor, she didn't get up there much. She led the crew to a tall table in the back.

The guys set down their mugs and grabbed a few more bar stools.

Karma poured the beer and took a seat, looking at each of her brothers and cousin. "So, what do we know about Angel Anderson?"

Fisher pulled up a stool, and then slid it away from her—the ninny. "He's a pitcher on the Jersey Jackals, and there's been some talk about moving him to the big leagues. He lives on the North Shore of Long Island—which, I'm told, is a really nice area. I think his family is rich—Grampa Joe rich. Other than that, we don't know much."

Of course, what was she thinking? She couldn't expect boys to do a woman's job. "One of us should meet him and feel him out. Since the adoption was private, we don't even know if he is Gina's long-lost brother. And if he is, we don't know if he's aware of the adoption. The situation has to be handled with delicacy." She sat back and smiled, knowing she was the perfect person to do just that. After all, she was a woman. Women were delicate creatures—okay, maybe not her—but hey, she understood more about delicacy than any of the four stooges ever would. Besides, she'd seen his picture. She wouldn't mind working on him and taking a few DNA samples of her own. Especially since her overprotective brothers would be twenty-eight hundred miles away.

Trapper looked up from under his low-set cowboy hat. "I'll do it."

Crap. She hadn't expected that. "You?"

"Yes, me. I have a few weeks off after this trial. I'll fly to New York after the New Year and handle it."

Ben shook his head. "Why don't I handle it? After all, he could be my brother-in-law."

"That's why. You're too close to the situation. I'm a disinterested party, not to mention a lawyer in the state of New York. I'm still licensed to practice there. It will work to our advantage, and Angel Anderson will have no way to connect us."

Karma really hated it when her über-intelligent

brother had a point. He effectively took all the wind out of poor Ben's sails.

Ben nodded. "Are you staying with me and Gina? We have plenty of room." And they lived right in Brooklyn, so it made sense.

"No. If Angel's family is the one who tried to scare Hunter off the scent when he was snooping around, they know where you live. I can't be anywhere near your place. I'll just get a hotel room or something."

The "or something" sent Karma's Spidey sense tingling up and down her spine. Trapper had another reason he wanted to be in New York, and she had a feeling it had nothing to do with that hot baseball player who might be Gina's brother, and everything to do with the nasty-ass mood he'd been in for a few months. Never one to beat around the proverbial bush, she tossed it right on the table. "Good, now that we have the whole Angel Anderson issue covered, let's talk about the weird mood you've been in, Trapper. What's crawled up your boxers and died?"

Hunter winked at her. "Yeah, you've been in a shit mood ever since one of your infamous flings had a last-minute cancellation."

Fisher joined in on the pileup. "You stomped around looking worried for a week after that, then you went from worried to pissed to…I don't know what. If it had been anyone other than you, I'd swear you were heartbroken."

Ben had the audacity to laugh. "Heartbroken? Not Trapper. No, Trap never gets involved with women. Sure, he likes them. And they certainly like him—a lot. But he hasn't had a relationship that lasted over seventy-two hours since he returned from his stint as a DA in New York."

Trapper set his mug down with a thunk. "You do realize I'm sitting right here and can kick all your asses into next week, don't you?"

Karma shot him a grin. "You can't kick my ass—Mom would kill you. But now that you mention it, Ben, Trapper hasn't had a real relationship since he became a judge. He's so well known for his seventy-two-hour flings, I've even heard them regaled at the bar. More than one of his women weren't happy with the 'no repeat performance' rule."

She looked around to make sure she still had the attention of the table. "Sure, he claims it's because he can't be nice for longer than seventy-two hours at a shot before he becomes an ass. I'll have to agree with him there. But a few months ago, something changed. Hell, he hasn't even looked at any women since. Curiouser and curiouser."

Trapper stood and speared each of them with his glare. He had that whole angry, strong, bad boy Judge Dredd thing going along with the I-can-have-you-hauled-in-with-one-phone-call look. It was scary and effective. "That's enough. I'm outta here."

His voice was low, menacing, and the vacant, haunted expression covering his face sent her Spidey sense skittering in a way that had her worried. Damn, her big brother was hurting, and she had no idea who had his balls in a noose.

Ben stood too, and stepped in front of Trapper, boxing him in the corner. "Hey, Trap, we're just concerned. You have to admit you've been off your game lately. What's going on?"

"Nothing that I care to talk about. Just leave it alone. Hell, leave *me* alone. Do I make myself clear?"

The guys exchanged looks and nodded.

Of course, no one looked at her. She'd be damned if she'd let him off with a flimsy little threat. Men could be such weenies. If Trapper was hurting, she sure as shit wouldn't allow it to continue. She didn't know what she'd do, but she'd figure it out. She had a new mission, and there was nothing her brothers could hide from her—at least, not for long.

Chapter 2

BIANCA DRAGGED HERSELF AND HER SUITCASE INTO her penthouse apartment and collapsed on the couch. She'd flown from Cincinnati to New York, via what seemed like the South Pole. After spending the holidays with her grandmother and putting on her I'm pregnant, happy, and healthy front for almost an entire week, she was exhausted.

She'd considered not making the trip, but since her grandmother was the only family she acknowledged, she couldn't very well let her spend Christmas alone. Nan had been the only one to stand by her when she was fifteen and filed for emancipation from her parents—the thieves that they were. They'd stolen all the money she'd made working as a full-time model from the time she was a baby, which numbered in the millions. Nan had supported her throughout her life. Even though Bianca bought her grandmother a home in the nicest retirement center in Ohio, she still needed to make sure her grandmother was being taken care of.

Bianca's stomach growled. She should get up and eat something, but she was too tired to walk to the kitchen—not that she had anything in the fridge anyway. She wished Five Guys delivered. Maybe she could bribe her doorman into making a burger run for her.

Her cell phone rang, and she answered without looking. "Bianca?"

Her heart leaped then sank, her throat closed, and her nipples perked up all in a split second. Oh, God. It was Trapper. And just the sound of his voice was enough to set her off. Damn pregnancy hormones. She didn't know if she wanted to laugh, cry, or come. Maybe all three.

She hit the end button and turned off her phone. How could she have been that stupid? Her home phone rang. She hadn't given Trapper the number. She never gave her home number out. She could count on one hand the people who had it. But, then, she'd brought him home—that had been a first. It had also been a mistake. She still wasn't sure why she'd done it. It could have been that he'd wanted to see her home. Or that she, just for a moment, wanted to have it all—a normal relationship with a normal man— albeit an extraordinarily hot, intelligent, and amazing man. Maybe normal didn't quite fit the bill. But then, it could have been that she'd been horny. She and Trapper in the same state were sexually combustible. In the same room, they were thermonuclear. Now, not only was she blessed with his child, she was blessed with memories of Trapper Kincaid everywhere she looked. They'd made love in this very spot. Heck, they'd made love everywhere she could have imagined, and a few she hadn't.

The phone continued to ring. She supposed Trapper could have gotten the number—after all, he had connections. Just in case, she didn't answer. She waited the ten rings for it to go to voice mail and closed her eyes. She was so tired.

—⁓—

Bianca awoke, disoriented to the sound of banging on the door. She wanted to roll over and pull the pillow over her head to drown out the sound, but she didn't have a pillow. She opened her eyes to find she was on her couch in her New York penthouse.

"Bianca. Open the door, or so help me, I'm gonna break it down."

James's voice sliced through the fuzziness in her brain. "I'm coming. Keep your pants on." Even to her ears, her voice sounded thin and reedy. She was a mess.

She rolled off the couch, got her balance, and dragged herself across the ocean of white carpet to the door. She opened it and, without even a hello, turned around and slogged back to the couch.

James's strong arm came around her. "Why didn't you answer the phone?"

"I answered my cell without looking, and it was Trapper. I hung up on him, and the house phone rang. I thought it might be him again, so I ignored it." She let out a breath. "I just want to sleep through the rest of the pregnancy and wake up after the baby is born. Bears do it. Why can't I?"

"I've heard you called a lot of names that start with the letter *B*, but never a bear. Sorry, sweetheart."

"Don't call me that. Trapper always called me sweetheart."

"I don't know why you won't talk to the man. If he's calling you after all this time, it's because it was a whole lot more than a fling to him." He helped her back to the couch.

"It's too late. He'll hate me now." Bianca rolled onto her side, and James pulled a throw her grandmother had made over her. She closed her eyes and had almost made it to oblivion when she was shaken awake.

"When was the last time you ate or drank something?"

"Breakfast." She didn't bother telling him she tossed it all in the airport bathroom before she boarded the first plane. "I sipped ginger ale through the entire flight, and the next."

"Damn. I have to find you something to eat. I'm thinking soup." He pulled his phone off his belt and speed dialed. "I need two quarts of wonton soup, white rice, chicken and vegetables with extra chicken. You'll get a twenty-dollar tip if you can have it here in fifteen minutes." He rattled off her address and left her on the couch to sleep.

A moment later, he pulled her to a sitting position and shoved a tall glass of water into her hand. "Drink this. Now."

Her hands shook, and she took a tentative sip. It stayed down—so far, so good. "James, what are you doing here?"

"Taking care of you since you refuse to do it yourself. What did the doctor say when you saw him?"

Bianca avoided looking at him and gave her belly a rub instead. It was getting bigger by the day. "Umm…"

James closed his eyes. "You missed another appointment?"

"I was in a meeting that ran late. I had to cancel."

"Did you reschedule it?"

"Not yet. I've been busy."

"You've been busy?" It wasn't often that James got mad. What he lacked in frequency, he more than made up for with ferocity. He was downright scary. "I've had it with you, Bianca. I'm personally calling your doctor in the morning, and I'll carry you there, if need be. Do you understand me?"

"Yes." She was sucking at this whole motherhood thing already, and she hadn't even started yet. "But, James, I'm fine. I'm just tired. That's normal."

"Sweetheart, you look like shit. I've seen pregnant women. I have three sisters and nine nieces and nephews, remember? And I've never seen them look as bad as you—not even after twenty hours of labor. Bianca, you're scaring me."

The intercom buzzed, and James took care of it while she drifted in and out of sleep.

"Come on, we're putting you to bed, and then you're going to eat some soup." He practically carried her to her bedroom, stripped her out of her clothes, and then cursed viciously.

"What?"

He looked at her in nothing but a bra and bikini panties—nothing he hadn't seen before. "I had no idea you'd lost that much weight. You're skin, bones, and belly. You would make Ethiopian refugees look obese. How could you have let this happen?"

"Let this happen? Believe me, I didn't plan to puke on a daily basis. Besides, I don't look that bad. Do I?"

He didn't answer, but he looked a little pale when he pulled a T-shirt that Trapper had left over her head. Of course, it would have to be Trapper's. It still smelled like him, and amazingly enough, the scent didn't make her want to toss her cookies. This was worse—much worse. It made her miss him, something she couldn't allow. No, she'd never let herself miss anyone, not her parents, not friends, not Max, and definitely not Trapper.

"Lie down, and I'll bring you something to eat."

She felt herself lowered onto the bed. He piled pillows behind her back and pulled the covers up. Her eyes closed of their own accord, and she felt a kiss on her forehead. "Try to stay awake for a few more minutes. I'll be right back."

James force-fed her chicken, rice, and broth and then let her sleep, waking her every few hours to make her sip orange juice cut with ginger ale and nibble on a few crackers—somehow, it all stayed down.

The next day she awoke and looked at the clock. It was almost ten. Shit. She had to get to the office. She had contract meetings with the lawyers, an interview with a new model, and an overseas shoot to set up—she was busy. She rolled over and found James sleeping beside her. "James, wake up. We're late. You're going to have to take that model interview for me. I'll have to rearrange my morning as it is."

"We're not late. I canceled all your morning appointments—Joanie is rescheduling them." He stretched. "I was going to wake you in a few minutes anyway. Here." He stuffed a handful of crackers in her hand. "Eat these before you sit up." He held her down until she did as he said. A glass of juice was shoved at her. "Now drink this. Slowly."

"Can I at least sit up now?"

"I don't know." He shoved a few pillows behind her back until she could sip the juice.

"What the hell did you do to it?"

"I cut it with some water. Too much acid in your tummy isn't a good thing, but you need the folic acid for the baby."

"I do?"

"Haven't you read any of those pregnancy books I bought you?"

"I've looked at some of the pictures."

He eyed the tome she'd been working on for her doctoral program, looking for sources for her possible dissertation on the Magi: who they were and who they became over the many dynasties. "Light reading?"

"You know I like to take courses. This is one of the texts I'm going through."

He picked up the book that must weigh ten pounds and flipped through it. "It's in German?"

"Yes."

"I didn't know you were fluent."

"Language is important in Egyptology. I'm pretty fluent in German and French. And I'm passable in Italian. It helps in modeling too."

"I see. You have time to read this, but haven't had time to read *What to Expect When You're Expecting*?"

"Hey, I saw the movie. Doesn't that count?"

"No. It does not." He slid out of bed and pulled on a pair of jeans before coming around to her side. "Okay, let's get up slowly and see if we can keep you from puking this morning."

Chapter 3

TRAPPER SWEET-TALKED HIS WAY INTO BIANCA'S OFFICE with a bouquet of flowers and chocolate. He liked her receptionist, Terri. He'd talked to her several times when he and Bianca had been seeing each other, and it didn't sound as if she'd heard he was persona non grata lately. He hoped he wasn't getting Terri into trouble, but damn, he didn't know what the hell to do. Bianca's doorman refused his bribe the night before and wouldn't let him into the building without announcing him first. This was his only other option.

Terri had been easy. He just dropped his sister-in-law Toni's name, and she let him wait in Bianca's office. She even promised not to tip off Bianca and spoil his surprise. Then she told him she wished her boyfriend was half as romantic, gave him a wink, and unlocked Bianca's office door.

He stepped into her corner office, and the scent of Bianca hit him—he was hard in a matter of seconds. He digested the differences between her office and her apartment. Her office was cool, modern, sleek, and so unlike her home. He'd been shocked when Bianca invited him to her place, opened the door, and he saw the collection of comfortable antiques—not like something you'd see in a museum. No, it looked like something you'd see in your grandmother's house—a feather-stuffed sofa with an old quilt hanging over the back. Beautiful, yet comfortable pillows were scattered everywhere. Low lighting from torchieres gave the place a romantic glow. Rolled arms to drape a lover over, and sturdy oak tables in the kitchen and dining room, perfect for dinner or sex—one memorable evening, both—added to the reasons he'd fallen in love with the place.

Trapper took a seat behind Bianca's desk and pulled his cowboy hat low over his eyes to cut the glare from the cold, hard-recessed lighting. He put his feet up and settled for a long wait. Terri had told him Bianca had canceled her morning appointments and was expected before noon. He sat back with his e-reader and caught up on law journals, while trying to keep his dick at half-mast.

At eleven thirty the door swooshed open. Bianca walked in, her black cape floating around her. Her hair was longer than he remembered, and she had big bags under her eyes that no amount of makeup could disguise. She looked beautiful, way too thin, and ill.

She still hadn't noticed him. She spun around, tossed her briefcase on the leather sofa, and turned her back, tugging off her cape. She might have lost weight, but damn, she still had the finest ass he'd ever seen.

He put a smile on his face—the one he was told made women swoon. He figured he needed all the help he could get. He had a strong feeling she wouldn't be happy being ambushed, but what choice did she give him?

He walked around her desk, leaned against it, watched, and waited for her to hang her cape—a difficult task since the darn thing had no sleeves.

She turned. The first thing he noticed was that her

breasts were larger, but maybe they just looked that way since she'd lost quite a bit of weight.

His gaze headed south and made an unplanned stop at her waistline. His smile froze. His jaw clenched. Blood rushed through his ears, making his temples throb. Every muscle in his body tensed.

Bianca—his Bianca—was pregnant? Definitely pregnant—past the point where a man would wonder. Not ready-to-pop pregnant, but just-about-time-for-maternity-clothes pregnant. He wasn't sure how pregnant that was, but shit, he was sure the baby she carried was his. He knew it the second she spotted him grinning like the fool he was and flashed him a guilty look. That was a nanosecond before what little color she'd had drained from the beautiful face that haunted his every waking moment and his dreams, leaving her looking like a corpse three weeks past her expiration date.

Bianca blinked, and her wide, green eyes rolled back in her head.

Oh shit. He raced for her.

Her long legs buckled, and he caught her just before she hit the floor.

His heart didn't beat again until he felt her shallow breaths against his neck. He carried her to the couch and laid her down, brushing the baby-fine hair off her face. He sat beside her, waiting for her to wake up.

Trapper had heard pregnant women sometimes fainted, but he didn't think they passed out for this long. It seemed like an eternity. He checked his watch. It had been less than a minute. He took a deep breath, felt her pulse strong and steady on her neck, and tried to keep the anger, terror, and helplessness out of his voice. "Come on, sweetheart. Time to wake up."

Nothing.

Panic scratched at his insides like a feral cat trying to escape a trap.

She didn't move.

Her lips were pale. The blue veins stood out in her forehead.

She looked like death.

He ran to the door and slammed it open. "I need some help here!"

In three strides, he returned to Bianca's side, took her cold hand, warming it between his. "Bianca, sweetheart, please, just open your eyes."

Terri ran in. She took one look at Bianca and stepped back.

"She passed out."

"I'll get James." She ran from the room, screaming James's name.

It seemed like forever until James ran in. "What happened?"

"I was waiting for Bianca when she arrived. She took one look at me and took a nosedive. I caught her just before she hit the floor."

"She pukes all the time, but she's never passed out that I know of." He looked as panicked as Trapper felt. He turned to Terri. "Call 9-1-1." When she didn't move, he screamed. "Now!"

The poor girl burst into tears and grabbed Bianca's phone.

Trapper placed Bianca's hand on her belly, on top of the other resting there protectively. He stared in wonder. They were having a baby. He was going to be a father.

He expected the fierce protectiveness, but he hadn't expected the fear or the joy or the awesome weight of responsibility that settled on his chest. But most of all, he hadn't expected the exhilarating feeling of knowing that together they had created a child. A child he loved. A child he would give his life for. A child who needed him.

His gaze rounded on James. He wanted to pick the man up and toss him out of the floor to ceiling window for allowing Bianca to get in this bad a shape. "What the hell happened to her?" His voice was low, threatening, and a hell of a lot calmer than he felt.

Terri's eyes went wide, and she skittered away.

James stood his ground like a man preparing for a shoot-out. He arched a scholarly brow. "Nothing that won't be remedied in five months. Where the hell have you been? Since I've handled the first four months, you get her for the finale. The woman is a full-time job. I recommend you clear your schedule." He handed Trapper a copy of *What to Expect When You're Expecting*. "Here, you might want to read this. So far, Bianca's only looked at the pictures."

Bianca floated through space feeling weightless, like she was in a weird dream. She heard voices far away, but she couldn't respond. She told her eyes to open, but they wouldn't. She tried to move her hand, but she couldn't. It was as if a lead blanket weighed her down.

Trapper's deep voice cut through the fog in her head. "Bianca, sweetheart, just open your eyes."

His voice sent a shiver through her. She tried. She really did. It was as if she were dreaming about him again. But this time she couldn't see him, and she really wanted to.

The ringing in her ears decreased, and she tried again. Okay, eyes open. They did, and there was Trapper looking angry, concerned, and something else. He always had the most spectacular face. He was really beautiful, but if you told him that, he'd be pissed. His too-long-for-the-Polo-set hair sticking out of his ever-present cowboy hat and his thirty-five-o'clock shadow only made her want him more. Good thing this was a dream. If he were here, she'd be so screwed.

"Welcome back, sweetheart." Even his beard couldn't hide the dimple that appeared only when he smiled at her.

She wanted to get up and throw her arms around him. Maybe take off that shirt of his, and then his pants. Hell, she tried to blink to see if she could fast-forward this whole dream sequence. It wasn't working. "I need to get up."

"Take it slow."

His hands were warm against her chilled body as he helped her. The scent of him assailed her. She'd always loved the way he smelled. She'd missed that.

When she looked past him, she spotted James. What would James be doing in one of her X-rated Trapper dreams? Then she realized she was in her office, on the couch, and like a flash, everything became clear. She'd come into work. She'd turned, and Trapper was there. He'd seen her, and then it was as if someone cut the tape.

Trapper was here.

Trapper knew.

This wasn't a dream.

"Oh God, I'm gonna be sick." She grabbed Trapper's hat and threw up.

Everything.

She'd die of embarrassment if he didn't kill her first.

She breathed through her mouth, trying to stop the gagging, and shoved the hat into his hands.

"Damn. That was a new Stetson."

James handed her a water.

"Thanks."

Trapper looked around, probably for a place to dump the hat.

She took a sip of water and held up one shaky finger, which, unfortunately, was like the rest of her shaky body.

Trapper shot her a questioning look.

She pulled the hat back toward her and spit the water out. No way she could drink anything—at least not yet. "Okay, now I'm good. Thanks."

His gaze flew from his hat to her. "Don't mention it. Ever. Please." Trapper tried to hand the hat to James and got a smile in return.

"Welcome to my world." James slid the trash can toward Trapper.

Trapper shook his head and dumped his hat. Funny, the barfing didn't seem to bother him. Barfing in his hat though, bothered him a lot. It was a shame. It had been a nice hat.

"Sorry. It was the only thing handy."

There was a commotion outside, and the next thing she knew two paramedics came in, followed by a stretcher.

"Oh, no."

Trapper stood and gave the paramedics a blow-by-blow of what had happened. Then James rang in, giving them the rest of the gory details. Shit.

"You are not going to—"

A blood pressure cuff was wrapped around her arm. The other paramedic knelt beside her and slid something over her forehead before rolling up her sleeve. "What are you doing?"

"Starting an IV. You're dehydrated."

"No, I'm not. I've had more to drink in the last twelve hours than I've had in the last twelve days."

"Sorry, ma'am. You're still dehydrated. But not for long." She shot Bianca a smile and slid a needle into her arm.

Before Bianca knew it, they had her strapped to a gurney and were wheeling her down to the elevator. "James, I'll never forgive you for this."

"I told you I'd make you see a doctor if I had to carry you there myself. This is a lot easier on my back."

"Very funny. Terri, cancel my afternoon appointments. If anything comes up, just call my cell. I'll be in later to pick up any paperwork."

"No, you won't." Trapper's deep voice cut through the chaos. "Terri, call James if there's anything you can't handle. We're not sure when Bianca will be back."

Bianca shot Trapper what she thought of as her Dirty Harriet glare.

He answered it with a pat on the shoulder.

"Terri, if you listen to him, you're fired."

"No, she's not." James interrupted. "Now lie still and behave, Bianca, or so help me, I'll come to the damn hospital instead of running your company. Is that what you want?"

"Yes. No. I don't know." She tried to run her hand through her hair but she was strapped down to the damn stretcher. "James, I don't want to go alone."

Trapper smiled down at her. "Oh, believe me. You won't be alone. Not from now on." That sounded way more ominous than comforting. Trapper was much nicer in her dreams.

Trapper walked through the hospital beside Bianca's stretcher and was stopped at the swinging door by a nurse.

"You wait here. Someone will talk to you once we've checked her out. How many weeks pregnant is she?"

He tried to remember what James had said. "I don't know, four or five months."

The nurse raised her eyebrows. "And you are?"

"Her fiancé."

"Uh-huh. Sure. Okay." The woman might as well have said, "Yeah, tell me another one."

"I'm the father of her baby." He tried to look tough, which was no small feat, while holding Bianca's suitcase-size purse. Damn, he missed his hat. He ran his hand through his hair. "Is she all right?"

"She's stable now. We'll know more once we're able to do an exam. Since you're her fiancé, why don't you go to the desk and take care of the paperwork?"

"Sure, okay." Paperwork. How in the hell was he supposed to do that? He didn't even know Bianca's date of birth.

The nurse must have seen the trepidation that was

quickly closing in on panic. "All the information you need should be in her wallet. Just go over to the desk and get started. Someone will be out to talk to you soon."

Trapper's definition of soon was vastly different from the nurse's. He was pacing and sweating and scared shit-less. He wiped his palms on his jeans and wished for the millionth time he had his hat. It gave him something to fool with. He felt naked without one. All he had was Bianca's purse.

He never realized how much you could learn about a woman by looking through her purse. And there were some things a guy shouldn't know. She kept a spare pair of panties and stockings in there. What were they for? She carried around condoms—nothing like closing the barn door after the bull was loose. But the most dis-turbing item was a well-worn black book full of men's names with some kind of star rating system. It was obvious she'd been keeping it since before PDAs were popular—several of the men had been through more than one wife since its inception. If the stars meant what he thought they did, she'd been with half of Hollywood, not to mention pro sports figures, and more than one Washington bigwig. The worst part was that his name hadn't even made the list. Shit.

His stomach burned, and he considered stealing a few of her Tums—not that she would miss them. She should take stock in the company. He'd found a half-dozen almost-empty wrappers and an industrial-sized bottle with only a handful left. Was she supposed to be taking this stuff while pregnant?

By the time the nurse reappeared, he had her purse

cleaned out and organized, and had eaten a handful of stomach stabilizers.

"We're getting ready to do a sonogram and thought you'd like to see your baby."

"Is Bianca okay?"

"She's underweight, her blood pressure is too high, and her attitude… Let's just say she'll be the talk of the ER for a while."

He could imagine. When Bianca wasn't happy, no one was happy. "She doesn't deal with fear well. She expresses it with anger."

"Will she be happy to see you or not?" The nurse turned and headed toward the doors of the inner sanctum.

Trapper followed closely behind, holding Bianca's purse in his sweaty hand. "I think she'll be happy, but she'll never admit it." He just hoped she didn't throw something at him.

She pointed to the curtained area. "She's in there. You're a brave man."

Trapper wanted to knock, but there was nothing to knock on, so he cleared his throat and stuck one hand through the partition in the curtains. No one screamed, so he slid through the opening.

Bianca lay with one hand gripping the bar on the side of the bed so tightly that her knuckles were as white as her face.

Shit, he should have brought her flowers or something. Hell, he'd do just about anything to erase the petrified look that covered her face. He slid into a smile and reached over to kiss her forehead. "Hey, beautiful, how are you feeling?" He pried her cold hand off the bar and was relieved when she gave his a squeeze.

She swallowed hard and blinked, staring at the ceiling tiles, as if she were trying to keep from crying.

Any anger he'd had evaporated. "It's going to be okay. You and the baby will be fine."

"How do you know?"

Her voice sounded paper thin—so thin, he could almost see through it. "Because I know you. You're strong and smart and determined. All you need to do is relax. That's the best thing for both of you. I'll take care of everything else."

"But you don't have to—"

Trapper looked at the nurse and the technician standing beside the bed. "Don't worry. We'll talk about it later. Right now, I think we're supposed to meet our baby."

He held her gaze while they adjusted her gown, exposing her belly.

The tech leaned over Bianca "This will be warm. It'll help us see the baby." She squirted a gel over Bianca's stomach. "This is the transducer. I'll just run it over your stomach, and you'll be able to see the baby on this screen." The screen facing the other direction. "But first, I have to take some measurements. It will only take a few moments, and then I'll turn the monitor so you can meet your little one."

Bianca nodded and held Trapper's hand in a death grip.

A second later, the transducer slid over Bianca's stomach, and then the tech's hand stilled. "Uh-oh."

Bianca's eyes went wide, and the pressure on his hand increased.

He grabbed the metal bar and held on. "What's wrong?"

The tech gave her head a tilt, and the nurse left. "Just give me a moment. We need to wait for the doctor."

Bullshit. Something was wrong. Suddenly, Trapper didn't feel so good.

A doctor rushed in and took one look at the screen. "Uh-oh."

Trapper didn't like the sound of two "uh-ohs" in under a minute when they were talking about his baby. "What's going on?"

The doctor took the transducer and slid it over to the side and shot Bianca and him a worried smile. "Congratulations. We're looking at two babies."

"What?" Bianca looked confused.

Trapper wasn't. "We're having twins?"

The doctor nodded and gave the transducer back to the tech. "That explains the extreme morning sickness. You have twice the hormones, twice the morning sickness, twice the exhaustion, twice the heartburn, and twice the love."

The tech looked up. "They're a little small for twenty-one weeks, but that's to be expected with twins. Let's see. That makes your due date May 16, but we're hoping you'll hold out until April 18—that's thirty-six weeks. Twins usually come early. Do you want to know the sexes?"

Trapper looked at Bianca. "It's up to you."

"Twins? Oh, God. Twins?"

The doctor chuckled. "Identical—they're sharing a placenta and holding hands." He turned the screen toward them.

Trapper had no problem picking out the heads. They looked big, and then he looked at the picture and squinted. Sure enough. They were holding hands. One was kicking his or her legs, but with the umbilical cord, he couldn't see much else. "They're beautiful, just like their mama."

He leaned down and kissed Bianca, who had tears dripping down her pale cheeks. He looked into those big, green, frightened eyes he'd missed so much. The eyes he'd dreamed of almost nightly. "You're amazing."

The tech cleared her throat. "Was that a yes or a no to the sex?"

Bianca tore her gaze from him and shrugged. "Can you tell?"

The woman smiled. "I can try. If not today, you might have better luck next time."

The doctor scanned Bianca's chart. "And there will be a next time—probably every office visit since you're high risk. After looking at your blood pressure, you're on bed rest for the next few weeks."

"I can't—"

He looked at her over the rim of his glasses. "You can, and you will. Get cleaned up, and I'll be back in a few minutes to talk to you both. Congratulations." The doctor left Bianca sputtering and staring at the screen.

The tech moved something and smiled. "If I had to place a bet, I'd say you have boys. But they're not cooperating, so don't go buy out the little boys section at Macy's on my say-so. You might get a more definitive answer with your next ultrasound. Be sure to drink a lot of fluids before your visit. It helps with the clarity." She took the wand away from Bianca's stomach, and the picture disappeared.

Trapper wanted to tell her to put it back. He wasn't finished watching his babies.

"I took pictures for their baby books. I think I got a few good shots of each of them." She handed Bianca several paper towels to wipe away the gel and handed the pictures to Trapper.

He looked at the pictures of his kids and couldn't keep the shit-eating grin off his face. He was a dad. Seeing the babies moving on the screen made it real in a way he'd never imagined. His boys. Or God, they could be girls. He didn't know what he'd do with girls. Girls like Bianca—beautiful, strong-willed, smart, or like Karma—all of the above mixed with just a little evil. He wasn't sure he could handle three women at once. Shit. He needed to sit down.

Chapter 4

BIANCA WIPED THE SLIMY GOOP OFF HER STOMACH, pulled the hospital gown down and the blanket up, and then girded her loins—or whatever the hell that had to be girded before looking at Trapper. He stared at the black-and-white snapshots, enthralled with the pictures of their babies.

Twins.

She was having twins.

She didn't think she'd ever be able to wrap her head around that one. Sure she'd seen them. They looked more like aliens than babies—but since she'd looked through a few baby books, the alien look wasn't a surprise. The twins thing was a complete and utter mind blower.

And there was Trapper staring at the pictures of their little aliens, wearing the biggest grin she'd ever seen on a man's face. His reaction was nothing like Max's. Max—her first lover—the man who wined and dined her, told her he loved her, and took her virginity when she was fourteen. No, Max had definitely looked pissed when she told him she thought she was pregnant. That was the only time she'd had visions of wedding dresses and happily ever afters.

Unfortunately, it was also the time Max saw fit to share the fact that he was already married with two children and that she had to have an abortion. With one fell swoop, he killed her idea of love and her position as the next Guess Girl. He'd conned her and used her just like her parents had. Her stomach soured with the memory—it was either that, or it was another bout of the never-ending-nausea-times-two of her new reality. But Trapper definitely wasn't Max.

Trapper looked tickled pink or possibly blue. Definitely not green. Of course, he wasn't the one puking every ten minutes and feeling as if he needed to sleep for an eternity. He wasn't the one who would get as big as a house and have to push not one but two bowling ball–sized humans through something his dick barely fit in. Why wouldn't he be pleased?

Having one baby had already turned into way more than she'd expected. She thought she could handle single parenthood. She knew enough to know having a baby on her own would be tough, but two? How would she ever be able to handle two—especially if they were anything like their father?

Contrary to popular belief, she had thought a lot about what it would be like having a child. She might not have gotten around to reading every baby book James had brought her, but it wasn't as if she was completely oblivious. She'd planned to keep the baby with her at the office. She'd even planned on building a little nursery in the office next door to hers. Having one child would have been pushing it—two seemed impossible. She'd have to hire full-time help. It wasn't as if she couldn't afford it, but she wanted to be the one to raise her child—make that children— not a paid employee.

"How are you doing, sweetheart?"

Why did he have to call her that and talk to her in that

sexy, bass baritone, do-me-baby voice of his? "Trapper, what are you doing here?"

"Here, as in standing in the emergency room at Lenox Hill Hospital? Or here, with you in New York?"

"What were you thinking just showing up at my office?"

"I came to see you to find out what the hell happened. But I think I've figured that one out myself." He ran his hand over her belly—a fatherly gesture that her body completely misconstrued. One touch from Trapper Kincaid, and even over four months pregnant, she was on fire. "I came to make sure you were okay. You're not. You weren't planning to tell me I was a father, were you?"

"No, I wasn't." She felt guilty as hell, but she'd thought long and hard about it and knew it was for the best. She'd never imagined he'd care enough to be bothered when she didn't return his calls, and she'd never suspected he'd come after her. No wonder she'd passed out when she saw him.

Trapper took a deep breath and looked as if he were wrestling with his temper. Only he could look sexier than ever when he was red with rage. It was a good color on him. "Why?"

"Because we had a fling. Because you didn't sign up for this." She shoved his hand aside and replaced his with both of hers. "Because I don't want you around out of some misguided sense of duty."

"Sweetheart, those are my children you're carrying. I signed up for that the second they were conceived, the same way you did."

"No, you didn't. It was my decision to have these babies. I didn't consult you."

"If you had, I would have told you that I want our

children with every fiber of my being. There's no way I'll have two children running around this earth and not be a part of their lives. Bianca, from this moment on, we're in this together."

"Oh no we're not. We're not doing anything together. Only one of us is having these babies—and as much as I'd love to assign that task to you, I can't. It's a one-person job. From the point of conception on, you have nothing to do with it."

He laughed. It wasn't a ha-ha-you're-so-funny laugh. It was a ha-ha-you're-a-fool-if-you-think-that's-going-to-work laugh. "Like hell it is. You're on bed rest for the next few weeks at least. You heard the doctor. And it's my job to make sure you get it."

"I'll hire someone."

"You can hire someone to take over for you at Action Models. I'll be the one taking care of you around the clock." He leaned over her, so close she saw the amber starbursts in his hazel eyes. "I'll make sure you get everything you need. And I do mean everything."

He was about to kiss her. She could see it. She could feel it. Hell, she could practically taste it. She fought the urge to wrap her arms around his neck and drag his mouth to hers.

His eyes dilated, his breath grew choppy and fanned her face. He moved closer, and then a throat cleared behind them.

Someone had seriously bad timing. It was as if they'd been sprayed with a cold garden hose.

Trapper gave her a we're-not-finished-with-this look, straightened, and stepped aside. The doctor came into view.

"Sorry to interrupt." The doctor smiled. "I don't believe I had a chance to introduce myself when we met earlier. I'm Dr. Schaeffer." He spoke to Trapper, which really ticked her off.

The two shook hands. "Trapper Kincaid."

"So, Ms. Ferrari—"

"Doctor, after all we've been through together in the last hour or so, I think you can call me by my first name."

"Very well. Bianca, how are you doing?"

"I thought I was doing fine until I found myself strapped to a stretcher. I have morning sickness. Morning sickness is typical, isn't it?"

"Not to the point where you're losing weight—which you are. And definitely not to the point of dehydration, which you were, until they put almost three liters of fluids in you." He looked over his notes. "At your age, Bianca, your pregnancy is high risk to begin with—"

"At my age? I just turned thirty-four. I'm hardly ready for the old folks home."

"Having twins amplifies the risk. Your blood pressure is very high, which means you will be spending the next three weeks on bed rest. You can get up to shower and go to the bathroom, but that's it."

She tried to sit up, but the damn buttons on the bed weren't cooperating. "That's ridiculous."

"That's an order. I'll see you in my office in one week." He gave Trapper an appraising look. "Bianca will be on a low sodium diet, no stress, and absolutely no work."

Trapper nodded. "Sex?"

She couldn't believe he would ask about sex. He had some nerve, not to mention the man was either delusional or would be severely disappointed. She had no intention of having sex ever again. He obviously hadn't noticed she looked like an emaciated whale. Who in their right mind would be attracted to her now? And how, exactly, would you do it? Not that she was even interested. Unfortunately, her hormones hadn't caught up with her brain.

The doctor patted him on the back. "It's a great stress reliever. Any other questions?"

"Can I take her home?"

"I'm keeping her here overnight. But if all goes well, which I believe it will, I'll release her tomorrow, provided she'll have around-the-clock care."

"She will."

"Good. I'll have the nurse bring over a meal plan that's easy to follow, along with her release papers, after I see her in the morning. She needs small frequent meals, nothing too heavy. Try to keep something in her stomach at all times. That will help with the morning sickness. Call or email if you have any questions."

"Great. Thanks, Doc."

Bianca had just about enough of the boys club. "Excuse me. Did you forget that I'm right here?"

Trapper shot her a smile, and that damn dimple winked at her. "How can we forget? We were talking about you."

"Right. You're talking about me, not to me."

Every muscle in Trapper's neck seemed to cord. "Would you rather stay in the hospital or go home?"

"Home."

"And I'm making that happen."

Her mouth slammed shut—she hated it when he was

logical and correct. But the last thing she wanted was to be trapped in her apartment with Trapper Kincaid. She was human after all, and he was too dangerous to her psyche, too dangerous when her hormones were running rampant, and way too dangerous to her heart. There was a reason their relationship had only been temporary. Small doses of Trapper Kincaid were all she could handle. Still, what choice did she have? Dr. Kildare wouldn't let her out of the damn hospital if she didn't have a prison warden for a nurse.

The doctor tried to cover a laugh with a cough and failed. He looked at her over the rims of his glasses again. "Is that okay with you, Bianca?"

If she said no, she'd be stuck in this godforsaken hospital for weeks. There was no other option. She couldn't very well drag her grandmother to New York. Nan was packing for a trip to Atlantic City with her Bunco group. Then she had a trip to Miami in February that she'd been planning for months. Bianca couldn't take Nan away from all that, and she needed James to run Action Models while she was on bed rest. She had no one else. "Yes." The word caught in her throat like a hook and tore all the way to her mouth. "Yes, it's just fine with me."

Trapper followed the doctor out of Bianca's spot in the ER and waited to speak until they'd reached the hall. "Doc, is Bianca okay to fly?"

The doctor's eyebrows rose. "She needs rest, not a vacation."

"I know. I believe the only way to get her to rest is to take her to my place."

"Which is where?"

"Boise, Idaho. I have the use of a private jet—there's a bedroom in the back, so she can sleep most of the flight. I could even have a doctor on board if that would make you feel better. It might make me feel better too."

"You have a private physician and a private jet?"

"The jet is my grandfather's. The physician is my brother—he's an orthopedist, but he did his residency at Rush. He's done a round of obstetrics."

"And how will you get Bianca on the plane? The way it sounds, you'll be lucky to keep her out of the office."

"She won't have much of a choice. If she's here, there will be little hope of keeping her from running the company from bed. Bianca doesn't know the definition of the word 'relax.' In Boise, I'll have a lot more control. All I'd need do is disconnect my router and take her phone away."

"Right. Good luck with that. Are you planning on her staying for the duration of the pregnancy?"

"Yes. She's alone here. In Boise, I have a big family, so even when I have to return to work, we'll have a support system—or, in Bianca's case—babysitters."

The doctor laughed and squeezed Trapper's shoulder. "I think Ms. Ferrari has met her match. Okay, Trapper, you can take Bianca to Boise. I have a colleague there I can recommend. We did our residency together. I'll give him a call and forward Bianca's records if you're successful in getting her on your grandfather's jet."

"Great, Doc, I'd appreciate it." Trapper pulled out his wallet. "Here's my card. Email me his contact information, and I'll make an appointment for Bianca to see him next week."

Dr. Schaeffer perused his card and laughed. "A judge, huh? That explains a lot. Bianca seems like a real handful. That's not a bad thing, if you can handle her. I married a tempest about twenty-five years ago, and the woman still keeps me on my toes. One thing is sure. I've never been bored. If you win this one over, I doubt you will be complaining of boredom either."

"Especially not with twins added to the mix. Which reminds me, I have a few phone calls to make. My family still doesn't know about Bianca and the babies." He ran his hands through his hair, wishing he had a damn hat. "Hell, I didn't know until a few hours ago."

"That will be an interesting conversation. If you need anything, don't hesitate to call. I'd be happy to help in any way I can."

"You wouldn't happen to know where a man can find a cowboy hat in these parts, would you? Bianca threw up in mine, and I feel naked without one."

"There's J.J. Hat Center on Fifth Avenue in the lower thirties. They have every kind of hat known to man."

"Great. Thanks for all your help. Now, all I have to do is get everything arranged for a trip home tomorrow." He shook the doctor's hand and took a deep breath before returning to Bianca. If she knew what he had planned, she'd kill him. Hopefully, she wouldn't put two and two together until they were on the tarmac of Teterboro Airport. Or maybe she'd fall asleep and not wake up until after they leveled off.

He found her staring at the pictures of the babies. That was a good sign. "I'm back."

"The nurses said they're moving me into a room for the night. Can you go to my place and bring me a few things? I'd ask James, but I don't want to pull him away from the office." She shot him a frustrated look. "Besides, he's not taking my calls."

"He probably thinks you're calling about work. He's worried about you and wants you to rest."

"I am calling about work. There are things he needs to be brought up to speed on. How am I supposed to rest when I'm worried he doesn't know what the heck he's doing?"

"So you're handing the reins over to James?"

"What choice have you and Dr. Kildare given me? I'm hoping that everything will be fine at my appointment next week, and the good doctor will let me return to work."

"Bianca, sweetheart, did you not hear what Dr. Schaeffer said?"

"I heard him, but he obviously doesn't know me. I've never been sick a day in my life."

"You're not sick. You're pregnant. The babies will get what they need. It's you who will suffer, which is why you've lost so much weight, why your blood pressure is through the roof, and why you're dehydrated. Sweetheart, you've been powering through and not taking proper care of yourself. That ends now. Your health and well-being are my number one concern. James can handle Action Models until after you've had the babies. Then we'll figure out what to do from there."

"We'll figure out what to do? As in, you and me?"

"First things first. What do you need from your place?"

She gave him a look that told him she'd humor him this time, but that wouldn't last past today. "I need a change of clothes, shoes to match, a nightgown, and my makeup."

"You don't need makeup. You're beautiful without it."

"You're insane. If I'm seen without makeup, it will hit the tabloids. I'm just thankful they haven't gotten wind of my pregnancy yet."

"Would that be a problem?"

"Yes. Don't you get it? Everyone will question if I can handle motherhood and my company. I've invested the last ten years of my life in Action Models. It's doing great, and I don't want my clients wondering if the company is still a good bet, or my models wondering if they're going to have a job."

"Okay, I'll bring everything on your list, including makeup. But you'll have to call your doorman and tell him to let me in. They weren't very accommodating last night."

"You went to my place last night?"

"Yes. I wanted to surprise you."

"No, you wanted to ambush me. They were doing their jobs by keeping you away. Remind me to give them a nice big tip."

Yeah, like that was gonna happen. "Bianca, just make the call and give me the key."

"Fine, but we need to talk."

"We'll have plenty of time to talk tomorrow after you're released." He didn't mention they'd have six hours of uninterrupted time to talk on the flight to Boise. "I have to go and get things ready. I'll be back later. Call me if you think of anything else you need."

She reached for his hand. "You're leaving?"

Shit. That scared little girl look eclipsed the superior businesswoman look she usually wore, and the grip on his hand tightened. "How about I hang out here with you until they get you settled? You look exhausted. You can take a nap while I'm gone, and before you know it, I'll be back and you'll be ready for more company."

"Okay." She rested against the pillows but didn't release his hand, and that was just fine with him. He couldn't think of another woman he'd rather hold hands with, and it had nothing to do with the fact she was carrying his children—the babies were an added bonus.

If the last few months taught him anything, it was that he wanted a lot more than a casual relationship with Bianca. The last thing he felt about her was casual, and that was before he knew about the babies. Now that feeling was amplified by a million.

He sat on the hard plastic chair beside her bed and watched her eyes drift shut. It was as if she was fighting sleep. He reached for his hat and remembered he was hatless. Damn. He sat back, holding Bianca's hand, and a feeling of rightness enveloped him. It was weird, considering their surroundings, his state of hatlessness, and his impending fatherhood.

Maybe this was the start of something wonderful. The beginning. The first step of the many steps he'd have to take to talk her into giving them a chance for something more than co-parenting, more than a casual relationship, more than anything he'd ever had with a woman.

For the second time in his life he wanted more. The first had ended in disaster—he just hoped this one had a better outcome.

Trapper didn't have much firsthand experience with fatherhood. The only thing his had taught him, other than how to fish, hunt, and trap, was what not to do. He would never be like his own father—a man who was only around when it suited him, and as far as Trapper could tell, marriage and fatherhood hadn't suited him at all. He hadn't seen his father in years. No one in the family had heard from him since Karma's eighteenth birthday when the support checks stopped. No, Trapper would be a full-time parent, and Bianca would have to get used to having him around—a lot.

Chapter 5

TRAPPER LEFT THE HOSPITAL AND JUMPED INTO A CAB. First things first. He couldn't imagine having the conversation he had to have with his mother without the aid of a cowboy hat. "J.J. Hat Center, Fifth Avenue between Thirty-First and Thirty-Second."

The cab pulled up in front of a store that looked as if it was a throwback from the nineteen twenties. He stepped in and looked around. He never knew there were so many different kinds of hats. In his world, there were baseball caps and cowboy hats—that was about it, unless you were looking at a knit ski hat.

"Can I help you, sir?" The gentleman's name tag read *Rod, Senior Hat Consultant*. This definitely was a gentleman too. There was only one word to describe Rod, and that word was dapper.

Trapper looked down at his Wranglers, boots, and wool sweater and felt completely underdressed. "I lost my cowboy hat, and I'm looking for a replacement. I need it."

The man nodded as if he completely understood. "We have the bushman." Rod picked up a round hat and passed it to Trapper.

"No. I need a cowboy hat, like a Stetson."

"Ah, this is an Australian cowboy hat. My mistake. I think I have what you're looking for—not a Stetson, but something I believe is even better." Rod disappeared into the back room and came back a moment later with three, honest-to-God, felt cowboy hats.

The added tension Trapper had been carrying since Bianca used his as a toilet bowl decreased to a manageable level.

Rod held the hats out for his inspection: black, silver, and brown.

Trapper already felt too much like a bad guy, so black was out. "I'll try the brown."

"This is the Dynafelt Rancher in Acorn."

"Yeah, okay." Trapper didn't give a crap what they called it, as long as it fit his head. He took the hat from Rod and slid it on. Damn, that was like stepping into a little bit of heaven. He felt a hundred times better already. He looked in the mirror, bent the sides up and the brim down. "Great. I'll take it."

"You don't want to try on the others?"

"Positive."

"Do you want to pick a custom band?"

"No, I just need the hat. I've been feeling like I've been walking around in my underwear for the last few hours without mine."

"I understand, sir." And the way Rod looked at him made Trapper believe he did. "I take it you're visiting?"

"Yes. I just flew in from Boise."

"Cowboy country."

"Close enough. Though the only place you see cowboys in Boise anymore is at a bar called Shorty's. Still, you can find a good cowboy hat just about anywhere. Here in New York, I was worried."

"If you ever get back, feel free to stop by for a steaming or a cleaning."

"Do you need the hat back to ring it up?"

"No, sir."

"Good." He followed Rod to the counter.

"You said you lost your hat. How does one lose one's hat?"

"My girlfriend grabbed the hat right off my head and threw up in it."

Rod's eyebrows went up to his hairline. "I see. That is a shame."

"Yes, it was a great hat."

"I do hope your girlfriend feels better."

"Me too, but she's not due for another five months, so I'm not counting on it. Just to be safe, I'm going to carry around air-sickness bags."

"A sound plan. Congratulations on the upcoming blessed event."

"Thank you. We're having twins." Trapper seemed to wear a permanent grin thinking about the ultrasound. That was one of the coolest things he'd ever seen in his life. He signed the credit card slip and tipped his hat to the man before leaving. "I hope you have more of these in stock. I don't relish the thought of being without a hat ever again."

Trapper left the store feeling more like himself and pulled out his phone. It was time to call his mother. He might as well deal with it on his walk back to Bianca's Fifth Avenue apartment—he figured he had thirty-seven blocks worth of talking to do.

There was a lot of packing ahead of him if he was going to whisk Bianca off to Boise tomorrow, but he had to set everything up first. He wondered if the doctor would keep her in the hospital until he had the jet ready.

His mother answered on the third ring. "Trapper, did you find Angel?"

Shit, he'd forgotten all about that. "No, Mom, I didn't."

"Is there a problem?"

He probably should have spent some time thinking about how to break the news. He cleared his throat, which suddenly felt swollen closed.

"Trapper, what's the matter?"

"How do you know something's wrong?"

"I know my son. It's written all over your voice. What's going on?"

Trapper waited for the light on Thirty-Third Street and spotted the Empire State Building. He remembered where it was compared to Bianca's place. He ripped his new hat off and hit his thigh. "You might want to sit down for this one, Mom." He walked past the gawkers and wondered if the thirty-seven blocks would be enough.

"I sat the moment I heard your voice." Damn, his mother's ESP never failed. As old as he was, his mother Kate "the great" Kincaid somehow seemed to know everything. It was a real bitch.

"Do you remember Bianca Ferrari?"

"Toni's old boss?"

"Yes, that's her." It didn't help that except for him, and maybe his sister-in-law Toni, everyone in the family disliked Bianca. "Bianca and I have been seeing each other since Toni and Hunter's wedding."

"I see." Damn, those two words spoke volumes. The worst part was, knowing his mother, she did see. She saw everything.

His face heated, and he was sure his mom knew that too. Even distance didn't make the situation less humiliating.

Trapper had been the one to grill his brothers about safe sex. He'd been the one to constantly remind them to suit up every time. No exceptions. Hell, he'd even talked to Karma—a conversation he'd had nightmares about before and since.

He was a thirty-five-year-old man, not a wet-behind-the-ears teenager. He was called Mr. Control for a reason—he'd never once lost it until the first time he touched Bianca Ferrari. He wished he could say it had only happened once, but that would be a lie. He seemed incapable of controlling much of anything when Bianca was in the vicinity. And now he had to explain to his entire family that he was the one who knocked up his girlfriend. He'd never live it down.

"I hadn't heard from her for a few months, so while I was in town I decided to stop by and see her."

"And?"

"Bianca's four months pregnant with twins. My twins."

His mother sucked in a lung full of air and was silent for so long, Trapper checked his phone to make sure they were still connected. "Bianca Ferrari is having your babies, and she didn't tell you?" She'd put on her momma bear voice. It was low. It was quiet. It was scary.

"Mom, in Bianca's defense, we didn't have that kind of a relationship."

"Your relationship changed the moment she conceived your children."

Yes, definitely scary.

He saw the New York Public Library in the distance. He thought about taking a walk around Bryant Park. This conversation would probably take longer than expected. He crossed the street and skirted the building. "I know that, and you know that, but Bianca didn't."

"She would have known if she'd called you. And what were you thinking having a relationship with a woman who knew so little about you? How could you have *that* kind of relationship without making sure she knew exactly who you are and what you stand for?"

A question he'd been asking himself since the moment Bianca canceled their meeting in Paris. She'd been sick. She'd said it was the flu, and he doubted she lied. Lying wasn't Bianca's style. He didn't know how he knew that, but he would bet a year's salary on it. She probably confused morning sickness with the flu. Hell, she probably found out she was pregnant in Paris, which explains why he'd never heard from her again.

He'd sat at home worried about her, and he hadn't known how to reach her. He hadn't known who to call. He didn't know who her friends or family were. He should have called James, but until today, he hadn't known that James was anything more than his sister-in-law Toni's friend and Bianca's employee. There were some things a guy couldn't ask his girlfriend's employee. Trapper hadn't known they were close—if he had, he would have swallowed a hell of a lot of pride and begged James for information. He hadn't known anything about Bianca—he hadn't even scratched the surface. He'd learn.

"Bianca's not doing well. She's in the hospital. She didn't know we were having twins until she was rushed there this morning. Her blood pressure is high, her weight is low, she's been sick since the beginning of October. The doctor put her on bed rest for the foreseeable future."

"And the babies?"

"They seem to be fine. I wish I could say the same for Bianca. She's having a really rough time of it. I want to bring her home so we can all help. I need one of Grampa Joe's jets, and I need it now. She'll be released in the morning, and my plan is to pick her up from the hospital and take her right to the airport. Can you talk to Gramps and arrange it?"

"Of course. How does Bianca feel about being so far from home?"

"I haven't told her yet."

"Trapper Stephen Kincaid, are you insane?"

"Mom, there's no way I'll manage to keep her from running Action Models without getting her out of the city. Besides, those are my children she's carrying. She and those babies are my responsibility. In Boise, I'll have a better chance of keeping her healthy."

"I think it's a mistake. If Bianca is the person I think she is, she won't take kindly to your he-man ways."

He knew that, but what choice did he have? "Let me worry about getting Bianca on the plane. You worry about logistics. Would you see if Fisher is available to fly out and back? I'd feel better having a doctor on board—even if it is Fisher."

"Your brother is a fine physician."

"Maybe, but I'm not sure I want my little brother checking out my girlfriend." He was lucky he wasn't standing beside her. The exasperated breath he heard come from his mother was usually followed by a smack to the back of the head. He almost ducked.

"You are such a man. But don't worry about Fisher. I'll handle him. He'll be on that plane. If my grandbabies are in distress, I want a doctor there. Is there anything else you need?"

"Not that I can think of."

"I'm assuming we'll be planning another wedding in the near future."

A wedding? Damn, he hadn't thought that far ahead. "I don't know, Mom. Bianca and I haven't had time to talk about anything but keeping her and the babies healthy. They look great though—identical. Bianca's still reeling from seeing me and finding out we're having twins. That's more than she can handle right now. Give us some time to get used to the idea and get used to each other. We'll work the rest out later. Please tell the family not to pressure her, okay? Especially Gramps. Bianca's under enough stress as it is. She doesn't need to deal with familial crap on top of all that."

"I wouldn't think of pressuring that poor woman." She sounded so innocent, but he'd been one of the many people she nudged in the right direction the way a good herding dog nudged its flock—sometimes taking a piece of his hide along with her.

"Mom, Bianca's a bit like Karma. If you push her, she'll push back in ways only God could imagine. We'll just have to be patient and see how everything else shakes out."

"Oh, yes. And patience is your middle name. That won't be a problem."

"Sarcasm doesn't become you, Mother."

"I think it works quite well for me.

"For the last three months, I've thought about her, worried about her, wondered what the heck I did to receive the silent treatment. That's why I jumped at the chance to track down Angel Anderson—because it gave me an excuse to come to New York. I had to make sure Bianca was okay. I had to find out what happened."

"I suppose it didn't take long for you to figure it out. Are you happy about the babies?"

"I'm still in shock, but yes.

"You will be a much better father to your children than your father was to any of you. So in case you're worried, don't be."

"I'm not worried about that. I'm worried about Bianca and our babies, and the fact that I have no idea if she feels anything but anger for me."

"She's angry at you?"

"She accused me of ambushing her."

"Did you?"

"Hell, yes. How the heck else was I supposed to see her?"

"And what happened?"

"She passed out and then threw up in my hat. She scared the crap out of me, Mom. First I thought she was dead, then she ruined my brand-new Stetson."

"Oh, that poor girl."

"Poor girl? She tossed her cookies in my hat. I mean, I'm sorry she felt sick, but did she have to puke in my hat?"

"Obviously, that was the only thing within reach. Would you have preferred it if she threw up on you?"

"Actually, yes. I could clean my clothes. My hat is toast."

"Oh, poor baby. Bianca ruined your security blanket."

"Excuse me?"

"When your Grampa Joe thought you were too old to be dragging your beloved blanket around, he took you to buy a big-boy cowboy hat. You exchanged your blanket for your hat and never looked back. You've never been without one since."

"I don't remember that." He couldn't remember ever not having a hat. "Hopefully, if all goes well, Bianca and I will see you tomorrow."

"Do you want me to go to your house and freshen it up? Stock the refrigerator?"

"That would be great if you have the time."

"I always have time for you, honey. Let me know if you need anything else. Now I'll go and make your grandfather's whole year. He's been dying for great-grandbabies—and now he has two to look forward to. It's gonna be a long five months."

"You have no idea."

———

Bianca sat in her hospital bed and put her signature on yet another contract then moved it to the stack of papers she'd already dealt with. "Make sure Monica follows the nutrition program. I need her to gain another five pounds for the Aruba shoot. She's no good if she looks like a waif next to the other models. And tell Xavier if he shaves his head again, we'll suspend him until his hair grows back. The shoot in Barcelona is in May. I want him there with a full head of hair, or he'll lose the cover."

James handed her another contract. "Yes, dear."

"I feel like I'm signing my life away. It's not as if I'm leaving the country. I'll just be uptown lying around my apartment."

"I'll be busy at the office. I won't have time to

messenger this kind of thing back and forth. If you're worried about me emptying your bank accounts, we could put a limit on my signing privileges."

Bianca looked up from her makeshift desk—the rolling table that slid over what was left of her lap—to her best friend. James had been with her through all the rigmarole with her parents—her emancipation, the lawsuits to retrieve at least some of the money they'd embezzled, the desolation, the devastation, the fear. Everything but Max. "I trust you, James. I'm not worried about putting limits on anything. You're like me—too honest for your own good." She let out a laugh, reached for his hand, and gave it a squeeze.

Instead of letting go, James tightened his grip and waited until she had no choice but to look him in the eye. "Are you being honest with Trapper?"

"Of course I am."

James gave her his better-than-a-lie-detector look. "Have you told him how you feel about him?"

It was all she could do not to give him a teenage eye roll. "What is this, a therapy session? Have I told Trapper how I feel?" Horny, irritated, and terrified. Had she mentioned horny? She would love to blame her sex drive on pregnancy hormones, but she couldn't. It was Trapper. She'd wanted to jump him from the first moment she'd seen him, and that hadn't changed with the pregnancy—unfortunately. "I don't know what you're talking about."

"Come on, Bianca. That's a lie. You care about him. You've missed him. Ever since you two conveniently disappeared from Toni and Hunter's wedding reception, I've caught you daydreaming about him repeatedly.

Your eyes glaze over, and you get this cute little smile on your face."

"I do not daydream about anyone."

"If you're going to lie, do it to someone who hasn't known you since you were twelve. And whatever you do, don't lie to yourself. The sparks the two of you put off are enough to scorch innocent bystanders like me— even after you puked in his hat. And since Trapper obviously knows the babies you're carrying are his, it sounds to me like the perfect time to explore the relationship."

"That's the thing, James. Trapper and I don't have a relationship beyond the bedroom." Or the living room, or the dining room, or that one time on the balcony of her hotel room in Milan. "All we had together was great sex, and unfortunately, that's not enough."

"No, but it's a start. A good one, if you ask me."

She didn't know if the queasiness she was experiencing was due to the food the nurses called lunch or James. Maybe both. "I'm not asking you."

"But if you had asked, I'd tell you that in my experience, those who are compatible in bed are compatible elsewhere. Give it a try. What do you have to lose?"

She tossed her pen on the stack of papers. "I've made peace with my life. I don't need any more heartache and disappointment. I don't think I could handle it. Besides, I'm happy alone."

"I hate to break it to you, my dear, but from this moment on, I doubt you'll be alone for the next twenty years. You're having twins. The idea of a partner to back you up, help you out, and share the joys and burdens of raising the children you're carrying—children who will invariably be as challenging as you and the good judge put together—shouldn't be something you toss aside like a Walmart T-shirt. It should be treated, fitted, and protected like a Coco Chanel original."

"I've worked for Coco, and I've always had to return the originals I modeled. It hurt. Losing Trapper—and that's if you can consider having his children equivalent to having him—would be devastating. No, I can't forget that the only interest he has in me is as a human incubator. He wants his children, and as much as I would prefer that he disappear, it's something I can live with. He doesn't need to be any more to me. He can't be."

"Bianca, he came here to see you before he knew about the kidlets. Explain that one."

She couldn't. She couldn't even explain why she'd watched Trapper on Court TV. He was a judge and a damn good one. A real judge. A criminal trial judge—not some traffic court bench jockey, like on that nineties sitcom, *Night Court*. The high-profile murder trial she'd watched him try had been fascinating. "He's not used to being the one who gets dumped. My lack of communication gave his ego a bruising. Instead of ignoring his calls, I should have broken things off after Paris. It would have saved me a lot of trouble."

"It would have been a lie. And while you might be a lot of things, you're no liar. Or so I thought until now—because if you actually believe the tripe you're spouting, you're selling yourself a false bill of goods."

Bianca pushed up to her full sitting height, shoved the table away, and crossed her arms. Her belly was getting so big, her arms rested on it. If she wore black and white, she'd be confused with Shamu. "You're getting dangerously close to crossing the line."

James shot her his serious model look. She had to hand it to him—he was good. Of course, it would have looked better if he were modeling men's underwear. "I'm your best friend in the world, and I love you like a sister—a much younger sister." He took the hand that was clasped around her arm and tugged it toward him. "I wouldn't be a best friend if I didn't tell you that I think you're making a mistake."

Bianca put her hand up to stop his soliloquy. He didn't even pause for a breath.

"I like Trapper. I always have. You two could be great together." He sat on the bed beside her and moved closer so he was in her face. "Not everyone is out for himself, not everyone sees you as a commodity, not everyone falls for the cold, self-assured, plastic veneer you show to the world."

She opened her mouth to begin a verbal assault, but James put a finger against her lips and gave her his don't-you-dare-interrupt-me glare—the same one he'd used when he helped her get through statistics. "Trapper's a judge—he can read people, and he cared enough about you to fly across the country to try to woo you. Give the man a chance."

"But—"

He increased the pressure against her lips. "Let me finish, and I'll drop the subject. I promise."

"For how long?"

"Until the next time I see you making a hideous mistake. Give Trapper a chance. If it ends, at least you won't have to spend the rest of your life wondering what if. Regrets suck. Take it from one who knows. I don't want you to look back and regret not taking a chance on love because you were afraid of failing or being hurt. You're strong, you're capable, and you have a lot of love to give. If you weren't completely wonderful after you get past the difficult bitch exterior, I wouldn't have put up with you all these years. Now I'm done."

Love? Was he serious? Love was something you read about in paperbacks. Love didn't happen in the real world, not to people like her. "Are you sure?"

"I don't want to hear an argument. I'll just give you a kiss good-bye and tell you to call me if you need me for anything but business."

James wrapped his arms around her, and Bianca curled into his chest. Tears stung her eyes, and she cursed her damn pregnancy hormones. She was turning into one of those women she hated—the ones who cried at the drop of a hat. The kind she'd always thought used tears against men and rational women. She always swore she'd never be one of them, and here she was crying like a baby.

"If you call me about business, I'll have to tattle on you, and you know how I hate to do that."

She peeked up through her tears and saw the laugh lines around his eyes. Of course on James, they added character. Her laugh lines added age.

"Take care of my nieces or nephews." He gave her a kiss on both cheeks and then on the forehead. "I love you, Bianca. Give the good judge a chance, and try to put a cap on that temper of yours—pregnancy hasn't done it any favors."

She felt James trying to release her, but she wasn't ready to let him go yet. She had a weird feeling that once he left, they'd never see each other again. Just the thought made the waterworks kick up a notch. "Don't go yet. Please. I don't know what's wrong with me. Maybe it's just pregnancy." She did her best to wipe her eyes. "Or maybe it's the twin thing. I don't know."

James pulled a crisp white hankie out of his pocket and handed it to her.

She took it and blew her nose, still keeping one arm around him. "Everything makes me cry. It's embarrassing. I've completely lost my marbles. It's as if I'm PMSing on steroids every day of the month."

James tried to cover his laugh with a cough. His execution needed work.

To her mortification, the tears really started falling. "Plus," she hiccuped, "I've got baby brain—I can't remember a thing."

"You're pregnant. You're dealing with a double dose of hormones. It's normal."

She shook her head and wiped her tears on his shirt. "I swear, if I didn't write it down, I'd forget my own name. I used to have a memory like an elephant. Now I just have the body of one."

"Bianca, you're beautiful. Once you stop puking, I bet you'll even get that pregnancy glow. You said yourself that pregnant women are sexy. Demi Moore proved that years ago, and you're way hotter than Demi ever was."

"Demi only had one baby at a time."

"Yeah, well, you've always been an overachiever. Leave it to you to take pregnancy to a higher level."

"James. I'm losing everything—my mind, my independence, and now my business. I don't know if I'm cut out for motherhood."

James rocked her and kissed the top of her head.

"You'll be a wonderful mother. You'll give your kids all the love they need. Besides, it's not as if you'll be doing it alone. You have Trapper and me."

"Trapper's only here because he feels responsible."

"He is responsible, and he cares about you. Everyone sees it but you. I might be gay, but I'm still a man. If you keep pushing him away, eventually, he'll give up. He's a guy. Guys can only take so much rejection."

"James, it's me who can't take the rejection. Everyone in my life but you and Nan has used me, bled me dry, and left me. My track record sucks."

"But Trapper hasn't, and he won't if you would just give him a chance. He cares about you. You care about him. Bianca, if I had a man like Trapper Kincaid look at me the way he looks at you, I'd hold on to him for dear life and never let him go. What do you have to lose?"

She didn't have much except her babies, her self-respect, her independence, and what was left of her heart. Trapper was a triple threat. "Everything," she whispered. "I can lose everything."

Chapter 6

TRAPPER STOOD JUST OUTSIDE THE HOSPITAL ROOM DOOR and eavesdropped on Bianca and James without remorse. He needed to figure out what was going on with Bianca if he wanted a chance of making a relationship work. Unfortunately, he wasn't used to sleeping with women who didn't drone on about everything that went through their heads after sex.

Bianca had always been as closemouthed as they came, unless she was slinging an insult—she was great at that. A woman who could take him down a peg or two and still have him half-hard while doing it was a woman with amazing looks, an IQ higher than her combined measurements, and a triple-digit ego. Truth be told, Bianca probably beat him in the IQ department, and that was saying something.

He'd only had one other relationship with a woman of Bianca's mental caliber, and it had ended in disaster. Paige Baker taught him several important life lessons— the first of which was that smart women were dangerous to his mental health. If he introduced himself as Fakie McNamerson, and the woman in question didn't blink an eye, she was perfect for a no-more-than-seventy-two-hour fling. Because of Paige, he'd come up with his personal dating rules:

1. *Never have sex with a smart woman.*

2. *Never have anything but casual sex.*
3. *Never spend more than seventy-two hours with a woman.*
4. *Never see the same woman twice.*
5. *Never talk about family.*
6. *Never give a woman your number.*
7. *Never lead a woman on.*
8. *Never promise more than you can deliver.*
9. *Never discuss anything that could be misconstrued.*
10. *Always wear a condom.*

He wasn't sure what it was about Bianca that had him breaking rules left and right. Hell, he'd broken every one—okay, rule number eight was still under consideration, but the nine rules he'd broken, he'd broken several times and enjoyed every second of it— every second until he'd gotten the call canceling the trip to Paris. From that moment on, it was like the Paige disaster all over again—but worse. So much worse, he couldn't believe it.

He and Paige had been together for three years. They'd been engaged, looking for a house, and had discussed a wedding date. After finding a positive pregnancy test in the trash, he stopped by her office with roses and a bottle of sparkling cider and caught his fiancée naked on the boardroom table doing the nasty with a senior partner of her law firm—the father of her baby. He'd expected emotional whiplash and he'd gotten it— times ten. He'd literally taken their history and put it all in a box—one he'd yet to reopen and examine. His reaction to the Paige disaster was understandable, but the whiplash Bianca blindsided him with was one that came as a real shock.

He still didn't know what the hell he was thinking going after Bianca the way he had. Well, other than the obvious—he had wanted her. Sure, she was physically one of the most beautiful women he'd ever seen, but it was her attitude that drew him in, grabbed him by the balls, and wouldn't let go until he figured her out. He was no closer to doing that now than he'd been then. Bianca was and had remained a challenge in every way. She was exciting and so multifaceted, he still hadn't seen all the sides of her—hard one moment and soft the next. Surprising at every turn and fun when he least expected it. But most of all, Bianca turned him on in ways he still couldn't understand. No matter how often he had her, no matter how often he spoke to her, no matter how many hours he'd watched her and held her in his arms, it wasn't enough. Bianca Ferrari was his addiction. He tried to go cold turkey after their first time together, but found himself flying to London just in case she could spare an hour or two. The worst part was he hadn't been able to look at another woman since—no other woman could compare.

Unfortunately, he'd just overheard Bianca tell James that they didn't have a relationship beyond the bedroom. He sure as hell hoped James was right about Bianca missing him and prayed there was more between him and Bianca than she was willing to admit. He kicked aside the resentment that James knew Bianca a hell of a lot better than he did. Feeling sorry for himself and resentful of the only ally he had would do him no favors.

Trapper leaned against the painted cinder-block wall,

letting the cold seep through his sweater. He closed his eyes and listened, wishing he understood her tears. Wishing his was the shoulder she cried on. Wishing he could go back in time and change the way they'd began.

He would have done everything differently. Everything except one thing—he'd never wish away their children. He'd have spent the time and laid a foundation on which to build a relationship. He'd have talked more, asked more questions—all the questions that had run through his head but were censored due to their fling status. He would have spent more time studying her library—a window to her very busy mind. He would have shared more—more of what he wasn't sure. Sharing was difficult since she seemed to struggle with her own internal censor. He would have brought her flowers just to see the hint of a smile she worked to control when he inadvertently did something nice or unexpected. He would have said the words he now knew she needed to hear, and he hoped it wasn't too late to correct his mistakes.

"Spying?"

Trapper's eyes shot open, and he stared into the face of an angry James Ness. The door to Bianca's room closed with a whoosh and a snick.

"How else am I supposed to figure her out?"

James shouldered a messenger bag and blew out a frustrated breath. "You might try talking to her."

"I have. You heard her, James. She refuses to see me as anything more than a sperm donor."

"Maybe that's because before now, that's exactly how you presented yourself."

"I can't go back and change the past. If I could, believe me, I would. I hadn't planned for any of this."

James shoved him against the wall and had his arm on his windpipe. "If you are talking about those babies— it's a damn good thing you're in a hospital. When I get through with you, you'll still be lucky to live—hospital or not."

If Trapper didn't admire the guy, he would have laid him out. "God, no." He pushed James away, caught the hat that had almost fallen off his head in the shoving match, and rolled the brim. "I'm talking about my relationship with Bianca. I never expected it to go anywhere past great sex. I never thought I'd want more. I do. I have since the wedding. Unfortunately, my wanting more won't make Bianca want the same."

James dropped his attack dog stance, let out what looked like a relieved breath, and leaned against the wall beside him. "Look, I've done my best to help you out. I've set everything up to make it possible for Bianca to be away from the business for an extended period."

"Thank you."

James turned, got into Trapper's face, and morphed back into his rabid wolf stance. "I've done everything you've requested to give you the time you need to prove yourself because with Bianca, that's what it will take. She needs to trust you. She needs to know you care about her beyond those babies she's carrying. She's a hard sell. But then, if you've been eavesdropping for as long as I think you have, you already know that. I've given you more latitude than you deserve. If you let Bianca down, if you hurt her, if you fuck up this chance, you'll answer to me. Do we understand each other?"

"Yes, sir." Trapper felt like a teenager getting threatened by a date's dad.

"Good. Do you need any help packing her things?"

"No, I took care of it. If I missed anything, you can send it along, or we can buy it there."

"Have you figured out how you're going to get her on the plane?"

"No. I'll have to wing it."

James shook his head and gave him a rueful smile. "I suppose that's my cue to wish you luck. You're gonna need it."

Bianca was having one of those dreams again. She wrapped her arms around Trapper's neck and deepened the kiss, thankful for the ability to duplicate the memory of his touch, taste, and scent.

She'd missed the feel of his hair in her hands, his hard chest against hers, the slight peppermint taste of his mouth, the scent of whatever aftershave he wore— faint but intoxicating—the way his mouth devoured hers, the way his hadn't-felt-like-shaving-in-days beard brushed her face, and the way she could feel his groan radiate through him into her. She'd missed this. She slid her hands down his chest and pulled his shirt out of his pants, wondering why he was never naked in her dreams. Getting into his pants always took way too long.

The beeping noise in the background was annoying, but not enough to make her stop what she was doing.

"Bianca, sweetheart, wake up."

Trapper never said that in her dreams before. The last thing she wanted to do was wake up. She hated waking up and finding herself alone. "No."

A light blinked on, shone through her eyelids, and

the buzz told her it was florescent. "What the hell?" She hated florescent lights—she refused to have them anywhere in her home.

"Bianca, sweetheart, wake up. The nurses are going to be here any second. Your monitors are going off."

Monitors? What monitors? The beeping got louder. She forced her eyes open and found herself with one hand buried in Trapper's hair, the other in his pants, and his smiling face wearing a superior smirk within kissing distance. She gave his hair a yank.

"Ow!"

She tried to extricate her hand from his pants, but it was hard. He was hard. And her hand was wrapped around his impressive erection. Obviously, his pants had gotten tighter with her hand in there.

"Bianca, sweetheart, calm down. I was just trying to kiss you awake." He grabbed her wrist in an attempt to protect his manhood. "Don't do anything you'll regret later."

She had half a mind to give his dick a twist and see how he liked that.

Bianca freed her hand just as the nurse ran in.

"What's going on?" she asked.

Bianca had never seen Trapper blush before. He was definitely blushing now as he tucked in his shirt. "I was trying to kiss her awake, and things got out of hand."

The nurse, who was old enough to be Bianca's mother, raised an eyebrow, put a blood pressure cuff on Bianca's arm, and tried to contain her laughter. "Maybe we should disconnect the monitors while he's in the room, Ms. Ferrari. He's enough to send any woman's blood pressure through the roof."

And wasn't that the truth. Still, she didn't want him

to end up with a bigger ego than he already had. "Only if she's unconscious."

"Bianca."

The way her name sounded when mixed with a pained growl brought a smile to her face. It was probably an evil smile—but hey, it worked for her. "He should come with a warning sign."

"I can see that. The nurses have been enjoying your visitors, Ms. Ferrari, but not much work has been getting done. We're not used to having male models coming and going."

Trapper wore a somebody-pissed-in-his-beer expression mixed with something she couldn't label. "Male models?"

A storm brewed behind Trapper's always composed facade—shit, was he jealous?

The nurse nodded. "Yes, you and Ms. Ferrari's other friend."

The storm disappeared and was replaced by a cocky smirk. "I'm a judge, not a model."

The nurse ripped the Velcro torture device off Bianca's arm. "I think he missed his calling," she mumbled.

Bianca didn't bother covering her laugh.

"Bed rest has been ordered, Ms. Ferrari. Not play. At least not yet."

"Tell him that. I was sound asleep."

The nurse turned toward Trapper—probably to repeat herself.

He put his hand up to stop her. "I got the message. It won't happen again until the monitors come off." He shot the nurse a wicked grin. Bianca was sure he probably practiced it in the mirror. "Hey, is it my fault she gets carried away when I kiss her?"

"Yes," she and the nurse said in stereo.

The nurse wrote something in her chart and gave Trapper a warning look that was ruined when she followed it up with a girlie sigh before exiting the room and leaving the door wide open.

Trapper cleared his throat. "I brought you a few things from home." He put her bag on the bed, and she rummaged through it.

"You brought me a see-through nightgown?" She didn't mention it was her favorite and the only one she could probably still fit into. She thought he'd throw together a T-shirt and a pair of sweats—yes, she had stooped that low. She needed something comfortable to wear around the house.

"It has a matching robe. And it's not as if there were any others less revealing—believe me, I checked them all." He leaned in close, so close she saw those gold starbursts in his green eyes, so close she wondered if he was going to kiss her again, so close, her heart monitor picked up speed. He wore that shit-eating grin—the one that formed an indentation in the side of his face and made her want to fill it with her tongue. "But damn, Bianca. I have to say, I do love your taste in lingerie."

"Too bad I'll never fit into it again."

"Is that a bad thing?"

Was he stupid? "Yes, look at me. I'm huge."

"You're not huge—if anything, you're too skinny. You're ripe, you're gorgeous, and you're over-the-top sexy—even wearing a hospital gown. Only you can make a hospital gown look that good. I can't wait to rip it off you." He stepped away from the bed and closed the door to her room. He was back, leaning over her, and before she knew what he was up to, he'd untied the string holding the damn thing together.

"What are you doing?"

"Helping you change."

"I don't need help."

He pulled her forward and got the second tie. "Sure you do. Now hurry up. The doctor will be in any minute."

That was all she needed to hear. She slipped her hospital gown down, tucking it under her arms, and pulled the nightgown over her head.

"You cheated."

"No, I just don't play by your rules. There's a difference." She shimmied the silky gown down over her belly and raised her rump, tugging it under her before she pulled on the robe.

"Sweetheart, I know every inch of your body—intimately."

How did he do that? With one look, one word in that deep gravelly voice, and her hormones were as out-of-control as a four-year-old let loose in a cotton candy factory. "You might have in the past, but now, there's a whole lot more real estate."

His smile widened, making him look a little intrigued, a little evil, and all kinds of hot. Damn, she was screwed.

"Just more of you to adore. For a little while, at least."

"Yes, we won't be together that long."

"Oh, no, we'll be together. But after you have the babies, you'll lose most of that sexy belly."

"We'll only be together until I'm released from bed rest."

Trapper crossed his arms over his chest and chuckled. Not a nice chuckle either.

"What's so funny?"

"We'll be together for much longer than that."

"Three weeks. That's all I've agreed to."

"We'll just have to see if I can change your mind."

—⁓—

Trapper sat beside Bianca in the back of the Lincoln Town Car they'd rented and waited for her to notice they were headed to Teterboro and not her apartment.

She pushed her long hair over one shoulder while she looked through the tinted window. "Trapper, the driver's going the wrong way."

That didn't take long. "No, he's not."

"What are you talking about? I'm on bed rest. Remember? Where are we going?"

"I'm taking you home."

"My home is uptown, on the East Side."

"I know."

"Then why are we heading to the West Side?"

"I told you I was taking you home. My home." Trapper held Bianca's hand. He was half-afraid that if he released her, she'd run as soon as the car stopped at a light, and half-afraid she'd hit him. Either way, he wasn't about to let her go.

"No." She leaned forward, pressed the control, and lowered the glass between the driver and passengers. Fisher turned from the front passenger seat, shot Trapper a grin, and held out his hand. "You owe me a Benjamin. I told you it wouldn't take two blocks before she figured it out."

Trapper pulled the cash out of his pocket with his free hand and slapped it on Fisher's open palm.

Fisher turned his grin to Bianca. "Hi, gorgeous. So I hear we're taking a little trip. How ya feelin'?"

Bianca's eyes widened, and her face paled. "Fisher? What are you doing here?"

"Me? I'm here to take care of you."

Bianca's eyebrows rose.

Fisher waggled his.

Trapper felt the rumble of a growl clear his throat.

Fisher continued as if he didn't have one foot through death's door. "In a medical sense, of course. I'm a doctor, remember?"

Bianca glared at him and then back to Fisher. "I thought you were an orthopedist."

"I'm an MD with an orthopedic specialty. Still, I've seen my share of pregnant women. Don't worry. You're in good hands."

"I'm not worried because I'm not going home with you or him. Now driver, turn this car around, and take me back to my apartment. I'm on Fifth Avenue between Seventy-Fourth and Seventy-Fifth."

Hunter turned and grinned. "Hi, Bianca. I wish I could help you out, but no can do. We're heading to Teterboro. James is meeting us there. He wanted to say good-bye. Everyone's waiting for you. Oh, and congratulations, by the way."

"Everyone?" Bianca was pale before. Now she looked ghostly.

Trapper groaned and reached for an airsickness bag. The last thing he wanted was to lose another hat.

Fisher's smile widened, if that was possible. "Oh yeah." He winked at Trapper. "We've got a full plane. It's gonna be like old times."

Bianca swallowed hard, grabbed the bag, and snapped it open before sitting back in the seat, quiet and subdued. She leaned against the leather headrest. He wasn't sure if she was taking one for the team, or if she was planning his murder. He had a feeling he'd be paying for this stunt for a long time—a long, long, long, long time. It was unfortunate, but how the hell else would he get Bianca on a plane to Boise? She'd given him no choice.

"I can't believe you're kidnapping me."

He pulled her closer, wrapping his arm around her waist. Her head rolled onto his shoulder. If she were going to be sick, he'd end up wearing it. At that point, he didn't care. He had a change of clothes, and Lord knew it wouldn't be the first time someone threw up on him. He was pretty sure it wouldn't be the last either. "Come on, sweetheart. Kidnapping is such a strong word. I like to think of it as the gift of a surprise trip. It's romantic."

"Romantic? You think this is romantic?"

"Need I remind you that the only reason you were released from the hospital was because I said you'd have round-the-clock care for the next three weeks? As much as I'd like to, I can't do that in New York. Sweetheart, I have a job. I've taken two weeks off, but I have to go back to work on the sixteenth. In Boise, we have plenty of family who are only too happy to help."

"Your family hates me."

"No, they don't. Toni loves you. Fisher's wife, Jessie, hasn't met you, but I'm sure you'll get along well. And everyone loves my mom. I think you met my mother, Kate, at Hunter and Toni's wedding."

"I did. Believe me, she's not a fan."

"She doesn't know you."

Bianca gave him her pissed-off-supermodel look, but it lost something since she'd turned green. With the weight loss, her cheekbones stood out in sharp relief against her pallid skin, making her look more like a vulnerable waif—if a waif could stand almost six feet tall. "Trapper, don't make me out to be anything but what I am. I'm no damsel in distress. I'm a pissed off, pregnant diva on hormonal overload who routinely eats men up and spits them out in the boardroom and the bedroom. Don't fuck with me."

"Sweetheart, I've already have, and you enjoyed it. I plan to do it again at the first opportunity. I can't tell you how much I'm looking forward to you returning the favor. I know you, Bianca. I might not know all of you, but I know what's an act and what's not. And believe me, I'm not being facetious when I call you sweetheart. You're sweet. Granted, you hide it well—hell, I might have even missed it if I wasn't looking closely. But you, my sweet, are my favorite subject to study. And so far, everything I've learned makes me just want you more."

—◦◦◦—

Bianca was awakened by sweet kisses on her forehead. She burrowed deeper into Trapper's chest and breathed him in. His beard brushed her skin and sent a series of sparks cascading through her.

"Come on, Sleeping Beauty, your carriage awaits."

Carriage? What was he talking about? Then all the pieces fell into place.

She was being kidnapped.

She was pissed.

She'd been betrayed. But she was too tired to fight it.

The door opened, and the smell of jet fuel filled her nostrils, sending her salivary glands into overdrive a nanosecond before she was hit with a tsunami of nausea. She tried to swallow. The pressure of her clothes on her throat engaged the gag reflex, and the bag she reached for lost the race with the rising tide of bile. She gripped the handle of the open door, leaned over, and puked—all over a fancy pair of cowboy boots. She looked up to find an octogenarian in a western-style suit complete with bolo tie smiling down at her. She couldn't speak. She was too busy trying to avoid a repeat performance.

Trapper made soothing noises and rubbed her back. It was nice, but she still wanted to reach around and tie his dick in a knot.

She breathed through her mouth and tasted the jet fuel hanging in the air. It was no use. She lost yet another battle with her stomach. At least the old man was smart enough and quick enough to step away, though his boots were already ruined.

"I suppose I'm happier to see you than you are to see me." He handed her a handkerchief and called over his shoulder. "You got any ginger ale in the plane, Marge? Send a can down, will you?"

Trapper had grabbed her hair and continued rubbing her back. "Hi, Gramps."

Great. She'd just puked all over the boots of Big Joe Walsh. The two hundred eighty-fourth richest man in the world now wore the previous contents of her stomach.

He rapped on the top of the car. "Pull up a few feet son. We wouldn't want the little lady to have to step in it."

The old man didn't bother closing the door,

something she was grateful for since she still had her head hanging out. The grip Trapper had on her waist tightened, and the car rolled forward. A second later, she heard a soda being opened, and the cold can came in contact with her hand. "Sip it slowly, then we'll give you a peppermint candy. Peppermint and ginger are great for what ails you."

"Thank you." She forced herself to meet his eyes. "I'm so sorry about your boots, Mr. Walsh."

"Don't you worry about it. It's not the first time I've been christened, and with you having my great-grandbabies, it won't be the last." He beamed at her. "And call me Joe, or Gramps. Welcome to the family, little lady."

"But I'm not—We're not—"

Joe waved a hand. "Now, don't go gettin' yourself all riled up. You're carrying my great-grandbabies, and that makes you family." He held her arm in a surprisingly strong grip and helped her out of the car. "Let's get you settled in the plane and get a little something in your stomach." He put his arm around her and led her over the tarmac toward a Gulf Stream. "Marge has been cookin' up a storm just waitin' for your arrival." He steered her around a patch of ice. Her cape whipped in the bitter wind. "We'll have a light lunch with James before we take off. That boy's wringin' his hands. He's been worried sick about you. Try to remember he only has your best interest at heart."

"He—"

"I know." He patted her back. "But put yourself in James's shoes. He loves you like family, and when you passed out the way you did, you scared ten years off his life. He feels responsible, and he's man enough to know that, right now, he's not able to take care of you. We are, and that's just what we're gonna do. So don't be too hard on James."

"I'm not—"

"Of course not." He smiled, and his eyes twinkled. "You save all that fire I see in your eyes for my grandson, Trapper. Now, that boy's a different story. You can give him all the hell you can stir up. Save me from having to box his ears."

"Excuse me?"

"Don't get me wrong. I'm happier than a dog with two peckers about you and those babies, but I raised that boy better than to get a beautiful girl like you in trouble."

"I'm not—"

"Oh, I know times have changed, but right is right and wrong is wrong. There are some things that don't change with the times, little lady, and bringing babies into this world is one of them things." He slipped his arm around what was left of her waist and tugged her close to his side. "Now watch these steps. They can be a little slippery."

She grabbed the cold railing, wondering just what had happened. "But your boots—"

"Never liked those damn boots anyway. But if you tell my Katie I said that, I'll call you a liar. She keeps hiding my favorites in the back of my closet. Now you've given me the perfect excuse to put them back into rotation. Shit, when I finally have a pair broken in just right she starts harpin' on me about lookin' like a street person. She wouldn't know a street person from the King of Siam."

"You still grousing about mom hiding your boots, Gramps?" Fisher came up the steps and winked at Bianca. "He's all talk when mom's not around. When he's within smacking distance, he's afraid of her."

Joe collected her coat and handed it to the flight attendant. "Don't listen to Fisher. Just because he's afraid of his mama, doesn't mean I am. No, Katie knows who wears the pants in my household."

Hunter poked his head through the door. "Mom does."

Bianca had been in plenty of private jets. Still, she had to admit, this topped them all. Especially when she took in the amount of pure testosterone contained in a relatively small area. She looked around for James—he was probably hiding. "Where's Trapper?"

Hunter grinned. "I left him with the luggage. That will teach him to pack like a woman."

James popped his head out of what was probably the bathroom. "He did pack for a woman."

"Yeah, and he can haul it. But be our guest, James. Do the honors if you feel so strongly about it."

James jumped at the chance to escape and brushed by her. "I'll be back in a few minutes."

Fisher took her elbow. "Let's get you situated, and I'll do a quick blood pressure check before lunch. After we get up to cruising altitude, you can finish your nap. We have a bedroom in the back."

"But your grandfather's boots—I should clean them."

He opened a medical bag and took out his tools of torture. "You're on bed rest, remember? Besides, did you see those boots before you ralphed on them? You really did do him a favor. Now Trap's gonna have to replace them with a pair Gramps actually likes."

"Oh, no. I'll replace them. I insist."

Fisher just laughed. "Yeah, don't waste your breath unless you want to press all of Trapper's buttons. Then go on. Just be sure to let me watch." Fisher gave her his toothpaste commercial grin, rolled up her sleeve, and then draped a stethoscope over his neck. "So I'm sure Dr. Schaeffer told you to decrease your salt intake, increase your fluids, get a lot of rest, no work, no stress."

"He told me the only time I can leave my bed was to shower and go to the bathroom."

Fisher raked his hand through his white blonde hair in an attempt to slick back his curls. "I'm sure that went over well."

"You have no idea."

Bianca rested her head against the leather seat and blew out a breath. "Fisher, Trapper's a great guy, but I never wanted or needed a man. Having Trapper's children won't change that."

Fisher looked over her head toward the front of the plane, and his smile fell.

"Trapper's behind me, isn't he?"

Fisher adjusted his stethoscope in his ears, effectively cutting off all communication, and focused on taking her blood pressure. Oh yeah, that would be an accurate reading—not.

Trapper sat beside her. "Hey, it's not a big deal. You've made it more than clear how you feel."

No, she hadn't. She'd never told him how she felt about him.

James gave her an I-told-you-so look.

Trapper might claim it wasn't a big deal, but the tight expression on his face belied his words. He didn't look angry; he looked resigned, fatalistic. She didn't want to lead Trapper on, but she wasn't comfortable being responsible for his reaction, his pain, or the worry that shadowed his eyes. She wasn't comfortable with her inability to reach him. She'd never tried. It had always been him reaching for her—until now. For the first time with Trapper, here in this plane filled with people, Bianca was alone.

Chapter 7

TRAPPER SAT IN THE PLUSH LEATHER SEAT OF THE plane, pulled his cowboy hat low over his eyes, and feigned sleep, hoping to avoid conversation.

Bianca had been quiet through lunch and during takeoff. When they reached cruising altitude, she gladly went back to the bedroom to nap. He had a bad feeling that although he won the battle—getting Bianca to Boise—he might have lost the war. And it was war. The looks she'd been giving him told him he'd have hell to pay for his high-handed ways. Yes, his mother called that one correctly, but then he'd never really known her to be wrong.

Someone sat in the seat beside him. He knew it was Gramps. Gramps was the only one who wasn't afraid of him. Not that he'd ever hurt his brothers—okay, not badly—but no matter how old they got, there was still that fear factor he'd spent years instilling.

"What are you doing pretending to sleep here instead of with Bianca?"

Trapper pushed the brim of his hat up. Once his grandfather set his mind to lecturing, there was little he could do to change it. "Gramps, I can't go in there. She's pissed. I'm probably the last person she wants to see. I didn't exactly invite her to Boise. She claims I kidnapped her."

"Son, the one thing you need to learn about women is that the sooner you have it out, the sooner that little lady will be able to sleep peacefully. So go on in there and set things right. Besides, the best way to win over a pregnant woman is with sex."

"Excuse me?" He couldn't believe he was having this conversation with his grandfather of all people. "Gramps, she's pregnant with twins. She's sick—"

"And probably horny as hell. Son, it's been a lot of years, but the female body hasn't changed. Trust me on this. Pregnant women are sexually insatiable. It almost makes up for the lack of sex after the kids are actually born."

Trapper would gladly volunteer for Chinese water torture before listening to any more advice from his grandfather. It would be a lot less painful. "Gramps, I don't want to talk to you about this. Stop. Please."

"I'm just giving you some damn good advice, boy. Get it while the gettin's good because after those babes are born, the only thing you're gonna be getting is too little sleep."

"Fine. I'll go." He stood and adjusted his hat, wondering if he should leave it in the front cabin where it was safe. Instead, he grabbed a couple of barf bags and went to the back of the plane. He stopped at the door, not knowing what the heck he should do. Should he knock? He tapped lightly on the door, and when he didn't get a response, he went in.

Bianca was out cold. So much for Gramps's theory about her being too upset to sleep. If there was one thing Bianca seemed to have no problem doing, it was sleeping. She slept on her side, her hair fanning out on the dark pillow, looking like a golden halo in the dim light of the small window.

Between being worried about her for the last few months, learning the news of the babies, her health crisis, and then planning the trip and packing up her things, he didn't think he'd gotten a good night's sleep in weeks. He was exhausted.

He unfastened his belt, popped the buttons on his Wranglers, and kicked off his boots. He tossed his hat on the bedside table, slid in beside Bianca, and snuggled up. His hand landed on her baby bump—their baby bump. The scent of her surrounded him and damned if his dick didn't jump in his jeans. He couldn't be in the same room with the woman and not have a woody. It was embarrassing. He'd been able to control himself when it came to that since he was a teenager, until he met Bianca. He was just lucky she was asleep.

Trapper closed his eyes and paged through his mental copy of the Idaho Penal Code. If anything would get rid of a woody, reciting the penal code should do it. Still, the scent of her, the feel of her body against his, the knowledge that his babies rested safe beneath his hand, made it hard to concentrate on anything but Bianca and their family.

His eyes shot open. He had a family—one of his own. Bianca and those babies were his—although Bianca would probably rip him a new one if she knew he was even thinking it. Well, she'd just have to get used to that. She was his. Hell, he might not have been aware of it at the time, but she'd been his since he'd first laid eyes on her. There was something about her that grabbed him and went far beyond the physical. He remembered the first morning they had breakfast, and she'd tossed cold coffee in his face. He might not have realized it while he was dripping, but he loved that she had no problem arguing with him and matching wits, even if he lost as many fights as he won.

He'd known early on that she was more than just a beautiful face. So much more. He never tired of reading her expressions and trying to figure out all the thoughts she kept to herself. The woman was a veritable human Rubik's Cube. But no matter what she was willing to give him when it came to her, he was a father, and that she could never take away. And someday soon, if he ever talked Bianca into it, he'd be a husband. He expected the idea to throw him like the bucking bronco he rode one drunken night in college, but instead, it just felt right. He fell asleep with a smile on his face, holding Bianca, and picturing a life with her and their kids.

He was awakened less than an hour later by a blow to the nose. His hands flew to his face as the white-hot heat of pain painted a galaxy of stars behind his eyelids. "What the hell was that for?" He hadn't expected it, nor had he expected the rush of blood.

"Trapper?" Bianca pushed herself to a sitting position. "Are you okay?"

He pinched his nose to stop the bleeding and tipped his head back. "Are you wondering if you need to finish the job?"

"I'm sorry. I didn't know it was you."

"So you wake up with strange men often?"

"No. You were on top of me, and I...I went to sleep alone. I wasn't expecting to wake up with someone holding me down."

"I wasn't holding you down. I was spooning with you."

"You threw your leg over me. I freaked and elbowed

you. Accidentally—on purpose. I didn't know it was you. It was instinct. I reacted."

He stumbled to the bathroom to check the damage. Damn, it was going to be ugly. Before long, he'd have a couple of colorful shiners. He didn't think his nose was broken, but then the way it felt, it could very well be. "Shit." The last person he wanted to ask was Fisher. His brothers would never let him live this one down.

"Are you okay?"

Trapper felt like saying "hell no," but then he turned around and saw her. Bianca looked worse than he did, and he looked pretty damn bad. "Sweetheart, I'm fine. It's you I'm worried about."

She covered her mouth with both hands and pushed past him into the small bathroom. She had the lid up to the can, fell to her knees, and lost her lunch before he could do anything to help.

Trapper looked around the cramped bathroom, pulled a glass out of the cabinet, and filled it with water. "Here." He went to hand it to her, but her hands were shaking so badly, he figured she'd just drop it. He flushed the toilet and knelt beside her, bringing the glass to her mouth. "You're okay. Just take a sip."

"I'm sss…sorry." The tears started. He cursed himself silently and repeatedly.

"Aw, sweetheart, don't cry. It's okay."

Tears streamed down her pale cheeks, and she wretched again.

"What will help? Ginger ale?"

She nodded and gulped air. He moved to get up, but she stopped him. "Don't go."

He slid the rest of the way down and pulled her onto

his lap, and she curled against him. Damned if he didn't like it. "Fisher," he yelled, hoping his voice would carry. "Bring me a ginger ale, would you? Oh, and an ice bag."

The door banged open. "An ice bag?"

"You heard me."

A second later, Fisher stepped in and handed the can of soda to Bianca, then he took one look at Trapper and laughed. "Broken?"

"Not sure."

Fisher handed him the ice bag, and before he knew what Fisher was up to, he'd squeezed the shit out of Trapper's nose, firing up the stars again. "Yup. Good one, Bianca. I always knew I liked you. I've been itchin' to break Trapper's nose for years, and here you did it for me. I take it he had it coming."

Bianca handed Trapper the soda and then tossed whatever she'd been able to get down.

Trapper wanted to kill his brother. "Now is not a good time, little brother. Can't you see she's upset?"

"She's not upset. She's sick." Fisher waited until she stopped heaving, rinsed out a washcloth, handed it to her, and put another one on her forehead. "Sometimes a cool compress helps. Now rinse out your mouth, and let's get you back to bed."

Trapper growled. "I've got her. Why don't you just get the hell out of here?"

"Because I'm the doctor, and I need to take her blood pressure."

Damn, what the hell was he supposed to say to that? "Fine, but keep the commentary to a minimum." He nudged Fisher out of his way, lifted Bianca off the floor, and wrapped his arm around her. If he could have, he'd have picked her up and carried her, but the damn bathroom was too small. "I got you. Don't worry about Fisher. I'll get rid of him as soon as he checks your blood pressure."

"I'm fine."

She was so far from fine it wasn't even funny.

Fisher sat beside Bianca on the bed, crowding him out. "Go get my bag, Trap, and put that ice on your nose to keep down the swelling. You're getting some real nice shiners. I was able to straighten that crooked nose of yours, so Bianca might very well have done you a favor." He shot a cocky grin at Bianca and handed her the soda. "Just take a sip, love, and let's see if we can get it to stay down this time."

Trapper stepped out of the bedroom with the ice bag on his face. He figured it was probably better if he covered up the swelling and bruising with a bag of ice then not. It was bad enough he had an audience. If he could get Bianca home without them knowing how bad it really was, he might survive with only his ego in tatters.

Gramps took one look at him and laughed. "I told you to have it out, but I didn't think she'd get physical—at least not that way."

"It was an accident. She rolled over, and I took an elbow to the face."

"Sure, that's what I'd say if I were you. Did I ever tell you about the time your grandmother went after me with the cast iron?"

"Gramps, I didn't come here to chat." He looked around the cabin wondering where Fisher stashed his bag. "Bianca's sick. Fisher needs his bag to take her blood pressure. Why don't you keep your comments to yourself and do something constructive, like tell me where the hell he hid his doctor's kit?"

Hunter grabbed it and passed it to him. "You two figure things out yet?"

"None of your fuckin' business."

Hunter held out a hand, and Gramps slapped a bill on it.

Great. His own brother had been betting against him. "Thanks for the vote of confidence, Hunter."

"Any time, Bro. I couldn't help it. Gramps thought you were going back there to get busy. Let's face it, with the three of us out here, I figured even you'd have performance issues."

Now Trapper wanted to hit Hunter too. "Bianca was sleeping."

Gramps looked him up and down. "Yeah, that's why your belt is hanging off you, and your jeans are undone."

"I was sleeping too."

Gramps looked over to Hunter and grabbed the bill out of his hand. "Likely story."

"Give Hunter back his money. Nothing happened and nothing will until she's feeling better at least." He turned and went back to the bedroom. "Here." He tossed the bag to Fisher. "Do what you have to do, and get the hell out. Bianca needs her rest."

<div style="text-align:center">~~~</div>

Karma stood between her sisters-in-law in Grampa Joe's hanger at the airport waiting for the arrival of precious cargo. She was beside herself with joy. She would soon have nieces of her very own—even if there was no love lost between her and the mother of said nieces.

Toni, Hunter's wife, stood with her arms crossed while she tapped out a death march with the toe of her combat boot.

Karma hadn't seen her pull out those boots in months. Toni had really toned down her Goth-princess look after she married Hunter, and not because he demanded it. As a matter of fact, Karma had a feeling Hunter missed his wife's wild clothing choices. Still, a girl didn't need to be Dr. Phil to realize Toni had used her sense of style as armor, which was why Karma hadn't seen Toni in her full Goth regalia since the last time she and Hunter had gotten into a row. Karma wondered what Hunter did to make Toni feel the need to wear her shit-kickers.

As a rule, Karma didn't like to get involved with her brothers' private lives, but realized there were just some things a sister had to deal with if her brothers were ever going to be happy. She liked to think of it as a form of community service. Besides, it had been her life's goal to finally have the women outnumber the men in the family, and it would help if she didn't have to include animals in the count.

Jessie looked content enough so Fisher must be in the clear, but then they were still in the honeymoon phase of their relationship and head over waders in love.

Karma couldn't count the number of times she'd been in the middle of a conversation with Jessie only to find her staring into space daydreaming about Fisher. Sure, she was happy for them, but jeez, sometimes being surrounded by the newlyweds made her feel as if she'd eaten an entire cake in one sitting and was suffering from insulin overload.

Karma elbowed Toni to get her attention. "So, Toni, who put the burr under your saddle?"

Toni kept a beat with the toe of her boot and blew out a breath ruffling her black bangs. "James called and told me Trapper, Hunter, Fisher, and Gramps kidnapped Bianca."

"What?" Jessie's I'm-still-having-honeymoon-sex starry-eyed expression fell faster than Evel Knievel over the Snake River Canyon. "No, they didn't. Kate told Fisher to fly to New York to pick up Bianca so there was a doctor on board in case she had problems. Trapper is a little overprotective."

Toni laughed and continued tapping. "From what James said, Trapper picked Bianca up from the hospital and let her think they were headed to her place, only to be taken to Teterboro and forced onto the plane." When Toni got upset, her New York accent gained strength. She sounded like she just got off the set of *The Sopranos*. "Believe me, the last place Bianca would willingly go is Boise. She'd never agree to be that far from Action Models no matter what the doctor said. The worst part is James aided and abetted Trapper. He feels guilty, but didn't know what else to do." Toni brought her thumb to her mouth and gnawed on the knuckle. "James is really worried about Bianca."

Karma shook her head. Her brothers were idiots. "Mom said the babies are fine, but the stress of running a business and having twins is enough to take down even Wonder Woman. No one mentioned Bianca hadn't agreed to the trip. I wonder if Mom knows."

Jessie copied Toni's pose. "It's not easy to deal with the Kincaid version of the three musketeers, especially when you're the odd woman out, and Karma hasn't given you a primer on *The Care and Manipulation of the Kincaid Male*."

Bianca Ferrari might not be Karma's favorite person, but no woman—not even Bianca—deserved to have the Kincaid men run roughshod over her. She was amazed Bianca allowed it to happen. Bianca was no wilting flower, which meant she had to be in pretty bad shape. Karma actually felt sorry for her and worried about the babies. How could her mother allow this? "Where's Mom?"

Toni and Jessie shared a look, and then Toni cleared her throat. "She's still freshening up Trapper's place, stocking the refrigerator, and making it more comfortable for Bianca. We were working there all morning. Kate should be here any minute."

"Why didn't you call me?"

Jessie burst out laughing. "We saw how you helped Fisher. He still has the pink shorts, underwear, and T-shirts to prove it."

Karma held up her hand. "I get the picture. What can I say? I'm domestically challenged." There was no need to rub it in.

"We know." Jessie didn't understand the hand gesture, obviously since she just kept going. "Kate figured it would be safer for us to handle the housekeeping."

"That's fine, you three take care of making sure Bianca and my nieces have everything they need to stay healthy. I'll deal with the boys. Man, are they in trouble."

—◦◦◦—

Bianca sat strapped in while the plane descended into Boise. How was she supposed to survive three weeks of nonstop Kincaids? Dealing with Trapper was bad enough, but to be stuck with Hunter, Fisher, their wily grandfather—oh, and Karma. God forbid she forgot the vixen who was out for blood. What would Karma think of her now? She didn't believe it was possible Karma's opinion of her could get any lower, but if there were a way, getting knocked up by her sainted brother and breaking his nose would probably do the trick. Oh yes, this will be as much fun as a barrel of rabid Madagascar monkeys.

Trapper sat across from her. Staring. Not saying a word. His silence was annoying. Almost as annoying as the way he watched her every move as if she was a human test subject in the midst of an experiment. She didn't like being on this side of the one-way mirror. And it was like a mirror. Oh, she could see him, but he put on that blank, emotionless face he wore when she'd seen him on the bench.

She couldn't take it anymore. "Would you stop looking at me like that?"

"Like what?" He moved over to sit beside her, buckled in, and wrapped his arm around her, drawing her close. "Like I want to strip you naked and lick every inch of you?"

Damn him. He was good. One sentence in his bedroom voice, and her hormones were in a tizzy. "You weren't looking at me like that. Your face was blank." She'd seen more expressive mannequins in Macy's—of course, they weren't nearly as colorful. He looked like a newbie on the losing side of a DSW shoe sale.

"Did you happen to look at my lap?"

"No."

"Yeah, well, that's where you went wrong, babe. We're not alone. Worse, we're with my brothers and grandfather. I can hardly give you the I-want-to-do-you-six-ways-from-Sunday look while under close scrutiny, can I?"

"Trapper, I'm here in a plane on my way to Boise. You've won. Congratulations. Now leave me alone. I'm not in the mood to be messed with any more than I already have been."

"You're accusing me of messing with you? How, exactly?"

"Don't insult my intelligence," she whispered. The last thing she wanted was for the rest of the plane's occupants to overhear this conversation, but she wasn't about to let it pass. "I might not be a highfalutin judge, but I'm no idiot. I have a mirror. I know what I look like, not to mention what I've done to you. I broke your nose."

"The nose was an accident, but what does that have to do with what you look like?" His voice sounded like gravel, and when she glanced at his face, her heart rate spiked and she did her best to move away. She preferred the blank face to the one she'd caught a glimpse of. By the way his jaw clenched—the muscle twitching beneath his five-o'clock shadow, combined with the popping and throbbing of the veins in his temples—his Pissed-O-Meter had spiked on totally. She'd never seen him this angry. Okay, that wasn't completely true. Trapper had been plenty pissed when he thought she'd tried to take advantage of his not-so-little brother, but she hadn't looked closely at him. She'd been too busy dying of embarrassment. Then there was the time she tossed lukewarm, bad coffee in his face, but he looked more amused than angry. No, she didn't think she'd ever seen Trapper Kincaid lose his temper, but right now, he looked like he was about to.

"If you hit me in the face to stop me from wanting you, sweetheart, you went for the wrong body part. Believe me, all my parts are in working order. My eyes might be black, but I can see just fine, and you look as incredible as ever—plus, you have that whole Madonna thing workin' for you. Babe, if I wasn't toast before, I am now."

"Madonna?"

"Oh yeah. Normal pregnant women are over the top sexy. And then there's you."

"What's that supposed to mean?"

"Don't play dumb, Bianca. You and I both know you're not. Not only are you physically one of the most beautiful women in the world, but your brain is a freakin' aphrodisiac."

Bianca had been in the business long enough to know that beauty had a lot more to do with makeup, lighting, and airbrushing than the model. There were makeup artists and photographers who could make even the homeliest person look beautiful. Bianca won the genetic lottery in that she had the height, the build, and the bone structure to model. There were a million other women who had more natural beauty and charm than she could ever claim, and they didn't have to work for it. She did. For her, beauty and charm didn't come naturally.

She thought it was just her stomach that dropped. When the wheels of the plane hit the runway, panic seized her. A minute later, everyone was up and moving around the cabin, and then Trapper was hustling her down the steps into a crowd.

Toni was the first person Bianca recognized. Her black hair hanging loose, her clothes less Goth than Bianca remembered, but then she saw her boots. It was good to know that some things stayed the same.

Toni pulled Bianca into a hug, and she was suddenly surrounded by women. "I know you might not be happy to be here, but I'm so glad you are. Let me look at you." She held her at arm's length and gave her a once-over, missing nothing. "Wow, you look—"

Karma pushed Toni out of the way. "Like crap. Sorry," she spoke to the group, "but it's true." Karma didn't look sorry. "Bianca, I never thought I'd say this, but welcome to Boise. It's really wonderful to see you, and it's a good thing you're here, but I'm still gonna kill my brothers for pulling that stunt on you." She leaned in to whisper in Bianca's ear, "I'll give you a crash course on Kincaid male management. I'll be over tomorrow for your first class." Then, as if things weren't surreal enough, Karma pulled her into a hug. "Don't worry. I'll make them pay. Leave it all up to me."

Karma was happy to see her?

"May I?"

Bianca was really confused. "May you what?"

Karma's green eyes sparkled with undisguised joy. "Those are my nieces you're carrying, and I heard that pregnant women get a little wigged out when people pat their baby bumps without permission. So I didn't want to just…you know, reach over and feel your belly, even though I'm just dying to."

"Your nieces? You're happy about this? I was afraid that you would…"

Karma smiled at her—something that had never hap-pened before. "You were afraid that I'd what?"

Bianca shook her head, hoping to make sense of Karma's turnaround. "Never mind."

"Well, can I?"

Trapper pushed through the women and pulled Bianca against him. "Karma, would you please leave Bianca alone?"

Karma's gaze went from Bianca's belly to Trapper's face, and she burst out laughing. "Oh my God! Did Bianca do that to you?"

Fisher came up beside them and put his arm around a tall brunette. "She sure did. Nice one, huh? She elbowed him in the face and broke his nose."

All eyes turned to Bianca, and no one but maybe Trapper's mother looked at all upset. "It was an accident."

"Sure it was," Karma said, but her eyes were filled with merriment. "Did anyone get pictures?" She waited a beat. "I didn't think so." Karma pulled out her iPhone and snapped one. "Now we'll have one for posterity." Karma stared at Bianca's middle. "You're not really showing much, are you?" She patted Bianca's baby bump. "See, girls"—she held up her phone—"Auntie Karma's already got the goods for your baby books."

Fisher leaned toward Bianca with a grin as wide as the Mississippi. "Karma, the babies can't see through the uterus. Bianca, this is my wife, Jessie. Jess, this is Bianca Ferrari."

Bianca tried to smile at the woman who looked at her with sympathetic eyes.

"Don't worry, Bianca. You'll get used to

them—eventually. They're really not as scary as they seem at first. They mean well. Mostly."

Kate clapped her hands. "Okay. Bianca and Trapper need to get home."

Everyone moved when this woman spoke. She was like a five-foot-four powerhouse.

"Trapper, I stocked your pantry and fridge with food for you and Bianca."

"Thanks, Mom."

Kate took both Bianca's hands in hers. "I hope you'll be comfortable. If there's anything you need, just call me. I was deathly ill with the twins for the first five months. I hope your morning sickness will pass too."

"Thank you. I hope you're right. I'm almost there."

Kate gave her hands a squeeze. "I'll stop by for a visit tomorrow if you're feeling up to it. I'll call first, as will anyone who wants to see you." She turned and met everyone's eyes. "Is that understood?"

A chorus of "Yes, ma'am" followed.

"Good, then. Fisher and Hunter will bring the luggage. Trapper, why don't you take Bianca home now and let her get settled?" She hugged Bianca. "There's soup in the Crock-Pot, dear, whenever you're up to eating."

"Thank you." Bianca didn't know what was worse, the thought of food, or how nice everyone was being. She was either going to barf or bawl—knowing her, probably both.

Chapter 8

TRAPPER TOOK ONE LOOK AT THE KINCAID'S VERSION OF the Welcome Wagon and wondered if bringing Bianca home had been a mistake. Especially since every female in the family had turned on him—every female, except maybe his mother. Right now, he was unsure if his mother was pissed at him or at the situation. She paid more attention to Bianca than she did to him, which wasn't a problem, but it made it impossible to get a read on her.

Hunter sidled up to him. "Thanks, Bro."

Trapper's broken nose throbbed, his head ached like a son-of-a-bitch, and all he wanted was to go home, take a handful of Motrin, curl up with Bianca in front of the fire, and hold her. He met Hunter's not-so-happy-to-be-home glare. "What are you thanking me for?"

"For whatever you did to get Toni pissed as shit at me. Look at her tapping the toe of her combat boot. I'm so fucked, and I don't even know what the hell I did."

"Toni and James are friends, and James wasn't a happy accomplice in Bianca's—"

"Kidnapping?"

"I didn't kidnap her, but Mom warned me that Bianca would not be happy about me bringing her to Boise. I had no choice. I didn't think I'd get her here any other way."

Hunter scrubbed his face with his hands. "Great. That's just great. I help you out, and I end up in the doghouse."

Trapper shrugged. "Hey, at least you get to look forward to the makeup sex."

Hunter looked at his wife and smiled. "There is that." He slung his arm around Trapper's shoulders. "I hope you appreciate all the sacrifices I make for you."

Trapper reminded himself that Hunter meant it as a joke. Probably, but it still made Trapper want to smack the shit out of him.

He spent his life taking care of his brothers and sister. He didn't mind being the big brother. He couldn't count the number of times he'd come to the rescue of one or both of the twins. He shook his head; he didn't even want to think of how many times he'd saved Karma's bacon.

In all the years, this was the first time he'd ever asked any of them for a damn thing, and it had just about killed him. He was the one who handled every problem. He was the one who led by example. But this time, for the first time, he was the one who had screwed up.

Being a screw up was new to him, and he didn't like it. Not one bit. The one thing he liked even less was catching shit from his little brother. He was in enough trouble with Bianca. He hadn't heard the end of it.

Trapper took a look at his mother hugging Bianca and saw all the signs of a meltdown brewing in her eyes. To say she was overwhelmed was an understatement of massive proportions. He needed to get her out of there. "I'll have you home in ten minutes, fifteen tops." He gave her a kiss while he buckled her into his Sequoia.

By the time he made it into the driver's seat, she'd lost the battle with the tears. "Are you okay?"

She waved a hand to brush him off while she sobbed into Gramps's hankie.

"Raging hormones?"

She nodded.

He patted her thigh. The sun had just set when they left the airport. Trapper headed downtown on Capital Boulevard. "Boise State University is there on the right. And that's the capital building straight ahead." The Christmas tree was still up and lit, making the grounds look like a picture postcard. The foothills beyond were covered with snow, but there wasn't any in the valley. They crossed the river and took a right on Main Street heading east, onto Warm Springs Avenue.

Bianca looked around and didn't say anything. It was a culture shock coming from New York, but the tree-lined street was beautiful and had some of the grandest homes in Boise all decked out with Christmas lights. His wasn't grand or decorated, but it was home.

He pulled into his driveway of the craftsman cottage he'd bought a few years ago for a song. He'd painstakingly refinished all the woodwork and built-ins—all of which had the gorgeous leaded glass insets. He'd gutted the kitchen and baths—only saving the woodwork framing the doorways and windows—and did his best to keep the flavor of the craftsman era.

It took two years, but when he finally finished, he loved the place. It wasn't one of the big estate homes the street was known for, but he'd never wanted one of them. They weren't his style, the craftsman cottage was—it had more than enough room for a family. He'd never planned to have a family, but was glad he had the space now. The motion sensor lights on the drive and backyard flicked on, and he parked outside the carriage house.

"This wasn't what I expected."

He went around to open her door. "What did you expect?"

"A condo or an apartment, I guess."

He took her hand and helped her out. "Nope, not my style. I like my space." He never thought he'd see her here. Oh, he'd dreamed of her coming to his place. He'd pictured her in every room, but he never actually thought she'd come. He just wished she were happier about it.

Bianca looked around the backyard he and his mother had landscaped. His mother was a force to be reckoned with, so a smart man just nodded and agreed to whatever she deemed necessary when it came to the yard. He'd learned that when she'd done Fisher's house. He couldn't complain though. No matter what time of year, it always looked great.

Bianca stared at the house. "It looks as if space isn't in short supply here."

He didn't consider a four-bedroom, two-and-a-half-bath home large. If she thought this was big, he couldn't wait until she got a load of Gramps's place. "It's comfortable." He opened the door and then entered the security code.

"You have an alarm system? In Boise?"

He raised an eyebrow. "I'm a sitting judge. We do have criminals here, and I tend to put them away. Unfortunately, sometimes they get out."

"I hadn't thought of that." She said it in a whisper.

Shit, he hadn't wanted to scare her. He let her into the mudroom off the kitchen. "I haven't had any problems, but with Karma living over the Carriage House, I thought it would be better to be safe than sorry."

"Karma lives with you?" Horror flashed across Bianca's face.

"No, she lives over there." He pointed out back to the carriage house. "It's a two-bedroom apartment. I rarely see her, but she takes care of the lawn and keeps an eye on the house while I'm away."

The house smelled like apple pie and chicken soup. His stomach growled. "So, do you feel like eating?"

She gave him the same look Karma did when she was three and had to eat her spinach before she could have dessert. The look may have said no, but they both knew she had to.

"Where do you want to lie down—in bed or on the couch?"

"I'd like to change, but my clothes aren't here."

"No problem." He took her hand and led her to the bedroom. "You can wear a pair of my sweats."

The look on her face was priceless. "Oh, that'll be real attractive."

"I think so, not to mention comfortable." He opened a drawer and took out a worn, red Dickinson sweatshirt and a pair of sweatpants. "I can bring in a bowl of soup and some crackers. Mom brought over a bed tray if you want to stay in here." He pointed to the fireplace. "I can turn the fireplace on, and we can curl up. Or, if you want, we can go to the den and watch some TV."

She looked from him to his king-size bed and back. "Where are you planning to sleep?"

"With you. The other bedrooms are upstairs."

"But—"

"Bianca, let's eat, and then we'll talk. You need to keep food in your stomach, and it's been awhile since you've eaten anything."

"Fine, but—"

"Get dressed. The bathroom is through there." He pointed to the door and left, closing the bedroom door behind him. The last thing he wanted was one of his brothers walking in on her.

He couldn't believe she actually asked where he'd sleep. They'd slept together every place they'd ever stayed—not that there was much sleeping involved, but still, it wasn't as if they'd never shared a bed. If he had anything to say about it, they'd be sharing a bed from now on.

Bianca looked around Trapper's bedroom. It was painted a Wedgwood blue with a rich brown accent wall and was dominated by what looked like an antique sleigh bed. Did they have king-size antique beds, or was it a reproduction? It was so nice, she couldn't tell, and she usually could. The room was beautifully furnished, homey, comfortable, and it smelled like him.

She took a deep breath and examined the framed pictures of his family. It was as if they'd been blessed with beauty and happiness. They were like *Father Knows Best*, but in their case it was *Grandfather Knows Best*.

Kate, Trapper's mother, was a formidable woman who kept her family close. She loved them—that was apparent. It showed in everything she did, even the way she looked at them with a combination of pride, love, and exasperation. Until she'd met Kate at Toni and Hunter's wedding, until she'd seen the family in action—that kind of love was something Bianca had only seen on TV.

She ran her finger over the group photo. They were

probably the most beautiful gathering of people she'd ever seen. Not that Trapper was beautiful—no, he was way too masculine to ever be considered pretty. Gorgeous, yes, sexy as sin, yup, and his body was a work of art. Still, his imperfections made all the rest of it work. Sure, he had a dimple, but the scar by his eye spoke of a bad-boy past. His nose, before she'd re-broken it, had been a little crooked. His lips... She swallowed just remembering the feel of them on her body. His lips were full, almost feminine, if they didn't twist into such a sardonic grin whenever he looked at her. His green eyes with golden starbursts held so much heat and emotion, they were enough to steal a woman's breath and heart. And when he got angry, the gold in them sparkled like freshly minted coins. Anger colored his face, highlighting his sharp cheekbones against the ever-present golden brown stubble. Trapper Kincaid angry was enough to make her want to piss him off on an hourly basis.

She set the picture down. Drooling over him wouldn't help the situation. She looked at the other picture and caught her breath. It was one of her at the lodge from last summer. She was laughing at something. He must have taken it when she wasn't looking. Just when she thought she had Trapper figured out, he went and surprised her. Why would he have a picture of her in his bedroom? She put it back exactly where she'd found it and sat on the bed. It was a gorgeous bedroom full of impressive pieces, but then everything about Trapper was impressive.

The house was beautiful, stunning really, in a totally Trapper way. She hadn't known what to expect. Part of her wondered if he'd have deer mounts hanging on the walls with his collection of cowboy hats dangling off the antlers. But when she'd walked in, she realized the house was just like him—simple, comfortable, with relaxed charm and understated elegance.

The kitchen was something out of a magazine. The man was either a gourmet cook, or he expected to marry one. Well, it wouldn't be her. She couldn't boil water without a microwave and a prayer.

She pulled off her clothes—the clothes he'd brought to the hospital. It seemed like a lifetime ago but was only yesterday. At least they'd matched. All black. With her recent state of constant nausea, wearing black made her look like a ghost. She would have thrown a scarf around her neck to give her some color, but then Trapper hadn't thought of that. James would have, though, and had even offered to lend her his when she saw him on the plane before she'd left.

She missed James already. He was her only friend, and now, he was almost three thousand miles away. Tears threatened to fall. Damn, she really hated these pregnancy hormones.

She dressed in Trapper's sweats and cinched the waist, happy she still needed to, and smoothed out the wrinkles on the bed. She really didn't want to sleep with Trapper. Okay, she wanted to sleep with Trapper, but not. She was huge and ugly and well, not attractive. Besides, they were together for a few weeks, and that was way longer than seventy-two hours. Shit, she could barely hold her own for three days. What the hell was she going to do for three weeks? She couldn't play house with him; it would be too painful once she had to go home. And with him in bed with her, there was no way she wouldn't be all over him. It would be like putting a diabetic with a sweet tooth in a candy store. It was bad enough she dreamed of him. If he was right there beside her, she didn't have a prayer of controlling herself.

She rolled up the sleeves of the sweatshirt and realized that it smelled like him. Just wearing it made her horny. She didn't think it possible to feel as bad as she did and still want to jump someone's bones, but then pregnancy changed everything—especially her sex drive.

There was a knock on the door, and then it swung open. Trapper carried a tray with a bowl of soup, a glass of milk, and a sleeve of crackers. "Dinner is served. Mom makes the best chicken soup this side of the Mississippi—don't tell her, but I've had better in New York. There they put matzo balls in it—hers has homemade noodles."

Trapper had taken his hat off. A precaution? It wasn't as if she didn't feel bad enough for barfing in his beloved Stetson. He should have hat-head, but he didn't. His hair curled in the back and almost hit his shoulders, and the smile he shot her showed off his dimples, beautiful lips, and his white teeth. His rolled sleeves exposed strong forearms. His feet were bare. Shit, the man even had sexy feet. And his jeans were worn to the point of being bleached on the fly and hugged him like a desperate lover. He was dangerous to her peace of mind.

"Do you want to get in bed, or do you want to go lie on the couch?"

"The couch." It would be safer, but then she remembered

all the things they'd done on her couch. Maybe the table. Nope, that wasn't safe either.

"Grab a few pillows and follow me."

She did and then got to stare at his ass the whole way across the house. By the time they made it to the family room, she was drooling, and it had nothing to do with the soup. She tossed the pillows on the couch, pushed one behind her back, and stretched out, hoping he'd take the chair.

Oh, no, he sat beside her, placed the tray over her lap, and rested her feet on his thighs.

Bianca was just about to take a tentative sip of the soup when his thumb pressed into the instep of her left foot and ran toward her toes, stopping at the ball to massage some more. He hit every pressure point before moving on to the other foot. She'd never realized that her feet were directly connected to other parts of her body—the girl parts. Her mouth dropped open, and her toes curled in pleasure. She'd dated a world-class masseur who wasn't as good with his hands.

"You're supposed to be eating."

She was too busy trying not to groan in ecstasy. He slid his hands up the leg of her sweats and massaged her calf while rotating her ankle and releasing stress she didn't know she had. It turned her on in ways that were all new to her. His thumbs caressed the back of her knee, and it felt as if it was connected to her nipples.

"You need to stop that." Her face flushed, she sounded breathless—maybe because she was—and her voice deepened, passing the point of recognition. She was strung so tight; one more touch, and she might just explode.

His gaze met hers, his eyes widened, and he picked up the tray with her uneaten food and put it on the coffee table. "God, Bianca." He lifted her foot, kissed the instep and dragged his teeth across it, while his other hand played havoc with the back of her knee. "You were always so responsive, but damn, you look as if you're about to come."

She was. It was all she could do not to. She pressed her legs together.

Trapper kissed her instep and slid his hand farther up the inside of her sweats and between her legs.

"You're so hot, so wet." He slipped his fingers beneath the elastic of her panties, pressed his thumb against the swollen bundle of nerves. Her hips rose of their own accord, her thighs flopped open, and she groaned.

"I've never seen anything more beautiful than you coming."

His deep, gravelly voice increased her need, her heart rate, her desire.

"Come on, sweetheart, just let go. You know you want to." He slid a finger into her, then two, and curled them hitting the target like a master marksman. Between that and the pressure of his thumb circling, she was a goner. She rode his hand, her heart raced, and she felt every muscle in her body strain toward release until she couldn't hold back. She flew apart, her back arching, her body quivering under the onslaught, and he didn't let up. If anything, he doubled his effort, making the orgasm last for what seemed like forever until she was limp, wrung out, and breathless.

Trapper groaned, and when she opened her eyes, she swore her heart skipped a beat. She'd never seen anyone look at her with such heat, such desire, such desperation.

A door slammed. "Trapper, we're here with the luggage. Where do you want it?" Two pairs of boots stomped across hardwood floors, and Bianca's eyes shot open.

"Fuck." Trapper pulled his hands out of her pants, stuck his fingers in his mouth, and licked them clean as if he'd just finished a messy ice cream cone. "It's Dumb and Dumber. I'll get rid of them." He stood and pulled his shirttails out of his pants, probably hoping to hide the telltale bulge. It didn't. His face was flushed, his cheekbones stood out sharply against his taut skin, his eyes were dilated, and his breathing was uneven. They were so busted. "Just put them in the bedroom," he hollered before kissing her full on the lips.

She hadn't expected that. Hell, she hadn't expected the way his tongue swirled in her mouth, and she definitely hadn't expected the little meteor shower that lit her up like a sparkler on the Fourth of July.

"Damn, sweetheart, you're not helping me here." He adjusted himself, blew out a breath, and put her food tray over her lap. "Eat. Believe me—you're going to need the nourishment."

———

Trapper took a few cleansing breaths, stuffed his hands in his pockets, and walked to the kitchen, stopping at the doorway. He leaned against the woodwork, wrapping the entrance, and caught his brothers eyeing the soup and sniffing the pie. Hunter held the lid to the Crock-Pot and met his gaze. "Damn, how'd you rate?"

"I had nothing to do with it. Mom made it for Bianca, and you're not welcome to join us. Just put her things in my bedroom and get out."

Fisher looked at Hunter with a raised eyebrow and checked his watch. "You owe me a twenty."

Hunter turned on him with a look of disgust. "Shit, Trapper, you couldn't even wait an hour and give the lady time to settle in?" He pulled a bill from his pocket and slapped it on Fisher's palm, ignoring Trapper's growl. "Damn, Fisher. How'd you know?"

Fisher rocked back on the heels of his boots, "A man learns a lot about women when he does a round in obstetrics and gynecology. Just you wait until you and Toni start down that road."

Trapper had heard enough. "Bring Bianca's things in, and don't let the door hit you in the ass on the way out."

Fisher looked him up and down, and a cocky grin split his face. He cleared his throat "Oh, so it was one of those." Fisher slid into his Bill Cosby voice doing his best impression of Dr. Cliff Huxtable, OB-GYN. "Don't worry. You can have normal sexual relations without hurting Bianca or the babies. Sex is good for all of them. Just watch the positions—"

Trapper held up his hand, cutting off his little brother. "I'm not talking to you about my sex life, thank you very much."

"I just thought—"

"Don't. Just bring in Bianca's things and leave. And be quick about it." He turned on his heel, and then stopped. "Oh, and don't you dare touch that pie, or I'm calling Mom."

Hunter grunted, "Shit, I hope he gets some soon. He's been a bear. At least now we know why. The man's gone without for months. I think that's a record."

Trapper didn't wait for Fisher's reply. He didn't need

to. He had been a bear. If he didn't get his hands on Bianca soon, he'd go nuts. It had taken all his control to watch her go over and not come in his pants like a teenager. When he stepped into the family room and saw the mortified look on Bianca's face, he knew two things: Bianca had heard every word, and it was going to be a long night. "Bianca, I'm sorry—"

Fisher popped his head in. The man was either very brave, or very stupid.

Right now, Trapper was going with stupid. "I told you to leave."

Fisher held up his medical bag. "I want to get Bianca's blood pressure before I go." He shot Bianca a wink that made her blush even more and sat down beside her. "Come on, sunshine, roll up a sleeve for me. I'll get a reading and let you two get back to whatever it was you were doing." Fisher put his stethoscope around his neck, and Trapper was tempted to use it as a garrote, but was more afraid of his mother than any grown man would ever admit. Fisher knew it and took full advantage.

Trapper would get him back for the hell Fisher put him through, and paybacks were a bitch.

"Look at that. Your blood pressure has improved. It's still a little high, but nothing like it was earlier. Being here seems to agree with you. I guess Trapper's doing something right." He stood, put his things away, and snapped the bag shut. "Get plenty of rest, drink lots of fluids, and call me when you get up in the morning. I'll stop by and check on you before I head to the hospital for rounds."

Trapper had just about enough. "Is that really necessary?"

Fisher put his hand on Bianca's shoulder, gave it a

squeeze, and morphed into his doctor persona. "Until Bianca is seen by her new ob-gyn, yes, it's necessary. I'll be over in the morning."

It was hard to be proud of the little shit and be pissed at him at the same time. Trapper shook his head and walked Fisher out. When they got to the back door, he grabbed Fisher's shoulder to stop him. "Is she really okay?"

"For sex or in general?"

"Both."

"She needs to eat. See how her stomach is afterward, and if everything stays down, I'd say she's fine. If she's sick all night, there's a cold shower in your immediate future."

"Hell, I know that."

"Well then, my job here is done. I'll see you in the morning. Good luck. You'll need it."

"Yeah, thanks to you and Hunter. Where the hell is he anyway?"

Fisher smiled. "He's out in the car. He doesn't have a doctor's bag to hide behind."

"Smart man." Trapper locked up after his brothers left and turned down most of the lights. He wasn't in any rush to get back to Bianca. He needed to get a hold of himself. He dished out another bowl of soup. When he returned, she was staring at her food. "I brought you a hot bowl. I'll just microwave that one, and I'll eat it."

"No, I'm not very hungry."

"You heard Fisher. You need to eat. Doctor's orders."

"Yeah, I heard everything."

He sat beside her and replaced one bowl with the other. "I know. I'm sorry."

"They took bets on our sex life?"

Shit, she had really good ears. "They're morons. What can I say?"

"Did you have to tell them?"

"Sweetheart, I didn't tell them a blasted thing. I just told them to get lost."

"Then how did they know?"

"Guys just know these things. Look, they're my brothers. We give each other shit on a daily basis. Don't you razz your siblings?"

She shook her head. "I'm an only child."

"Oh." How could he not know that? "I can't imagine not growing up with Ben, the twins, and Karma. It must have been lonely for you."

She shrugged and stirred her soup. "It's all I knew."

He ate a spoonful of his. Damn, it was good, and he was starving. "You'll get used to it."

"That's what Jessie said, but I don't see that happening."

"It might surprise you. Jessie is an only child too, and she's survived the Kincaid family welcome. Hers was far worse than yours, believe me."

"How could it be worse?"

"Everyone thought Jessie was a man."

"A man? How is that possible? She's one of the most beautiful women I've ever seen. I was tempted to ask her if she was interested in modeling."

"It's Karma's fault."

Bianca looked like she was fighting a smile. "Karma's pure evil. You know that, right?"

He couldn't help but laugh. "Yes, but she means well. Usually. We hope."

"You know what she's like, and you still fall for her stunts?"

"Every freakin' time. Maybe we're all morons. What can I say? The girl's really good at playing us. She's been practicing her entire life." He stilled Bianca's hand that was stirring the soup. "Eat that, and I'll tell you about what happened with Jessie and Fisher. If Jessie can get past her introduction to the family, you should have no problem."

Chapter 9

BIANCA WOKE WITH THE FEELING OF BEING LIFTED. SHE just missed hitting Trapper's nose again when she startled and screamed.

"Shh. I've got you." He held her against his chest, the way he'd carry a child.

She clung to his neck.

He'd stepped away from the couch where she must have fallen asleep after eating.

She remembered he'd been telling her a funny story about the family walking in on Jessie and Fisher in bed, and then it was as if someone had just cut the tape—there was nothing else. "Put me down. I can walk."

"No need. I'm taking you to bed." They were moving out of the family room, and if she remembered correctly, he was headed straight for the master bedroom.

Great. Just what she'd tried to avoid. She made the mistake of looking at his face. If the heat in his gaze wasn't enough to make her raging hormones take their positions at the starting line on the race to completion, the pheromones he emitted warranted a meteorological warning. Bianca was woman enough to admit she fought a losing battle, especially when every fiber of her being wanted to hold up a white flag, possibly green—go full-speed ahead.

Trapper set her on the bed with a gentleness that belied the sexual urgency pumping out of him in waves.

The tension in the room spiked, and she didn't know how much more she could take. She wasn't sure why he wanted her, but it was clear he did, and damned if it wasn't mutual. She didn't release his neck. She held on, pulling him over her.

His arms braced his upper body above hers.

She tugged him into kissing range. If she was going to have sex, she wanted to do it now before she lost the unusual spurt of energy that hit her upon waking.

She smiled when she realized that kissing a man with Trapper's injuries needed to be done carefully. Or that's what she thought until their mouths met, and he stole control of the kiss. The man was like a master pick-pocket. She didn't know she'd even lost it until his hand cupped the back of her head, tilted it to his satisfaction, and then hit her with the sonic boom of his groan.

His tongue filled her mouth, and she tensed, waiting for the inevitable gag reflex to start. It didn't.

Lately, she had a hard time just brushing her teeth but thanked the sex gods his tongue didn't cause the same reaction. After a few seconds of success, she relaxed into the kiss, dragged her nails over his scalp, and slid her other hand under the waistband of his jeans, grabbing his ass.

His taste was familiar. Exciting. His touch ramped it all the way up. She didn't want to take the time to rip clothes off; she wanted him with an urgency she'd never felt before. It went beyond want. It went beyond need. It was primal.

She wrapped her legs around his waist, arched her back, and ripped her mouth from his when they made full contact. "Oh God, yes!"

It had been so long since she'd felt his weight on her, so long since she'd felt the length of his erection against her. Hell, it had been months since she'd felt remotely sexual while she was awake anyway. She yanked the button band of his jeans and heard the satisfying slide of the zipper.

"Bianca, sweetheart, wait—"

"Wait? No. I can't wait." If she didn't have her hand wrapped around his dick, she'd wonder if he wasn't into it. But by the way his dick jumped and throbbed, she knew that wasn't the problem.

"The babies—"

"Are just fine. Dammit, Trapper. I'm the one who's hurting here."

Trapper bounded off her so fast, you'd think he'd been hit with a cattle prod. "I hurt you?"

He was killing her, but anything she was about to say evaporated when the color drained from his face. She took a deep breath. "Calm down. I was speaking metaphorically, not literally."

He collapsed beside her, his breathing ragged. "Don't scare me like that."

"Then don't leave me hanging."

He lay on his side facing her, his jeans open and tugged down, making her thankful either he wasn't a fan of underwear or it was washday. Either way, it worked for her. "I'm not leaving you hanging—believe me. We need to be careful how… I mean, I've never…not with a pregnant woman."

"Oh, yes, you have." She slid onto her side and kicked off the sweatpants she wore.

His gaze traveled the length of her legs. At least pregnancy hadn't changed them—yet.

She ran her hand over the front band of his shirt before starting in on the buttons. He wore way too many clothes. "You had an amazing amount of sex with a pregnant woman." She kissed the skin of his chest she bared. When she reached his belly button she stopped. She wanted to slide that dick of his right into her mouth, but figured that would be asking for trouble. "We just weren't aware I was pregnant at the time." She pushed the shirt off his shoulders, catching the glint of disappointment in his eyes. "Remember that long weekend in London?"

Oh, he remembered all right. His dick just about waved hello at the mention of it.

She hid a smile as she pulled her sweatshirt off. She wore a thin, stretchy tank top beneath it. Her breasts had gotten larger, but then so had her middle. She wasn't sure what his reaction would be and didn't have the guts to look. "Then there was Milan." She slipped out of her panties and kicked them onto the floor, rolling back to face him, avoiding his gaze. "Oh, and we had sex all over New York." She shoved him onto his back, climbed aboard without permission, and settled onto his thighs. "We can't forget that now, can we?" She walked her hands from his belly to his shoulders, and finally got the guts to look into his eyes. Trapper and she were swollen-nose to nose. Her long hair curtained his face. His erection slid between them. All it would take was one move on his part to do the deed, or one word to kill whatever she hoped was brewing between them.

"God, Bianca." He sat, drawing her up with him, so she rested on his thighs. His gaze raked her from head to belly and back again. "Do you have any idea how sexy you are?" He grabbed the hem of the tank she'd made sure covered her belly and pulled it up so fast, she couldn't even catch it before it stopped under her arms, leaving her breasts and belly exposed.

"You're so beautiful. So hot." His arms wrapped around her, and his mouth found her nipple, sucking it gently, but since her pregnancy her breasts had become a million times more sensitive. One hand worked her other breast, the other hand palmed her baby bump, his fingers sliding farther south. Sitting this way, her belly didn't seem as large as it did when she was trying to squeeze into her clothes. "Bianca, you have me so on edge, this first time is gonna be fast. It's been a long time—since New York. I'm about ready to go off just looking at you."

She couldn't believe her own ears. Then she noticed the way his jaw clenched, all the muscles in his chest and stomach delineated, and the tremor that ran through him.

"If I were more of a gentleman, I'd make sure you were taken care of first, but damn, sweetheart, I'm about to come. I need to—"

She slid down onto him, and he groaned as he dragged her other breast into his mouth and sucked hard. Between his hand circling the bundle of nerves, his mouth on her breast, and his depth and angle—he hit all the right places, throwing her right into an orgasm.

Trapper took control when all she could do was feel. He rocked into her, guiding her movements, thrusting, and sent her over again before he found his release. He pulled her against him, shaking, and held her so tight— tighter than he'd ever held her before. His face pressed against her neck, his every labored breath sent a little shiver of orgasm through her.

She never wanted him to catch his breath. She moved over him again. She was so close.

He hissed out a long breath, as if he was in pain, and then rolled his hips, hitting the exact spot that shot her higher until she swore her eyes rolled back into her head and her vision dimmed. Every muscle in her body convulsed—even her toes were getting in on the action.

"Bianca, are you all right?"

She still couldn't speak. All she could do was nod and hope he felt it.

"Sweetheart?" He slid down and rolled them onto their sides, pulling her leg over his hip, and making her gasp with delight. "Please, say something."

"Don't move. Okay, do move. Moving is good. Yeah, just like that. Just don't stop."

Trapper rolled over, reached for Bianca, and felt nothing but the sheet. His eye opened a crack. The clock said it was ten after eight. He sat and rubbed the sleep out of his eyes. He'd slept better than he had in months, and he woke with a smile on his face for the first time since he'd left her in New York.

He didn't know if his happiness was a product of thankfulness or relief—because shit, he was relieved that he hadn't hurt Bianca or the babies when they'd made love, and he was every bit as thankful that he was able to hold out as long as he had. If it had been over a minute, he'd consider it a freakin' miracle. He was just glad Bianca seemed to have developed a hair trigger.

He'd spent the night holding her while she slept. He couldn't stop touching her, exploring the body he knew so well, reveling in the changes he found, and realizing that they turned him on even more. If anyone had told him he'd want Bianca more now than he had before, he wouldn't have believed it possible, but he did. Everything about her fascinated him.

The shower turned on—that was his cue. There was nothing he loved better than Bianca in the shower. He rolled out of bed and was glad he got the high efficiency, fifty-gallon water heater. With any luck, they were going to need all of it.

He stepped into the shower at the perfect time. Bianca had her eyes closed, her back arched, head tilted back, and water cascaded through her long hair.

"Good morning." In his estimation, mornings didn't get any better.

Bianca's eyes shot open and widened. Then her hands flew to cover herself—her breasts, her belly. "What are you doing?"

He turned on the other showerhead. "Joining you. What does it look like?"

She turned her back to him. "It looks like you're interrupting. You could have asked."

"I didn't think I had to."

"I'm naked."

He stepped closer and slid his arms around her. "That's one of the perks of showering together." He nuzzled her neck. "Sweetheart, we've always showered together."

"That was then. This is different."

He turned her around and kissed her, holding her close. "How is it different?" He was obviously missing something. Something big. And navigating around a pregnant Bianca was like walking through a minefield with size fifteen feet and his eyes closed. "If you haven't noticed, Bianca, I'm a guy. If you have a problem, maybe you'd better spell it out."

She didn't look him in the eye. She stared at his chest. "I'm not comfortable being naked in front of you."

"Since when? I remember a time when the only clothes you wore was the hotel bathrobe, and that was only until the room service guy left."

"That was before I was almost five months pregnant with twins."

"What's that got to do with anything? Pregnancy hormones make you modest?"

"I'm not modest. I just don't want you to see me naked looking like this."

Not that he could see a thing, which was a damn shame. She still had her arms covering all the fun stuff, and those arms were stuck between them. He grabbed the bar of soap and ran it over her back, massaging tense muscles. Her skin felt like silk beneath his rough hands. "You were naked last night, and you didn't have a problem with it then."

"It was dark last night."

"Not that dark. Have I ever told you how beautiful you are in the moonlight?"

She laughed, and it wasn't a you're-so-funny laugh. It was more of a you're-lying laugh. "Light of any kind is not my friend."

"I disagree." He stepped back, took her hands, and tugged them away from the body he'd spent most of the night caressing while she slept. He took a good long look at her and let her see his reaction—hell, she'd have to be blind to miss it.

He'd seen Bianca scared, sick, and embarrassed. He'd seen her in all-business bitch mode, taking on difficult situations like William "The Refrigerator" Perry took on an offensive line, but he'd never seen her vulnerable—until now. "Bianca, sweetheart, look at me." He tipped her chin up until their eyes met. "I don't think I've ever seen you look more beautiful than you do right now. Not even in the swimsuit issue. Everything about you is beautiful—inside and out."

"You don't know me, and you don't need to tell me that to make me feel better. I look in the mirror, and my vision is fine." She wet her hair and squirted shampoo into her hand.

He watched her and did his best to push down the anger. He soaped his chest and counted to ten. "I might not know everything about you. I might not know where you went to school, or even if you did. But I know you—I know the stuff that counts."

The light of anger brightened her eyes, and she pumped the conditioner into her hand with way too much pressure. "You don't know squat. I've spent my life selling an image, and you bought into it."

"Bullshit. I read people for a living. I've spent more time reading you than probably anyone else. If it were only your image I saw, I wouldn't have wasted my time—at least not more than seventy-two hours. After all, I'm a guy, not a monk. But it was never the image I was interested in. At first it was the body, but then it was the stuff between your ears. And although you're the most beautiful woman I've ever seen, that's not what keeps me coming back. Oh, no. It was all those things I saw that you try so hard to hide."

Her vulnerability eclipsed the supermodel expression she showed the world. She went from looking at him as if he was like every other stupid guy who jacked off to her spread in *Sports Illustrated*, to something else entirely. Her face spun through a carnival wheel of emotions, slowing on self-consciousness, tripping over denial, and then bouncing back and forth between the pegs on either side of something that looked a hell of a lot like fear. She closed her eyes, stepped under the shower, and took her sweet time rinsing the conditioner out of her hair.

Bianca did her best to ignore Trapper, something that was nearly impossible even in the huge, doorless, walk-in shower. It was the kind of shower that made her want to take her time—just not today. Not with him there. Not even after what he said. She stood under the showerhead; the side jets made sure every square inch of her was drenched in luxury and warmth. It should have been cold. After all, it was January, but it wasn't. She wasn't sure if it was because of efficient heating, her own natural pregnancy heating system, or the fact that Trapper Kincaid stood next to her naked.

The shower was all grainy white rolled marble with black marble trim and built-in benches—a shower made for wet and wild trysts. Oh yeah, she wasn't going there. It was bad enough she'd gone there last night for real, not counting the dreams she had of him teasing her. She finished rinsing and turned off her share of the water.

Trapper was either delusional or deluded—she wasn't sure which. She grabbed a towel, wrapped it around herself, scurried out, and headed to her suitcases. She wanted to get dressed before Trapper got out of the bathroom. She'd die before she let him watch her tug clothing over her belly.

She hoped James had packed all the maternity clothes she'd bothered to buy. It seemed as if her girth had increased an inch overnight. She'd been wearing her stretchy leggings, but those were tight last week, making her look and feel like an overstuffed sausage escaping the casing.

She unzipped the first bag and pawed through the contents, tossing piece after piece of her useless pre-pregnancy wardrobe onto the bed. "No, this can't be happening."

She tugged the second bag onto the pile of clothes. She was going to kill James. Was this some kind of sick joke?

The third suitcase held all the bras and panties she'd already outgrown. Her eyes filled with tears. She reached for the fourth bag—shoes and toiletries—her last hope was dashed.

"What was James thinking?" He knew she kept all her maternity clothes in the spare bedroom. She just hadn't had the energy or the intestinal fortitude to ferry her fabulous wardrobe from the master to the spare closet and replace it with matronly maternity wear. She sat in a pile of clothes strewn all over the bed and let loose. She couldn't stop the torrent of tears; it was useless to try.

"What's the matter?"

She rubbed the tears out of her eyes and saw Trapper wearing nothing but a towel tied around his waist, looking more beautiful than any man had a right to.

"I have nothing to wear."

He looked at the explosion of clothes scattered all

over the bed, falling onto the floor and laughed. "What do you mean? I packed just about every piece of clothing you had in your closet—well, except for the evening gowns. I didn't think you'd have much use for them here."

"You did this?" She didn't realize she'd screamed until her vocal chords protested. She'd completely lost it and wasn't able to dial down the volume. She stood and got right into his face. "You not only kidnapped me, but you packed every piece of clothing I own that I can no longer fit into?"

He took a step back to avoid the finger she poked into his bare chest. "I packed your clothes. The ones in your closet. How the heck was I supposed to know they were the wrong ones?"

"You could have asked. Oh right, you couldn't because then I'd know I was being kidnapped!"

"I didn't kidnap you. I told you I was taking you home."

"You just failed to mention that it was *your* home you were referring to. Now what am I going to do? I don't even have a clean pair of panties to wear, and the only bra that fits, I've worn two days in a row because you didn't bring one to the hospital."

"I'm sorry?"

Oh, he's sorry. That makes all the difference. "You'll be sorry, all right. I'm leaving."

"Oh no you're not."

"Who's going to stop me?"

Someone behind them cleared his throat. "I am."

She turned to find Fisher stepping into the bedroom. She'd called to tell him she was awake, thinking she had plenty of time to get dressed. That was a joke. Now she stood there in nothing but a skimpy towel that barely covered her, crying and snotty and dying of embarrassment.

Trapper pulled her behind him and swore. "Fisher, did you forget how to knock?"

Fisher leaned against the doorjamb and crossed his arms, as if walking in on two people wearing only towels, having a knock-down, drag-out fight was a daily occurrence. "I knocked. I even rang the bell. I could hear the screaming from outside. Besides, I was invited. Bianca called. Didn't you, love?" The side of his mouth twisted into a cocky grin she wanted to wipe right off his face.

She slid her hand into the back of Trapper's towel so if he went after his brother, he'd do it naked. All she could see was Trapper's back muscles ridge out like a dog's, ready to attack. Her hold on Trapper's towel was the only thing protecting Fisher's life. The man was way too cocky for his own good, but she didn't think he deserved to have the wrath of Trapper come down on him.

"I thought I better come in to protect you, Trap. You can thank me later."

She released her hold on Trapper's towel. After that last crack, Fisher deserved whatever Trapper could dish out. Besides, if Trapper killed him, she'd have one less Kincaid to get through before leaving this madhouse.

Trapper took a slow, measured step toward Fisher, like a superhero gathering energy and preparing to blast his tormentor. "Get the hell out of here. Now." He didn't yell, if anything he'd gotten quieter. His voice was so low and deep, it reminded her of the far-off rumble of thunder—a prelude to one hell of a storm.

Fisher's smile disintegrated; gone was the happy-go-lucky Dr. Welby wannabe, only to be replaced by a grinning Dirty Harry. "Make me."

"Fisher Michael Kincaid." A female voice—Kate Kincaid's—flew into the room, and both men froze. "One more word out of you, and you'll be eating through a straw for the next eight weeks." Kate pushed Fisher aside as if he was no bigger than a toddler and stomped up to Trapper, hands on hips, expression fierce. The woman was a good foot shorter than her son, but somehow looked down her nose at him. "Trapper Stephen Kincaid, you wipe that smirk right off your face before I do it for you. Bianca's had quite enough. It's amazing the girl hasn't keeled over from testosterone poisoning."

Kate didn't spare either of the men a second glance, but Bianca felt her gaze as sure as she felt her nausea increasing. Kate went right to the closet, opened the door, reached in without looking, and somehow pulled out a beautiful, thick terry bathrobe. "Here now, Bianca. Let's wrap you in this. I don't want you to get chilled."

Bianca slid into the robe Kate held open and closed it before dropping the towel. "Thank you." She stepped back and sat on the bed, exhausted, and prayed she wouldn't end up barfing. She was embarrassed enough as it was.

Kate turned on the men. "For God's sake, Trapper, put some pants on, and you and your brother get out of this room. Oh, and if you're going to fight, take it outside. I refuse to clean up any blood splatter."

Bianca stared at her hand. She'd wrapped the belt around it so tightly, her fingers turned red and throbbed with every beat of her heart. She couldn't believe Kate kicked Trapper out of his own room. The slide of a drawer broke the thick silence, punctuated by the snick of a door closing. She looked up to find Kate picking clothes off the floor and neatly folding them. "Do you feel up to telling me what happened?"

The tears started again, and she ran for the bathroom, barely making it before losing what little was in her stomach.

—⁓—

Trapper stomped out of his bedroom feeling like a freakin' teenager. He was a thirty-five-year-old man, a sitting judge, for God's sake, and his own mother threw him out of his own bedroom in his own home.

Damn, faster than Trapper could pound his gavel, his day had gone from top-ten incredible to a knee-in-the-nuts nightmare. The only thing remotely redeeming about this clusterfuck was that his mom had all but given him permission to beat the crap out of Fisher. That was something. And right now, opening an industrial-size can of whoop-ass would feel fan-fucking-tastic.

"Oh, no." Fisher held up his hands. "Don't even think about it. If you pound on me, you'll have to answer to Jessie—and we both know you're not strong enough to take her on. My kickboxing, fifth-degree black belt–wearing wife will not only have you bloody and bruised in under a minute, but if you hurt me, she'll break a few ribs and an arm for good measure."

Fisher was probably right. Jessie was a hell of a fighter, and the girl fought dirty.

"Oh, and let's not forget that I'm the only person

keeping Bianca from getting on the next plane headed east. I just saved your ass. You owe me."

"The only thing I owe you little brother is a swirly. Don't push your luck. Hiding behind your wife is effective, but it will only get you so far. I might just tell Jessie what you did—walking into our bedroom like that—and let her kick *your* ass." He shot Fisher an evil smile. "Then I can tell everyone you got beat up by a girl." He rocked back on his heels. "Oh yeah, I like that."

Fisher took a seat on one of the bar stools, obviously seeing the error in his ways.

Trapper watched his little brother's mind spinning, searching for a change of topic.

Fisher's smile took shape when he hit on an idea. "So, now it's our bedroom, is it? I remember when my bedroom became our bedroom. Good times. So what happened?"

Trapper pulled out the coffee to make a pot. He needed caffeine, and having something to do besides kill Fisher wouldn't hurt either. "I came in from the shower, and she was crying. I'm not talking a few tears. I'm talking a-full-box-of-tissues-minimum weeping, complete with hiccups and the shoulder shake."

"The shoulder shakes too?" Fisher rubbed the back of his neck. "Man, that's rough."

"I thought something was wrong with the babies. She scared the crap out of me. And then, as if that wasn't enough to cut me off at the knees, she blew up like a chemistry project gone awry and told me she was leaving."

"What did you do to get Bianca so damn upset?"

He pressed the brew button, turned, and leaned

against the granite counter, gripping the edge so hard, he was surprised it didn't crack. "Apparently I packed the wrong clothes."

"What are you? An idiot?"

"How was I supposed to know she didn't keep her maternity clothes in her bedroom closet and dresser?"

"You couldn't tell?"

"Could you? Do you even know what maternity clothes look like?"

Fisher shot him a look that showed exactly how afraid he was to even contemplate it, no less go there. "I guess not."

"Me either. You'd have made the same mistake. Now the question is, what the hell am I going to do about it?"

"Go shopping?"

"Shit, Fisher. I can't go shopping for Bianca. Hell, I couldn't even pack for her."

"I hate to say this, Bro, but you might have to get the women involved."

"The only one who could do it would be Mom—after all, she's been there and done that, times three or four, depending on if you count pregnancies or progeny. God, I hope she offers. The last thing I want to do is shop for Bianca, and she can't shop for herself unless you can buy that kind of stuff online."

Fisher perked up and sipped the coffee Trapper had poured for him. "You can buy anything online."

"That would mean giving her access to a computer and Internet—and the first thing she'll do is start working. I was hoping to keep her away from the computer all together."

Fisher let out a laugh. "You took her computer away?"

"Shh. Not so loud. She hasn't realized it yet. I took away her phone too. I stuck them in my gun safe."

"And you thought she was upset about the clothes. Just wait until she realizes you've effectively unplugged her. She's going to come unglued." He stood. "I have to get to the hospital, so I guess I'll brave your bedroom again. I'll knock first this time." He grabbed his bag and left Trapper in the kitchen.

He should probably follow Fisher, but then, maybe not. Sometimes discretion was the better part of valor—or maybe, it was just an excuse to hide.

Chapter 10

TRAPPER SHOULD HAVE KNOWN HE'D NEVER BE ABLE to hide from his mother. She came through the kitchen pulling Fisher by the ear. Of course, Fisher had to bend down to allow it. Still, it was safer for him to do that than to further piss off Mom.

Any evil tendencies Karma had, she came by honestly. After all, the crab apple doesn't fall far from the tree. When it came to scariness, Kate Kincaid made Karma look like an amateur—but, then, Karma was still growing into her power, and that thought alone was enough to make Trapper's ass twitch. Karma might wield her power more often, but his mother had better aim, and right now, she had both Fisher and him in the crosshairs. She had no problem smacking them down at the same time.

Trapper wasn't stupid. He did what any smart man would do: he stepped back and ducked. He knew his mother's reach and stayed well clear of it.

His mother backed him into the island, grabbed his ear, and literally knocked his and Fisher's heads together. "What in the name of all that is holy have you two boys done to that woman? Trapper, you first."

"I packed the wrong clothes. I didn't know Bianca kept her maternity clothes in her spare bedroom."

"And, Fisher, what the hell were you thinking walking into Trapper's bedroom unannounced?"

Fisher shrugged, as much as he could, since he was bent over with Mom hanging onto his ear. "Paybacks are a bitch?"

That earned him a smack upside the head.

"That's for Bianca. Like she doesn't have enough on her mind—you have to embarrass her?"

"I kept her from walking out on Trapper. She practically had one foot out the door."

"In a towel. In January. With no car. Oh, yes, I can see why you were concerned."

"You can't blame me. Trapper was fighting with her. I was trying to help."

"Fisher, you stuck your nose in where it didn't belong and just made matters worse. Now, not only is Bianca sick and tired, she's justifiably upset and humiliated."

Trapper groaned. "Sick?"

His mom put her hands on her hips. "What the hell do you expect? She had nothing in her stomach."

She shoved Fisher's bag at him. "Get in there, take her blood pressure, and then leave. And if she's asleep, for God's sake, don't wake her up, or you'll answer to me."

Fisher nodded and scurried away.

"Trapper, take her crackers and ginger ale while I make breakfast. Then I'm going to the mall to buy Bianca maternity clothes."

"Yes, ma'am." He grabbed what he needed and slipped quietly into the bedroom.

Bianca was sound asleep wearing his robe, and Fisher sat beside her doing his best to take the Velcro cuff off her arm without waking her.

"Is she doing all right?" Trapper whispered.

Fisher shrugged. "Her pressure is still high but not

as bad as I've seen it. You might want to get these bags out of here while she's sleeping. When she wakes up, the last thing you want her to see are all the clothes she can't wear. I'll stop back to check on her on my way home. Keep her fluid intake up, and make sure she eats small meals." Fisher tossed the blood pressure cuff and his stethoscope into his bag. "I'm sorry I walked in on you two earlier. I was just concerned." Fisher stepped toward him and shook his head. "Do your best to keep her calm today. Meltdowns are not recommended."

"Yeah, I got that. I'm working on it." He just didn't know what to do to keep her happy, and healthy, and safe, and right where she was—in his home, in his bed, in his life.

Fisher shook his head. "Looks to me like you have about a four-month window to get it done. Don't fuck it up. Those are my nieces or nephews she's carrying, and I don't want to be a long-distance uncle." Fisher walked out leaving him looking at Bianca, who slept curled up, one hand on her stomach.

Trapper refused to be a long-distance father. Hell, if he had to, he'd sell the house, pack up, and move back to Manhattan. He left the DA's office on good terms, so there would be no problem getting a job there, or maybe even another judgeship. Heck, with his experience as a judge, he could probably have his pick of jobs at any law firm—except for his ex's. Damn, he didn't even want to think about Paige and shut the steel door on that part of his life.

He stuffed a pile of clothes back into one of the bags, zipped it up, and did the same for the other, tossing the bag of shoes into his closet. Then he carried all the clothes he'd packed to a guest room. When he returned, she was still sleeping soundly, so he took her toiletries into the bathroom. After setting everything out, hoping to make her feel more at home, he was glad he'd gone ahead and paid through the nose for the dual sinks. He had done it for resale because everyone told him to. Now looking at all the crap Bianca had, he understood why they insisted it was a necessity.

The scent of food wafted in from the kitchen. Trapper had a hell of an I-told-you-so coming. He might as well get it over with before Bianca awoke. He didn't want an audience and hoped he could charm his mom. He'd always been her favorite, and it wouldn't be the first time he'd coaxed her out of a tirade.

He strolled into the kitchen, gave her a hug from behind, and kissed her cheek. "Thanks for helping, Mom. I love you."

The spatula she held flew up like a weapon. "Back off, and don't you dare try to sweet talk me. I'm still pissed at you on Bianca's behalf."

Trapper held up his hands and did as he was told: he backed way the hell off and leaned against the counter out of spatula range. "Bianca's pissed enough on her own behalf. She doesn't need your help with that. Now buying maternity clothes is a whole other matter."

"Bianca's scared, sick, and so…I don't know…alone. Solitary. I don't know why, but I have a feeling everything about us, about the way we live, is foreign to her. Did you see the way she looked at us when she came off that plane? The girl looked like she was in a zoo, on the wrong side of the bars."

Trapper hadn't seen Bianca's face, but he'd imagined

it. And his imagination must have been deadly accurate. "Mom, Bianca's very independent."

"I know that. My question is whether Bianca is independent by choice or by necessity?"

"I don't know." He nabbed a piece of sausage and avoided the spatula his mother swatted at him. He'd never thought about it. Bianca had always seemed so damn strong and together and in charge. The only time she ever let loose was when they were having sex. Okay, well, before the pregnancy at least. Now she seemed to go off like a damn grenade launcher with a newbie at the trigger whenever the mood swing struck her.

"Where is her family?"

"I don't know."

His mother gave him a look that made him take another step back.

"She's an only child."

"Trapper, this is the kind of thing you learn on the first date."

"I never dated Bianca, Mom. I don't date anyone."

"And why is that?"

He shrugged. He was not interested in discussing his lifestyle choices with his mother—the lifestyle choices he'd made since the Paige disaster. He'd refused to make the same mistakes with another woman. It wasn't so much the cheating; it was the months of living in limbo that got him—the stark reality of having no control of his own life for almost a year.

He hadn't believed Paige's son had been his. He'd always used condoms since she couldn't take the pill, and at the time of conception, they'd hardly seen each other. She had been embroiled in the case of a lifetime—her

words not his—and was second to the senior partner. The
timing was wrong. Still, it kept him living in limbo through
the months of her pregnancy and waiting for the results of
the paternity test. He'd never forget the sense of relief he
felt when the test came back negative. "I know I went about
this all wrong. But the time Bianca and I spent together"—
when they weren't going at it like bunnies—"was nice.
She's sweet, intelligent, and funny." Intriguing. "But she
never mentioned a family, and she had already met mine."

"And that didn't strike you as odd?"

"Sure it did. But it's not as if I could force her to talk."

She raised an eyebrow. "So all those years of law
school and the time you spent in the DA's office taught
you nothing?"

"Mom, I'm not going to interrogate Bianca."

"There's interrogation, and then there's interrogation.
If you make it fun"—she waggled her eyebrows—"I
doubt Bianca will complain."

"Fun?" She couldn't be suggesting what he thought
she was suggesting. And, God, if she was, he certainly
didn't want to talk to his mother about it.

"You never 'dated' Bianca, but I think if you want
to turn this into a lasting relationship, it's high time you
started." She pulled a tray of biscuits from the oven and
blew her hair out of her eyes.

"And how am I supposed to do that?" He swiped a
biscuit and tossed it between his hands to cool it. "She's
on bed rest for the foreseeable future."

"What is it with the male mind? You boys always
take everything so literally. Just because she can't leave
the house doesn't mean you can't have a romantic dinner
and a movie, does it?"

"No. I guess not."

"Buy her some flowers, a nice candlelight dinner, get a romantic comedy—not one of those shoot-'em-up films you prefer—make her feel beautiful and special and—"

"Mom, Bianca has been voted one of the fifty most beautiful women in the world. She *is* beautiful and special."

"I said to make her *feel* beautiful and special. Women, especially pregnant women, don't. It's your job to see that she does."

"Bianca is anything but a typical woman."

"Bianca has the same feelings and insecurities that every other woman alive suffers—maybe more so. Think about it. She spent her life practically starving herself to stay a size two, and now she's pregnant with twins. That would do a job on a normal-size woman. Can you imagine what she must be going through? Just because photoshopped pictures of her face and body have been plastered all over every magazine doesn't make her invincible—if anything, it makes her just the opposite."

She fixed a plate and handed it to him on a tray that already had a glass of milk, juice, coffee, and several kinds of jelly and butters. "There, now take this in to her, and if you know what's good for you, you'll wake her with a kiss."

"Coffee?"

"It's decaf, so don't get your boxers in a knot."

"Thanks, Mom. I love you and appreciate you, you know."

She pinched his cheek. "Remember that when you get the bill. I'm off to shop and do some real damage to your bank account. Oh, and I'm leaving you with the dishes."

—◦◦◦—

Bianca took another bite of a flaky biscuit. Normally she never allowed herself to eat things like this, but since there was a good chance it wouldn't stay in her stomach long enough to be digested, she figured it couldn't hurt to indulge just this once. She slathered the decadent brown stuff over it and took another big bite. "God, Trapper. This is amazing. What is this spread?"

Trapper sat at the foot of the bed facing her and looked as if he was having the time of his life watching her eat. The man was strange. "It's apple butter."

Bianca swallowed and chased it with a few gulps of milk. She'd never been a milk drinker. Not even the two percent kind—too much sugar, but she couldn't believe how good it tasted to her at the moment. "Apple butter, huh? I've never heard of it, but I can't stop eating it. It's incredible."

"It's just applesauce slow-cooked with apple cider and spices. Mom makes it every year."

"Seriously? Kate made this?"

"She cans all the vegetables she grows. We've always had a big garden. She makes pickles, jellies and jams, applesauce, apple butter, sauerkraut, the usual."

"You think that's usual?"

"Didn't your mom ever can?"

That was laughable, but she couldn't really laugh because her mouth was too full. "My mother never did anything." She licked apple butter off her fingers. Her mother did nothing good anyway, but then, neither had her father.

"You've never mentioned your family. Where are your parents?"

She took another bite of the biscuit, but it didn't taste nearly as good as it had before. Maybe it needed more apple butter. "I don't know, nor do I care. I haven't seen them in almost twenty years."

"How can that be? You're barely thirty-five."

She pushed the tray away. "I'm thirty-four. It was relatively easy, actually. I was emancipated when I was fifteen."

"Why?"

"I've been modeling since I was a baby—you know, diaper commercials, Gerber baby, that kind of thing? My parents managed my career and embezzled millions from my trust. When I figured it out, I took steps to stop them." She wiped her mouth on the napkin and took a sip of coffee. "This coffee tastes funny."

"It's decaf."

She returned the cup to the tray and wished Trapper would stop staring at her as if she'd grown a third boob. "What?"

"You're not in touch with any of your family?"

"I'm close to my grandmother. I spent Christmas with her in Cincinnati. I bought her a home in a retirement community there a few years ago. She's happy. She has friends, a good life."

"But you didn't call her to help you."

She gave him another shrug. "She has a few trips planned, and I didn't want to intrude."

"Intrude?"

"She's going to Atlantic City with her Bunco group, and then they're planning a trip to Florida in February. She's been looking forward to it for months."

"So? Don't you think your health and the health of our babies would mean more to her than a trip to Florida?"

"Trapper, she helped me when I was a kid. Now, I take care of her, not the other way around."

"You're her granddaughter. Does she even know about the pregnancy?"

"Of course she knows. She's not blind. I visited her for Christmas and stayed through New Year's. It was hardly something I could hide."

"Did you hide how sick you were?"

"I'm not sick. I'm pregnant."

"That's a definitive yes. Bianca, you're so busy being independent you don't let anyone care for you."

"That's not true. I care for James and my grandmother."

"Like I said, you don't allow people to care for you. Do you even know what that means?"

She knew exactly what that meant. It meant giving someone else the ability to hurt her, use her, and let her down. Everyone except her grandmother and James had done just that. Truth be told, she stopped giving people the opportunity to hurt her after her experience with Max. She'd bought into the lies and dreams and promises often enough to learn her lesson. Now she expected nothing from everyone, and she hadn't been disappointed or hurt since. It always worked. "I've been taking care of myself for most of my life. I've done a pretty damn good job of it. I don't need anyone."

She expected Trapper to get angry. Anger, she could handle, but she saw a flash of something that left her aching inside. She wasn't sure what it was—pity, sadness? It was an expression she'd never seen directed at her. She didn't like it or deserve it. "Don't look at me like that."

"Like what?"

"I don't need your pity. I have everything I need in life, and I've earned everything I have—including the Bitch Badge I wear with pride. I have a great home that's paid for, savings and investments, Action Models, a best friend, and two children on the way. What else could I possibly want?"

"Someone to share it with."

"The last thing I need is an alpha-male pitying me or trying to take care of me."

Trapper moved, leaning over her, his arms on either side of her hips, boxing her in. She leaned farther into the pillows at her back, trying to get some much-needed distance. They were nose to nose—his eyes were still black and blue, but breaking his nose hadn't dimmed their color. If anything, it made the green look brighter and the gold sparkle. "I don't pity you. I care about you." His breath brushed her cheek. "And before you say a word about the babies, I cared about you long before I knew our children existed. I missed you and wanted you and worried about you the entire time we were apart. I went to New York to get you back."

"Get me back? Trapper, I hate to break it to you, but you never had me in the first place."

"Oh yes, I did. You might not want to admit it, but I know the truth. I had you, and believe me, I'll have you again in every way that counts. You can rationalize it any way you want, Bianca, but you're mine. You've been mine since that first day you tossed coffee in my face."

"You're delusional."

"Maybe, but the fact is that I care about you, dammit, and that's not going to change. So you're just going to have to get used to it. Hell, you might even like it."

"Like it? Oh, I like the sex okay, but the rest of it—no freakin' way."

"You like the sex okay? Sweetheart, we've never had sex—not once."

"Really? I beg to differ. These babies I'm carrying are not immaculate conceptions, that's for sure."

He moved even closer, if that was possible, so close she stared at those golden flecks blazing in his irises. "I've had all kinds of sex. I know the difference. What you and I do between the sheets and everywhere else is not sex." He looked so damn sure of himself, like he really believed it.

"Fine." She wanted to cross her arms, but he was too close to allow it. "Let's go with it then. Tell me, if it's not sex, what the hell is it?"

"It's called making love." His voice did that deep gravelly thing so that when he leaned into her, it rumbled right through his chest into hers.

"No, it's not. Love has absolutely nothing to do with it." Just the thought of the *L* word shot something cold and icy through her blood and made her feel like someone was cinching her into the mother of all corsets.

"The hell it doesn't. When I touch you, when I'm with you, it's unlike anything I've ever known or felt. What else can it be?"

"Really good sex." It was hard to breathe. She could only manage a half breath. This was so not good.

"No." He shook his head, his curly blond hair sweeping his shoulders. "I've had a lot of really good sex before too. This is more. It's like comparing a jump on a trampoline to a space launch—they both get you in the air, but one is way over the top."

"Trapper, you're mistaken." She tried to take a mini breath, but that wasn't enough, so she took another and another.

"No, you're in denial."

She couldn't get enough air.

"And you're hyperventilating. Shit, Bianca, calm down. Take slow, deep breaths."

"I'm fine." But she'd be a hell of a lot better if he would stop throwing around the *L* word.

"Right. I can see that. Dammit, Bianca, cup your hands over your mouth and concentrate on breathing slowly and not on fighting."

"Get out of my face, and I'll be fine."

He backed off to the footboard and waited.

Okay, maybe she did need to slow the breathing down some—she was huffing like a freight train on an uphill climb, and worse, she was getting light-headed. She cupped her hands over her nose and mouth and concentrated on breathing slow and deep. It seemed to do the trick, but then, maybe it was because she couldn't do that and concentrate on Trapper and the *L* word while she was doing her best to un-cinch the invisible corset.

Her breathing evened out, and he relaxed against the footboard, looking way too pleased with himself. "Trapper, just because you were right about the breathing doesn't mean you're right about everything else."

"How do you know?"

"Because I know me. Do yourself a favor, and don't read any more into this than it is."

"Bianca, this thing between us is bigger than you or I ever imagined. It's not the kind of thing you plan. The universe doesn't give warning signs before it throws people off their trajectory. It happens if you're very lucky, and all you can do is protect and nurture it."

"Oh, no. The only things I'm nurturing are these babies. Get with the program, Trapper. I'm here until I'm allowed to leave. And I will leave. I had a full life that had nothing to do with you and these babies. My being pregnant hasn't changed who I am—it just added dimension. And no matter what you think, or who the hell you think you are, I am a lot more than an incubator. I'm not going to let you, or the fact that I'm having your children, change that."

"I know who you are, and I've never thought of you as an incubator, so just get that idea out of your head."

"Right. The only reason I'm here is because I'm pregnant."

"That may be, but that's not the only reason I want you here. I've wanted you here—I've imagined you here—since the first day I met you. I know I'm damn lucky you're here now, although I would have preferred it to be under different circumstances. But know this, Bianca, I'm going to do everything in my power to make you want to stay."

"That's not going to happen."

"Sweetheart, you've been flying solo for so long, you don't know what it's like to be a part of something bigger than yourself."

She had to laugh. "I'm getting so big, there's going to be nothing bigger than myself soon."

Trapper ignored her little dig.

She might as well have been a prisoner awaiting a bail hearing. "What are you getting at, Trapper?"

He moved back to his place beside her, crowding

her against the pillows. "Nothing sinister. There's no need to start hyperventilating again. I'm just telling you that you're already part of something bigger—and not because you're carrying our children. It's because I care about you."

"You don't know me well enough to care—"

He ignored her and kept talking. "I've made you part of my life, and that happened long before I knew about the babies. You're not alone anymore. I might not have been with you physically, but you haven't been truly alone since I made that trip to London."

"I can't believe the gall—"

"What you have to understand is that having people who care about you doesn't make you weaker, sweetheart. It makes you stronger. What you do with that strength is up to you. But no matter what, you have me, and my entire family, watching your back. And whether you want to admit it or not, I suspect that James and your grandmother have always watched your six too. You just never trusted anyone enough to accept help. As of right now, I'm taking point."

"Okay, you can call yourself judge or point man or whatever you want. It makes no difference to me. I'm only here until my sentence is up. Once the doctor gives me my walking papers, I'm history."

Chapter 11

KARMA LOOKED INTO TRAPPER'S BEDROOM AND TOOK in the scene. For a second, she mistook it for a war zone. It looked as if she stepped into the middle of an emotional standoff. Trapper and Bianca were on the bed; he leaned over her so close they were practically nose-to-nose. They stared at each other defiantly, and with so much intensity, the air around them practically shimmered.

Karma tapped on the open door, drawing Bianca's and Trapper's focus. "Did I come at a bad time?"

Bianca's gaze held relief, and Trapper's settled right into annoyance—an emotion Karma was used to bringing out in people and didn't mind in the least. She considered the ability a God-given gift and one of her best qualities. She kicked the wattage of her smile up a notch just to get under Trapper's skin because she could. Poking at him was like taunting a big grizzly bear caged safely behind the bars at the zoo. He couldn't retaliate with Bianca there as a witness. At least Bianca looked happy to see her, which was odd. Bianca had never been happy to see her before.

The lady in question gave Trapper a shove and smiled. "Karma, no, it's not a bad time. As a matter of fact, your timing is perfect. Trapper and I are done here."

Trapper might have eased his big body away from Bianca's, but he wasn't happy about it. The set of his shoulders was so rigid, it would make a steel beam look relaxed. His stare returned to Bianca and drilled into her. "We're as far from done as Earth is from Mars. We'll finish this conversation later, sweetheart." His gaze slammed back to Karma, and the annoyed look took on a decidedly evil glare. "You were supposed to call for permission before stopping by."

Karma didn't bother hiding her glee—really, what was the point? Boys were such fun to play with—even when the boys were her brothers. She could play them like a game of Parcheesi, and she loved Parcheesi almost as much as she loved them.

Karma didn't often get a rise out of Trapper without getting into trouble with the rest of the family, so this opportunity was extra special, and she was going to take full advantage of it. Let the games begin. "I know dropping by without warning or an invitation is a no-no. Mom has questions for Bianca about sizes and preferences—that kind of thing—and you haven't answered your phone, Trap. She called me from the mall and told me to come over and talk to Bianca."

He smacked his hands against his thighs in apparent frustration and then rose from the bed. "Fine. Give Mom a call, get the questions answered, and then get out. Bianca needs her rest." He grabbed his hat off the corner of the headboard, smashed it onto his head pulling it low over his eyes, and stomped past her.

"Nice to see you too, Trap. Oh, no need to thank me for coming by—"

The slam of the back door echoed through the house.

Score. Karma took the point and the match.

Bianca winced and blew out a breath.

Okay, that wasn't good.

Karma watched Bianca deflate against the pillows. Her eyes went glassy, and the color drained from her face.

"Hey, don't let Trapper's little hissy fit get to you. He's like this when he can't control something or someone—not that he's usually a control freak—he's just überprotective. All of them are—all of them, meaning Kincaid males. They can't help it. It's just how they're wired." She reached over and patted Bianca's hand. "You'll learn how to get around Trapper. It's difficult but definitely doable. Just ask Toni and Jessie. They've learned the skills needed to manage Fisher and Hunter. Of course, they were probably easier than Trapper will be since they don't have the whole judge persona. Give a man a gavel, and the power goes right to his head."

Bianca laughed and seemed to loosen up a little—a very little.

Karma still had work to do. She took a deep breath and went back to Operation Save Trapper's Ass. "To Trapper's credit, he's acting like a butt-head because he's worried about you. If he were able, he'd move an entire mountain range to make sure you were all right. Unfortunately, there's not a whole lot he can do, which only serves to piss him off. Kincaid men are men of action—the helplessness is enough to drive Trapper nuts."

"I'm fine. The babies are fine."

Karma raised an eyebrow. Bianca looked anything but. She really looked unwell—in the beautiful, totally ethereal way that only finely boned supermodels could pull off. If Karma were the jealous type, she'd hate

Bianca just for being over-the-top gorgeous. Any other woman would look like a skeleton. "Bianca, nothing personal, but you're not fine. If you were, you wouldn't have been put on bed rest for weeks, would you?"

The defiance was back on Bianca's face, which was a real improvement over deflated and defeated paleness.

Karma took the opportunity to relax on the bed and stuffed a throw pillow between her back and the footboard. "You know, Bianca, there's not much Trapper can't do—the man has crazy skills—but even he can't control your blood pressure."

Grooves wrinkled Bianca's forehead like a spring runoff. If she kept that up, she'd be a candidate for Botox.

"Okay, I guess he can raise it. I'm sure you two fighting doesn't help matters."

"No, it doesn't. He makes these commands and expects me to agree with him. The man is exasperating."

"Most men are—it's part of their charm. Still, there's always a way around them. The first lesson in Kincaid Male Management is to pick your battles wisely. Only fight about what matters a lot to you and needs to be dealt with immediately. Never fight about something that can wait until later. This gives you the element of surprise. The boys will never see it coming. If Trapper's giving you crap about something you feel strongly about, and you know there's no way he'll see your side of it, just smile sweetly and let him think whatever he likes. He'll think he's won, so he'll leave you alone and then you can do what you need to do to stay calm and healthy."

"He thinks he's going to make me stay here."

"And you don't want to?"

"No. Why would I want to stay in Boise? I have a

life in New York, and the fact that I'm pregnant doesn't change that."

Oh, it changed everything all right. The pregnancy made Bianca need Trapper and the rest of the Kincaids; Bianca just didn't know it yet.

Everyone in the family wanted Bianca and the baby girls with Trapper. After all, they were a close-knit bunch. There was no way any of them would be happy to have Bianca and the twins twenty-eight hundred miles away—including Bianca. Karma was certain that she would figure that out on her own eventually. Unfortunately, Trapper's pushiness wouldn't do anything but make a stubborn mule like Bianca Ferrari dig in her five-inch heels and jump the first plane to the Big Apple.

Bianca needed all the love and support they had to give, and Karma would see to it that she had all that and more.

A situation such as this needed to be handled with delicacy and finesse, which left Trapper out. He was great at a lot of things, but he didn't excel in either. He was too used to being treated like the all-knowing judge. When he spoke, people were forced to listen and do whatever he commanded within limits—limits of which he was certain. He might be able to order around everyone in his courtroom, but he'd never get away with ordering Bianca. No, she wasn't one to kowtow to anything or anyone—especially not a man. Trapper was just damn lucky he had a talented sister who excelled in finesse and delicacy.

Karma rubbed her hands together and envisioned pulling one over on Bianca and Trapper. Just because she was doing a good deed didn't mean she couldn't enjoy herself, did it? "Bianca, I understand where you're coming from. The only way to handle Trapper in this situation is to make him think you're considering staying for the duration. He doesn't need to know that you have your mind made up to go back to New York as soon as you're allowed to fly, does he?"

"But that's lying."

"Not if you don't verbally agree to stay, it's not. By letting sleeping babies lie, you'll gain a modicum of peace, and not be forced to fight with him every second of the day. I think it will do wonders for your blood pressure."

Not to mention what it would do for Bianca and Trapper's relationship. If Trapper thought he was getting his own way, he'd be able to show Bianca the real him, the one who wants nothing more than to take care of her and love her. Bianca would finally see the man who would make the best daddy, the man who would do anything in his power just to make Bianca and their not-so-little family happy. She would see Trapper in the best light, not the frantic, scared man who had been desperate to see her for months, worried about her, and then when he found out about the babies, worried about them too.

No one, not even a woman like Bianca Ferrari, could resist the Kincaid charm for long. If she weren't fighting with Trapper, Bianca would have no choice but to fall head-over-stilettos in love with him. Karma just prayed she could pull it off before the doctor gave Bianca the all clear to go back to New York.

"You said Kate needed something from me? Sizes?"

Karma waved her question away. "No, that's what I told Trapper. Mom called to see how you were feeling.

When Trapper didn't answer, she was worried. She asked me to stop by and check on you and make sure you were all right." She shrugged. "Mom always knows what's going on—it's like she has ESP or something. It's kind of scary at first, but you get used to it. She doesn't abuse her sixth sense so it's okay. She probably knew you and Trapper were in the middle of an argument and didn't want your blood pressure hitting the boiling point. Mom sent me to diffuse the situation and protect you from testosterone overload."

Bianca laughed. "Kate doesn't need ESP to know Trapper and I were butting heads. We've been doing that ever since the first day we met."

Yeah, when they weren't bumping heads, they were bumping uglies. There was more electricity between them than any couple Karma had ever seen. They made Ben's, Fisher's, and Hunter's relationships seem almost boring. It was like the difference between static cling and a lightning strike. With all that energy, Karma couldn't wait to meet her nieces—they were going to be handfuls for sure.

"I don't think we've stopped fighting since I threw up in his hat, but he was more concerned about me passing out. He did seem a bit put off about me not telling him I was pregnant."

Karma could believe that—Lord knew she had to do some deep-breathing exercises to control her rage when she found out about that, and she wasn't nearly as interested a party as Trapper. She was surprised he handled it as well as he had. "Yeah, well, that was just wrong. Really, really, really wrong."

Bianca shrugged but pinked in embarrassment. "I

know. But I honestly didn't think Trapper would want anything to do with a baby. He's the man who can only commit to a seventy-two-hour relationship, remember?"

Karma sat back and smiled. "I seem to remember Trapper disappearing three or four times since Toni and Hunter's wedding. I have to assume he was with you."

Bianca didn't look too sure of herself now. Her face turned an odd shade of red. "We met a few times—"

She'd known all along something big was up with Trapper. "Bianca, to Trapper—the man who has sworn off repeat performances—four seventy-two-hour trysts *is* a committed relationship. But no matter what kind of relationship you two had, Trapper would want to know about his children. Even if you were a one-night stand, he would take care of his kids and make sure he was a part of their lives. A big part."

"I know that now." She didn't look at all happy about it. "That's why he wants to marry me. He hasn't asked me yet, but I'm sure he's just waiting until we know everything's okay with the babies."

"Whoa, marriage? Oh, no. Where did you get that idea? Don't get your hopes up, Bianca. Trapper wouldn't marry you or anyone he doesn't love. He'd be with his kids, pay his share of support, and make sure the mother of his children was taken care of, but he would never marry a woman just because she was having his children. Trapper would never marry someone with whom he wasn't madly, insanely in love. That's not the way he is."

"Karma"—Bianca shot her what she was sure was meant to be a conciliatory smile—"I know you're close to your brothers, but this isn't something most men talk to their little sisters about."

"You think not, huh? Well, you're wrong. Trapper was the one who talked to me about the birds and the bees in the first place. And believe me, I keep trying to erase that discussion from my mind—talk about awkward in the extreme."

"No need to go further. I have a mental picture."

"Oh yeah, he had pictures too." She shivered. "Still, Trapper would be the first one to say that children are never a reason to marry. Both parents should be a part of their children's lives, and the parents should support each other, but marriage takes a lot more than the mutual love of a child to work. Heck, Trapper knows that better than any of us; he's the only one who remembers the way it was with our parents. Believe me, the last thing he wants to do is put his children through the hell he went through when he was a little kid. It was plenty ugly. There is no way Trapper would ever marry you or anyone he didn't love—and I'm not talking about lust either. I'm talking the till-death-do-us-part kind of love."

"Oh good, that's a relief." Bianca let out a breath, the muscles of her face relaxed, and she took on a more natural smile. "I hope you're right because I'm not about to marry anyone—ever." Bianca's shoulders, which had been up around her ears, dropped to their normal position, and she sank back into the pillows. "I'm sorry to hear about your dad."

"We had Grampa Joe. He was more of a father figure to us than our own father ever was. Gramps was always there when we needed him—he still is."

"That's nice. I've been on my own since I was a kid. I'm close to my grandmother though—she's great. She reminds me of the female version of your grandfather."

"She's your only relative? No brothers or sisters or anything?"

"I'm an only child, thank God. My parents weren't meant to have children."

"You turned out okay."

"If I did, it was despite my parents. I met James when I was pretty young, and he looked after me like a big brother. If anyone deserves credit for me, it's him. He kept me on the straight and narrow—he still does."

"I'm glad you have James. I like him a lot. And now you have Trapper and all of us."

Bianca looked confused.

"You know, you're not alone anymore, Bianca. You and Trapper have been together since this summer. And when you have one Kincaid, you're stuck with the lot of us."

Bianca looked like she was about to throw an embolism—her face got a little mottled looking. "Karma, Trapper and I aren't together…and we're not going to be."

"Right." Karma couldn't contain her laughter. "Just because you're not planning to do the Marriage Mambo with Trapper doesn't mean you're not part of the family. Heck, you're carrying my nieces—therefore, you automatically have all my love and devotion. It's the same for all of us. I think you're Grampa Joe's favorite. He's wanted great-grandbabies forever."

"But that's not how it works. Families just don't take on people like me."

Karma leaned forward. "Bianca, that's exactly how it works. We're not really related to Gramps—not by blood—but that doesn't matter. And now we have you too. And you have us. Cool, huh?"

Bianca didn't look at all convinced, but that was okay. It might take some time, but she'd definitely get used to being loved. And surprisingly, Bianca was a lot more lovable than Karma had ever expected. "You know, I was thinking that you might want to have your nails done or do something girlie. We can get Jessie and Toni to come over maybe tomorrow night since that's the guys' weekly poker game. We can throw Trapper out and do a spa thing. How's that sound to you?"

Bianca's eyes were glazing over.

"Jessie won't like it—she's so not the girlie-girl type, but it's fun to torture her. I look at it as a cheap form of entertainment."

"Has anyone ever told you that you have some deep-seated evil tendencies?"

"Who me?" Karma let out her evil witch laugh. "Never."

Trapper sat with his head in his hands, beside both his brothers at Fisher's kitchen table. He had never dealt with anyone as hardheaded as Bianca Ferrari in his entire life. He didn't know whether to strangle her or kiss her half the time.

He looked from his beer into the wary eyes of Fisher and Hunter. "I called an emergency meeting with you two hoping to learn how you handle the stubborn women in your lives, but the only thing I've gotten is a pretty good buzz."

Fisher shook his white blond head, his curly hair brushing his collar, in dire need of a trim. "We should never have started on the tequila. That was a mistake."

Normally, Fisher didn't drink much, but today he

didn't have office hours, he wasn't on call, and he wasn't even scheduled to make rounds at the hospital. Luckily, his wife, Jessie, wasn't expected home until much later so they were safe from females.

Trapper took a slug of his beer and contemplated pouring another shot of 1800. "What do you do when they don't listen to you?"

Fisher and Hunter looked at each other, and the two of them looked back at him with twin smiles and laughed.

Hunter wiped the lemon and salt from his lips with the sleeve of his flannel shirt—the cotton stretching taut around his linebacker-size shoulders. "Damn, Trap. Women are not trained seals or your bailiff, which, when you think about it, is about the same thing. Except that Traci, your hot little bailiff, is packing, carries handcuffs, and has been trying to get under your judge's robe since she retained the position. Have you told her about Bianca yet?"

Trapper shook his head. "No, why would I?"

Fisher poured another shot. "No reason. Maybe you like being chased around your chambers by your bailiff. I never thought you'd be into handcuffs, but, then, what do I know? What do you think, Hunter?"

"Me?" Hunter looked up from pouring his next shot. "I think the last thing I want to know about is my brother's sexual appetites." He winged an eyebrow. "But, on the other hand, I wouldn't mind borrowing a few pairs of handcuffs."

Fisher and Trapper stared at Hunter in shock. Then Fisher laughed and took a shot. He let out a fire-shooting breath and cleared his throat—as sure a sign of his pulling on his doctor persona as if he donned his white coat with his name embroidered on the chest and wrapped a stethoscope around his neck. "Metal cuffs leave marks. Silk ties are the way to go, unless you can get a pair of fuzzy handcuffs."

"Duly noted." Trapper definitely needed more tequila for this discussion so he poured one and raised it in a toast when something occurred to him. "Hunter, you've been pretty quiet, little brother. Do you actually expect us to believe Toni doesn't already have at least one pair of handcuffs?"

"No, Toni doesn't."

Trapper groaned.

The answer hadn't come from Hunter—whose gaze shot to him, so startled and wide that red could be seen surrounding the whites of his eyes and every muscle of the man's body tensed to the point that even the chair he sat on creaked.

Although the voice was deep and a little husky, it was definitely female. Trapper cringed, downed the shot for Dutch courage, and then turned to smile at his sister-in-law. "Well, damn, Toni. You weren't supposed to hear that, darlin'. But you can't blame me for wondering with all the collars and Goth stuff you wear. You gotta admit it's not a far stretch to assume it doesn't stop at the door to your bedroom, now is it?"

Toni fingered the D-ring on the spiked black leather collar she wore around her neck. "No, I suppose it's not. Especially seeing how you've obviously had too much of this to drink." She picked up the bottle of tequila and put it back in the liquor cabinet then turned to him and, with her hands on her hips, speared him with her steely glare. "Trapper, what are you doing here? Shouldn't you be home watching over Bianca?"

He sat there, with his hat in his hand and looked down—that wasn't even correct. It was worse. His hat was on his lap. "I called these bozos for advice on dealing with difficult women." He swallowed hard and tried not to piss off Toni. He imagined the woman could be scary, especially when she was wearing her shit-kickers, which she was. "No offense."

"None taken."

Trapper sent up a quick prayer of thanks to the Goth Gods. "I thought they'd have some words of wisdom to impart."

"And how are they doing? Are they helping you out?"

He relaxed a little and sat back in his chair, curling the brim of his new hat in his hands. "Honestly? They've been pretty much useless, unless you're interested in the advantages of silk ties over metal handcuffs when it comes to leaving marks. I suppose I could try tying Bianca to the bed—it's probably the only way I'm going to keep her in Boise. The woman's been here less than twenty-four hours, and she's already driven me to drink. Which is why I'm currently one and a half sheets to the wind."

Toni blew out an exasperated and alcohol-free breath. "Trapper, if you wanted help dealing with Bianca, why didn't you just call me for advice? I know her better than most—after all, I worked with her for years."

Trapper didn't bother hiding his skepticism but found himself turning in his chair toward her and leaning in. "Don't you women have some kind of sisterhood code when it comes to dealing with the enemy—namely me? Because right now, Bianca sees me as nothing more than an adversary. It seems the only thing I'm able to do is piss her off so much her blood pressure is going through the roof. I thought I'd do us both a favor and left her with Karma until Mom came back."

One of Toni's dark brows drew up so far it was completely hidden by her bangs. "You left Bianca with Karma?"

He'd wondered if that had been a mistake, but at the time, it seemed the lesser of two evils. "Well, yeah, Bianca was happy to see Karma, or so she said. Anything to get away from me, I guess."

Toni pulled out the chair next to him and sat, kicking her combat boot out in front of her and leaning back, wearing a smile that made the hair on the back of his neck stand on end. "From what Hunter said last night, it sounded as if Bianca was treating you like a sex god. What happened?"

Trapper spun around to give Hunter a what-the-fuck look and realized he probably shouldn't have had that last shot. Especially since all he'd eaten was that biscuit he swiped from his mom. He'd watched Bianca eat—and he'd been thrilled to do it, but now he realized drinking on an empty stomach was probably a bad idea. "I didn't know my sex life was fodder for you two." Hunter had the manners to look ashamed; Fisher just wore his usual happy-go-lucky-surfer-dude smile. "I suppose Jessie knows about it now too."

Fisher shrugged. "I had to tell her about winning the bet, didn't I? Besides, you'll learn the secret to a happy marriage is never to keep secrets."

Toni shook her head, her twin pigtails dusting the shoulders of the tight-fitting black T-shirt she wore sporting the words: *You're Too Mainstream for My World.*

"Hunter, you didn't tell me you lost a bet. What the hell were you thinking betting on Trapper's sex life? No less betting against him? Damn, I thought you were smarter than that. I've seen Bianca and Trapper *together*—on our wedding day no less—and they're combustible. Bianca didn't stand a chance." Toni blew out a breath that made her bangs fly. "And neither, it seems, did you. Never bet against the infamous Kincaid charm."

"I guess it's a good thing you didn't marry me for my brains." Hunter kicked Fisher under the table. "Way to get me in trouble, Bro."

Trapper couldn't stand to see another man in the position he was quickly becoming accustomed to living in. "Aren't we a little off-topic here, people? We're supposed to be talking about what I can do to keep Bianca calm and in Boise, not about your insane predilection to bet on anything and everything."

Toni tapped him on the shoulder, making him spin his head around the other way. Good thing she put away the tequila.

"What can I do to help?" Her voice was still deep but had definitely softened. That was a good sign—he hoped. "And if you don't feel comfortable talking to me, why not call James? He's been handling Bianca since she was twelve. I'm sure he'd help you out. He wants to see Bianca happy, and he never would have allowed you to fly her here if he didn't think you were man enough to handle her."

Hunter laughed. "Babe, Trapper's still learning that women don't take orders—even if he is a judge. Hell, you know he's always threatening to put us behind bars. I think he should try that with Bianca."

Toni crossed her arms and stared him down, making him feel like the crap one level below whale shit. "She'd likely kill you in your sleep. Really, you can't be that clueless. I always thought you were the smart one in the family."

Dumb and Dumber shot him twin dirty looks—obviously, they thought they were the smart ones. He had to diffuse the situation "Don't look at me. When it comes to brainpower, I'll put my money on Karma." That seemed to appease everyone. "Now, back to my not-so-little problem."

Fisher sat forward. "Did you and Bianca have another fight after I left this morning?"

Shit, he really hated asking for advice. "We had a disagreement—not a fight exactly."

"What happened?"

"I just told her that she's not alone anymore. She has me and the whole family."

Toni brought her hand to her forehead and groaned. "Oh God, no. You didn't! What the hell are you trying to do? Scare her? Bianca's been on her own since she was like...I don't know...a teenager."

"Yes, I heard. She said she hasn't seen her parents since she was fifteen when she was emancipated."

"And you think the thought of more people having control over her is something that would make her feel all warm and fuzzy? Trapper, Bianca has done everything in her considerable power to avoid emotional entanglements for the last twenty years."

"She's all alone. That can't be comfortable."

"For someone like Bianca, it is. She knows she can rely on herself, and maybe James and her grandmother, but she's been used by everyone else in her life. Men just wanted her as a trophy on their arm, someone who can get them on the A-List. Bianca and everyone else knows that if she's seen with someone, his name gets into the tabloids. Every up-and-coming actor and model wants a piece of her—male and female. Bianca Ferrari is a hot commodity, and she's smart enough to know it. Hell, she hasn't worked in front of the camera for almost ten years, and they're still trying to use her. The last thing she wants is to add the Kincaids—a collection of people she hardly knows—to the mix. Bianca doesn't understand how a family like ours works. We're foreign to her, and she hasn't a clue what to do with all of us. Think of it from her perspective—no one in the family would give her the time of day if she weren't pregnant with your children."

Trapper didn't believe that, but Bianca would. Hell, Bianca told him that herself. "Toni, you cared about her before we got together."

"Fine. I'll give you that. But even when we worked together there was a definite line drawn in the sand. I could get close, but not too close. Bianca's the strongest, most independent person I've ever met. I've even heard her say, 'Expect nothing from everyone, and you'll never be disappointed.' That's the mantra she's lived by for her entire adult life. She's spent the last twenty years making sure she would never be put in a position to need anyone."

Trapper rocked back on the legs of his chair. "She needs me."

"Yes, she does, but she's not at all happy about it. She's going to fight it every step of the way."

"Yeah, I'm getting that. Now, what the hell do I do to change it?"

Toni pulled her cell phone out of her pocket and hit speed dial. "James, it's Toni."

She sat back and smiled at something James said. "Yes, last I heard, Bianca was fine. And, yes, Trapper is still alive, which is the reason I called. Trapper needs a little help dealing with Her Royal Bitchiness and isn't finding it in the bottom of a tequila bottle or in the well-meaning, yet equally inebriated minds of his brothers."

She fingered her collar and smiled. "I was hoping you'd want to see Bianca happy. Would you help Trapper out? For me? Pretty please? With a skull-and-crossbones on top?"

Trapper rolled his eyes and took the phone from Toni. He got a kiss on the cheek from her before she shuffled Fisher and Hunter out of the kitchen and into what was once called Fisher's man cave. Now, it was referred to as the Toy Room. He didn't even want to know what was behind the new moniker. "Hi, James. Yeah, I was hoping you could help me out. When it comes to Bianca, I always seem to be doing the wrong thing."

Chapter 12

BIANCA HEARD SOMEONE IN THE KITCHEN AND ROLLED over to find Big Joe Walsh still watching over her. Okay, maybe watching wasn't the right word since he was sitting in a chair with his feet up on the ottoman, snoring. "Joe, it sounds as if Trapper's home." When she received no response, she tried again. "Joe?"

She interrupted him mid-snore and the old man came awake. "What did you say, little lady?"

"I think Trapper's home."

"Oh." Joe stood and stretched. "I suppose he wouldn't be too happy to find me here taking a catnap while I'm supposed to be keeping an eye on you. I started to appreciate taking naps after my bypass surgery. Hell, I'm pushing eighty-three. I deserve a few extra winks during the day." He winked and smiled wide, showing off his pearly whites…maybe dentures, she wasn't sure. "You'll keep that just between us, right?"

"I'd be happy to."

"I knew I liked you. How are you feeling?"

"I feel good, actually. I just woke up myself. I don't think I've slept as much in five years as I have over the last five months. Pregnancy is exhausting."

"Especially with twins, or so I'm told. Well, not told— hell, I googled it. Damn fine thing that Google. I got in on the ground floor of that one back in 2004—it would have made me a very rich man if I hadn't already been one."

"You do have a great business mind. One I'd like to pick someday when I'm not suffering from pregnancy brain."

"Anytime, Bianca. Just between you, me, and the doorknob, you don't seem as if you're suffering from anything except the lack of a good meal. You've lost a hell of a lot of weight, little lady. I hope that with Kate and Trapper cooking for you, you'll be able to put a little meat on your bones."

"It's not a lack of food, Joe. It's just that I don't seem to be keeping much of what I eat down. The good news is I've only been sick once today. That's a new record."

"Glad to hear it." He retrieved the cowboy hat he'd tossed on the corner of the headboard when he'd come in to relieve Karma and placed it on his head at the same angle Trapper wore his.

Bianca wondered if either of them saw the similarities. She could imagine a young Trapper following the larger-than-life Big Joe Walsh around, imitating him from the angle of his cowboy hat to the brand of cowboy boots. A surge of something made its way around her— envy, warmth of some kind, maybe indigestion—she didn't want to look too closely. Feelings were something she always tried to avoid. They had a way of coming back at her and biting her on the ass.

"I'd better be gettin' before Kate sends out a search party. I'll be back soon. I've really enjoyed our time together."

Bianca pushed herself farther up in the bed and rested against the pile of pillows. "I have too." And surprisingly enough, she had. "Come back anytime."

Joe came toward her and bent to kiss her forehead. His blue eyes shone with a youthful expression, making him look decades younger. "If you behave yourself, I'll bring you a little treat next time, as long as you can keep a secret."

She hadn't expected a kiss, or the feeling of rightness that came along with it. Who would have thought Big Joe Walsh was such a softy. When she smiled up to Joe, she spotted Trapper.

"Are you making moves on my girl, old man?"

Joe winked at her. "You bet your ass I am." He placed a hand on her shoulder. "If you're worried about a little competition, you'd better do something about it."

"I can just tell mom you're planning a visit to your favorite fast-food joint and eliciting vows of secrecy from unsuspecting women."

The men wore twin smiles, and Joe gave Trapper a push. "Come on, boy. It's bad enough I have your mother breathing down my neck, making me eat reconstituted tree-bark for breakfast, and hiding my whiskey. I don't need her following me around too. The damn woman acts like she wants me to get as old as Moses. And who the hell would want to live that long if all a man gets to eat is roughage? Now that Fisher's married, I don't even get to sneak one lunch a week with Jessie. Damn, but I do miss our greasy lunch dates."

"Bianca's supposed to have a low sodium diet. That means there will be no Westside Drive-In food for her— at least not until after the babies are born. Do you hear me, old man?"

Joe took his hat off and slapped it against his thigh the same way she'd seen Trapper do more times than she could count. The two were so similar; it was amazing they weren't really related. "Okay, you know I wouldn't do anything to endanger Bianca or my great-grandbabies." His eyes searched hers. "Don't worry your pretty little head about it. I'm still planning to bring you a surprise, just not something to eat. Okay?"

That last word was directed to both her and Trapper.

Trapper tossed his hat on the corner of the headboard and sat beside her, throwing his arm over her shoulder. "That's fine, Gramps. And thanks for coming by to keep Bianca company."

Joe returned his hat to his head. "My pleasure. You know how I love spending time with all my granddaughters—you boys sure know how to pick 'em. I don't think I could have found four more different young ladies, but, damn, if they don't all fit right into the family. At least all my grandsons have great taste in women. And it's a good thing because the Lord only knows what kind of man Karma will bring home."

Bianca's mouth dropped open. "But I'm not…I mean, Trapper and I aren't… Just because I'm—"

Joe waved and walked out. A minute later, she heard the back door shut, and the second it did, Trapper moved, shifting her back into the pillows, his chest sliding across hers. "Hi." Then he kissed her like he'd been stranded on a deserted island for a decade and she was the first woman he'd seen. Like if he didn't kiss her, he'd lose his mind. Like he needed to taste her as much as he needed his next breath. He kissed her with a desperation that was contagious.

She went from shocked to sexually ravenous with the swipe of his tongue. Damn, how did he manage that? She was just sinking into the kiss when he pulled back and stared into her eyes.

"Come on, dinner's waiting. I thought we could watch a movie after dinner. It's date night. I have everything set up in the dining room."

"Date night? Why?"

"Because I like you, and I want to get to know you better. It occurred to me that two adults who are attracted to each other and like each other usually date."

"Considering our predicament, isn't dating now a little backward?"

"Maybe, but I want you to be comfortable here with me, and I thought since we never did the traditional thing, we might give it a try. Let me wine and dine you, Bianca. What do you say?"

"I'm not allowed to drink wine." She blurted out fast—she was so not prepared for dating.

He took her hand and helped her out of the bed. "I got nonalcoholic wine and sparkling cider so we can at least pretend."

She looked down at the new clothes she wore—the ones Kate had bought her earlier. "I guess if this is a date, I should change."

"Only if you want to." He took in her long sweater and leggings. "I think you look perfect just the way you are, but then, you always take my breath away."

Bianca had heard that line before, numerous times, but the way Trapper looked at her made her think for once it wasn't just a line, it was the truth. Warmth surfaced on her cheeks, and her heartbeat kicked up a notch. She toyed with the hem of her new scarlet sweater. It was soft and cuddly and warm—comfortable, yet really stylish. "Your mom bought it for me. She has great taste." The sweater was a V-neck and showed a little cleavage without being slutty, and had a band going under the bodice that flowed over what was becoming one hell of a baby bump. The black leggings fit perfectly too—which was amazing. She'd have to find out where Kate had purchased them. When a woman had a forty-three-inch inseam, finding anything long enough was a feat.

"I have a feeling she could have bought you a potato sack to wear, and you'd be beautiful. And Lord knows we have enough potato sacks in this state." He cleared his throat and stepped back. "So, are you ready for our date?"

Not really, she hadn't dated anyone in ages, but if she were to date, she had to admit, it would be with Trapper. That when added to the fact that she'd missed him while he was gone for hours, and worried about him, and regretted their argument, just made this whole dating idea dangerous.

She'd been okay with seventy-two-hour flings because that didn't give her time to get too attached; it didn't give them time to get too cozy. Now she was stuck living with him for weeks, and that made the whole dating idea all the more frightening. She ran her hands through her hair. She probably had bed-head—after all, she'd been napping. "Let me brush my hair and splash my face. I just woke up a few minutes ago."

"I know. I've been home for over an hour. I thought I'd let you sleep while I rustled up dinner. Still, it was surprising to walk in on the two of you snoozing together."

"Trapper, when I need sleep, even your grandfather can't keep me awake. He was talking, and I don't know what happened. I guess I dozed off."

"I don't think he minded much since he fell asleep too." Trapper's grin shifted into a naughty smile. He stepped closer and ran his hands from her shoulders down her arms. Her pulse picked up when his fingers encircled her wrists and pulled them behind her, tugging her against his chest. "Should I be worried now that you're sleeping with my grandfather?"

He carried the scent of beer, pine, the outdoors in winter, wood smoke, snow, and something that was intrinsically him. It made her want to curl into him and sit beside a roaring fire. She leaned back, her belly pressed against his so she could look him in the eye. "Oh, I think you're safe. He slept on the chair." She kissed his scratchy cheek and nuzzled his ear. "Besides, he snores."

"Is that a deal breaker?"

She headed for the bathroom. "I don't know. You're the only man I've ever spent the night with, not counting James."

When she came out of the bathroom, Trapper stood where she'd left him.

"You've slept with James?" His voice was deep, his expression hard and serious.

She shrugged. "Yeah, just the other night, but we've shared rooms and suites for years. Why?"

"James is a man."

"James is not only openly gay, but he's like a brother to me. He slept in my bed the other night because he was worried about me. He woke me and made me drink watered down orange juice every few hours." By the look on Trapper's face, she knew he wasn't getting the point. "Trapper, until you showed up the other day, James spent the last few months holding my head while I was puking. He forced me to eat and drink, and he hounded me to make my doctor appointments."

Trapper stared into her eyes and was clearly dumbfounded. "You think I'm overreacting?"

She laughed. She thought a lot of things, the least of which was that he was overreacting. She took a calming breath, trying to control her blood pressure and her temper. "I think you're being ridiculous. Even if James wasn't gay, he's been my friend since I was a kid. He's the closest thing to family I have next to my grandmother. My sleeping with him would be like you sleeping with Karma."

Trapper looked sufficiently horrified.

"Yeah, believe me, I don't relish the idea of sleeping with James any more than you would Karma, even with no touching involved. I was so out of it, I didn't realize he'd fallen asleep beside me until I woke up with him the next morning."

"Come on." He took her hand and walked her toward the dining room.

The scent of food made her stomach grumble. She was suddenly ravenous.

"I'm sorry, sweetheart. I'm usually not an ass, and I've never been possessive or jealous, but when it comes to you—" He pulled out her chair, and after she was seated, he stood there staring at her as if he was trying to sort out a problem. He shook his head and ran his hands through his hair. "I don't know what it is. Bianca, with you, everything's different."

She supposed it was. After all, how many girlfriends would a man like Trapper knock up? The table was set, but there was no food. She tore her gaze from his. The way he stared at her made her nervous. "Because I'm pregnant." She meant to say it as a question, but it came out sounding like a statement.

"No." He grabbed the wine from the wine bucket and poured two glasses. "Everything with you…with us… has been different from the beginning. I don't know how to explain it. I don't understand it myself. But there's something about you…about us…that brings out the caveman in me. It's never happened before. I'm not sure I like it. Believe me, if I could have stayed away from you, I would have. I've never been a repeat performance kind of guy."

"Never? You've never had a real relationship?" But then she wasn't one to talk; she'd never had a real relationship—at least not one that she'd admit to.

"I've had a few. They didn't work out—obviously." He didn't look at her. As a matter of fact, it felt as if he was doing everything not to look at her. He might as well have held up a Do Not Enter sign and installed a gate across the road she'd wanted to travel.

Trapper looked at his watch and held up his hand to signal her to wait, and then disappeared into the kitchen. He returned carrying two plates. "Mom told me to serve you something bland but not tasteless, so I came up with salmon steaks braised in white wine with mint, carrots, and peas. Don't worry. The alcohol cooks out, and I went light on the garlic."

He put a plate in front of her that looked like something served at a fine restaurant. Even the mint and lemon slices garnishing the plate looked professional. It was served with risotto—the long-cooking kind. The kind you'd get from an Italian grandmother, not the instant stuff even some restaurants served. She hadn't seen risotto like that since she'd left Milan.

He disappeared into the kitchen again and returned

with a salad that was to die for. Feta cheese crumbled over romaine, and what looked like chopped kale, endive, artichoke hearts, along with slivers of carrots, olives, dried cranberries, and pumpkin seeds. Her mouth watered so much she had to swallow it back. "Where did you get all this? Is there a Michelin three-star restaurant in Boise?"

Trapper looked a little smug—not something she was used to seeing outside the bedroom. "There might be. I'm not sure. When I'm home, I cook for myself—and now for you too."

She didn't know anyone who could cook like this except the chef she'd met at that hot restaurant—Daniel in Manhattan. He'd asked her out. One night at his place had been enough to turn her off food entirely. Pregnancy, however, changed that. Maybe it was pregnancy and Trapper. "You cooked this? By yourself?"

"Yeah, I came home and caught you sleeping with Gramps, so I decided to let you two snooze while I fixed dinner. I would have invited him to stay if this wasn't a date."

So they were back to the whole date thing again? "I don't understand why you're so insistent on dating. I mean, the food looks great—" She took a bite of risotto and groaned. Great wasn't a strong enough adjective, but then she wasn't sure there was one she could use to describe a multiple mouth orgasm. "It tastes even better than it looks. My God, what did you do to this?" She asked around a mouth full of food, not even bothering to hide the fact her manners were MIA.

He shrugged and dug in. "I cooked it. What do you mean, what did I do?" He filled his mouth, chewed, and seemed pleased with the end result.

"So you came home and threw together a gourmet meal? Just like that?"

"No." He cut into his fish. "I had to shop first. I didn't have any salmon, and I wanted to get fresh veggies for you."

He had shopped and cooked for her? She didn't think anyone had ever gone to that much trouble for her before. She cut into the salmon steak with the side of her fork and watched the tender fish flake. It was done to perfection. She should know. She was a total food snob. She refused to ingest caloric food unless it was exceptional. Life was too short and her workouts too hard to waste calories on crap. Well, crap that wasn't Five Guys burgers and fries. So, pregnancy did change a few things when it came to her eating habits. "Thank you. It's amazing. If that whole judge thing doesn't work out for you, you could always become a chef."

"It's good to see you eat."

And she was eating. Everything. God, she was suddenly so ravenous. She'd be as big as a sumo wrestler soon if she didn't watch herself. She devoured all of the food on her plate and had seconds of salad.

When she looked up from cleaning her plate, she found Trapper watching her. She'd been too busy stuffing her mouth to notice and realized she hadn't been much of a conversationalist.

Trapper had pushed his chair away from the table, crossed his legs, and sat back. He rested his glass of non-alcoholic wine on his knee as if he'd been at it awhile. "There's more if you're still hungry."

Her face heated, and she felt as if she could eat for another hour, but she'd already made such a pig of herself—at breakfast, lunch, and now dinner. And that wasn't including the snacks Kate had left for her. "No, thanks. I shouldn't. Who knows if it's going to all stay down?"

"I guess we can have a midnight snack, or a nine o'clock snack, since ten seems to be your new bedtime. Come on." He helped her out of her chair. "I have a movie all cued up I think you'll like. Go ahead, and I'll bring out the popcorn. It'll just take me a few minutes."

"I'll help with the cleanup." She grabbed her plate and reached for his when he stopped her. His hand firm but gentle against her wrist.

"No, you won't." He kissed her, a simple kiss on the lips, as if he did it without thinking, as if kissing her was something he did all the time, as if it was second nature. No one had ever kissed her like that—it was the kind of kiss she saw in movies that showed the characters were in love. A simple peck that meant nothing and everything.

No one had ever kissed her without an agenda. Usually the agenda was to bag Bianca Ferrari, super-model. Trapper kissed her just to kiss her. Not that he didn't want to sleep with her—he did, even now, which was just inexplicable—but he hadn't had an agenda when he'd done it. And the fact that he'd done it left her speechless.

Trapper smiled at her discomposure and then pushed her hair behind her ear. "You're on bed rest, remember? I can do the few dishes left while the popcorn is popping. Go lie down on the couch. Just try not to fall asleep."

She could only nod and do what she was told. She made her way to the den. The fireplace was blazing, and candles were lit on the mantel. There were even flowers—her favorite flowers in the world—baby pink roses. They conveyed admiration and joyfulness. She much preferred them to tacky red roses that were as common as a cold in December. These roses were the softest of pink, so pretty, soothing, and they smelled heavenly. He was sure doing a bang-up job on the dating front, and she was turning into a sucker.

———

Oh shit. What had he done now?

Trapper walked into the den and found Bianca crying—again. She wasn't bawling this time. No, she was just brushing the tears from her face and sniffling. It was an improvement over the meltdown she'd had that morning. Still, the sight of Bianca crying in any way was enough to bring him to his knees, which was exactly what happened. He set the massive bowl of barely salted popcorn on the coffee table and knelt beside her. "Sweetheart, what's wrong? What did I do?" He wrapped his arms around her and pulled her close. "I'm sorry. Whatever it is, I'm sorry."

"You bought me roses. Not just any roses, you bought me my favorite roses."

And this was a bad thing? "I didn't buy them to make you cry. I'll get rid of them." He rolled back on his heels to do just that, and she grabbed him.

"No. Don't you dare. I love them."

"Then why are you crying?"

"You bought me my favorite roses." She spoke slowly as one would when talking to a person with a very low IQ—which was exactly how he felt. Damn, he was so confused. She must be going through some kind of hormonal overload because Bianca was not the type of woman to cry over a dozen roses—even if she knew he had to go to three damn florists to find them. Baby pink roses—he cringed remembering the humiliation of asking for them. He was less weirded out buying Karma tampons—at least with those, he didn't have to ask anyone for help. "You like the roses, and you're crying? Pregnancy hormones then?"

"Probably not. I'm just…" Her hands went up as if she were gesturing for help from the gods. "I don't know…touched, I guess. No one has ever bought me flowers, or cooked me dinner, or kissed me just to kiss me, unless they were trying to get into my panties."

He couldn't help but smile. "Who says I'm *not* trying to get into your panties?"

"You don't have to *try* to do that. My panties seem to disappear whenever you're around. That's the point. You don't have to do any of this, and yet you did, and I'm…I'm…"

"Happy?"

"Overwhelmed."

He took a deep breath and rested his forehead against hers, closing his eyes tight and drinking in her scent— the woman could make a mint if she could bottle it as perfume. "I kiss you because I can't help myself. I see you, and I want to touch you. I want to hold you and kiss you and make love to you—I don't even think about it—it's just a natural reaction to being close to you. The first time I laid eyes on you, I wanted to pick you up, throw you over my shoulder, and carry you to my cave."

"You did?"

"Yes, I did." He rubbed the back of his neck. "That

had never happened to me before, and I was not at all happy when I saw you sneaking into Fisher's cabin."

"I thought it was Hunter's and I thought I had an invitation."

He cleared his throat. "That doesn't make it go down any easier, sweetheart."

"Sorry."

"It's okay. I got over it." The memory still bothered him, but shit, there was nothing either of them could do about it. He wasn't comfortable with the thought of Bianca wanting anyone but him—the fact that it had been one of his brothers made it worse.

"I don't understand why you're doing all this?"

"This—meaning buying you flowers?"

"The flowers, the dinner, the candles, the date?"

"I bought you flowers because I thought you'd enjoy them. Making you happy is important to me. You're important to me. I cooked for you because I like taking care of you, I want you to be healthy, and I want you to choose to stay here with me—and not just while you're on bed rest. I want you to stay because this is where you belong." And since he was doing his best to start a real relationship, trying to lay a foundation for their future, he decided he'd step even farther out of his comfort zone and go for an emotional Full Monty. "And because I want to impress you."

Her eyes went wide. He didn't know if it was from shock or revulsion. "I'm very impressed, but I was wrong. You do have an agenda after all."

He shrugged. It was true. He definitely had an agenda, and he refused to feel sorry about it. He'd do whatever it took to change Bianca's mind about leaving him, and help her see that they could have something special together, if only she gave their relationship a chance. But he wouldn't tell her that now—it was a little heavy for a first date. "We should get to the movie before the popcorn gets cold. I put a little salt on it, but not as much as usual. Popcorn without any salt kind of sucks. I tried it."

She let out a relieved laugh. "I agree with you there. Thanks for the little cheat." She gave him a peck on the lips that looked as if it surprised her as much as it had him. She wasn't one for handing out thank-you kisses for something like salted popcorn or even her favorite roses. She scooted back against the pillows piled against the arm of the couch as he stood. "What movie did you pick out for us to watch?"

"How do you feel about Jane Austen?"

She laughed then, a full belly laugh that made him wonder if he'd made another mistake. "You really do have a serious agenda, don't you? God, I didn't think any man would voluntarily sit through a Jane Austen flick, even if it was the only way to get what he wanted."

"I'll have you know that I double-majored in history and English in college and took an entire class on Jane Austen's writings. I considered going for my MFA before I decided on law school. I planned to do my dissertation on Austen from the male perspective. She's one of my favorite authors."

"You're serious?"

She thought he was feeding her a line. "Yes, and I can prove it." He pointed to his bookshelf. "I have the first Brock edition set of Jane Austen's complete novels. They cost me a pretty penny. The collection was the first thing I purchased when I paid off my student loans."

"You had student loans?" She stammered and stopped. "I mean…I'm just surprised. I can't believe your grandfather didn't pay for your education."

Trapper sat back and pulled Bianca's feet onto his lap. "So was he. And, no, Gramps didn't pay for my education, but it wasn't for lack of trying on his part."

"And you accuse me of being stubbornly independent?"

He shrugged. "I got through college on a scholarship and had scholarship money for grad school too—but not enough to cover everything."

"So you're telling me that Joe Walsh, a man who has been at the top of the *Forbes* list since its inception, was willing to pay for your education, and you refused to accept his generous offer?"

"Yes."

"And he let you get away with it?"

"Not without a fight, but that's the way it is with Gramps. He wasn't happy about it. We had more words than *Webster's Dictionary* over my decision. You haven't lived until you see Big Joe Walsh in full fury—the old man is scary when he doesn't get his own way. Still, it was nice to know he and his money were available if I needed either more than I needed my pride. I'm glad I didn't. I really hate to eat crow. As for Gramps, he got over it—eventually."

"You're just as stubborn and hardheaded as he is, aren't you?"

"I choose to think of it as bound and determined."

She let out a laugh and wrinkled her nose like she got a whiff of sour milk. "You would."

He wondered if she knew how cute she looked when she did that? He wasn't in the mood to fight, so he didn't mention that sometimes she didn't look anything like a supermodel—not when she was with him and relaxed and thinking about something other than work. The Bianca persona was nothing like his Bianca. The one he saw glimpses of when they were in Stanley together last summer—glimpses of that Bianca was what drew him in. It was the Bianca people didn't see through the lens of a camera—the lightning-quick flash of emotion you'd miss if you weren't focused on her expression and not her words. The way she ran from the emotional spotlight, even while smiling pretty for the camera. The woman who avoided connecting with people, as if she saw everyone as a possible threat.

"Which Jane Austen movie did you pick?"

"I thought we'd start the BBC miniseries *Pride and Prejudice*. That way we can watch it in sections." He looked at her closely—even after napping, she still looked tired. "I doubt you're up for a five-hour miniseries."

"Have you seen the most recent film with Keira Knightley and Matthew Macfadyen?"

"Sure, but I thought the BBC version was closer to the book—most of the dialogue is word for word, and I think they did a better job of capturing the character of Mr. Bennet. And, let's face it, Jennifer Ehle is hot."

"And Keira Knightley isn't?" She smiled and rolled her eyes. "I thought you would prefer Jane Bennet over Elizabeth anyway."

"Because Jane's a blonde?" He wondered if she knew Jennifer Ehle was a blonde in real life. "No, I like women with spunk, obviously." He gave her calf a squeeze and shot her a smile. Her toes curled in his hand. "Look at you—you're the definition of spunky." And difficult, but he kept that little tidbit to himself. "Hair color doesn't matter. I don't have a type, if that's what you're inferring. I will admit to having a real weakness for women who give me a hard time, which explains both our relationship and why I have yet to kill Karma. I love that you can stand up to me in an argument. You aren't only capable of it; you excel, and usually win. I knew that as soon as you threw that cup of coffee at me."

She nudged him in the ribs with her stocking foot. "You deserved it."

"Maybe. But could I help it that you took me for a stupid cowboy? You made a false assumption and then didn't like the way it made you look."

She poked him again. Harder. "I didn't think you were a stupid cowboy. I just didn't know you were a judge. You could hardly blame me. How many thirty-five-year-old judges do you know—other than yourself, that is?"

She had him there. "Not many." He grabbed the remote, hit play, handed her the bowl of popcorn, and watched the emotions crossing her face as the story of *Pride and Prejudice* unfolded.

Trapper saw the moment her exhaustion overtook her interest and paused the show. She didn't open her eyes, and since she looked as comfortable as he felt, he sat watching her sleep, not willing to spoil the vision of Bianca Ferrari with every one of her protective shields down.

She'd been more relaxed than he'd ever seen her. She looked happy and entertained and comfortable. Normally he couldn't touch her without feeling as if she were a skittish horse waiting for the jab of a spur. If Fisher had made an appearance and taken her blood pressure this evening, Trapper was sure it would have been as close to normal as it would likely get. "Maybe this dating thing wasn't such a bad idea after all," he mumbled as he slid out from beneath Bianca's feet. She was out for the count, so he went to the bedroom and pulled down the covers. If she didn't wake when he picked her up, he'd put her to bed in her new clothes—it wasn't as if she hadn't already slept in them.

Chapter 13

HALF-AWAKE, BIANCA SNUGGLED CLOSER TO THE warmth. Her head felt heavy so she rested it against the solid chest of the man who carried her. Trapper—his scent and strength wrapped her in comfort, the steady thump of his heart against her ear lulled her, leaving her mind to float into a place she wasn't used to occupying.

Trapper was the only man who had ever carried her when she wasn't working as a model. He was also the only man who made her feel secure in his arms, sure in the knowledge he'd keep her safe. She was a big girl. She might not have weighed a lot until recently, but she was six feet tall—a handful, even if she had worn a size two.

"Don't worry. I've got you." Trapper's gravelly voice rumbled through his chest right into the ear resting on it.

She hadn't been worried. She would have told him so if she weren't mostly asleep. She'd never been a heavy sleeper, but since her pregnancy, she felt so out of it. She wasn't sure she could wake up if she wanted to. She was content to stay just where she was. She should shake herself out of the twilight zone and go to bed on her own, but she was tired of fighting. She was too tired to walk, she was relaxed and warm, and she trusted Trapper to take care of her.

A little niggle of fear raced up her spine, zinging her with an ever-present danger warning. She was used to it, and for the first time, she was able to ignore it.

She didn't have the energy to fight her feelings for Trapper that constantly bombarded her. She didn't want to. She wanted to grab them, hold them close, and never let go.

Whenever Trapper did something like this, something selfless and caring and sweet and sexy, her defenses broke down like the walls of a cliff attacked by the constant rush of a raging sea. She could almost see another section tumble into the abyss.

Every day Bianca found herself trusting Trapper a little more than she did the day before. She admitted, if only to herself, that a man lifting her dead weight off the couch and carrying her to bed, knowing he would get nothing in exchange for his heroics—except maybe a hernia—was one of the sweetest, most caring, and sexiest things she'd ever experienced. Then to top it off, he had cooked dinner, bought her favorite flowers— flowers that weren't the easy-to-find grocery store kind, picked out a movie she'd enjoy, and rubbed her feet until she was so relaxed she almost oozed off the couch into a near comatose pile of goo. The date had squelched even her ability to second-guess his actions and discount his intentions. All she could do was smile when he kissed the top of her head and lowered her into the downy softness of his bed.

"Do you want to change?"

She wanted to float in the comfort of her fuzzy, semi-conscious state, but she liked her new clothes, so with hands that felt too clumsy and heavy, she tried to pull off her sweater.

"I'll get it." Trapper's deep, soothing voice rumbled against her ear. She realized she was still leaning against his chest, his arm holding her up.

She concentrated on sitting under her own power long enough for Trapper to pull her sweater off and release the clasp of her bra. Cool material of a nightshirt slid over her head, and she did her best to find the armholes. She wasn't sure how, but by the time she dragged her hands through the sleeves, he'd gotten the rest of her clothes off, and then laid her against the pillows and covered her with the duvet.

When she awoke in the early morning light just before full dawn, she found herself on top of Trapper. Her head used his chest as a pillow, the sound of his heartbeat slow and comforting under her ear. He radiated heat, and in her sleep, she'd wrapped herself around him like a desperate lover. She was perfectly comfortable. It was as if their bodies were meant to fit together like two pieces of a 3-D puzzle.

Her bladder was near bursting, but she didn't want to leave the circle of his arms. She feared that when she did, the spell would be broken, and with it, the feeling of comfort and safety—no, that wasn't precisely how she felt, she wasn't even sure how to describe it. It wasn't so much safety, but a lack of fear—one she imagined a tightrope walker would feel walking with the earth solidly beneath her feet without the need to reach for balance. Balance that, while walking a tightrope, was achievable but, at any given moment, could be lost or elusive. Unfortunately, due to her full bladder, she had to chance it. She tried to slip out of bed without waking her human mattress.

Trapper's eyes shot open, and he rolled toward her, his hand staying her, trying to draw her closer. His sleepy grumble could have been, "Where are you going?" Or maybe, "Everything okay?" She couldn't make it out.

"Go back to sleep."

He sighed and stretched. "Not without you."

When she returned, he was awake and waiting.

"Are you feeling okay?"

"I'm fine." She slid back into bed.

Trapper tugged her closer, his hand warm against her neck, until her head rested over his heart and her leg shifted over his. She felt him relax, his hand slid down her back to rest on her side, where the dip of her waist had once been. Warm, sure, comforting, and just like that, she was on solid ground again.

"I'd forgotten what it felt like to sleep through the night. Until you came home with me, I hadn't slept worth a shit for months."

Had he missed her that much? She couldn't imagine it. She'd dreamed of him almost nightly, but she slept—sort of. Still, a cloud of exhaustion had been her constant companion. She thought it was due to the pregnancy, but the last few nights with Trapper, she'd slept better than she ever had without him.

"I'm sorry I fell asleep on you last night. And I don't remember if I even thanked you." When she lifted her head, his eyes were on her. She leaned farther over and kissed him. "Thank you for everything. It's been years since I went on a real date, and I've never enjoyed a date more."

"You're welcome. But you know it wasn't really a date, don't you?"

"You said it was." She felt him shrug.

"It was the best I could do while following your doctor's orders. It turned out to be a pretty typical night in. You know, a nice dinner, conversation, a movie, or a few hours in front of the boob tube."

"Nonalcoholic wine and roses?"

"Sweetheart, I'd gladly give you roses every day if that's what it took to make it a nightly occurrence."

She snuggled closer, loving the rumble of his voice through his chest. "I don't need wine and roses every day."

"No, but I need you."

"Now?" She raised her head to look him in the eye—not sure if he was serious. It was early, and she hadn't even brushed her teeth yet. She guessed that she could avoid kissing him, but she really liked kissing him.

He rolled them both over, but he wasn't wearing an I'm-about-to-get-lucky grin. He slid down so they were eye to eye. No, he was definitely not happy. "I wasn't talking about sex."

Not happy and possibly angry—it was hard to tell with his early morning gravelly voice.

"I said I need you. Sure, making love to you is amazing, but so is watching TV and rubbing your feet. I love having you with me. Watching you fight sleep, and wondering what you're dreaming about when you smile after you lose the battle. I love coming home knowing you've spent the afternoon charming my crusty old grandfather. I even love the way you pop into my mind at the weirdest times. I love that I see something, and the first thing I think is how I want to tell you about it. When you were…out of touch, I was going crazy not knowing where you were. Not knowing if you were okay. And not knowing why you'd disappeared? Nothing made sense without you. With you here—everything feels better."

She stared into his eyes and saw nothing but sincerity. What does a person say to that? Her heart sped up, and she did her best to ignore the urge to run. He had his arms wrapped around her, and when she tensed, his arms tightened, making her fight or flight response useless— the man was strong.

"You're not going to start hyperventilating again, are you?"

God, she hoped not.

"What's got you so scared?"

"You." He was throwing around the *L* word the way a major-league pitcher throws fastballs. She didn't want to look at him. Just looking at him did things to her mind and her body—things that made her not trust herself. "This scares me. It's like I'm drinking the Kool-Aid. Sure, everything last night was wonderful and romantic and you know…"

"No, I don't know. Explain it to me." His mouth twisted into a combination grimace and snarl. If she were in front of him in the courtroom, she'd expect to be sentenced to death.

"It was perfect, okay. It was like a fairy tale, or one of those cheesy Lifetime movies. It's not real life."

"Of course it's real life—what do you think this is? A movie set?"

"No, but, Trapper, no one is that amazing—not even you."

"I've never lied to you. What you see is what you get."

"So, you're telling me that you're amazing? Okay, fine. You're amazing."

"When someone says something like that, there's always a 'but.'"

"But I don't know when it will happen, sometime soon—probably a lot sooner than I want or expect. You'll see the real me, and that will be the end of it."

"I see the real you now."

"No, you don't." If he did, he wouldn't use the *L* word. "Trapper, you see the woman who is carrying your children—but that's only going to last a few more months. Then I'll just be me again and the real me and the real me inside—" She closed her eyes and shook her head. "You know nothing about her." She whispered, hoping he wouldn't hear it. If he knew what she was really like, he'd run as fast as he could in the opposite direction. Everyone else had. Even her parents, and they were supposed to love her no matter what.

"Bianca, I've seen the real you since the day we met."

"Oh no you didn't. You just think you did—Mr. All-Knowing-Judge. Maybe you're not so damn perfect after all. You think you have some kind of power to see through me, but you see exactly what I wanted you and everyone else to see—nothing more. You saw the Bianca Ferrari I spent years creating and perfecting— she's a fantasy. She's not real."

"You don't know what you're talking about." He gave her shoulders a little shake. "Bianca, I love you, dammit."

She wasn't the only one drinking the Kool-Aid.

"I know exactly who you are, and I love every diffi-cult, independent inch of you. I have a knack for read-ing people. And don't kid yourself by thinking I bought into some apparition you've sold to the world. I'm not infatuated—I'm a grown man, and I'm anything but blind to your faults."

She didn't believe him, and it must have shown on her face because he held up one finger.

"You kick in your sleep." His second finger popped up. "You leave your creams, hair stuff, and girlie crap all over the bathroom and my dresser—usually uncapped. Number three—though I don't really know if I'd consider it a fault—I know you well enough to know you do. You're a natural blonde, but you still color your hair. I can't imagine why—"

"It's a dark blonde. I prefer it lighter."

"Fine, whatever makes you happy, sweetheart." He ran a hand over her hair. "I wouldn't care if you wanted to color your hair purple or shave it off. Nothing's going to change the way I feel about you. But since I know you care, I checked online, and it's fine to keep dying your hair while you're pregnant and nursing."

"Nursing?" She swallowed hard. She hadn't even thought that far ahead. But, of course, he had—Judge Dad.

"Now, where was I?"

She tore her mind away from wondering how one woman could nurse two babies and back to the topic at hand. "Number four."

"Oh, right. Shoes. You have more shoes than any ten people I know put together—that's including every female I'm related to, and they're no slouches in the shoe department. When it comes to collecting pricey footwear, it's as if you're in a race with those women on *Sex and the City*, and I would venture to guess you've got them all beat."

He held up his right hand, fingers spread wide. "Five—you have a type A personality and a hair-trigger temper. When it comes to targeted insults, you have lethal aim." A smile crawled across his face like a worm, thinning as it spread. "That's actually two faults, isn't it? So we're up to number seven—you're demanding. Number eight—stubborn. Number nine—difficult." He took a breath. "Do you want me to continue?"

"There's more?"

"Sweetheart, you are the most competitive, fascinating, and multifaceted person I've ever known. Every day I learn something new—good and bad. That's one of the things I love most about you. Even when it drives me nuts, the fact that you're doing the driving makes all the difference. I could study you for the next fifty years and never discover all there is to know about you. Maybe it's because you keep so much hidden. You'd make a hell of a poker player with everyone but me."

"Why not you?"

"Because I know all your tells. My law degree and experience in front of and behind the bench, not to mention living with Karma, has made me a veritable bullshit meter. I've spent my life spotting lies and untruths—even the ones people tell themselves—like the one going through your mind at this very moment. Out with it. What are you thinking?"

"I think you're the one lying to yourself. You don't love me. How could you considering all the faults you so easily named and numbered? I suspect you missed a few, but you got all that in what? Fifteen days that we've spent together?"

"That's not counting our time in Stanley. I think we're pushing twenty, if I'm correct."

"We weren't *together* in Stanley."

"Weren't we?"

"No, we got together at Hunter and Toni's wedding, remember?" She certainly would never forget it. It was crazy and amazing and incredible. Given the choice, she wouldn't change a thing—after all, she loved her little aliens and had since she'd first suspected she was pregnant. But a relationship with Trapper was clearly a mistake.

"Hunter and Toni's wedding was the first time we made love, but we were together since our first breakfast."

"The one we ate, or the one you wore?"

"The one I wore."

"We were so not together. I hated you."

He looked as if he remembered it fondly. She only remembered how pissed she'd been. From the very first, Trapper had always been able to push her until she lost her temper.

"Love and hate are the opposite sides of the same coin, sweetheart. It only makes sense."

No. It didn't make sense at all. She squeezed her eyes shut. Nothing made sense, not since he said he loved her. She had to set him straight. "I don't love you."

"Oh yes you do."

When she got the guts to look at him, she found him smiling. How could he smile like that after what she told him?

"Don't feel like you have to say the words. No pressure. Take your time. It'll probably be quite awhile until you're comfortable with the idea of falling in love, no less admitting it. But don't worry about me. I understand, and I'm not going anywhere." He kissed her and seemed smugly satisfied.

If his kisses were emoticons, this one would be the big yellow happy face with a wink.

He shifted away. She wasn't sure if she was relieved or bereft. "Okay, I'm going, but only to the kitchen. Since you're awake, you need breakfast, and Lord knows, I don't want a repeat of yesterday morning—at least not the part where you were throwing up." Trapper's gaze searched her face, and the corners of his lips drew down. "I have a feeling there will be no getting around the fight. Just remember your blood pressure okay, baby?" He got out of bed and pulled a pair of sweats over his perfect bare ass.

"Baby?"

He spun around to face her. "What?"

"I wasn't calling you 'baby.' You called me 'baby,' and I don't like it."

He gave her a clinical once-over. "Maybe low blood sugar is making you cranky."

She sat and punched the pillow behind her. "Maybe it's just my fault number ten."

"No, fault number ten is the whole breaking and entering thing. No matter how you spin it, sweetheart, that's definitely a fault."

"Of course you'd bring that up again. I thought Hunter had issued me an invitation. I misread the situation—a first for me, but definitely not a fault. Faults are repeated. That was a mistake."

He ignored her outburst and her excuse. "Your morning crankiness is either low blood sugar, or you're pissed and not able to control your temper on an empty stomach. Either way you need something to eat." He dragged on a T-shirt. When his head popped out, he laughed. "Besides, if mom finds out I waited this long before I got something in your stomach, she'll have me drawn and quartered and bury my body in her compost pile to feed her rosebushes come spring—at least that's what she's threatened since I was just a little cowboy."

Leave it to Trapper to have her sputtering mad and still laughing. A picture of a miniature Trapper, with his blond hair curling out of an overly large cowboy hat, baggy jeans, beat-up boots, and sporting the same mischievous glint in his eyes, popped into her head. The image made her sigh.

She imagined what their little aliens would look like. She couldn't picture it, but she knew exactly how Trapper would look at their children. After all, she'd seen the look of love and wonder on his face when he watched the screen during her ultrasound. It was the same look she'd seen every time she caught him staring at her. But his wonder and love for her was as much a fantasy as her image—she was sure of it. So, okay, maybe he loved her the way a man loves—for loss of a better word—the mother of his children. That didn't mean he was *in* love with her. If she were smart, she'd remember there was a very big difference between loving someone and being in love.

She rested against the pillows and concentrated— doing her best to come up with a plan. Then she realized she didn't have to do a damn thing. All she had to do was be herself. After all, Trapper wasn't the first man who thought himself in love with her. In her experience, the emotion was more elusive than Bigfoot and wore off faster than the shine off a cheap piece of costume jewelry. For her, even that kind of phony love left a virtual green stain on her heart that lasted longer than the man's presence in her life. Once he saw through the smoke and mirrors of his own design, he'd feel nothing but relief when she left him, his family, and his home.

She was on an emotional merry-go-round. She could

handle it when it was only revolving slowly, but the merry-go-round he'd set her on kept picking up speed, and she wanted to get off, wanted to hold on to something solid. Her whole world was spinning out of control, and that was unacceptable. She tried to envision herself walking away from Trapper, but she felt anything but relieved. She felt scared and alone and…shit—she felt empty. She hadn't expected that.

Bianca took a deep breath. It was a bad visualization— she needed to visualize herself walking away without a backward glance and a smile on her face. She was secure, happy, independent and…shit, she couldn't do it. She couldn't see herself leaving him—not of her own volition. She was too weak. That meant he'd be the one leaving her, and all she could do now was damage control. She had to control the situation. She had to control herself. The trick was to get through their time together while protecting her heart. Because when it came down to it, even with all Trapper's cocky smugness and his annoying habit of thinking he knew her better than she knew herself, he was the one man who had the power to hurt her. She thought she'd put her heart in a deep freeze, but even she knew that a frozen heart would still shatter if dumped. In the past her heart had been broken and left in so many pieces, it was held together with Elmer's glue, duct tape, and a prayer. When it happened again, her heart would be broken beyond repair.

She knew Trapper would be busy in the kitchen for a while, so she picked up the phone and did her best to remember James's number.

"I was wondering how long it would take you to call me."

Just the sound of his voice started the waterworks.

"Bianca, are you okay?"

"Noooo."

"Physically?"

She took a deep stuttering breath. "I'm fine. The babies are fine."

"Okay. Calm down and tell me what's the matter."

"Trapper thinks he loves me."

"Of course he loves you. I told you it wasn't a fling. I knew that before Thanksgiving, remember?"

"Not a fling and love are not the same things."

"They are to the good judge, apparently. Why are you so upset?"

"He's wrong. And when he realizes it—God, James, what am I going to do?"

"Bianca, men like Trapper don't go off willy-nilly and tell women they love them."

"He's confused."

"I sincerely doubt that. If there's one thing Trapper Kincaid knows it's his own mind and what he wants."

"Exactly—he loves the babies, and he's transferring that love to me."

"He's loved you since before he knew about the babies. Explain that."

"How can he love me, James? He doesn't even know who I am. He doesn't know anything."

"You claim he can't love you because he doesn't know you. Maybe if you stop hiding behind your image, he'll just love you more. There's no way he can win. God, you're a royal pain in the ass."

"Yeah, that he knows—he gave me a list of my faults."

"Well, that's certainly very Darcy-esque."

"What?"

"Don't you know that scene in *Pride and Prejudice* when Darcy proposes to Elizabeth and tells her all the reasons he shouldn't marry her?"

"We were watching the movie—I must have fallen asleep before that."

"You never read the book?"

"No. English lit was never my thing."

"That's right. If it doesn't have mummies or pyramids, you're just not interested."

"Trapper majored in English and history."

"What kind of history?"

"I didn't ask."

"Because if you had, you might have to tell him about your studies. You know, I've always wondered how you get away with never telling him about yourself. I think I'm beginning to see your methods."

Not surprising—James noticed everything. She wished her methods worked better. "I don't like talking about myself, that's all."

"God forbid you show someone something that would not fit the mold you've poured yourself into for years. Bianca, what the hell happened to you that made you so afraid of being three-dimensional? Did you ever think that people treat you like a paper doll because that's all you ever show them? I'm sure Trapper's noticed that you hide things from him. He might not know what they are, but he knows. It's not fair to withhold parts of yourself and then blame the poor man for not knowing them."

"I don't hide."

James laughed. "Darlin', don't bullshit a bullshitter.

You even hide things from me. Don't think I don't know how you've shut me out."

"James." She gave him her normal warning. One that he usually ignored.

"I have several theories, but I've given up asking."

He may have stopped asking, but he had yet to stop mentioning it—over and over and over again. "It's still not working." Yet the mention of it never ceased to throw her back to that one moment her entire world had blown up. And no matter how mature she'd thought herself at fifteen, no matter how mature she had been compared to every other fifteen-year-old on the planet, she hadn't been prepared for the fallout. It was painful, scary, and incredibly embarrassing, and what's worse, she'd never really gotten over it.

"Don't worry, I'll drop it for now, but I've often thought about getting you rip-roaring drunk and trying to drag it out of you. It looks as if I'm out of luck with that too—at least for the next four months or so."

"Well, that's helpful, James. I'm so glad I called."

"So you called for advice?"

"Yes, and maybe some sympathy. I should have known better."

"Oh, poor baby." He drew the words out like a five-year-old. "Feel better now?"

"No."

"Okay, you asked for advice, so here it is: let it fly. Tell him everything. It's the only way you'll know if he'll stick, or if he'll run, like you think he will."

"But then he'll know." She couldn't believe she was actually whining.

"Exactly. And so will you. Bianca, if your worst

fear is going to happen, wouldn't you rather know now, instead of waiting and wondering and letting your angst affect your blood pressure?"

"No, I just want it to all go away."

"Sorry, kiddo, that's not going to happen, so it's time to pull up your big-girl granny panties and do the deed."

"I don't wear granny panties."

"You will soon."

"Thanks for that, James."

"Hey, it's my job to keep it real, sweetheart. I love you."

"I know. I love you too. I just wish I were home. I wish Trapper had never found me."

"No you don't. You're just afraid. Take my advice. I think you'll be pleasantly surprised. Be sure to call me afterward, and then you can thank me. A raise would not be inappropriate."

"Since you're running the company for the foreseeable future, you definitely deserve one. Consider it done."

Bianca looked at the phone and pressed the end button. She'd really hoped that James would make her feel better. He didn't. Right now she didn't think anyone could.

―⁓―

Trapper should never have told Bianca he loved her. It was too soon, and she hadn't been ready to hear it. Now, not only had he overheard her crying to James, he'd overheard her wishing that he'd never found her. So much for their date. One step forward, ten steps back.

He was in the middle of whipping nine eggs into a froth when a soft knock on the door interrupted his self-flagellation. He turned to see Karma poke her head through the door. "What are you doing up so early? Didn't you have to work last night?"

"I worked. I'm just getting home. The crew and I had a meeting over breakfast."

She was lying, and he didn't want to know where his sister had spent the last four or five hours, what she'd done, or with whom. No, he had enough problems of his own without having to worry about Karma too. It didn't keep him from doing just that.

"How did your date go?"

"Where did you hear about my date?"

"You know how it is. You can't go to three florists looking for baby pink roses and expect me not to hear about it. I have my sources, and they all came into Hannah's to tell me about it. When was the last time you bought a woman you weren't related to roses?"

He'd bought Paige flowers the day he'd found the positive pregnancy test. That was years ago, and he wasn't about to tell Karma. "Never. But that still doesn't explain how you knew about my date."

Karma leaned against the counter like she was too tired to stand on her own. "Once I found out about the flowers, I called Jessie and Toni."

"To spread the rumor."

Karma shrugged. "Yeah, so? Anyway, Toni told me that the date was Mom's idea."

Oh, this was just great. The one problem with having so many females in the family was that they talked. Constantly. About him. "Are you expecting me to feed you?"

"Would you mind? I'm starving."

He knew she hadn't gone to an early breakfast

meeting. He'd keep that pointy arrow in his quiver to shoot at her later. "How many eggs?"

She shrugged. "Two…no, three. I haven't eaten since lunch yesterday."

He cracked three more eggs into the bowl he'd been taking his frustration out on, making it an even dozen, and added more sour cream.

"What are you making?"

"A potato, leek, and mushroom frittata. Once it's done, you can take your portion to your apartment and leave Bianca and me alone."

Karma poured herself a cup of coffee, not bothering to offer him any. She fixed her coffee with cream and a half cup of sugar, made a mess of his clean counter, and then plopped her ass down at the breakfast bar. "I take it the date didn't go well?"

"According to Bianca, the date was perfect."

"Then what's got your boxers in a knot."

He gave the pan with the potatoes and vegetables in it a toss and got out the cheese grater and the Fontina. "I'm not wearing boxers." He didn't need to see Karma's face to know she wore a horrified expression. He mutilated the piece of cheese, took a handful, tossed it in the egg mixture, and then retrieved a bunch of fresh parsley and proceeded to eviscerate it.

"Have you ever considered anger management classes?"

"For me or Bianca?"

"Both? Tell Karma what happened."

What was the point of keeping it to himself? The family had a way of finding out everything—they probably had the bedroom bugged. "I told her I loved her."

Karma spit out the coffee she'd just sipped. "You

didn't!" She wiped her face on the sleeve of her Humpin' Hannah's sweatshirt and didn't bother reaching for the paper towel to wipe up the rest of her mess.

"I did. Not that Bianca believed me." He'd spent his entire life cleaning up after Karma and knew he'd be at it for a while longer. He grabbed the washrag out of the sink and mopped up her mess.

"Oh, this is so not good."

"I know. I told her I loved her faults and all, because Lord knows she has enough of them."

"I hope you didn't say that."

"No. I just listed the first ten or so."

"You didn't." Karma glared at him as he poured the egg mixture into his prized number ten cast-iron skillet.

What was she so mad about? "Of course I did. I wanted her to know I wasn't behaving like some infatuated fool. I love all of her—even her faults."

"Trapper, you have to take it back."

He looked up to find Karma worrying her bottom lip between her teeth. He turned down the heat under the frittata and checked to make sure he'd preheated the oven. "What did you do, Karma?"

"I don't know if I should tell you."

"Because I'll kill you if I found out?"

"Well, that's definitely part of it. The other part is it was a private discussion between me and Bianca."

"About me?"

"Of course it was about you, you meathead. You and those babies are the only thing we have in common. What else did you expect us to talk about?"

"The Seahawks season? How the Steelheads are doing? The fuckin' weather?"

"Bianca doesn't seem like the typical football or hockey fan."

"No, but she has the phone numbers of half the New York Giants' defensive line in her little black book."

"Jealous much?"

"When Bianca's involved? Hell yes. So spill."

Karma stomped up to him, turned her back, and held her arm behind her. "Go ahead and twist it. Make it good so I have an excuse."

"You don't need an excuse. You need to grow the fuck up." Still, he gave her arm a twist because right now it was either that or strangle her, and he wouldn't have a prayer of explaining the latter to his mother.

Karma rose up on her toes and let out a yelp. "You didn't have to enjoy it so much, Trap." She rolled her shoulder. "Fine. Bianca thought you were going to propose because of the babies, and I told her you would never propose to anyone you didn't love."

"Fuck."

"Exactly."

"Now what the hell am I going to do?" He tossed the rest of the cheese on top of the frittata, stuck it in the oven, and set the timer.

"Personally, I'd give Fisher a call to come over and check Bianca's blood pressure. I'd bet you a Ben Franklin you and your 'I love you' just shot Bianca's high blood pressure right into the stratosphere. Then I'd get a few self-help books. I can't believe you told Bianca you loved her and then made a list of her faults. What kind of idiot does that?"

"She told me I didn't know her. Shit, Bianca thinks she's got me, and everyone on the planet, fooled into believing that's she's nothing more than her cover girl image. Like I was out to bag a supermodel. I'm not some ass who spent the last ten years jerking off to her *Sports Illustrated Swimsuit* issue. I love Bianca. Hell, I couldn't help myself. Believe me, I tried. It's not as if falling in love with anyone was part of my five-year plan—why do you think I have the no-repeat-performance rule?"

"I always thought it was because you were a horn-dog." Karma slid off her stool and came around the center island. "What happened to you that was so bad it turned you off to love and relationships?"

One word—Paige. But he'd be damned if he would tell Karma about how stupid he'd been. Thinking back now, he wasn't even sure he'd ever really loved Paige. He thought he had at the time, but what he felt for Bianca was so much more—comparing the two would be like comparing the spray of a kitchen faucet with low water pressure to Old Faithful. He could only shrug.

"It's going to be okay." Karma wrapped her arms around his waist and gave him a hug. "Bianca will come around. How can she resist you? After all, you're related to me—that makes you utterly irresistible."

He gave Karma a squeeze, hoping he hadn't deceived himself when he saw what he'd swear was love lurking in Bianca's big green eyes. "She loves me. I know she does. She just doesn't want to. Someone did a real number on her. Maybe her parents, maybe a guy—I'm not sure. She loves me, but she'd be the last to admit it."

"First things first. I'm texting Fisher. How did she look when you left her?" Karma typed a message on her phone.

"She wasn't hyperventilating, if that's what you're

asking. She was as ornery and skittish as a twelve-point mule deer on the first day of hunting season. I thought it might be from low blood sugar so I escaped to make breakfast."

"Should I go talk to her?"

"I guess that's up to you. Just try not to piss her off."

"Okay. I told Fisher if he was here in the next fifteen minutes, he could have breakfast."

Good thing he'd made a large frittata. "At least we know he'll be over fast."

Karma smiled and slurped her coffee. "Wish me luck. I'm going in."

"Knock first. No need to piss her off more than she already is."

Chapter 14

BIANCA LAY IN A COLD EXAM ROOM WEARING A paper gown, staring holes into a poster of a cute, chubby-cheeked kid blowing the fuzz off a dandelion puff. And this was somehow supposed to be calming? Talk about a major fail.

It would take a fifth of scotch she could no longer drink to calm her after all the indignity she'd suffered in the last eight hours. First, Trapper had told her he loved her and then proceeded to list her faults as proof of the miracle. Then there was the conversation with James that was nothing more than a reality slap across the face. And that was immediately followed by having to deal with Karma and Fisher without the aid of drugs or caffeine. She had a real problem living without caffeine.

The ob-gyn visit merely upped her indignity factor into the triple digits. She was forced to weigh herself in public—okay, not public. The big ugly scale was in the hallway, but the nurse practically shouted her weight and then gave her a hard time about it being too low. As if she hadn't spent the last two days eating everything that wasn't nailed down. Obviously the nurse's definition of low weight gain and Bianca's were diametrically opposed. After all, she'd gained weight. What she wanted to know was how a person who barely kept half her caloric intake down could gain ten pounds in under a week?

If lover boy hadn't been standing beside the scale to catch her, Bianca might have ended up on her ass from the shock, and the nurse would have definitely had strangle marks around her chubby little neck.

The only time that Trapper let her out of his sight since their nightmare breakfast was at the doctor's office when she was ordered to pee in a cup—and that was only because she'd slammed the door in his face and locked it.

Trapper leaned against the wall, watching her. She didn't need to look; she could feel his gaze. "You're still not talking to me?"

"I have nothing to say."

His face blocked her view of the stupid poster hanging on the ceiling.

"Look, I was just working on going to my happy place. You're not helping me get there."

"I'm sorry." And he really did look sorry. Damn, why did he have to pull that puppy-dog expression out of his bag of tricks? He slid his hand over hers, and the anxiousness that had her heart racing decreased markedly. When it came to anxiousness she had more than her share. After all, it was never comfortable to assume the position—feet in stirrups—with an audience no less. "Bianca, I didn't mean to upset you. And I might have gone about expressing my feelings the wrong way."

"You think? Honestly, Trapper, I've never heard another declaration of love that was worse. Not even in the movies."

"At least it was memorable. If it had been out of *Declarations for Dummies*, it never would have made an impression."

"Oh, yours made an impression—a bad one. You obviously haven't perfected the art of sweet talk, that's for sure."

"Sweetheart, I was trying to make you understand that what I feel isn't a passing infatuation. It's the real deal."

"And you thought that by pointing out all my faults, it would cement that in my mind?"

"It worked a lot better in theory than in practice. Can you forgive me?"

"There's nothing to forgive. It doesn't matter." She wished she could take the words back as soon as they left her lips. She hadn't meant to hurt him, and from the look on his face, she had. "I didn't mean that the way it sounded, Trapper. What you said—"

"That I love you."

"Yeah, that. The way you said you loved me doesn't matter. I know you think you do, and you think you know me, and you think we can have a relationship. But, as much as I hate to say it, you're wrong. I just wasn't cut out for anything long-term with a man, even a man as wonderful as you." Especially a man as wonderful as him. She was anything but wonderful—and he'd done a good job of listing just a few of her many faults.

An adorable look of confusion crossed Trapper's face and was quickly replaced by a look of shocked curiosity. "I never thought. I mean—together, sexually, you and I are off the charts compatible. Hell, we're explosive. Do you expect me to believe you're interested in long-term relationships with a woman? Not that there's anything wrong with that."

Did he just ask her if she was gay—or bi? That sent

her into a fit of laughter so violent, she was glad she'd just peed in a cup. She was still doubled over laughing when the doctor knocked and stuck his head in. Tears rolled down her cheeks, and her ass was hanging out of the paper gown.

Trapper's look of relief and the way his big he-man body relaxed sent her into another fit of giggles.

He waved the doctor in while she tried to collect herself. She definitely had to hand it to Trapper, he made her nerves over the worst kind of doctor's exam disappear like no one else could.

The two men shared a handshake and a shrug and waited her gigglefest out.

Once she calmed down, Dr. Weaver introduced himself, asked her the usual questions, and did the usual things that kind of doctor did. Bianca could do nothing more than concentrate on him. If she so much as looked at Trapper, she was sure she'd start laughing all over again.

The exam was painless, and when he was finished, Dr. Weaver helped her up. "I'm going to send the ultrasound techs in to do a quick look-see. Then we'll let you get dressed and have a little talk."

Trapper bundled Bianca up, led her out of the doctor's office, and helped her into his truck.

By the time he got behind the wheel, she'd opened the front of her cape to show off another new outfit his mother had purchased. This was a long-sleeved top made out of the same fabric as his favorite Henleys over a pair of black skinny jeans that had a panel sown in the front for expansion. The top was the same deep green as her eyes, which was quickly becoming his favorite color. He noticed it everywhere. And every time he did, he thought of Bianca. She'd taken the time to put on full makeup, probably hoping to fool the doctor by covering up her pallid complexion. It hadn't worked, but as usual, she looked camera ready. "I can't believe Dr. No You Can't, won't let me off bed rest."

Trapper, on the other hand, had no problem believing it. It sounded to him like the doctor had damn good reasons to keep her flat on her back. And she hadn't taken the news well. Which, when it came to Bianca, wasn't at all surprising. "Fighting with him probably hasn't helped your blood pressure any. Why don't you just think of it as a vacation? When was the last time you took one of those, Bianca?"

She pulled the seat belt across her and secured it. "A vacation?" She shrugged, looking like she couldn't remember. "I don't know. I was sick for a week in Paris before I found out it wasn't the flu—does that count?"

"No."

"What about you?" She pulled one long leg underneath her and then turned toward him. "When was the last time you took a vacation?"

He remembered that disaster. "This time last year. I went skiing for a week." Three days with what's-her-name—the lawyer from Seattle. He'd made up an emergency to get away from the woman. He couldn't even put up with her for the whole seventy-two hours and caught the first available fight out. He landed in Boise, and without even going home, headed straight to a friend's cabin in Sun Valley and finished out the week alone. He had a much better time skiing by himself than he'd had with what's-her-name. That had been his last fling before he'd met Bianca.

"I have a business to run. I can't take vacations like everyone else."

"You're taking one now. Think of it as a vacation at a beautiful bed and breakfast with a really hot gigolo." He looked at her and had to stifle a chill, her gaze was so cold. That went over like a fart in church. "Hey, it's not my fault your blood pressure is through the roof and your sugar is climbing. At least you're gaining weight—that's good, right? And the babies are getting bigger. They're almost starting to look like little people."

She smiled at that. "They still look like little aliens. Cute little aliens."

"They're healthy. You heard their heartbeats banging away. We just need to make sure they stay that way."

"Right."

"So we're okay?" He hated sounding like a whiny girl, but, damn, she'd been so pissed, she'd hardly spoken to him since he'd dropped the *L* bomb—and that was only to tell him he was wrong. He wasn't. She'd figure it out eventually. He hoped.

"It's hard to be pissed after seeing Thing One and Thing Two."

"That's good. So what do you say we start talking about names. Calling them Thing One and Thing Two or the aliens could hurt their little psyches."

"We don't even know what they are yet."

"We know they're either girls or boys, so why don't we just come up with four names—two of each."

"Do you want one to be Trapper Junior? Is Trapper

even your real name?" A look of horror crossed her face. "It's not a nickname is it?"

"Calm down. Trapper is the name on my birth certificate—Trapper Stephen Kincaid—Stephen with a *ph*. And no, I don't want one named after me." He'd be damned that he'd tell her that for years his nickname had been Crapper—only because Karma wasn't too good with her *T*'s. "Maybe we can name one of them after Gramps. I like Joseph. I think the old man would get a kick out of it, and it's a nice name."

"Okay, what about a middle name?"

"I thought you might want your last name as their middle names—you know, since we're not married, and they will have my last name." He looked over at her to see how she was going to take that one. He'd be damned if his kids would have a hyphenated last name.

She didn't seem pissed. He let out a breath he'd been holding, hoping to God she wouldn't explode. "Ferrari is just the name I chose to model under—kind of like a pen name. When I turned eighteen, I changed my name legally. I didn't want anything to do with my parents and didn't want their name either. So I'd just as soon give them a nice, normal middle name. Joseph Stephen Kincaid is nice. What about Thing Two?"

"I guess it's your turn since I named Thing One."

"How about James? He's my best friend, and it doesn't look as if he's going to have any kids of his own."

"James and Joseph. That works. And for a middle name?"

"I don't know. I'm kind of out of men's names— well, men I like, especially if we're taking Trapper off the table."

"I don't think we should use Benjamin, Fisher, or Hunter, since they might want to use their names for their own kids."

"Your father's name?"

Trapper shook his head since he didn't like to curse in front of the little aliens.

"Well, damn, what's Joe's middle name?"

"Benjamin."

"I guess that's out then. How about your mother's father's name?"

"No, they cut Mom off when she married my dad. They never spoke to her again."

"We definitely have a real shortage when it comes to male role models."

"I guess we can use Benjamin for now, unless we come up with something better later. I don't think Ben would mind as long as we called him James or Jim or Jamie."

"Okay, so Joseph Stephen and James Benjamin for boys. Big names for little aliens, but they'll grow into them."

He reached over and took her hand, relieved to see a smile on her face. "They definitely will."

"Now, about the girl names. I was thinking Kathryn after your mom, and Charlene after Nan—but we'll call her Charlie, because no kid can pull off Charlene until she hits at least thirty."

"Charlie—that's cute. And Katie. I like it. Thanks. I know it would mean a lot to my mom."

"That's good, because I really like your mom. Heck, even Karma's growing on me. What about middle names?"

"Mom's middle name is Ann. And Gramps's wife

was as close as a real grandmother to me. Her name was Lynn. So how about Charlie Ann and Katie Lynn?"

"Imagine that. I like them all, and we didn't even fight about it. Maybe we should write them down so we don't forget—I swear, lately I have a hard time remembering my own name."

"I won't forget, but we can write them down in their baby books when we get home."

She leaned closer, and he breathed in her scent. She was the only woman he knew who could get him half-hard just by leaning into him. "We have baby books?"

"That we do. Mom bought two at the mall when she was shopping for your clothes. She even did some furniture shopping. She didn't buy anything, but she gave me a list of stuff we'll need and took a ton of pictures."

"Trapper, I'm going to have the babies in New York."

He looked over, and the smile was gone. She looked serious and sad. He returned his gaze to the road, not wanting to talk about her leaving. "Maybe, but either way, I'm going to need a couple cribs here for when the babies are with me."

"You're going to take them away from me?"

He heard the tears before he saw them. Fuck. He looked for a safe place to pull over. By the time he did, she was in a full hiccuping cry. He stopped and drew her to him, well, as close as he could, considering there was a console between them. Sometimes he really missed bench seats. He kissed her temple. "No, sweetheart. I'm not going to take the babies away from you. But God, Bianca, that's exactly what you're planning to do to me. What do you want me to do? Never spend time with my own children?"

"No." Her face was held tight to his neck; her tears were dripping all over him. Not that he minded getting wet, but her crying just about killed him.

"Do you think I love our babies any less than you do?"

"No, but I can't imagine being away from them. Even for a little bit."

He scrubbed his hand over his face. "Neither can I." But then he couldn't imagine being away from Bianca either. Unfortunately, she didn't feel the same way about him. He was doubly fucked. "Don't worry. We'll figure it out."

She hiccuped. "How?"

"I don't know, sweetheart, but we will." They would have to.

"I guess I can come with them to visit you, but what's going to happen when you get married?"

"What's going to happen when *you* get married?" Just the thought of her marrying someone else had him grinding his molars together with such force, he was surprised he didn't have dust in his mouth. "I doubt your future husband will approve of you coming out here to stay with me."

"I'm never getting married. But you will. And then what will I do?" Then the shoulder shakes started, she was on her way to full-blown bawling—as if the thought of him married to someone else bothered her as much as the thought of her married to someone bothered him.

"Hold on. Why would I get married and not you?"

"You're perfect, remember? You'll have women knocking me over to get to you."

"I'm not perfect. Besides, I'm not going to marry anyone. I happen to be in love with you, and you say you're never marrying, so it looks as if I'm not either—unless our little aliens and I are able to change your mind."

"Trapper, you don't want to be married to me. Just wait, you'll see. It won't take long."

"What won't?"

"For you to realize you don't want me."

"Why wouldn't I want you? Why would you think any man wouldn't want to marry you?"

She dried her eyes and shook her head, as if she couldn't speak though her bawling. He just waited it out. After a few deep breaths, she said, "You'll see soon enough." The way she said it, the look of sadness etched on her face, was enough to rip his heart right out. God, she really believed there was something so wrong with her that he couldn't love her.

"How about I make a deal with you."

"What's that?"

"I'll prove to you that I love the real you—warts and all."

"I don't have any warts."

"I know that, sweetheart. You're the only one who doesn't seem to get it. Let's table the discussion about sharing custody until later. It's nothing we need to decide now. Let's get home and get you back into bed. Our little aliens are probably starving."

"The little aliens would feel better if we could drive by a Five Guys and get some burgers and fries."

"No, they wouldn't." He checked his rearview mirror for traffic and pulled back onto the road. She was still sniffling, but the all-out bawling was done. "If you or the aliens want burgers, I'll make them, and fries too—just no salt."

She rubbed her belly and sniffed again. "Anyone ever tell you you're a buzzkill?"

"Yes, all three of my siblings. Any other questions?"

"Just one."

He looked at her. Tears still welled in her eyes, making the green brighter, and killing him slowly. "What's that?"

"Promise you'll never take my babies away from me, Trapper. They're all I have. I don't think I can lose them too."

Shit. His own eyes were starting to burn. He looked at her, and he saw no lies. She really believed it. She believed that their babies were the only people she had, the only people she loved—her only family. He didn't want to promise, but he had to. "I promise I'll never take our children away from you."

She let out a shuddering breath and relaxed against the back of the seat. "Thank you. I promise I'll never keep the babies away from you either."

He knew at that moment she believed her words as much as he believed his. He just wasn't so sure she wouldn't change her mind.

Chapter 15

BIANCA AWOKE AND FOUND KARMA, TONI, KATE, AND Jessie standing around the bed she occupied in Trapper's room. Okay, sometime since coming to Boise, she started thinking of it as their bed. She figured that as long as she never said it aloud, it didn't count. She lay there with four women staring at her. She'd never woken up in the presence of four females before and hoped never to again. She wiped her mouth, thrilled to find she hadn't been drooling. "What are all of you doing here?"

Karma stepped front and center as Bianca had learned Karma was wont to do. "Other than waiting for you to wake up and killing ourselves trying to be quiet so Mom didn't come after us with a handy cooking utensil?"

"Yes, other than that." Bianca smiled at the group. They were a unit—there was so much love between them, it was palpable. She'd never experienced anything like it, and she'd spent her life around women.

Toni pushed Bianca's feet aside none-too-gently and took a load off, sitting on the corner of the bed. "It's poker night. All the guys go off to one of the houses—I think it's at Gramps's house this week, to drink, smoke, and try to steal each other's money. Us girls thought we'd be nice and give you the night off. We kicked Trapper out." She sat forward, getting closer to Bianca. "The boy didn't want to go so we sicced Karma on him. He took off real quick. God only knows what she's holding over his head. Kate cooked, which is good because she's the only one of us who knows how, and we're drinking virgin daiquiris. I'm just warning you, Bianca. As soon as Kate lets the snacking start and turns her back, I'm hitting the liquor cabinet hard. I love you, but, shit, I need some booze. You have no idea what you getting knocked up has done to my life."

"Or mine." Jessie took another corner of the bed. "I think Fisher and Hunter have a bet to see who will be the first to knock up his wife. I don't know if they're jealous of Trapper, or if it's just plain dumb twin competition."

Kate and Karma looked thrilled and shocked. Karma was the first to speak—naturally. "You're both trying to get pregnant?"

Jessie and Toni shared a look and paled. "No!" they said in stereo.

Jessie cleared her throat. "I mean, not yet. Heck, Fisher and I have been married less than a year, and I want to have time for the two of us before we start having little rug rats. It's going to be awhile—a long while, if I have anything to say about it. Thank God for birth control."

Bianca's eyes bugged out. "Fisher doesn't know you're on birth control?"

Jessie laughed. "Of course he does, he just thinks his little guys can beat the odds. I'm praying he's wrong. Toni?"

"Same. I think Hunter's trying to talk me into going off the pill. The boy doesn't want to know what I'm like off the pill—I give PMS a bad name. And he'd have to be crazy to think I'm ready to go through what Bianca's going through. I mean, there's the twin thing, and the stretch mark thing, and then the puking thing—I'm so not ready for that yet. No offense, Bianca, but I can't imagine anyone doing that to themselves on purpose. I like doctors even less than I like being stuck alone in the woods." She shivered and rubbed her arms. "Although I can't complain about the sex—"

Kate cleared her throat. "Please, have some compassion for my ears, girls. There are just some things a mother doesn't want to know—ever."

Toni didn't bother hiding her smile. "Sure, Kate. Sorry."

Karma smiled sweetly, but Bianca wasn't fooled. "Mom still thinks I'm a virgin."

"Karma Lynn Kincaid, shut that mouth right now, or I'll shut it for you. I swear you're responsible for every one of my gray hairs."

"Sorry, Mom."

Kate let out a breath of disgust. "Like I believe that." She pushed Karma toward the door. "Now go put the food out in the den. Toni, you grab Bianca's pillows, and Jessie—you get that throw. Come on, Bianca." Kate looked at Bianca. "Honey, do you need help?"

"No, thanks. I'm fine. I'm just going to the restroom to freshen up. I'll be out to join you in a minute."

Bianca watched everyone leave before getting out of bed and heading to the bathroom. What the hell was she going to do with all those women? She wasn't prepared for something like this. How could Trapper throw her to the she-wolves?

Bianca and women didn't mix. She didn't have girlfriends for a reason. She'd never gotten along with anyone who didn't have a Y chromosome. She never had.

Since starting her career, she was always seen as competition, and since starting her agency, she was known as the bitchy boss. Or maybe she was just unlikable.

In any case, she didn't know how to let her guard down, and she wasn't even sure it was safe to. And right now, she was hiding in the bathroom because there were four women in the other room falling over themselves trying to be nice to her. It made her feel a little sick. It could just be all the food she'd stuffed in her mouth at dinner. She'd been ravenous again, or should she say, still. She wasn't sure if she was happy to be keeping everything down or horrified.

She brushed her teeth and took a deep breath to steady her nerves. Kate seemed to genuinely like her. That was scary too. She didn't want to lose that. And Karma—who had always scared the crap out of her—was definitely growing on her too. A person had to respect a woman who said exactly what she thought—Lord knew, no one, including Karma, could stop *her*. And Toni—she was the closest thing to a girlfriend Bianca ever had. Especially since she'd apologized to Toni for the whole Hunter-Fisher fiasco. Jessie even seemed nice, and that was saying something. Bianca was surprised to find out that Jessie and Fisher had only been married a few months—and yet she seemed to fit in with everyone so seamlessly.

Jessie poked her head into the bedroom. "Are you okay, Bianca?"

"I'm fine." How many times had she said that in the last week?

"I was just wondering. I mean, it wasn't too long ago I was in your shoes—not exactly, of course. But I was the new girl on the block, and, well, I've never been much of a girlie girl. The whole thought of being around a bunch of women was enough to make me contemplate barricading the doors. Karma was my first real girl-friend. My best friends have always been guys—girls still scare me a little."

Bianca couldn't help but smile. "I know how you feel. So how did you deal with it? I mean, Karma can be scary. And Kate—she's so nice."

"Karma's a force of nature. There's not much we can do but go with it and try to remember that in Karma's mind, she's really just trying to help. Of course, her help usually involves devious maneuvers."

"And Kate?"

Jessie leaned against the dresser and picked up the picture that Trapper had taken of her in Stanley. "Kate's really as nice as she seems, but she loves her boys—and even Karma—like a momma bear. I wouldn't want to get on her bad side."

"Yeah, that's what I'm afraid of. I don't want to make enemies out of any of you."

Jessie put the picture down and turned to look at her and shrugged. "Then don't."

"It's not that easy."

"It's not that difficult either. Just be yourself, and tell the truth. I know you're not planning to stick around, and so do they. Sure, we all want you to change your mind, but Ben and Gina live in Brooklyn most of the time, and everyone is okay with that. They come out here every few months, and it seems to keep Joe and Kate happy enough."

"I'm not marrying Trapper though."

Jessie just smiled as if she knew something Bianca didn't. "All I'm saying is that with the Kincaids, it doesn't have to be all or nothing. There's always a way to work things out. The thing to remember, and the one thing I didn't understand about this family at first, is that they want nothing more than all of us to be happy. They wouldn't want you to be here with Trapper and the babies if you were miserable. So there's no pressure."

"Right, no pressure at all."

Jessie laughed. "Come on." She threw her arm around Bianca. "We're probably missing the bitch fest. And believe me, we don't want to miss that."

"What's the bitch fest?"

"It's when we drink and bitch about the men in our lives. Karma usually gives us a blow-by-blow of someone at the bar, one of the bartenders or a customer. I talk about something Fisher did or one of the guys I work with. There's never a lack of fodder when you're dealing with professional sports. Believe me, I have stories that would curl your hair. Toni bitches about everyone, and Kate goes off on Grampa Joe or her boyfriend."

"Kate has a boyfriend?"

Jessie tugged her toward the den. "Oh yeah, though she refuses to acknowledge it." She stopped in the kitchen and pulled two glasses out of the cupboard as if she lived there, filled them with the pink concoction, and handed Bianca one. "His name is Buck, and he's a long-distance trucker. He's a big bear of a man, and he's been sweet on Kate for years. We're hoping that with all the boys marrying she'd finally throw Buck a bone, but it hasn't happened yet."

Bianca followed Jessie into the den and looked at the women who had taken over Trapper's man cave. There was finger food covering every flat surface. She went around and made herself comfortable on the other side of the couch where Kate had placed her pillows.

Karma lay sprawled out on the couch. Kate took the leather chair and put her feet up on the ottoman.

Toni had the love seat and was in the middle of pouring a healthy shot of rum into her daiquiri. "So I walk into Fisher's yesterday to pick up that bag that Jessie borrowed for Halloween." She turned to Jessie. "I forgot to grab it by the way." Her attention went back to the group. "I find all three of the guys sitting around the kitchen table complaining about us. They didn't even hear me come in. They were giving each other bad advice on dealing with difficult women over beer and tequila—at two in the afternoon. Then Trapper asks Hunter if I have handcuffs. Do you believe them?"

Karma sat up straighter. "So do you?"

"No!"

Karma looked a little put out. "What were they doing drinking at Fisher and Jessie's place?"

Toni stirred the booze in with her straw. "Trapper called an emergency meeting looking for advice on how to deal with Bianca." Toni smiled at Bianca and raised a glass in a toast. "I don't know what you did to Trapper, but I've never seen Mr. In-Total-Control-Of-My-Universe so completely out of his depth that he'd turn to his brothers for advice. Way to go."

Karma smacked her glass down and grabbed the bottle of rum. "Why didn't they call me? Everyone knows I'm the only one to call in times of crisis."

Jessie shook her head and held out her hand for the bottle. "Come on, admit it, Karma. You're the one usually causing the crisis."

Karma shrugged. "Hey, can I help it if I'm a little unconventional in my methods? And you can't blame a girl for having a little fun while helping cupid out, can you?"

Jessie shot Karma a dirty look. "Why, yes, I can. How about you, Toni?"

"I have no problem blaming Karma." Toni shot Bianca a grin. "Karma is always playing the guys—it's her favorite pastime. What I don't get is why the guys never see it coming? I mean, Jessie and I didn't know her when she was moving us around like pieces on a chessboard, but the guys don't have that excuse. Yet she pulls the wool over their eyes all the time."

Jessie took a healthy swig and grabbed the rum. "I have a theory on that. I think the Kincaid men were born without the devious gene—Karma hit the jackpot."

Karma held her hands up. "Stop, you're making me blush."

Kate sat there like Bianca, trying her best to follow the conversation. She reached for a chip and then pushed the vegetable tray toward Bianca. "So, I heard you had a doctor's appointment this afternoon. How did that go?"

"It was okay, but humiliating." She picked up a carrot and dipped it in the ranch dressing. "The doctor's still confining me to bed. The nurse yelled at me for not gaining enough weight, even though I've put on ten pounds in a week, and Trapper's my new shadow. The man tried to follow me into the bathroom."

"Did they do an ultrasound?"

"I think that's standard operating procedure from now on. The little aliens are starting to look like little people."

Karma almost spit out her drink. "You're calling my nieces aliens?"

"Well, that's what they look like—and I'm not sure if they're your nieces or nephews. They had their legs crossed this time. They're modest little buggers."

Kate smiled. "So they're growing and gaining weight?"

"So far, so good. They were pretty active, which is fun to watch, and their heartbeats are in the normal range. We put some of the pictures in their baby books if you want to see them—"

Karma jumped up. "Of course we want to see them."

Bianca slid her legs off the couch."

Karma stopped her. "No, don't move. I promised Trapper I wouldn't let you do too much, so just tell me where the pictures of my little nieces are, and I'll get them."

"They're in the baby books on the shelf beneath my bedside table."

Karma was off like a woman on a mission.

Bianca stretched out again. "Kate, thanks so much for buying the baby books—I hadn't thought of that." She couldn't imagine what else she was missing.

Kate actually looked a little choked up. "I hope you like them. I didn't want to overstep. I mean, I know you can't get out to pick up things for yourself. And you know, when Trapper has to go back to work, I'd be happy to take you to your doctor appointments. I promise I won't try to follow you into the bathroom."

"I'd like that, thanks. I have a driver's license but haven't driven in years."

Toni laughed. "Kate, you might have to fight Trapper over that. He's in such a state; I don't think he'd trust anyone to take Bianca to the doctor. So, Bianca, you never did tell us what Trapper did to piss you off so badly that he had to call in reinforcements?"

Bianca didn't know what to say. She didn't want to rat him out, but then it would feel good.

Karma ran back into the room, plopped down with the baby books on her lap, and bounced. "Oh, I know. He told Bianca he loved her and then made a list of all her faults."

Every eye in the room was on her, and her face felt like it was on fire.

Kate choked on her virgin daiquiri and reached for the rum. "I'll kill him." She poured a healthy amount into her glass, capped the bottle, and put it on the table with a thunk. "I'm sorry, sweetie. I don't know what he was thinking."

Jessie laughed. "He wasn't—obviously. I swear, for a smart man, he can be a real imbecile."

Toni shook her head. "I got nothin'. But I have to say I'm impressed with your self-control. I'm surprised you didn't kill him in his sleep."

Kate laughed. "Me too. I tell you—I wouldn't have been so kind. You have my permission to break his nose again." She turned to Karma. "How did you find out?"

"He told me."

The look of shock on everyone's faces would have been funny if Bianca hadn't wanted to disappear.

Karma shrugged. "I stopped by hoping he'd feed me breakfast, and he was all upset—he beat those eggs within an inch of their lives. Watching Trapper cook when he's pissed at himself is pretty entertaining. Only he could turn cooking into a full-contact sport."

Bianca wished she could pour some rum into her drink. "It's okay. I told him he was wrong, and Trapper doesn't take kindly to someone disagreeing with him. He's just confused. I mean, I know he cares about me and the babies—but that's not the same as being in love. That was his way of proving that he knows all my faults and loves me anyway. He wasn't trying to hurt my feelings."

Kate was up and sitting beside her in a flash and pulled her into a hard hug, rocking her back and forth. "Oh, honey, my son might truly be an idiot when it comes to his delivery, but don't doubt his words. Trapper isn't the type to say he loves someone unless he's damn sure of the feeling. He loves you. I've known he was down for the count for months. I just didn't know it was you he'd fallen in love with. He keeps everything to himself. He always has." She pulled away, holding Bianca by the shoulders and looking at her with eyes so similar to Trapper's it was scary. "Bianca, if any of my boys tells a woman they're in love with her, they are. They don't fall easily, but when they do, it's the forever kind of love."

Jessie and Toni both nodded.

Karma saved her from doing something embarrassing like bursting into tears when she opened Thing One and Thing Two's baby books. "Oh God, they do look like little aliens!"

Kate slid in between her and Karma holding the books. Jessie and Toni went around the back of the couch to see the pictures. Bianca was surrounded by women and for the first time in her life, she felt a part of a group—a family. They examined each and every picture oohing and ahhing. Comparing the two ultra-sounds and smiling as if they were the most incredible babies ever in utero.

Kate hugged her again. "You're doing so well, honey. I can imagine how hard it is for you to stay in bed, away from home and all your friends and family. But I'm so happy you're here with us and that we have time to get to know you. I couldn't have done a better job of picking out the mother of my grandchildren. I know you might not believe it now, but I think you're perfect for Trapper and that he's perfect for you."

"You do?"

"Trapper needs someone as strong, if not stronger than he is. I don't know if you've realized it, but he can be a little on the bossy side."

"No. Not Trapper."

"I always knew the woman for him would have to be as smart and as driven and determined as he is. Personally, I think you might have him beat when it comes down to it. I've never seen Trapper try so hard and still fail so miserably when it came to something or someone he wanted. If he weren't in such a bad state, I'd almost enjoy watching him fumble his way through this. But between trying to win your heart, and worrying about the health of you and the babies—he's in way over his head. So try to be kind to him, Bianca."

"But he's always so sure of everything. Heck, he told me I loved him."

Kate just gave her a smile as if she knew something Bianca didn't and then patted her hand. "He's always been sure of himself, and as much as I hate to admit it, he's rarely wrong."

"Trapper?" Gramps hit him with his cane. "Are you ever gonna ante up, boy?"

Trapper raised his gaze and found his brothers and Grampa Joe staring at him. "Sure. Sorry." God, he'd been playing horribly. He couldn't concentrate on cards. He was too busy wondering what Bianca was doing and how she was handling the hen party the girls decided to have. Bianca didn't strike him as someone who would be comfortable with that.

"Either get your head in the game, boy, or get out."

Fisher grinned and reached over, took a chip from Trapper's quickly dwindling pile, and tossed it in the center of the table. "He's in. He's just missing Bianca."

"I'm not missing her." He had no problem lying. He missed Bianca a lot, but he refused to look like a pussy in front of his brothers.

Fisher dealt, cards flew, and Trapper didn't even bother picking his up. "I'm worried about her. The doctor's appointment today didn't go well: her sugar is up—gestational diabetes was mentioned; she's not gaining enough weight—although she almost passed out when she saw she'd gained ten pounds in the last week; and her blood pressure is still too high. If that wasn't bad enough, she had another meltdown on the way home. I had to pull the damn SUV over until I could calm her down. I had to promise I wouldn't take the babies away from her."

Gramps slammed his cane on the table, making all the chips jump. He wielded the damn thing like a sword. "Of course you wouldn't take those babies away from their mamma. What kind of man would?"

Shit, he hated feeling a complete lack of control over his life and the lives of his children. This isn't the way it should happen. "Bianca's planning to take my children away from me, and that's okay?"

"Son, if that little lady goes back to New York, you follow her. You do whatever you need to do to be with my great-grandbabies. Children need a full-time father."

"I know that, Gramps, and I will. But I want Bianca and the babies to stay here with me. I can't imagine raising kids in New York." Hell, he couldn't imagine not waking up every morning next to Bianca or sleeping without her in his arms, even if she did kick the shit out of him half the night.

Gramps smiled. "So there's nothing saying you have to live in the city. Brooklyn is nice, and I hear there are some decent communities in Connecticut and New - Jersey to raise a family."

"I want my kids to grow up here with the love and support of the entire family. It would be better for all of us. Lord knows Bianca's never had a real family. It sounds as if she's never had anyone she could count on before."

Gramps laid two cards down. "Let's hope she gets used to having our support. Give her some time, son. She might even have to leave us and go on home to the big city before she realizes how much she loves and needs us all." He kicked Trapper under the table. "Oh, and you too."

Trapper's hand sucked. He tossed his cards, reached for his beer, and waited for the inevitable lecture. Gramps had that look in his eyes—the one that said he was in for a verbal hide-tanning. Trapper would honestly prefer the belt, not that Gramps had ever used one on him, but his own father had, and frankly, those swats with the belt always hurt a hell of a lot less than one of Gramps's lectures.

"And you might try romancing the little lady."

That didn't take long.

Gramps looked at him the same way he did every time he'd done something stupid as a kid. He took a shot and tried to prepare himself for the you-screwed-up-but-I-believe-in-you lecture. "We're counting on you, Trapper. You've had women following you around all your adult life. I never thought I'd see the day that you'd have trouble making even a woman like Bianca Ferrari fall for you."

"A normal woman, no problem." Not that Bianca would ever be confused for a normal woman—hell, the woman was on a level all her own and way out of his league. "A pregnant woman is a whole other animal completely."

Gramps raised an eyebrow. "She wasn't pregnant the whole time you were together. It seems to me, you weren't getting the job done then either."

"How was I supposed to get the job done when I didn't even know I wanted to put in an application?"

"And that's the problem with your generation. It used to be if you wanted to get into a lady's bloomers you had to romance the panties right off the girl. You had to sweet-talk her into doing a two-step down the aisle, or at the very least, put a ring on her finger before you could get the goods. Nowadays, you can wet your wick any time you want. You don't even have to work for it—which, at first blush, sounds pretty damn good. And it would be, if everything else had stayed the same. But like you all are so fond of saying, times have changed.

Now women like Bianca are smart, strong, and finan-
cially independent. They don't need to get married. Hell,
they don't even need a man—not with those newfangled
vibrators and artificial insemination. Men have become
expendable. All a woman needs to get everything she
wants is a doctor's appointment and a trip to Costco for a
mega-box of batteries. The shoe's on the other foot now,
boys. There's no reason for the cow to put up with one
bull and all his orneriness for a lifetime when she can
sample the whole herd or just do without all together."

Trapper stifled the urge to bang his head on the damn
table, and, with as few chips as he had left, he had plenty
of room to do just that. Was that what happened with
Paige? She decided dealing with one bull and all his
orneriness was too much trouble? Was she sampling the
herd or was she going for a prize steer? Whatever the
reason, he wasn't enough for her. Had he made the same
mistake with Bianca? "What about love?"

Gramps leaned forward, and disappointment brewed
in his eyes. "Son, love is supposed to come before the
sex. Love makes sex better, not the other way around."

"So I'm screwed?" And not for the first time apparently.

Gramps threw his cards on the table. "It seems so.
There's no easy way out of the situation you dug yourself into. Now you not only have to prove to Bianca
that you're in love with her, but you have to prove that
love is just for her. Those babies she's carrying, while
blessings from heaven, sure do complicate the question
of love. For a man, it's hard to separate the love you feel
for the mother of your children and the love you feel for
the woman. Bianca knows that."

"I loved Bianca from the first moment I saw her. I

just didn't know it. And I didn't know anything about the babies when I showed up at her office with candy and flowers. I was there to get her back."

"Have you told her that?"

"Of course I have. She doesn't believe me. She doesn't believe anyone can love her—the real her. She's so invested in her image, she thinks that's all anyone could want." He wasn't going to tell them how he fucked his declaration of love up, and that it took him hours before she'd even speak to him again—so much for their theory of how women throw themselves at him. Smooth, he was not. At least not when it counted.

Gramps, Fisher, and Hunter stared at him with their mouths hanging open—clearly stunned into silence. That was a first.

"What, no helpful advice?"

Fisher tossed his cards on the table. "All I can say is it sucks to be you. Here you are, you have the woman of every man's dreams in your bed, and there's not a damn thing you can do or say to prove that you love her for all the right reasons."

Hunter grabbed the bottle of whiskey and poured them all another shot.

Trapper wasn't about to push it away. She'd driven him to drink again.

Hunter passed the glasses around. "Trapper, as much as I hate to say it, I think Gramps is right. You might have to let Bianca go, pray she needs you more than she thinks she does, and hope to God she feels more for you than just your run-of-the-mill lust. You better pray that woman loves you."

Bianca told him she didn't love him. But then he'd catch her looking at him, and he'd swear the look in her eyes was more than just like. He hoped to hell he was right.

Hunter emptied his glass and set it aside. "I certainly don't envy you. Your situation makes the hell I went through with Toni look as easy as a run down the bunny slope after a nice sprinkle of powder."

Chapter 16

BIANCA ROLLED OVER AND LOOKED AT THE CLOCK. IT was past midnight, and Trapper still wasn't home. It was pretty late for a weeknight—especially since she knew from Toni and Jessie that Fisher had early rounds in the morning, and Hunter was working the morning shift on the cats. Toni said they were expecting snow so the trails would have to be groomed at first light.

For all she knew, Trapper wasn't even with Fisher and Hunter. After all, Joe was part of the poker party too since it was at his house. He might be sharp as a 600 DPI image, but he was still an octogenarian. Didn't all old people go to bed early? Okay, maybe not her grandmother, but then Nan couldn't be considered normal.

Bianca was tempted to call Jessie or Toni. She had Toni's number, not that she knew where Trapper had hidden her cell phone. God forbid she have access to the Internet or be able to call her office. She'd have to call their landlines, and that would be embarrassing, especially if his brothers were already home. The last thing she wanted to do was wake them up and sound like a needy lunatic. No, she wouldn't be calling all over town looking for him. Trapper was a big boy, and he could go wherever he wanted. It wasn't as if he had to answer to her. He could do anything with anyone.

She punched her pillow and rolled over. She was the one under house arrest, not him. He was on vacation—maybe he played a few hands of poker and then decided to go out on his own. She imagined anything would be better than coming home and doing nothing but watching her belly grow.

She closed her eyes and tried to get comfortable. She was exhausted. She should be sleeping, but even the exhaustion couldn't keep her worry at bay.

Joe lived somewhere in the foothills—at least that's what she'd thought someone had said. She got up, pulled on one of Trapper's big sweatshirts, and then tugged it up against her nose for another sniff. It smelled like him, and she wasn't sure if that was comforting or not. Wrapping her arms around herself to quell the shiver of fear going through her, she looked out the window and stared at the snow. Big fat fluffy flakes fell from the sky and covered the grass but seemed to melt as soon as they hit the pavement. She imagined that wouldn't be true at higher elevations though…like the foothills. Where was he?

Maybe Trapper had gotten into an accident. After all, while Trapper seemed to have no problem leaving her, he did have a problem leaving her alone. It wasn't as if she needed someone with her twenty-four-seven. Lord knew she was fine alone. But whenever he had left in the past, she was sure that he'd arranged to have someone stop by, and invariably, they'd stay until Trapper or another of his replacements came to relieve them. In Trapper's mind, she needed a babysitter—except tonight. And that's why she was worried.

He had to know that the hen party—as Kate called it—had ended hours ago. The Kincaid women had tucked her into bed and cleared out by nine thirty. She'd been alone for three hours.

By one thirty Bianca was pacing. Maybe Karma was awake. She headed to the kitchen to see if the lights of the carriage house were still on. If they were, she'd call Karma. She pressed her nose to the cold pane of glass in the back door. The carriage house was dark, and Karma's little yellow Jeep was still parked in front of the garage.

Shit. Bianca stomped across the kitchen, not sure if she was hungry, angry, or both. She threw open the refrigerator door and searched its contents looking for something decadent to eat. Trapper's refrigerator looked like it belonged in a photo shoot for a healthy eating magazine—full, sparkling clean, with no old containers of takeout, nothing growing, nothing even questionable. It was all neatly arranged and incredibly healthy. What she would give for a jar of Nutella and a big bar of dark chocolate to use as a tasty spoon?

She abandoned the fridge and headed to the pantry. If Trapper wasn't home by two, she'd swallow what little pride she had left and call Karma. Karma would know what to do. That decided, she hit the pantry looking for junk food. Even guys like Trapper had to have a stash, didn't they? Right now, all she wanted was something sweet and something salty. She poked around the shelves and shook her head at the organization she found—his pantry was practically alphabetized within sections— canned goods, dry goods, but no junk food that she could see. Nothing. Not a damn thing worth cheating with. Maybe he hid things on the top shelf. She wasn't sure, but it was worth a look. She just needed a chair.

—⁂—

Trapper climbed out of Fisher's car and wove his way through the falling snow to the house, thankful his brother was a regular teetotaler. Trapper wasn't quite drunk, but he wasn't sober—not sober enough to drive in any case.

He should have come home after his mother had made her appearance at the poker party. She'd scowled at the booze his grandfather drank and the cigar smoke that hung like a cloud of exhaust over the poker table. She'd been pissed, and Trapper was grateful that for once, she wasn't pissed at him. He was having a difficult enough time with the women in his life—the last thing he needed was his mother angry with him too.

When he'd stood to leave, she put her hand on his shoulder to stop him. She'd explained that they'd tucked a very tired Bianca into bed before they left, so there was no need for him to rush home and every reason to keep drinking. Okay, so she hadn't said that last part, but hell, after the wisdom Gramps had imparted—wisdom that had the horrible ring of truth—he thought tying one on couldn't hurt. After all, he'd completely fucked things up with Bianca, and what was worse, he had no idea how to fix it, and neither did anyone else.

He'd wished he'd known then what he knew now.

He wished he'd done everything differently—almost everything—he couldn't regret the babies.

He wished he'd told Bianca he loved her before they were conceived.

He wished he'd known.

The cold, wet wind whipped Trapper's hot face. He wasn't used to being the fuckup of the family—he was so ashamed, he was surprised the snow didn't turn to steam. He fumbled his key into the lock, got through the kitchen door, and reset the alarm.

All he could think about was getting to Bianca, curling up with her, holding her, and making sure she was okay.

He hadn't wanted to leave Bianca earlier. She'd been asleep so hadn't even had a chance to say good-bye. If Karma hadn't threatened to make him join their hen party, he would have stayed, but Karma was very good at getting her own way, and even better at scaring the bejesus out of him. He'd folded like a house of cards in a windstorm.

Trapper made his way through the dimly lit kitchen as quietly as he could in cowboy boots, tiptoed into the dark bedroom, and tossed his hat on the headboard.

The scent of Bianca filled the room, and his shoulders dropped as his tension receded like the tide. He wasn't sure when Bianca's scent had ingrained itself in his mind as the scent of home, but it had, and he prayed that never changed. He went to her side of the bed, wanting nothing more than to put his arm around her, bury his nose in her neck, and drink in her warmth, her scent, her softness. The room was dark so he leaned against the side of the bed and reached for her only to find it empty.

His heart rate bounded like stampeding horses—something was wrong. His mom said Bianca had gone to bed. He tamped down the niggling thread of fear. He was overreacting again. Maybe she was in the bathroom. The light wasn't on, but the night-light gave off enough of a glow to get by without turning on the overhead lights. She had to be in the bathroom. He took the few steps to the door, rapped on it. "Bianca, are you in there?" When he heard nothing, he opened the door and flipped on the light. Empty.

Had she left him? No, she couldn't have. Okay, she could have, but if she had, it would be against doctor's orders. Besides, they hadn't fought in the last few hours. They were fine when he'd left. Maybe she was in the den asleep on the couch. She was probably there. Maybe the alcohol racing through his system was making him paranoid. He made his way to the den, flicked on the lights, and found it empty. Fuck. A needling sensation ran up his spine to the back of his neck. "Bianca?"

What if something happened to her? He dragged his phone off his belt to check for messages, but the damn thing was dead. Shit. What if someone had been trying to call him? Where was she? "Bianca?"

Visions of the way she looked passed out—pale and lifeless—clawed their way to the surface. He choked back a groan. He'd left her alone, but Karma was close by. If something had happened she would have called Karma, wouldn't she? Shit, he'd taken her phone. But the phone by the bed had everyone on speed dial—if she'd remembered. Besides, Karma's Jeep was parked in the driveway. Bianca was fine. She had to be fine. Unless Karma called an ambulance.

His heart felt like it traded places with his stomach, and he couldn't breathe. "Bianca!" He ran to the kitchen, grabbed the phone to call Karma. His hands were shaking, his throat closed, and sweat beaded on his forehead. He couldn't even remember Karma's speed dial number.

Bianca stood on a chair in the pantry searching for chocolate. What house doesn't have chocolate? Trapper's, or so it seemed. She thought she heard footsteps, but then with all the rustling she was doing in the pantry, it was hard to tell. She stopped digging and held her breath, listening.

Nothing. False alarm. Not that she wasn't alarmed—she was. But the worry for Trapper was quickly eclipsed by anger. How dare he leave her here alone for hours like a teenager grounded for staying out past curfew?

She was tired, worried, hungry, and damn it, lonely, which was doubly odd, because she didn't do lonely. Well, not usually, but she'd never before been surrounded by people for days on end. Maybe she was just going through Kincaid withdrawal.

She'd concentrated on angry—it beat lonely any day and fit her like a tailored suit before her pregnancy. Trapper could be lying in a ditch somewhere dying. Or lying in someone else's bed. That thought was somehow almost as painful as the first. God, she'd never before had a normal relationship, although her relationship with Trapper couldn't really be considered normal could it? No, he'd never said he wouldn't see anyone else, and why should he? She was pretty much a sure thing—besides, it wasn't as if anyone else would want her. She looked down at herself wearing his huge sweatshirt over her nightshirt, a pair of socks because her feet get cold when he's not around to warm them, and her belly sticking out. Definitely not the sexy woman companies paid millions of dollars to hawk their wares. Shit, she looked ridiculous. What if Trapper didn't want her anymore? Maybe that's why he hadn't come home and why they'd only had sex once. Maybe the sight of her in a paper gown at the doctor's office and the ten pounds she'd gained killed what little interest he'd had.

And wouldn't that just be her luck? No one told her that pregnant women have the sex drive of a dozen horny teenagers. The worst part was she didn't want anyone other than Trapper, even if she could have her pick of men. She'd never thought about it before, but she hadn't wanted another man since she'd met him. It wasn't as if she went out with many men, because of the whole agenda thing, and, well, she didn't have much time. But she'd never not looked at men and enjoyed it—until Trapper.

Now he'd ruined her for all other men, and for all she knew, he was out with some beautiful woman who wasn't five months pregnant.

She thought she heard someone call her name—if it was Trapper, he sounded funny, not to mention far away, which, when she thought about it, was probably a good thing. The man got nervous when she had to step three inches off the floor to get on the doctor's scale. Of course, for her, scales were way scarier than chairs, but she didn't think he'd agree with her about that. He'd probably freak if he saw her perched up here reaching for the back of the top shelf. She wondered if he was always so damn overprotective or if it was just because of the babies. In any case, she didn't want to get caught.

She turned to face the pantry door. The chair wobbled—one of the legs had ended up on the first shelf. She'd been in such a rush to get chocolate she hadn't paid attention. She sucked in a breath when she saw Trapper standing beside the island in the kitchen. The small pendant light they'd left on highlighted the lines of his face. He looked frantic, his hands shook, and he was furiously dialing numbers and cursing. She hadn't heard Trapper curse before, neither had she ever seen him visibly upset. He was well beyond upset now—he looked completely out of control. What had happened to him?

"Where in the hell could Bianca have gone?"

He was upset about her?

"She couldn't have left me. She wouldn't do that. Would she? Christ, what the hell is Karma's number? If something happened to Bianca—" He let out a strangled growl and threw the phone. The battery popped out, and it skittered in three pieces across the granite counter and fell to the floor. "Useless piece of shit." He stomped to the door, not even bothering to put on his coat.

"You're leaving again?" She pushed the door to the pantry open farther. Of course, she had to hold on to a shelf and lean to reach it. She had long arms, but they weren't that long. "I'm right here."

He stopped and turned slowly, looking directly into the pantry. It was as if someone took a flamethrower to the mask of distress and anguish that covered Trapper's face—hell, his whole body shook with it—puddling like melting snow around his feet and morphing into relief. He took three deep breaths while she held hers, watching the transformation.

She stood perched on the chair in the pantry, waiting for him to say something, waiting for him to move, waiting for his smile. He'd been worried about her—not the babies. She knew he would have eventually gone down that road, but his first thought had been of her. He'd been afraid that she'd left him, and he looked as if he needed her. He wanted her. He loved her—really loved her.

She felt the heat of his gaze that raked from the top of her head to the socks covering her feet. All parts of her body fired like a jet engine set on a fast burn.

Then his eyes hit the chair, and the change in his expression was as swift as it was dramatic. In a millisecond the look of stunned relief was replaced by what could only be labeled as white-hot fury. If she'd blinked she would have missed it, but she hadn't. She could do nothing but hold on to the damn shelf, her knees weak with her own sense of relief. Trapper had come home. He wasn't lying dead in a ditch or in some strange woman's bed. He'd come home to her.

—⁓—

"You're leaving again?" Bianca's voice cut through the static filling Trapper's mind.

He had one hand on the doorknob, ready to run to Karma's and knock down the door to find out what had happened to Bianca. Now he was afraid to move. He'd been crazy with worry, with grief, with fear.

"I'm right here." Bianca's voice—soft and gentle, and God help him, so fucking welcome.

His heart beat again, hard and fast. It was drowned out by the rush of blood flowing through his ears into his brain. He turned, needing to see her and afraid his mind was playing tricks on him. Maybe he was hearing things.

His eyes locked on her—the overhead light shining on her golden hair, making her look like a tarnished angel. There was no white gossamer gown; she wore his beat-up, faded Dickinson Law sweatshirt over her nightshirt and a pair of his rag wool socks that slouched at the ankles of her million-dollar legs.

Relief swamped him, making it difficult to swallow past the lump of pain and fear he'd spent the last week trying to hold back.

Then she wobbled, and he felt his world tilt off its axis. "What the fuck are you doing standing on a fucking chair, in my fucking pantry? Are you trying to kill yourself?" The voice that rang through his ears didn't sound like his—it was hot and cold and strangled with terror and rage. Rage he could handle—it was the terror that paralyzed him.

"Looking for chocolate. I'm hungry."

She shifted again, and the chair wobbled. He didn't even realize he'd moved until her weight filled his arms. He set her down and wanted to pick up the offending chair and break it into a million pieces to insure she would never stand on it again.

His breath, hot and painful, raked through his lungs and his throat. He grabbed the chair and slid it toward the table where it hit and fell backward onto the floor with a satisfying crash.

Bianca's eyes widened. "What the hell is your problem?" She stomped toward him, her face red, her hair wild, and her lips so thin, he wondered if she'd swallowed them. "I wake up surrounded by four Kincaid women only to find you gone. You sicced the she-wolves on me without warning, without so much as a by-your-leave. You didn't even have the guts to say good-bye. You just slithered out when your baby sister threatened you."

He took a step back to avoid the finger she pounded into his chest.

"Oh, that's right." She stepped forward, going up on her toes to get into his face, pointing at his still healing nose.

He took another step back.

"Big, bad Judge Trapper Kincaid is afraid of his baby sister."

She stepped toward him again, and the granite counter hit his back. "And you have the balls to stand here and yell at me?"

God she was beautiful when enraged.

"You want to know what my problem is? Fine. You're my problem." Her eyes went glassy. "I'm under house arrest. You took my phone and my computer away, punishing me like you would a recalcitrant child when I haven't done a damn thing wrong."

His mouth opened but said nothing—she thought he was punishing her?

She took a stuttered breath and blew it out. "All the while you're God knows where gallivanting around until two in the morning. In the snow. For all I knew you were dying in a ditch somewhere or warming someone else's bed."

She thought he was with another woman? Was she mad? Okay, of course she was mad, but he hadn't thought she was crazy.

"I've spent the last five hours worried about you. You…" Her voice shook so hard, he saw the movement in her throat. "Inconsiderate, thoughtless, self-centered, egotistical, narcissistic jerk!" She pounded on his chest like a battering ram hitting a door. "I couldn't sleep, I couldn't think of who to call without sounding like a lunatic, and I couldn't find any chocolate!"

God, then there were tears. His throat closed, and he fought back the helplessness he felt whenever Bianca cried.

"Then you stomp in here, and you have the nerve to be mad at me? Well, let me tell you, buster—"

She was worried about him. That was good, right? Maybe not good exactly, but it was something. And the whole part about him being with another woman—what man in his right mind would leave Bianca for another woman? She might be crazy—he'd chalk it up to pregnancy hormones—but it also meant she cared. A lot. He grabbed the hand headed right for his face and fought a smile he swore she was about to wipe off with her fist. From the sparks shooting from her eyes, he could tell he failed at the whole not smiling thing. "You were worried about me?"

"Of all the things I said, that's the only one that registered?"

"Well, yeah. That—and you didn't find the chocolate." He held her close and slid around the island. "If I let your hands go to get the chocolate, do you promise not to hit me and swear you will never again climb on another chair for as long as you live?"

He actually felt a shiver run through her. "You have chocolate?"

"Of course I have chocolate. I'm not a complete idiot."

—◊◊◊—

Trapper had chocolate, so she might just let him live—at least until she ate her fill.

He pulled down a decorative canister and removed

a handful of Dove Dark Chocolate Promises—the ones with the sayings in the wrapper.

She was toast. "I promise not to hit you if you give me chocolate."

He held up a piece. "And?"

She blew out a breath and wondered how hard she'd have to kick him to get the canister out of his hand. "And I promise not to climb on chairs."

He wore that cocky-ass smile of his that made her tingle and pissed her off at the same time. "I love you too, sweetheart."

She snatched a chocolate out of his hand and didn't bother to hide the moan when it melted against her tongue. God, it was heaven. Even "I love you" couldn't spoil this moment. She took another without even reading the message.

"I was playing poker with Fisher, Hunter, and Gramps. Gramps was in a lecturing mood. I didn't mean to worry you."

"You didn't even think about me," she said around a chunk of heaven. He'd left her all alone, and dammit, she'd missed him.

"I thought about you so much, I couldn't even concentrate on the game."

"Not enough to come home."

"I lost over a hundred bucks. I never lose—you're hell on my poker game. But I love that you're calling Boise home."

She didn't say anything. There was no reason to argue. Maybe she should take a page from Karma's book. Besides, it was difficult to speak with her mouth full of chocolate and Trapper's tongue. She was in a chocolate fog and couldn't believe even Trapper could drag her out of it with a kiss. But he could. He did. And God help her, she liked it. Who needed chocolate when she could have Trapper?

She didn't know how many times he'd kissed her, but every time, she was surprised by his effect on her. She melted faster than the chocolate in their mouths. Her hands dug into his shoulders because if she didn't hold on for dear life, she'd end up in a puddle on the floor.

She dragged her mouth away from his and was caught in his gaze, so intense, so hot, so damn volatile. Sparks of need clawed at her. Even the soft fabric of her nightshirt against her nipples had her shuddering.

His hand lifted her thigh, his other arm held her against his hard body, and damned if his erection didn't hit the exact right spot. "I came home, and all I wanted to do was hold you. Feel you against me."

"And now?"

"Now I want to make love to you, spend the night holding you, and wake up with you. That's all I've ever wanted. What do you want, Bianca?"

She remembered how she felt trying to visualize leaving Trapper. She remembered how she felt when she didn't know where he was. She remembered the feeling she got when she thought he could be hurt. "I want that too." She swallowed hard and felt just a little sick. "I want you. I want all of it."

"All of it?" His voice was soft, but for the first time she thought she heard some vulnerability. "What exactly does that mean?"

She needed to tell him. God, she heard James's advice on how to handle Trapper. *Let it fly. Tell him everything.*

It's the only way you'll know if he'll stick, or if he'll run like you think he will. "It means I want to make love to you. Then I want to sleep in your arms and wake up with you in about eight hours."

He kissed her neck, breathing deep against her. "I'm sorry. I wasn't thinking. It's late. You're probably exhausted. You should be sleeping."

"No." She held him closer, not wanting to leave the warmth of his arms, his home, his love. "We should be making love. The rest will wait until later."

"The rest?"

She didn't want to talk—the morning would come soon enough. Right now, all she wanted was to feel. If everything was going to fall apart, she wanted one last night with Trapper. She wanted to make love with him one more time when he thought he loved her. She wanted to grab one last bit of heaven before reality invaded. Before she told him. Before she had to watch all the hopes and dreams she'd tried desperately not to dream, crash all around her. She wanted to love him once without reservation. She wanted to show him everything. And then when she lost it—lost him—at least she could claim to have had it once, even if it was only for a few hours. At least then she'd have the memory—something to hold on to when he went back to being nothing but the father of her children.

Chapter 17

TRAPPER CARRIED BIANCA INTO THE BEDROOM. HE KNEW he should lay her down and leave her the hell alone. She needed sleep. She'd obviously been upset, and that wasn't good for her or the babies. But, shit, he was a man, and she said she wanted him. And damn him to hell, he needed her. It was the need running through him that killed any trace of gentlemanly behavior he'd held in reserve. It was the need that drove him. The need to mark her heart, her body, her soul.

Bianca had pulled his shirt out of his jeans before he even got her out of the kitchen. She was a master in the art of the quick change and could unbutton just about any piece of clothing in record time. He wasn't sure how she managed it, but by the time he set her on her feet in the bedroom and made sure she was steady, she had his shirt unbuttoned, his belt unbuckled, and his jeans hanging off his hips. He loved a woman with talent.

He struggled with his boots and tossed the last one over his shoulder desperate to get to her, only to find her laid out on the bed like a vision. A goddess. A woman in love. God help him, he prayed he wasn't imagining it.

He stared at all those curves, the way her breasts rose and fell with each breath, the ridges of her ribs, the nip of her waist, her still evident hip bones, and the gentle swell of her belly. He let the vision of her burn into his memory—not wanting to ever forget how she looked at that moment. Because tonight was different than all the nights they'd had before. She'd always been beautiful—that was a given, but never more beautiful than she looked right now. It wasn't so much the pose. Bianca didn't have to try for provocative—it was just her natural state. Tonight it was her eyes that got him. She looked at him with an openness he'd never seen in her before. For the first time, she wasn't hiding, and she wasn't holding anything back. It was as if she'd finally taken down all the barriers she'd built between them.

Trapper didn't register moving, but he must have, because before he knew it, he was lying beside her, his arms wrapped tight around her, his face buried in her hair, drinking in her scent, losing himself in the feel of her body against his. Home. With Bianca, anywhere they were was home. "I love you."

Her body tensed against his.

He pulled away and looked into her eyes. "What's the matter?"

"I just hope to God you know your own mind. I hope you're right, because I'm beginning to believe you. So help me, Trapper, if you're wrong—"

"I'm not wrong. I'm not going to change my mind. Bianca, I'm going to love you for the rest of my life."

"I—"

He cut off whatever she was going to say with a kiss. He didn't want to hear her say she didn't love him—not again. It might just kill him. Instead, he poured everything he felt into the kiss. He made love to her mouth like he planned to make love to her body. All he could do was show her how he felt and pray she believed him.

Bianca pushed away. "Trapper, wait."

He focused on her eyes. Damn, he was beginning to recognize her we-need-to-have-a-talk look—the one she was currently drilling into him. "You want to talk? Now? Sweetheart, there's a lot I want to do with you involving your mouth, and none of it has a thing to do with talking."

"Are you trying to make this hard for me?"

He didn't think anything could be harder than he was at that moment. Her body pressed against his, and everything in him wanted to get inside her. Bad. "No." He blew out a breath and prayed that a really bad case of blue balls wasn't fatal. If it were, he'd be toast. "I'm going to have a really difficult time concentrating on talking while you're lying in my arms naked, looking and feeling like my every wet dream." He removed his hand from her ass and put some space between them before tugging the sheet over her. Covering her didn't help much because knowing she wore nothing but a sheet only made her that much hotter. He lay on his back and stared at the ceiling while silently reciting the Idaho Penal Code—again.

Bianca rolled onto him—her breasts resting on his chest, her face inches above his, wearing her we-seriously-need-to-talk expression. "You're not even going to look at me?"

"Not looking at you would help if you want me to concentrate on what you're so intent on saying instead of what's under that sheet. Namely, you. Naked." He snuck a glance. Her fist clenched the sheet at her breast. Was she getting ready to hit him? Her lips were disappearing faster than his erection—which probably wasn't a good thing. "Damn, Bianca. I'm a guy. In case you don't know already, let me clue you in on a fact of male anatomy—when a man's big head is in competition with his little head, the little head usually wins."

Her eyes stared into his and started glistening in the low light.

Oh shit, not tears. Not again. "Don't cry. I'm sorry. What do you want to talk about?"

"It's nothing."

"Sweetheart, I'm sorry." He was so screwed. Every man in existence knew when a woman said it was nothing, it was something—usually something big—and not in a good way. "I'm looking at you, and I'm listening. I want you to tell me. Really." Her use of the word "nothing" had the desired effect on his libido—it squashed it like a bug under one of her five-inch heels.

Bianca raked her hands through her hair, making it even more of a mess than it was before—but then she'd also forgotten that she had been holding the sheet.

Trapper knew when he was in deep shit, and he didn't want to make it any worse, so he made an exerted effort to keep his eyes on her face. Staring at her breasts like the animal he was definitely wouldn't help matters.

Bianca's hands flew through her hair and then curled into fists—not a good sign. "I'm certainly not going to tell you now." She remembered the sheet, pulled it up to her neck, and sat, putting more distance between them.

"Why the hell not?" Frustration colored every word. This was just great. He sat and tugged what little sheet was left over his lap—his hard-on was history. "You might as well just tell me because fighting with me has made sure that the little head is no longer a variable in the little head/big head equation."

"I'm not telling you because I refuse to tell someone I love him for the first time in the middle of a fight! That's why." She wasn't crying now. No, she was pissed. She was yelling. And damned if he wasn't the happiest son of a bitch on the planet.

She scooted away, and Lord knew, she was fast, but he was faster.

He grabbed her before she could get her cute ass out of bed, did a little wrestling move to get her hands safely under his control and her body beneath his, careful not to disturb the babies too much. He didn't bother trying to hide his smile this time. Hell, it would have been a lost cause anyway. "You love me?"

Her eyes spit fire, and she tried her damnedest to get out of his hold. "Let me go."

"Oh, no. I know you, Bianca. You're either going to take a swing at me or throw something."

"You're a jerk."

"Yeah, maybe, but you love me anyway." He kissed her quick, hoping to avoid her teeth.

She blew out a breath and relaxed beneath him. "I tried to tell you nicely, but, no, you were more intent on shoving your tongue in my mouth."

"I was trying to keep you from telling me you *didn't* love me." He kissed her again, nibbled on her lips, and then moved to her ear. "I couldn't handle hearing that again, not after everything that happened tonight."

"I wouldn't have said that even if it were true. I'm not cruel. I saw how upset you were. I'm really sorry. I didn't mean to scare you."

"I know you're not cruel, just honest. Still, if I had any idea what you wanted to say, I would have kept my tongue to myself, at least until after you told me. I'm sorry." He nuzzled her neck waiting to hear it.

She didn't say a word.

"Bianca?"

"Hmm?"

He kissed up to her ear. "I thought you had something you wanted to tell me." He slipped her earlobe between his lips and raked his teeth over it.

"Nope. Nothing else."

"Oh, no. You're not getting off that easily. As a matter of fact, I'll make sure you won't get off again—not until you tell me exactly what I want to hear. I'm not above using a little sexual torture to get what I want, and right now, I want to hear you say the words."

"You're incorrigible." She gave him a shove, but he didn't move.

"Wrong words. Try again." He kissed her slow and deep, and damned if he didn't almost forget his mission.

She moaned when he pulled away. "Trapper?"

"Yes?" Keeping her hands in his, he pushed them over her head, clasped both wrists in one hand, and ripped the sheet out from between them with the other. His gaze traveled the length of her body, her hands held high, her back arched forcing her breasts up, her nipples dark and tight from the heat of his gaze, the chill of the night air, or the electricity between them whenever he touched her. Her skin was so pale, opalescent in the light spilling in from the doorway. "God, you're beautiful." He felt like he had when he skied down a frozen waterfall, taken a jump he had no business taking, and landed harder than he thought possible. It was as if something kicked him in the diaphragm and forced all the air from his lungs. "I'm waiting." He slid his cheek over her breast, his two- or three-day stubble abrading her sensitive skin.

She shivered beneath him, her nipples tightening to hard points, and he hadn't even touched them. Not yet. Bianca moaned but didn't say a word.

He let his free hand glide slowly down the length of her long arm, teasing the side of her breast. "Cat got your tongue?" He waited for her to speak while his callused fingers scraped against the baby-soft skin beneath her breasts.

Bianca let out a frustrated groan and rolled her hips beneath his, trying for more contact, more pressure, more pleasure.

He loved that for once in their relationship, he was in total control. He knew this was an anomaly, one he was going to enjoy while he had the chance. He didn't expect it would ever happen again, and maybe that was okay. Being out of control with Bianca sure beat the hell out of having total control of his life without her. He slid to her side because having her beneath him was too much of a temptation and giving in was not an option. No, tonight he'd make sure she'd tell him what he wanted to hear. And until then, neither of them would have any satisfaction.

He kissed his way across her breasts, his tongue skittering over her soft skin without touching the areola, while his other hand slid over her ribs to cup her baby bump, his pointer finger slipping in the dent of her naval.

He ignored her sounds of utter frustration and spread the fingers of his hand over the babies—amazed at how small they were, amazed that he and Bianca had created their two little miracles together, and amazed that in a

few months those miracles would make him a dad and
Bianca a mom.

Bianca's breathing grew erratic, and her eyes were a
little bit wild. She'd always been so damn responsive—
especially since her pregnancy. He prayed he could pull
this off. He slid his lips over her nipple and dragged it
farther into his mouth.

Bianca freed her hands—her fingers dug into his
hair, making sure he was unable to move away from her
breast. Not that he wanted to, except to pay attention to
the other—after all, he was a fair guy.

He did his best to remember his mission while tor-
turing her breasts. It was a difficult task, but someone
had to do it.

Her moans grew louder, her nails raked his scalp, so
he backed off one breast and moved to the other, and he
drew his hand down her thigh to play with the back of
her knee. He remembered how sensitive she was there.
Her legs opened in invitation. He kissed his way down
the long length of her body, paying special attention
to the baby bump, slipping his tongue into her naval.
"Anything you want to tell me?" he asked as he drew his
teeth over the sensitive skin just below their babies and
slipped between her gorgeous thighs.

"Trapper, stop toying with me."

"Not what I want to hear." Her scent was overwhelm-
ing and called to him on a primal level. He wanted a
taste. Hell, he wanted to drown in it—in her. He wondered who he tortured more with this little game of keep-
away, Bianca or himself? He was so hard he ached with
it. He'd been on edge since the last time they'd made
love. He settled, pressing himself into the mattress, and

opened his eyes only to find her swollen and glistening before him. He blew out a breath, and her hips rose.

"Trapper, please."

"Oh, I plan to. Right after you have your say." He kissed his way from her knee up her inner thigh, his hands filled with her ass. He was testing them both. Unfortunately, he was the only one who seemed to be suffering. Especially when she reached down and grabbed both his ears, pulling him up her body. He went with it. It was either that or losing body parts he was kind of fond of. Without ears, how would he keep his hat from falling over his eyes?

Trapper held himself above her, not wanting to put too much weight on the babies.

As soon as he got within kissing range, she had her mouth on him. Bianca's mouth was amazing, but unfortunately, she wasn't using it for what he needed.

He broke the kiss. "Say the words, Bianca."

She rolled her hips, and his dick nudged her opening. God, she was trying to kill him.

He held back a groan and stared into her green eyes, darkened with desire, still full of love. What the hell was she waiting for?

She wrapped her long, long, long legs around his waist and did her best to pull him closer.

He made like a statue, only raising one eyebrow, and watched the emotions cross her face like subtitles on a foreign film. Anxiousness, desire, anger, frustration, and fear. She needed a nudge—and not with his dick. "I love you, Bianca."

She looked him dead in the eye, and her lips trembled. "I love you too."

Trapper let out the breath he felt he'd been holding for the last hour. "I promise you'll never regret it." He slid into her body while he slid into her kiss and swore he saw fireworks. He loved her slow, watching her come, watching her climb back up again only to shoot her higher. He wanted the night to last forever—this love, this meeting of hearts and minds and bodies. He fought his urge to follow her over as long as he could, and finally, gave in.

Trapper lay spent beside her, having rolled them over on their sides to keep from crushing her and the babies. He held her close, still inside her, her belly and breasts against his, and watched her come back to earth. Her eyes were closed, a smile playing on her lips.

Bianca reached over and wrapped her arm around his neck, pulling him closer for a kiss.

That's when he felt it. A shift, a thump…something against his stomach.

Her eyes shot open wide.

Neither of them breathed.

There it was again. So faint.

Bianca sucked in a breath. "Did you feel that, or was it just me?"

"Is that the first time you felt them move?"

"I don't know. I wasn't sure. I mean, it was so soft before, I didn't think it was anything more than my imagination, but this time—"

"I felt it too." He slid his trembling hand over the babies and held his breath, waiting and praying the speed of his pulse didn't drown out any movement. Sure enough, there was another little nudge. "Oh man, that's amazing." He couldn't believe it. He looked into her smiling face, and for once her tears didn't freak him out. He was feeling more than a little misty himself. Even with the tears, he saw nothing but love and happiness shining from her eyes. He leaned over to kiss her. He couldn't have kept from kissing her if his life depended on it.

—·∾∾·—

Bianca woke up, opened her eyes, and found Trapper with his hand on her baby bump, staring at her belly. "How long have you been doing that?"

He gave her his heart-stopping smile. "Awhile. I'm waiting for the babies to wake up."

She rose onto her elbows. "We could try making love again—that seemed to do the trick last night." She wouldn't mind that at all. She couldn't believe she wanted him again so soon. She thought last night would be their final time together, but maybe not. Maybe she could love him one more time. She didn't know if it was Trapper or just pregnancy hormones, but she was beginning to think horniness was a perpetual state during pregnancy. "But since the babies have half my DNA, it could be the chocolate that got them going and not the sex."

He sidled up against her and slid his leg between hers and pulled her in for a kiss. "Did you get enough sleep?"

"If not, I'll nap later. I'm hungry."

His smile grew wider and showed off his dimples. "Are you hungry for me or food."

Her heart did a little somersault, and her tummy grumbled. "Both?"

He rolled away, and she watched while he pulled on a pair of sweats. The man looked as good going as he did coming. A shiver ran through her just remembering the way he looked last night when he finally let go. He'd held her gaze and let her see into his soul. She felt his love right down to her toes—which he ended up curling more times than she thought possible. She just prayed he didn't change his mind about this whole love thing, but she wouldn't bet on it. Actually, she'd bet against it. Either way, she'd know soon enough. But first things first—the other secret of pregnancy no one mentions beforehand is that when you're pregnant, you have to pee, constantly.

By the time she did her thing, brushed her teeth, and washed her face, Trapper was almost done whipping up pancake batter—and she wasn't talking Bisquick. He made pancake batter from scratch. Who did that? Hell, she thought she was a culinary goddess when she managed to toast her Eggo waffle without torching it. "Do you always cook like this?"

"Like what?"

"You know, using ingredients. Everything I make just needs to be toasted or nuked and usually comes out of a can or a box."

He made a funny face.

She shrugged and headed to the coffeepot, thankful that for once, the scent of coffee wasn't making her yak.

Trapper stuck a full mug in her hand. "Decaf for you."

She took a sip and wondered why she bothered. "That's just so not fair. I'd love to see you live without caffeine for nine months."

He gave her a kiss, another one of those kisses he seemed to plant on her without thinking. "No, you wouldn't. I lived on the stuff all through law school. It's my only addiction—well, other than you."

"Yeah, about that."

Trapper tossed a hunk of butter on the hot grill. "How do you like your eggs?"

"I thought you were making pancakes."

"You need protein too. Pancakes, ham, and eggs."

"Seriously? I'm going to get fatter than I am already."

"You're eating for three, and you're anything but fat. I believe I kissed every inch of your body last night. No fat; I looked."

"Right." She didn't believe him, but she wasn't going to waste her breath.

He stopped moving the butter around the griddle and stared at her.

"What?"

"You're not going to argue? Are you feeling all right?"

"Would you stop looking at me as if you're expecting my head to explode? I'm not that difficult."

Trapper made himself very busy at the stove and didn't comment. Figures. He was probably doing his level best not to laugh in her face.

She held the warm cup between her suddenly cold hands and sat on one of the bar stools across from the stove. "I talked to James the other day."

Trapper looked up when she said that. "That's good. Everything at work going well?"

"I didn't ask, but he hasn't called screaming, so I guess it is. He did tell me he wanted a raise."

Trapper poured the batter on the griddle.

"I told him what you said."

That got his attention. Not that he stopped filling the griddle.

"You didn't invite your family to join us for breakfast, did you?"

"No, why?"

"Because you're cooking enough for a crowd."

"I'm hungry. I worked up a hell of an appetite last night. So back to James. What did you tell him?"

She felt her face heating so she stared into her cup of useless coffee. "I told him that you thought you loved me."

"I don't *think* I love you." His tone held an edge of something—a little angry, no, more put out. Yeah, when he got that deep gravelly quality, he was either turned on or put out. He definitely didn't look turned on. "I *know* I love you."

"That's pretty much what James said."

"Smart man." He plopped the ladle into the bowl of batter and leaned toward her over the stove, his eyes glittering in the morning light. "What I don't get is why it's so hard for you to believe."

She pushed the coffee away. Suddenly, she didn't feel so good, but she couldn't back down now. So she told him about Max, about thinking she was pregnant, about telling her parents, about losing the biggest modeling contract of her young life and discovering that her parents had embezzled all her money, about losing the one man she thought she loved. She wasn't even sure she'd made any sense. She kind of vomited the whole thing out.

Trapper hadn't said anything; he just listened. She felt him watching her, and she wanted nothing more than to disappear. She'd been such a fool. A fool for Max—a man who was more than twice her age. Max had told her he loved her, and she believed him—until the day she told him she was pregnant. She hadn't known he was

married. God, when she'd learned that, she'd wanted
to die. He had kids. If that weren't bad enough, she'd
found out that not only had her parents been robbing
her blind, they'd practically pimped her out to Max to
ensure she'd be the next Guess Girl. All the embarrassment and pain she'd felt exploded in her again. It
was as if talking about it brought it back—all the pain,
all the humiliation, all the loss. When she'd told her
mother she thought she was pregnant, her parents had
planned to force her to abort the baby. Everyone knew
pregnancy killed modeling careers, and she'd been their
meal ticket. That's when she ran. She'd snuck out of her
hotel room in the middle of the night, grabbed a cab to
LaGuardia, and flew to Cincinnati. To her grandmother.
She never saw her parents again outside of a courtroom.

Silence. The only thing she heard was Trapper turning the stove off.

"What happened to the baby?"

She still couldn't look at him. "False alarm. I dieted
too much. I needed to lose some weight for the Guess
Girl contract, and a celery and water diet, while good
for dropping ten pounds in a week, was not condu-
cive to reproductive health. Five percent body fat is
too little to menstruate—I didn't even know it was a
possibility. I was left with no baby. No boyfriend. No
parents. No contract. No money. Not that the money
mattered. At the time, I'd have traded all my money to
have any one of those back. I lost everything I thought
I loved. I lost everyone."

"Bianca?"

She heard anger in his voice. She knew that little
tremor she heard whenever she pissed Trapper off.

She'd known how it would be. He didn't have to draw her a picture. "And now, I've lost my appetite." She slid off the stool and stared at the floor. "I'm sorry. I'm just going to sleep for a while."

"This is why you didn't believe me when I told you I loved you?"

"I don't know." She refused to cry. She would not cry.

"This is why you didn't tell me about the babies?"

"I don't know." She blinked back her tears. They burned her eyes and her nose. Shit. She was crying. She covered her mouth to stop the inevitable sob. She wasn't able to hold it back. Not when he put it like that. God, she hadn't even been aware—she told herself he wouldn't have wanted to know, but maybe he was right. Maybe she didn't tell him because she was afraid he'd want her to have an abortion.

"At least it's making sense now. You don't trust me, or anyone, because a pedophile raped you when you were a child. Because your parents abused your trust, abused you, and treated you like a fucking ATM." Suddenly he was there in front of her, his big body blocking her exit.

"Max didn't rape me. I was a willing participant."

"You were a child."

"I was fourteen, almost six feet tall, and I'd been in the business my whole life. I was hardly a child."

"You were a little girl in the body of a woman. That doesn't change the facts. Max belongs in a prison cell full of big men who want to make him their bitch, and your parents belong there with him."

"Trapper, I knew what I was doing with Max. That was on me. It was my fault. I asked for it. I got what I deserved."

"You were desperate for love. God, Bianca. Give yourself a fucking break. Your parents, Max, and anyone else who knew about it abused your trust. They broke the law. I'm a judge. I've seen this time and again, and believe me, there's always an excuse for the perp's behavior, and the victims always blame themselves. You deserved to be loved and protected, and they used you, abused you, and threw you away."

"I allowed it."

"No, baby, you didn't allow it. You just didn't know how to protect yourself."

"I learned."

"Maybe too well. Does James know? Was he there then?"

"God, no. That summer he was modeling in Europe. I've never told anyone. Even my grandmother doesn't know the whole story."

"Yet you told me."

She still couldn't look at him. She stared at his throat. The muscles of his neck tense and chorded. "I had no choice. You thought you loved me. You're so stubborn you wouldn't let it go. You wouldn't believe me when I told you that you didn't know me. But I was right. You didn't know me, but now you do. That changes everything."

"You think so?"

"I know so. And believe me, I understand. I do." She patted his chest. "I'd do the same thing if I were you. It's fine. I'm fine. You didn't know who I was, and now you do. So, when I can leave, I'll go back to my life, and you can go back to yours. We'll figure out this whole co-parenting thing. Maybe we should just let the lawyers come up with an equitable arrangement."

"So that's it? You lied to me last night? You lied when you said you love me?"

"No. I don't lie. I would never—" He took her hand and pulled her against him, then tipped her chin up so she couldn't avoid looking into his eyes.

"You said you'd never take our babies away from me, but you're planning to do that too."

"You don't want me. You can't." God, this hurt. She was doing all she could not to fall apart. "Trapper, what the hell do you want from me?"

"I want you to trust me. I want you to believe I love you and that nothing is ever going to change how I feel. Jesus, Bianca, you were abused. That doesn't make you unlovable. That makes you a survivor."

"No, that makes me a slut. I'm not some pitiable victim, Trapper. Don't make me out to be one. The only thing I suffered from was my own stupidity. I trusted the wrong people."

"They were your parents."

"I allowed Max to play me. I believed every line he fed me. Lesson learned. I got over it."

"You're wrong. That asshole should have paid for his crimes. Unfortunately, the statute of limitations in the state of New York is only five years for statutory rape."

"How the hell do you know that? What do you law-yers do, memorize the statute of limitations for every law in every state in the union?"

"No, only the ones in which you take the bar exam. I was a DA in Manhattan for a few years before moving back to Idaho."

"It doesn't matter. I told you it wasn't rape. It was consensual."

"That's where you're wrong, sweetheart. It was rape, and you were a victim. And, God, Bianca, I'm so sorry you went through that. I'm so sorry for all of it."

"I don't want your pity."

"I don't pity you. I love you. I admire you. I'm amazed by you. I always knew you were strong, but I had no idea how strong."

"I was stupid."

"Do you think you're the only one who ever fell for the wrong person? You should have been passing notes in school and going to Sadie Hawkins dances. Hell, I fell for the wrong person, and I was an adult with a degree in law. I don't have your excuse."

"Do you really believe that?"

"I do. I believe every word. I love you." He leaned forward and kissed her. Just a soft kiss. "I love you."

"Still?"

"Always." He looked so strong and certain and determined. "I will always love you."

She heard the words. She felt them rumble through his bare chest. She saw the truth in his eyes. She dropped her head to his shoulder and felt safe and loved and warm for the first time, maybe the only time in her life. She wanted to hold on to him and never let go.

Trapper kissed her forehead. "Now, are you keeping any other secrets from me?"

"Just one."

Every muscle in his big body tensed against hers.

"I'm working toward my doctorate in Egyptology. But the babies have kind of thrown a monkey wrench in my plans."

"Seriously?" He set her away from him and stared, clearly shocked.

"I have two more classes to take before writing my thesis." She shrugged. "I had to take an incomplete in both classes this semester. Between all the traveling and then the morning sickness, I just couldn't—"

"Wow. I had no idea."

"I don't advertise it. It kind of kills the whole brainless, blonde bombshell image."

"I never thought you were brainless. As a matter of fact, I've always thought that if we compared IQs, you'd have me beat. But, man, Egyptology. That's intense."

"I don't know about intense—fascinating, sure, but intense? Maybe if I was able to study in Egypt. I mean, I've been there, but not to study."

"So, we're okay?"

She looked into his eyes and saw all the love and acceptance she'd seen before. Another piece of her heart melted. He looked at her like he looked at their babies on the ultrasound screen, like he looked when she'd caught him staring at her belly an hour ago. "Yes, we're okay."

He wrapped his arms around her and held her tight. "I know you're probably tired, but do you think you could eat something before you crash?"

"I'd better let you feed me." She reached up and gave him a kiss. "I can't have your mother killing the man I love and putting your body parts in the compost pile to feed her roses now, can I? Besides, I don't cook. The babies and I would be shit out of luck."

Chapter 18

TRAPPER CAME HOME FROM HIS FIRST FULL DAY AT work, breezed through the kitchen, and headed straight for the master bedroom. Bianca wasn't there so he tossed his hat on the headboard, pulled his hair out of his queue and ran his hands through it, before heading to the den. He found her curled up on the couch dozing.

He let out a relieved breath just like he had every time he found her at home when he returned. He wasn't sure if it was because he invariably missed her when he was away, or if part of him still expected her to run. The feeling was one he didn't want to examine too closely, so instead, he pushed it to the back of his mind. He slid behind her, replacing the pillows she leaned against with his body. "I'm home," he whispered and kissed her temple. He wrapped his arms around her, spread his hand over her belly, and breathed in her scent.

"Trapper?" She sounded half-asleep, all soft and warm and sexy.

"Of course it's me. Who else kisses you and holds you?"

"You'd be surprised."

He chose to let that one go without reply. He didn't like the habit his brothers had gotten into of kissing Bianca's cheek whenever they said hello or good-bye. He was sure they just did it to piss him off. Of course, he'd followed suit with Jessie and Toni. "I thought the day would never end. How are you doing?"

Bianca shot him a warning glare. Not good, obviously. "I feel as if I've grown another appendage—your hand." She removed the offending addition from her belly and gave him a kiss in exchange.

The kiss was nice, but he wanted both. "Oh, come on, Bianca. I haven't been home all day. I missed holding you and feeling the babies move."

She elbowed him in the ribs and struggled to sit up. He didn't have to be a rocket scientist to catch her back-the-heck-off warning. "You might have been away, but I've yet to be alone. Unfortunately, feeling the babies move happens to be every Kincaid's favorite pastime. I've had someone's hand on my belly all day."

"Gramps's too?"

"Joe spent hours waiting for the twins to wake up. And once they did, he didn't want to miss a kick or punch. There was a veritable boxing match going on in there earlier. Joe had the time of his life. He said it was more entertaining than his first television."

"That's because there was only one channel. What about Fisher and Hunter?"

"Oh, yeah, they're tummy-touchers too."

"Well, shit. I don't know if I like my brothers feeling up my girl."

"You have a problem with your brothers having their hands all over my belly, but your grandfather's okay?"

"No, but that's Gramps. I just can't go there, Bianca. Sorry, sweetheart, but you have to own that one. After all, what do you expect after sleeping with the old man." God, he loved making her blush with embarrassment, almost as much as he made her blush with desire. He decided not to mention the fact that she'd also tried to sleep with his brothers too. That would sign his personal death warrant. And she'd make sure it was a slow and painful one to boot.

"Thanks for all your support, Trap. I knew I could count on you. You're a regular knight in rusty armor."

"I have one or two redeeming qualities. I even brought you a surprise."

"You did?" She snuggled closer and didn't swat the hand sliding around her belly. "A good surprise or a bad surprise?"

"Why would I bring you a bad surprise?"

"I don't know, but most of the surprises I've received haven't been all that good."

He could imagine.

"So what is it?"

"I was in such a rush to see you, I forgot to bring it in."

"I'm guessing it's not a puppy, then."

"Do you want a puppy?"

"No. I don't know. Maybe. I asked for a puppy for Christmas every year when I was a kid. Well, until… Anyway, Gina brought Jasmine, her pointer, over today. She's a doll and such a little lady."

"Gina or Jasmine?"

"Both."

"Jasmine weighs seventy pounds—she's hardly a puppy."

Bianca rolled her eyes. "Gina doesn't weigh much more. But Jasmine is so cute. I've never seen such a well-behaved animal, and she's so gentle."

"She's also a dog. Dogs and puppies are two different things. Dogs don't usually chew through furniture and crap in the house."

"I've never had either. My parents wouldn't allow

me to have any pets. When I was out on my own, I was traveling so much." Her voice sounded odd, almost wistful—he'd never heard Bianca sound wistful, not even close.

"Did you see Ben too?"

"No, but Gina said something about them stopping by tonight. Ben and Joe went to the office today for a board meeting, so Gina and Jasmine belly-sat until Karma came over."

Belly-sat? What the heck was that? And where the hell was Karma? He looked around. "I didn't see Karma."

"I'm guessing that was her plan. She said something about getting away before you discovered she drank your last beer."

"I'll kill her. She works at a freakin' bar, and she comes here and steals my beer. What's wrong with this picture?"

"Nothing—it's a game for her, Trapper. Karma loves nothing better than to get under your skin or pull a fast one on you. Today, she accomplished both."

"She's very good at it."

"I have a feeling Karma would be good at anything she puts her mind to. The trick is to get her to expend all that energy toward good instead of evil."

"Yeah, good luck with that. We've been trying to accomplish that her whole life—it hasn't worked yet." He kissed the side of Bianca's neck because, shit, he couldn't resist. "The kids are quiet tonight."

"Feed me something sweet, and they'll probably start boxing again."

"I can do that."

"I know. It's one of your redeeming qualities."

"Cooking and the great foot rubs."

"And the sex. Sex is a biggie."

"It's nice to know I'm not the only one who missed our afternoon nap today." He stood and took both her hands to pull her off the couch and into his arms. God, he loved coming home to her. He could do this for the rest of his life and be happy. "Come on out to the kitchen, and I'll get your surprise. You can open it while I make dinner."

∼∾∼

Trapper hefted a large box into the kitchen. It was bigger than a bread box, and from the sound it made when he dropped it on the counter, it was heavy. That's when she noticed what he wore—a sweatshirt, jeans, and his cowboy boots.

She'd been asleep when he left for work that morning—she hadn't even heard him. Waking up alone after waking up in his arms for almost two weeks really sucked. She'd missed him. Of course, Kate and Joe had stopped by with breakfast, so she hadn't been alone for long. "Did you change when you came home?"

"No. Why do you ask?" He pulled a bunch of vegetables out of the refrigerator and shot her a smirk. "What do you want me to change into? And don't think I'm going to run around in those silk boxers you found. The one time I wore them, I almost slid out of bed and ended up on my ass. It's not happening again." She happened to think he looked really good in those black silk boxers—of course, he looked really good out of them too.

His sweatshirt was red with a big solid black rectangle

on it above the words "Boise at Night." "Do you mean to tell me you wear jeans and sweatshirts to work?"

"Only in the winter. I wear T-shirts and shorts all summer."

"But you're a judge."

He looked up from the eggplant, peppers, onions, and asparagus he chopped. "Yeah, so?"

"Aren't judges supposed to wear suits and ties?"

"Some do, but not me. Not unless I have meetings anyway, and I really try to avoid those. I hate wearing suits, and I've learned silk ties are better used for things other than neckwear. I have to wear my robe when I'm on the bench anyway, so no one knows what, if anything, I'm wearing beneath it." He gave her an eyebrow waggle. "I have a collection of off-color T-shirts and sweatshirts for when my least favorite lawyers are before me. It always makes running into them in the hall fun."

"You really are incorrigible."

"Pretty much." He shot her a grin she could imagine he'd have worn after successfully hiding a frog in his teacher's desk drawer, or supergluing a stapler to her hand. "It keeps life interesting though, doesn't it?"

"Definitely interesting." She'd been in Boise for almost two weeks. She'd never had such a good time doing absolutely nothing. She even loved having her belly-sitters around. If someone had told her a year ago that the highlight of a very enjoyable day would be giving Hunter Kincaid a hard time by browsing through a book on pregnancy with him, she'd have offered to give that person the number of her therapist. She couldn't keep from smiling. Hunter was a nervous wreck around pregnant women. She couldn't wait until he and Toni started a family—she could only imagine how protective he'd be. Toni was not one to take kindly to being kept in a gilded cage. It was going to be fun to watch the fireworks—and there would be fireworks. Not that Bianca would be around to see them. She'd be back in New York by then.

Her eyes burned with sudden tears she was thankfully able to blink back. Leaving Trapper and Boise was what she wanted, or at least, that's what she told herself. Her life was in New York. She let out a sigh. Maybe Karma would keep her filled in on all the news. Still, she was probably going to miss Trapper more than she expected. He'd been her constant companion until today—and she'd missed him something awful, even knowing he'd be home in eight hours. She couldn't imagine how it would feel to be thousands of miles away. And if that wasn't bad enough, she'd miss his family too—even Karma.

"Something wrong, Bianca?"

"No." Nothing new anyway. Since she arrived she'd been wondering how she'd leave when the doctor let her off bed rest and gave her the okay to go home.

When she finally did leave, she'd have to figure out how to sleep alone again. And she'd have to hire a cook. After living with Trapper and eating real food, she was afraid the babies would revolt if fed anything that wasn't homemade. She'd be alone. She'd spent her life alone, and she'd been okay with that—after all, it wasn't much different than having her parents around. But now, after being here with the Kincaids, she couldn't imagine going back to her solitary life, and that's what scared her.

"Are you going to wait all night, or are you going to open your surprise?" Trapper dragged her from her thoughts, and when she looked at him, she could have sworn he looked nervous.

"What's the rush? Did you not put enough airholes in the box?"

"Bianca, it's not a pet."

"Okay. It's not a pet, but you think I'll like it?"

"I hope so. Why would I get you a surprise I thought you wouldn't like?"

She received nasty surprises all the time. Maybe bad surprises were a new concept to Trapper, but she'd had more than her fair share. She examined the box and tried to decipher its contents. It hadn't been posted, so she couldn't even tell the point of origin. "Where's it from?"

"What's it matter? Would you just open the damn box?"

She slowly lifted the edges of the top, stepping away so her face wasn't over it, just in case something popped out.

Trapper had been so closemouthed; she couldn't imagine what it was. The least he could do was give a girl a hint.

She removed a layer of tissue and sucked in a breath. "My books? You brought me my books? How did you know?"

He shot her a half smile and a one-shoulder shrug. "I thought since you were taking classes, you must have had a bunch of books at your place. I called James and asked him to pack all the books he could find for your classes and dissertation. Gina and Ben picked them up on their way to the airport. It's not that big a deal."

Her mouth must have been hanging open.

"I thought you'd want something to do while I'm at work all day. And just because you had to take an incomplete in your classes this semester doesn't mean you can't go through the work at your own pace, does it?"

She didn't even know what to say.

"I'm sure you plan to finish your doctorate after the babies are born. Don't you?"

He assumed she'd go back to school? "I guess I will eventually. I hadn't really thought about it. I was overwhelmed with the thought of one baby, but with two, I don't know how I'll manage it."

"We'll work something out."

"We?"

"You're so close to your degree, I can't imagine you wanting to give up on all your years of hard work. It couldn't have been easy juggling the agency, your traveling, and school."

It hadn't been that difficult—she just didn't have a life. Hell, she hadn't even wanted one. No relationships meant no pain and plenty of time to bury herself in her studies. Now her life was so full of relationships she'd never looked for, but found anyway. The whole idea still had her head spinning. What was she going to do when she left?

"I set up an office for you upstairs. I thought if you wanted to do a little schoolwork it would be okay. It's not as if you'll be under deadlines or stress, right?"

She grabbed one of her books and hugged it close to her chest. "You set up an office? For me? When?"

"The twins and I moved the furniture in while you were asleep."

"Furniture?"

"It's not much—just a desk, a few bookcases, and a chaise longue. I thought you might want to be able to stretch out and read. It's not a big deal."

Not a big deal? God, she needed to sit down.

"But if you don't want to go up the stairs, you can use my office down here. Or we could switch—"

Oh God, the tears she'd been holding back started rolling down her cheeks like someone had turned on a faucet. Damn pregnancy hormones. But then, maybe it wasn't even that. No one had ever done something that nice for her in her whole life.

"Damn."

She heard something fall, and then in a heartbeat, Trapper's strong arms wrapped around her, drawing her right off the stool and into his chest.

"Shit, I'm sorry. I thought you'd be happy. I didn't mean to upset you. I'll buy you a puppy. Any kind you want. Just stop crying." He held her tight and rubbed her back until she could speak. It took awhile.

"I'm not upset about not getting a puppy." God, she was embarrassed. "I can't believe you would do all that. I didn't ask for an office or my books or anything—"

"It's okay, sweetheart. I'll get rid of everything. You don't even need to look at it."

She wiped her cheeks on his sweatshirt. "No."

He tipped her chin up to face him. She wasn't much shorter than Trapper, but he was wearing his boots, and she wore his wool socks. He searched her face and then let out a relieved breath—relieved and just a little angry. "Give a guy a break, will ya? You can't start weeping and expect me to know what the hell is going on with you. Seeing you cry kills me."

"I don't do it on purpose. I can't control it. It just happens."

"We need to have a hand signal or something, because when you start—you're too busy sobbing to speak. So, just to clarify, this is like the roses? You're not mad or upset?"

"I'm happy."

"That's good, right?" He gave her a kiss, one of those little kisses that melted her every time. "Sweetheart, do you think you can do happy without the waterworks?"

Probably not until her hormones went back to normal, but he looked upset enough as it was—no need to make matters worse. "I'll try."

"Does this mean we're going to be puppy shopping or not?"

"You were serious?" She was an adult. She shouldn't even be considering it. What would she do with a puppy? But then she didn't know what she was going to do with two kids—that didn't mean she didn't want them. "We can get a puppy?"

"We can get anything you want. Just, you know, don't cry."

The look of fear that crossed his face was priceless. She couldn't squash the laugh that escaped. "That's a nice offer, cowboy, but it was obviously made under duress."

"Maybe, but I sure like seeing your eyes sparkle like a teenage boy's with his first Victoria's Secret catalog. It doesn't happen often."

"A big decision like that should probably be slept on. Still, it's tempting as all get-out. Almost as tempting as you."

"Temptation is part of my plan."

"Right. I keep forgetting about your agenda." The

funny thing was her agenda seemed to be getting closer and closer to his.

<hr />

A week later, Trapper drove back to the house after Bianca's prenatal appointment. She hadn't said a word since he started the engine. She didn't even look at him. She just stared out the passenger-side window.

He wished he paid more attention in his college psychology class. Hell, he didn't know what to do or say. All he could do was pray she didn't start crying again. Not that the silence was much better than tears. He didn't know if she was upset about what the doctor said, or the fact she couldn't leave—with his luck, probably both. She was off bed rest, but her sugar was still high, so that meant a fasting blood test first thing in the morning. "Want to talk about it?"

"There's nothing to say until we find out the results of the test."

"There's plenty to say. Your mind is whirling—I can hear it from all the way over here. You're just not telling me what you're thinking."

Bianca was so far over, she was one with the door. "I'm trying to figure out what I'm doing wrong. I've done everything the damn doctor told me, and it's just not good enough."

"Sweetheart, it's not you. It's difficult to carry twins. You heard the doctor. He said they're being overly cautious, which is a good thing, right? We don't know anything yet. We'll cut down on the carbs, up the protein like he said, and wait for the tests to come back. The babies are fine. They're getting so big—it's amazing to see how fast they're growing, and you're gaining weight the way you should—it's all good."

"You don't know that."

"Yes, I do. If there were a real problem, you'd be in the hospital like you were before. He's playing it safe by ordering the blood test, so relax. You stressing out won't help." He reached over and grabbed her hand.

"Easy for you to say. You don't have the dynamic duo sitting on your bladder."

"Do I need to stop?"

"No, I can wait until we get home. I'll be fine."

"I can call into work and reschedule my afternoon." As much as he'd like to get away from the nasty custody case he was hearing, it wouldn't be fair to any of the members of the splintered family. They were all going through their own version of hell, and prolonging it would be cruel. Sometimes the unknown was worse than the pain his decision would bring to most of them—one of the two parents who loved their kids but not each other, and both children caught in the middle. There was no good decision he could make. These cases were as hard on him as any murder trial. By the time the family hit his courtroom, things were so out of hand, there was little he could do to help matters. Sometimes it came down to determining which living situation would do the least damage to the children, who already had their lives torn apart.

She shook her head. "No, you need to go back to work. I'll be fine. Besides, it's not as if I'll be alone."

He let out a relieved breath and wondered if he could manage to talk the parents into shared custody. It's what would be best for the kids. If the parents would think more about the welfare of their children than their need to punish their exes, it would be better for everyone concerned.

"Are you okay?"

Trapper shook his head and tried to erase the images of little Lucy and Sam. They were great kids and were being used as pawns in their parents' war. "Yes, I'm fine. I'm just in the middle of a difficult case."

"Criminal?"

"No, I'm in family court this week. Family court is worse—at least in criminal court, most of the people who come before me deserve prosecution. The people who come before me in family court rarely deserve the pain my decision will create. No matter how I rule, the kids are always going to lose. They're six and eight— they think they somehow caused their parents' divorce, and now they're being fought over like valuable pieces of artwork."

"That's horrible."

"The trick is to figure out which of the parents— who both obviously love their kids—wants custody more because they want to care for their children and less to use their children as a weapon against their ex. Although, in this case, I think to some degree, there will always be a little bit of that. It's been ugly."

She turned her whole body toward him and focused all her considerable attention on him. "I watched you on Court TV—the Madison trial."

He forced himself to remain expressionless. He couldn't believe it—he didn't want to. He knew it was news in Idaho, but he hadn't known it garnered national attention. He'd okayed cameras in the courtroom—he had expected to see film clips on the nightly news, but he hadn't known it would be shown anywhere else. It was a horrible trial, and he wished she'd never seen it. "You watched the whole thing?"

"I did. You're very good at what you do. I can't tell you how stunned I was to see your face while I was flipping through channels. I was really impressed. I never realized until then how difficult your job must be for you—the stress, the pressure—it must be incredible, and it has to take a toll on you. How do you handle it?"

"I just do. But when it comes down to it, I don't matter—it's the law that matters. The people. Justice."

"On the bench, yes. But you and your feelings matter to me. You never talk about your work and the stress you must feel."

"Sweetheart, by the time things get to me, they're ugly and horrible—it's my job to make sure I find the most equitable way to see justice served. It's nothing I want to share. I want to protect you and the family from the ugliness I see every day."

"But who protects you? Who listens to you? Who do you talk to?"

"No one. I'm fine with it. I've learned to handle it. It's part of the job."

"Trapper, you don't need to protect me from your feelings. Don't you see? I need to support you just like you feel the need to support me. I want to be there for you. I love you."

"I love you too."

"But you still keep a huge part of who you are and what you do from me."

"Bianca, I can't talk about a lot of what goes on—"

"I don't want specifics about a case, Trapper. I just

want to know what's going on inside you. What you feel. I want to know if you have a crappy day, or a great one. I want to know that you won't keep that part of yourself and your life from me."

He'd never thought he'd hide anything from Bianca, except Paige, but he had a damn good reason for that. Still, he hadn't realized he'd kept anything else from her, not since he'd brought her home, but he had. Distance kept in the name of protecting her was still distance, and he knew from being on the other side how that felt. "I'm sorry. I never had anyone who wanted to be part of my life in that way. I didn't know—"

"That you weren't alone?" She smiled. "Yeah, I've got your six, Trapper. It's not so easy when the cowboy boot is on the other foot, is it?"

"Not easy, no, but I think it's something I can get used to."

"Maybe we both need to work on it."

"Maybe we do."

She took his hand and bounced a little in her seat. "So, you'll go back to work, and we'll talk about it later."

"Yes."

"That's good. Now don't worry about me. I'm sure you have the belly-sitters all lined up for the day. You're a master scheduler."

"They're not belly-sitters, they're concerned family. I couldn't keep them away if I wanted to—you know them well enough by now to know that. The schedule keeps you from having to deal with them all at once. If it's too much, I'll ask them to back off."

"No, I don't mean to sound as if I'm complaining. I

love your family. I actually like the company, really. I'm just cranky, and worried, and hungry. I'm sorry."

"Are you sure?"

"Positive. I'm disappointed. I thought with my blood pressure down, I'd be in the clear."

"You're off bed rest. That's a plus, but remember you're still supposed to take it easy."

"I know, and I will. I'm just going a little stir-crazy, I guess."

"Do you want me to take you up to Gramps's house for a change of scenery? Mom's there with Gramps. Ben and Gina are probably there too, if they're not off skiing."

"You don't think they'd mind?"

"Mind? Hell, they'd love it. You could nap there just as easily as at home if you get tired. It's not as if they're lacking for guest rooms. I'll pick you up after work. Knowing mom, she'll even feed us. It'll be a nice change. You're probably getting sick of my cooking."

"Hardly. You have no idea what I usually eat."

"Yeah, I do. I cleaned out your refrigerator before I brought you home, remember?"

"You did?"

"There wasn't much to clean out. The only things in there were condiments and batteries."

She didn't say anything, but her face flamed. At least he took her mind off the babies.

"So, do you want to tell me what those batteries were for?"

"None of your business."

He slid his hand up her thigh and under her skirt. "Yeah, that's what I thought they were for." He meant to tease her and only succeeded in getting himself hot and bothered. Damn, he took one look at her in that skirt when he'd picked her up that morning for her appointment and just about swallowed his tongue.

"I'm not talking about this with you."

Trapper looked over at her. Her blood sugar might be a tad high, but she hadn't been sick in over a week, and even without makeup, he couldn't help but notice Bianca was glowing. All he wanted to do was slide that sexy skirt up her long legs and take her back to bed. He hadn't had the time then, but there was nothing standing in his way now.

He turned into the driveway, and she realized where they were. "Hey, I thought we were going to Joe's."

"Later." He got out of the car, went around to open her door, and kissed her—long and slow and deep. He stepped back and waited for her eyes to refocus. "Court isn't scheduled to reconvene until two o'clock, and it isn't even noon."

"So you thought you'd bring me home, ravish me, and then drop me off with your mother and grandfather?"

He took her hand to help her down and couldn't keep the stupid grin off his face. "Yeah, pretty much. Do you have a problem with that?"

"I know I probably should, but surprisingly, I don't." She sashayed toward the house, putting a little extra sway in her step.

"Thank God." He didn't think Bianca could have gotten any sexier than she already was, but damn, since she stopped throwing up everything she ate, the woman practically radiated sex. The stress of the case that slipped off his shoulders earlier was now replaced by a whole different kind of tension—the good kind.

Chapter 19

"Nan, I'm fine. Really. There's no need for you to come to Idaho." Bianca looked around the office Trapper had set up, a space just for her. The desk was beautiful—definitely not something he picked up at Target. No, it looked like a vintage 1940s French Napoleon III desk, ebonized with drawers, and hoof-shaped feet. She ran her hand over the leather top. It was gorgeous and something she would have chosen for herself. The chaise longue he bought was a ruby red color that made you want to curl up with a good book or lie there daydreaming. It sat before French doors that opened onto a deck. The late March sun spilled in, and a view of the mountains with ever-changing colors filled the mullioned doors and surrounding windows. The room was painted a rich antique gold, calming, soothing, inspiring.

Bianca sat on the chaise and took the throw pillow and stuffed it behind her sore back. The sky was blindingly blue, and she stretched out like a cat in her own patch of sun, letting it warm her. This time of the year was never nice back east. In New York, March was usually cold and gray, but here in Boise, it was different. She gazed at the snow-covered mountains and thought it pretty cool that although there was no snow in the valley, there was still plenty for the skiers just a half hour up the mountain. If she weren't thirty-three weeks pregnant, she'd have loved to be up on the mountain spring skiing and getting a suntan. But then, if she weren't pregnant, she'd be in New York, working.

If she weren't pregnant, she would have missed out on all the time she and Trapper had spent together. She'd have missed out on all their date nights—nights that, no matter how stuck she felt due to her condition, Trapper always managed to make a special occasion. Some nights they shopped online for books, movies, or baby furniture. He usually cooked, but always made sure she had fresh baby pink roses. During their several dates a week, they'd succeeded in watching all the Jane Austen movies in what she liked to call pregnancy segments—making time for pee breaks and naps. They'd spent an evening playing board games, and she'd even managed to beat him twice at Scrabble.

Sometimes they just cuddled up in front of the fire and talked. He was getting much better about sharing how his work affected him. Every evening when he came home, they talked about their work, and the one who had the more difficult day got the longest back rub. So far, she was winning when it came to receiving rather than giving. She hoped that changed soon. Trapper had become so much a part of her life that she couldn't imagine not having him around, and that scared her.

"Nan, the gestational diabetes is under control. I'm even working a little—just a few hours a day."

"I hope you're not overdoing it."

"No chance of that. James is handling the majority of the workload—I'm here for questions and okaying things he's not sure about." James was doing an amazing job. She didn't know if she should be impressed or distressed.

He'd hired a replacement for himself and had totally taken over her job and her office. He said they'd need the help even after the babies were born, and when she took into account how active the babies were in utero, she had no doubt they'd be two handfuls once they arrived.

"When will you go home?"

"I don't know. I'm going to have the babies here in Boise. They don't allow pregnant women to fly after seven months, and definitely not with the complication of twins and gestational diabetes. I'll be fine here. Trapper's whole family is around, and I like my doctor. I'm well taken care of."

"Bianca, if I had known you were having twins, I would have canceled my trip to Florida, or at the least, not extended it." There it was—a little of her frustration cut across the line like a scissor over curly ribbon. Pretty, but sharp. Oh yeah, Nan was definitely a little miffed. Good thing the anger was tempered with the thrill of hearing about the twins.

"I know, Nan. That's why I didn't tell you. You had the trip planned for months, and all your friends were counting on you to be there. Tell me all about it. Did you have fun?"

She lay back to listen. Once Nan got started, she was unstoppable. The woman may be in her midseventies, but didn't look a day over eighty. She was beautiful—okay, she knitted beautifully—she was vibrant, outspoken, and her life was one long good time. She enjoyed thrills, mostly because she could barely see over the dashboard of her car. Nan went on and on, so Bianca said a lot of ahs and ohs in all the right places. Or at least she thought she had.

"Bianca? Bianca, are you there?"

"Yes, I'm sorry. I guess I'm just tired." She wondered how long she'd been asleep.

"Make sure you give Trapper my number just in case. I'm here if you need me—I can drive out or fly. And I'm planning to be there for the babies' birth. You said your due date is May 16?"

"Yes, but twins usually come early. We're trying for no earlier than April 18."

"Oh, maybe you'll have them on your birthday. Lord, can you imagine having three bullheaded Tauruses in one house? I do hope that man of yours has a strong constitution."

"Nan, he's not my man."

"It certainly sounds as if he is."

"I don't know what Trapper and I will do. We haven't really discussed it lately."

"And why is that?"

"I don't know." She'd been wondering why too. Not that she was really looking forward to the discussion, but she couldn't help but think that maybe he was second-guessing his whole idea of a happily-ever-after.

"Are you being difficult?"

"No." Well, no more than usual. "We've been getting along very well." Better than she could have ever imagined. She looked around her office, and for the first time in her life, felt truly at home. Okay, it wasn't just her office; it was the whole house. But it wasn't the house. It was Trapper. Her life here with Trapper was almost surreal—perfectly wonderful if she had to label it. Even with the backaches, swollen feet, and the constant peeing.

Trapper had returned her computer and cell phone after she'd been taken off bed rest and hadn't given her a hard time about the few hours a day she worked. Except for him being a food and blood sugar Nazi, she couldn't complain about anything. Their time together had been surprisingly easy—they fit into each other's lives almost seamlessly. She loved spending time with him and his entire family. Everything was perfect—so perfect it made her nervous. She'd been in Boise almost three months, and she kept waiting for something to pop the ideal little bubble they lived in. Heck, even the sex was incredible, which was amazing, considering how big she and the babies had gotten. She couldn't see her feet, and soon she'd probably have to start screwing on her underwear. Sure they had to get a little creative in the sex department, but Trapper was nothing if not creative. He seemed to enjoy the challenge.

"Don't you think you should bring it up? You've never been the shy type, and those babies need two parents."

"They do have two parents."

"Call me old-fashioned, but I think babies need two parents who are married to each other."

"What do you want? Do you expect me to propose to him? That's not old-fashioned."

"Do you love him, Bianca?"

"Yes, I love him."

"Does he love you?"

"He says he does."

"So, what's the problem? One of you should propose. I don't see why it shouldn't be you—although you might have a difficult time getting down on one knee in your condition."

"Very funny. What would be the point? It's not as if I need to be married. And I certainly don't want Trapper to marry me only because we're having children together."

"It sounds to me like there's a lot more between you than just those babies. You need to stop paying for a mistake you only think you made when you were little more than a child yourself."

"I did make a mistake. There's no question about it."

"Get over it already. No one gets through this life without having a broken heart. You had yours broken earlier than most, but that's not what's kept you alone. It's that type A personality that just won't accept the fact that you're not perfect. I've been waiting for twenty years for you to take another chance on love. Now seems like as good a time as any."

"I doubt there will ever be a good time for that."

"I just hope your young man feels differently. He's certainly not going to get any encouragement from you."

"I'm tired. I think it's time for my nap." She checked her watch. It was later than she thought. Trapper would be home any minute.

"You'd better call me again soon, Bianca. And no more keeping secrets from me, young lady."

"I promise. I love you. Bye." Bianca ended the call and twisted to set the phone on the table beside her, only to find Trapper in the doorway. "How long have you been standing there?" He looked angry. She thought about what she'd said—what he could have heard.

"Long enough."

"You were eavesdropping?"

"Not intentionally. But yeah, I guess I was. Do you care to explain yourself?"

"I have no need to explain anything. If you're rude enough to listen in on a private conversation, you can figure it out for yourself. I'm tired."

He sat beside her and boxed her in with his arms. "Tough. I don't appreciate being referred to as a mistake."

"And this is why it's wrong to eavesdrop on half a conversation. You don't know what I said was a mistake. Trapper, here's a news flash: the world does not revolve around you."

"You said you didn't need to marry, and you didn't want to marry me because of the babies. I think that's a pretty good clue you were talking about me. The next thing out of your mouth was, and I quote, 'I did make a mistake. There's no question about it.' So was I the mistake? Or were you talking about our babies?"

"I was talking about Max, you ass." She pushed him and did her best to get off the chaise and away from him, but the chaise was so low. She wasn't all that good at getting up from the damn thing, especially when half of it was covered with an angry man. She finally put one hand on the back of the longue and one hand on his shoulder trying to push herself up. Instead, he lifted her, which only served to piss her off more.

"You told some guy you loved him."

"I told my grandmother I love her. Or is there a law against that too?"

"Your grandmother?"

"Yes. She just got back from Florida, so I called her to tell her about the twins and hear all about her trip. Next time, I'll wait until you get home so you can better monitor our conversation. Or would you prefer a transcript?"

"Bianca—"

"Oh, no." She held up her hand to stop him. "I'm finished discussing this. I'm tired, and I'm going to lie down. Alone."

"Sweetheart—"

"I mean it, Trapper. Drop it before I say something we'll both regret."

"I'm sorry. Wait. Let me help you down the stairs."

"No. I don't need your help. I just need you to leave me the hell alone."

—∾∾—

Trapper stood in the kitchen and put the finishing touches on the stew he'd started in the Crock-Pot that morning. He set the spoon down and looked over the island where Hunter sat. God, he hated asking for help, but what choice did he have? "Bianca needs to eat, and then she needs to check her blood sugar. All you have to do is bring her dinner, and then make sure she tests her glucose level twenty minutes after she eats."

"Sounds simple enough. Why don't you do it?"

"Last time I tried to walk into the bedroom, she threw something at me."

Hunter's grin spread across his face like a banner. "Something hard?"

"No, it was a pillow, but she's got good aim and there are only so many pillows within reach." Did his big linebacker-size younger brother look scared? Hmm, interesting.

"What did you do to piss her off so much she won't even let you feed her?"

"I overheard a conversation and then talked to her about it."

"Oh, come on, it has to be something more than that."
He waited a second, took a sip of his beer, and then his
eyebrows popped up like a jack-in-the-box. "You overheard something and jumped to the wrong conclusion—
one that made you say something stupid. Am I right?"

Trapper didn't need to answer.

"Way to kill a relationship, dude. Didn't you learn
anything from the hell I went through with Toni?"

"Are you going to help me out or not? I really
don't want to have to call Karma." Then he'd really
have to explain, and explaining his relationship faux
pas to Karma was not on his list of things he wanted
to do again.

"Sure, I'll take care of Bianca. Why don't you take
off? It's poker night. I'll hang out with Bianca and
smooth her ruffled feathers."

"Just try not to brush them the wrong way, and make
sure she eats—"

"I know what you want, Bro, but beggars can't be
choosers—you can have me, or you can call Karma.
Your choice."

"Fine. I'll go. That should make her happy. You'll
stay until I get home?"

"I'll stay. But if she pulls out those books about
giving birth again, you're gonna owe me big."

Trapper dished up Bianca's dinner and set it on a bed
tray. "When you find out her sugar level, just text me."

"Will do." Hunter took a sniff of the stew. "What? I
don't get to eat?"

"Sure, knock yourself out."

He pulled down another bowl and handed it to Hunter
before heading to the bedroom and rapping on the door.

"Leave me alone."

He said a quick prayer, opened the door, and stuck his head in. Bianca was curled up on the bed. "I know you're mad, and I know you don't want to see me."

She didn't bother to even look at him. "Then why are you here?"

Shit, she was speaking to the damn wall—again. "I need my hat."

She slid across the bed, grabbed it, and threw it at him. He wondered if she bent it out of shape on purpose. Probably.

"I didn't want to leave without saying good-bye. Hunter's here. He's bringing you dinner, so please don't throw anything at him. Eat and then test—"

"I know. I'm a big girl. Just go."

He put his hat on and curled the brim. "I really am sorry, sweetheart."

Bianca said nothing. Anger radiated from her in waves.

He wondered how long she planned to be pissed at him. "I love you." He stepped out and closed the door behind him. It was better if he didn't hear her response— he'd really rather not know what it was. He had a feeling it wouldn't be good for either of them.

Trapper drove to Fisher's house, and there wasn't a second that went by that he hadn't considered turning around and going home. Leaving Bianca to build up a bigger head of steam was probably a bad idea. He'd been wrong. Hell, he admitted it and said he was sorry. What more could he do?

He'd walked into her office to give her a kiss and find out how her day was, only to overhear her say she still didn't want to marry him. She couldn't have done a

better job of poleaxing him if she'd used a six-ton wreck-
ing ball. Then, in her next breath, she said she'd made
a mistake. What the hell was he supposed to think? But
what really got him was when she said "I love you" to
someone other than him. He kind of lost it. All he could
think of was how he'd felt when he caught Paige with
the senior partner she was screwing. Bianca wasn't the
type to throw I love yous around like confetti—no, she
was downright miserly with them. He had to practically
torture her to admit she loved him.

Wasn't it natural to assume she was talking to a man?
Shit, he didn't know. Maybe not. It wasn't like she'd
said, "I love you, Nan." How was he supposed to know
she'd called her grandmother? Especially since today
was the first time she mentioned talking to anyone in her
life other than James.

Trapper pulled up in front of Fisher's house. He
didn't see Gramps's car—he didn't know if he was
relieved or not. When he walked in and found Toni and
Jessie in the kitchen, he cringed. Damn, he was screwed.

The two women eyed him, wearing twin accusa-
tory smirks.

"Hi, I'm surprised to find you both here." It was
poker night. No females invited—ever. And, yes, Toni
and Jessie were definitely female and definitely smirk-
ing. A chill that had nothing to do with the night air and
everything to do with the frost of their gazes ran up his
spine like a herd of elk. "Aren't you ladies doing a girlie
thing tonight?"

"A girlie thing?" Toni looked at Jessie and mouthed
something he hoped was not a silent battle cry. She
shook her head, her pigtails swaying. "No, our plans

were canceled thanks to you. Hunter called. Bianca's too upset to even have a bitch fest."

Jessie poured them both margaritas. "Your mom is on her way though, so you might want to run and hide. I doubt you're her favorite son right now."

"Mom knows?"

The front door slammed behind him. He spun around. "Karma." Her green-eyed glare shot through him. He was in trouble. Big trouble.

"Of course Mom knows." Karma tossed her hair over her shoulder and rolled her eyes. "Mom knows everything."

He took a menacing step, wanting to kill her. "You told her?"

Karma gave him a push back and then held out a hand just as Jessie slipped a margarita into it. They practically had it choreographed. "I didn't want her coming all this way without warning her. You know Mom hates poker."

"Poker?"

"Oh yeah." Toni tossed her arm around him. "Since you spoiled our get-together, we decided to join yours—we're amazingly flexible that way. But don't worry. We're supplying the booze and snacks."

Fisher walked in carrying three Guido's Pizza boxes and wearing his you're-making-me-rethink-my-Hippocratic-oath look.

Trapper avoided his brother's eyes. The guys were currently outnumbered—a new phenomenon and not a good one. "I thought you said that you were supplying the snacks."

Toni gave him a not-so-innocent shrug. "Hunter was scheduled to pick up the pizza, but it looks as if he's on duty at your house, so one of our other minions had to fly."

"Minions?"

Fisher looked as if he wanted to amputate one of Trapper's appendages and beat him with it.

Toni took the boxes and laid them on the dining room table. "Did you know the owner of Guido's is from New Jersey? He makes the closest thing to real New York pizza west of the Hudson."

"No, I didn't." The only thing Trapper knew was that his stomach was so tied up in knots, he didn't even want pizza, and he loved Guido's.

His mom didn't bother knocking; she and Gramps just walked in.

"Hi, Mom." He helped her off with her jacket. "I'm surprised to see you here. I didn't think you liked playing poker."

She put her hands on her hips and got that you're-in-deep-shit tilt to her head. All she needed was a wooden spoon in her hand to bring back his childhood nightmares. "I don't. I came to see you." She was a foot shorter than him but somehow looked down on him. He wasn't sure how she managed it. "What the hell were you thinking, Trapper?"

"Mom, you know I love you, but I'm not a child. I don't need a lecture. Whatever problems Bianca and I have, we'll work out on our own."

She didn't back off; she poked him. "Not if she locks you out of the bedroom, you won't. And what did I teach you about eavesdropping?"

He took a giant step back. "That nothing good can come from it. I know. I didn't do it on purpose."

"No, but that didn't stop you from forcing her to explain herself."

"If you want to help, why don't you stop yelling at me and tell me how to get her to listen to me instead? I feel bad enough as it is."

"You feel bad?" She took another step toward him. "*You* feel bad?"

God, his mother looked like she was going to guilt him to death. She was going for the jugular; he could see it in her eyes.

"Why don't you think about how Bianca feels? She's almost eight months pregnant with twins and can't even have a conversation with her grandmother without you jumping all over her and accusing her of cheating."

"I didn't accuse her of cheating." Did he? "I just asked her who the hell she was professing her love to." Shit. That's exactly what he had done. "I didn't mean to."

His mother shook her head. "It doesn't matter. The fact is you did."

Gramps rocked back on his heels, seeming to have a jolly good time at his expense.

Trapper didn't like being the object of his entertainment or anyone else's, and he was center stage in front of his whole family. Perfect. "What is it, Gramps? Don't you have any words of wisdom to impart, or are you just going to stand there enjoying my misery?"

"I'm not enjoying your misery, son. I'm just enjoying watching Kate give you what-for. It's been awhile since I've seen the old girl in action."

Mom swung around and aimed her ire at Gramps. "Who are you calling old?"

Gramps ignored her and kept talking. "I certainly do miss having front row seats at the almost daily fireworks show we had with you kids underfoot. It brings back good memories. Real good. Pretty soon we'll have two more underfoot. That's if you get your head out of your ass and don't screw it up."

—⁓—

Bianca did her best to eat, but she had constant heartburn, and nothing tasted good when you knew you were going to spend the rest of the night burping it up—not even Trapper's stew.

Her belly was too big to eat with the bed tray over her lap—after all, her lap had disappeared about two months ago.

Hunter lay sprawled beside her on Trapper's side of the bed with the bed tray sitting between them.

She set the bowl of stew on her belly—holding it with one hand in case the babies got rambunctious—and looked over at Hunter.

The guy made himself right at home, pushing Trapper's pillows against the headboard behind his back.

"If you're going to put your feet up on my bed, you'd better take those hiking boots off first."

He did as she asked, so she didn't even bother to give him a hard time about joining her on the bed. What was the point? If there was one thing she'd learned about the Kincaid men, it was that they did what they wanted to do, and they weren't the least bit shy about it. They also said whatever came to mind—filtering wasn't their strong suit.

Hunter cleaned his bowl in about two minutes flat. The man was an eating machine. He nodded to her food. "Are you going to finish that?"

"No, I'm done." She returned the bowl to the tray and took a sip of water.

"Trapper's not going to be happy when he hears you barely touched your dinner." He looked at his watch and slid her bowl onto his empty one. "You don't mind if I finish it, do you?"

"Be my guest."

"So, what's up with you and Trapper? I thought you were getting along really well. What happened?"

She stuffed another pillow behind her aching back. Her feet were so swollen they hurt, and her fingers looked like sausages. Pregnancy really didn't agree with her. "He eavesdropped on a private conversation and misconstrued the whole thing—then he had the nerve to get in my face about it."

"So what? He acted like a jealous jackass. Give the man a break, would you? Trapper can't help it. He's a guy. Guys are territorial when it comes to their women. And before you say anything, let me tell you from experience, women can be just as territorial about their men. You gotta admit that if you overheard Trapper saying 'I love you' to someone else, even over the phone, it would get your dander up."

"I was talking to my grandmother."

"He didn't know that."

"I'm eight months pregnant."

"What's that got to do with anything?"

God, were all men really this clueless? If they were, she hoped she was having girls. "You're kidding, right?"

"As a matter of fact, your pregnancy probably makes it worse. You're his whole world, Bianca, and you're carrying his entire future too. Face it, lady: you're holding all the cards in Trapper's poker tournament of life. His hand sucks. The only way he has a prayer of winning is if you decide to fold. Otherwise, he's pretty much powerless."

"Trapper Kincaid has never been powerless a day in his life."

Hunter just laughed. She couldn't believe it. He was sitting on her bed, eating her dinner, and laughing in her face. "Don't tell me you're buying into Trapper's whole I-Am-Judge facade? He's my big brother, and I love him. He's one of the smartest and best men I know, but he's as human as the next guy. Trapper might walk around in a robe in public—which, just between you and me, is downright embarrassing—but it's a robe, not a cape, darlin'. When it comes to matters of the heart, that robe don't make him Superman or even supersmart, apparently. All Trapper knows is that he loves you. He's just going about showing it all wrong, and frankly, he's scared to death of losing you. It's not as if you have a ring on your finger. In everyone's eyes you're single— you're theirs for the taking."

"I'm no one's for the taking. Besides, Trapper's never proposed to me. He hasn't even mentioned marriage in months."

"And do you blame him? You've spent the last three or four months repeatedly telling him you don't want to get married, you don't need to get married, and I think you've gone as far as to say, you'll never marry. As far as I know, there was no clause there that said: 'except if you ask me nicely.' It would take a pretty strong guy to propose to a woman like you."

"A woman like me?"

"Oh yeah, you know—the strong, independent, and difficult type. The whole fragile male ego they talk about is true. No man wants to get shot down—not when he's got his heart on the line. Men like to know they have a better than even chance of scoring the winning point before getting down on one knee. Take it from someone who knows. Asking Toni to marry me was the single bravest thing I've ever done—not to mention the scariest. And she wasn't nearly as difficult as you. No offense."

"None taken."

"Bianca, I hate to break it to you, but this is your own damn fault."

"My fault?"

"You put Trapper in an untenable situation. I don't envy him." Hunter's watch dinged. "It's time to do the blood test. Do you need my help, or can you handle it on your own?"

"I can do it."

Hunter let out what looked like a relieved breath. "Thank God. I'm good with a lot of stuff, but blood, not so much."

"It's just a pinprick, Hunter. I don't have to hit an arterial vein."

He paled and swallowed hard. "It doesn't matter. If it's red and involves needles, I get the heebie-jeebies. And if you tell anyone, you can bet that sweet ass of yours I'll sell those baby shower pictures Toni took of you last week to the tabloids."

"You wouldn't dare!"

He shot her an evil smile. "Try me. But don't worry; I'll put all the money I make off them into a college fund for the twins. I'm good like that."

She took the meter out of the case. "Are you going to turn around so you don't swoon, or are you going to run?"

He grabbed the dishes. "Guys don't swoon, they pass out. I'm just going to take these to the kitchen and do the dishes like any other respectable man. Holler when you have a reading and stop the blood flow."

He ran out like his hair was on fire and the only water source was in the kitchen.

"Men are the reason God created women—because she knew no man would ever be man enough to go through labor and delivery."

"I heard that."

"You were meant to, which is why I said it out loud." She pricked her finger and then stuck the blood-smeared tab in the meter and waited for the reading. "It's 162."

"That means nothing to me."

"It's a little high."

"How little is a little? Is Trapper going to freak or just start foolin' with his hat?"

"I don't care." He'd probably freak, but chances are it was still coming down. She wasn't too worried. She had too much to do before the babies were delivered, and it wasn't often she had slave labor at her beck and call. "Come on. I'm going upstairs to clean out my clothes, and I need your help."

Hunter walked into the bedroom with a kitchen towel thrown over his shoulder. "Help with what? You're not moving out, are you?"

"No, not yet. Trapper brought all my pre-pregnancy clothes here by mistake. I'm not fool enough to believe I have a prayer of being able to fit into them for months—if ever. I'm just going to ship them back to my place in New York."

"Why?"

"Because that's where I live."

He leaned against the door frame and crossed his arms over his big chest, giving her the Kincaid imperious glare. "You really shouldn't do anything strenuous."

"I agree. That's what you're for. You're going to do all the strenuous stuff, and I'm going to do what I do best."

"And what exactly is that?"

"Direct. Now help me up."

"You want me to what?"

"Just come over here to the side of the bed and pull me up."

"Lift you?"

"God, Hunter. Breathe. It's not that hard. Just hold out your hands, and when I tell you to, pull."

"Wouldn't it be easier if I just, you know, picked you up?"

"No. I weigh as much as a small elephant."

"Right—I'm not buying it, sister."

"There's no way in hell I'm allowing you to pick me up, no matter how very big and strong and manly you are. It's not happening. Just hold out your hands. Oh, and you might want to lean back a little—it's a counterbalance thing."

"Trapper is going to owe me so big. It's gonna make puking on his boots look like a freakin' shoe shine."

"Who puked on Trapper's boots?"

"Fisher."

"Wow, he loves his boots almost as much as his hats."

"Exactly."

Hunter was a real sport, not to mention strong as an ox—as long as there was no blood involved. He helped her out of bed, up the stairs, and even onto the chaise longue. She'd wanted to sit in the desk chair for an easier exit—the chair had arms. After trying to get off the chaise earlier, she wasn't looking forward to trying it again. She figured if she were going to do any lying around from now on, she'd do it in bed. At least that way, she could roll herself off of it. Just not in mixed company.

Hunter even lifted her up so she could stuff a pillow behind her aching back, and then moved the whole longue, with her on it, so she faced the closet. She'd learned the hard way that twisting was not a good thing when you had ten pounds of mobile humans in utero, unless you wanted a foot sticking between your ribs.

He opened the closet door, looked inside, and cursed. Three huge suitcases lay open, crammed full of clothes—most of which weren't even folded. "This could take awhile."

"I don't need you to fold the clothes. Just drag them out here, and I'll fold them."

"I'll do the folding." He gave her a don't-mess-with-me look that all of the Kincaids must have inherited from their mother.

"Fine. If you want to fold my unmentionables, be my guest."

"I've spent years doing all the laundry for the entire family. I doubt you have anything I haven't seen already. There's nothing worse than folding your mother's bras and panties—well, except that time I found Karma's crotchless panties. She said they were a gag gift."

"And you bought that?"

"Hell, yes."

"If they were a gag gift, what were they doing in the laundry?"

He looked at her, blinked a few times, and then turned a little green.

God, he was so easy. No wonder Karma toyed with her brothers as often as karmically possible.

"Bianca, you do realize you've just scarred me for life, right?"

"I'm sorry to burst your bubble, big guy." She couldn't very well sit there doing nothing. "Grab those boxes on the shelf so I can go through them, since you're a master clothes folder."

When he didn't look as if he was going to move, she gave him a little incentive. "Don't make me get up and drag a chair over there, because I will. Just ask Trapper."

He looked over at her and blew out a frustrated breath—of course he took it like a man. "Threats will get you pretty much everything, but have some mercy, will you?" He stood and piled the three boxes up and laid them beside her on the chaise. The largest was full of her shoe collection. She removed a pair of Salvatore Ferragamo Royal Booties and sighed. She looked at the boots and then at her swollen feet and wondered if she'd ever be able to wear pretty shoes again—she'd taken to wearing Trapper's slippers, or his old sneakers, because they were the only things she could squeeze her feet into. "Take this—it's nothing but shoes I can't wear. You can probably fill it with some clothes. Just, you know, don't crush the boots."

"No, we can't have that."

She slipped the top off a shoe box and watched Hunter fold one of her tailored suits just the way she liked it, folding the jacket outside in, cupping one shoulder over the other. The man really could fold clothes. She looked into the box and found a bunch of pictures—pictures of a gorgeous woman she'd never seen before.

Pictures of a woman with Trapper.

On the beach.

Skiing.

Curled up with each other in front of a fire.

Whoever she was, she was blonde and beautiful... and pregnant?

Bianca swallowed back the wave of nausea. Her head throbbed, and she was having a hard time catching her breath. The woman wore an incredible formal gown—it looked like a Valentino from a few years back—five maybe? She looked adoringly at a tux-clad Trapper who stared straight into the camera. She had her right arm through Trapper's and her left hand on a definite baby bump, and that hand sported a diamond engagement ring.

Bianca took one of the other pictures and held it up. "Hunter, who is this?" She was surprised to hear her voice sounded normal, even though she felt as if every muscle in her body jumped—as if zapped by the TENS machine her chiropractor hooked her up to. Her skin was too tight, too sensitive; it felt as if a thousand ants crawled up her spine and down her arms.

Hunter turned and squinted. "Oh, that's Paige Baker— one of Trapper's exes." Hunter got up and reached for the box. "Why don't you give me that, and I'll put it back?"

Bianca held on, her fingers crumpling the cardboard. "Trapper and she had a baby?" It sounded like a million bees built a hive in her head. The buzzing ebbed and flowed like the tide.

"No."

She held up the formal picture of Trapper and Paige

with the baby bump. "She definitely looks pregnant to me. Engaged and pregnant. She's wearing his ring."

"Look, Bianca. I don't know whose ring she's wearing, or whose baby she's carrying, but it's not my brother's."

She dug through the contents and found a velvet ring box, opened it, and there sat the very ring Paige Baker had worn, along with a note: *I'm sorry, Trapper. I never meant to hurt you.* Her scalp tingled, and her fat sausage fingers felt clumsy. She dropped the ring, not even bothering to close the velvet box.

Oh God, Trapper had loved this woman so much that he'd asked her to marry him.

She felt so stupid. She'd started to believe the reason they were together was because Trapper loved her, not just the babies. She never dreamed of being married, but over the last three months, it felt as if they were. She felt as if she fit. As if she belonged. As if she was loved. Now she just felt stupid. She'd fallen for it again. She felt stupid and hurt and sick—her ears rang, and everything looked fuzzy.

She looked up at Hunter's crestfallen face and shoved the whole collection at him. "I don't feel so good. I just want to lie down."

Hunter dropped to his knees in front of her and held her shoulders. "Bianca, don't jump to any conclusions. I know my brother. If he had a kid, there's no way he'd ever—"

"The baby wasn't mine." Trapper's deep voice somehow rose above the buzzing in her ears.

Chapter 20

TRAPPER STARED AT HUNTER HOLDING BIANCA LIKE HE would a fragile child. It was like watching his own personal horror flick.

Bianca had found out about Paige.

He should have told her, but how? If he had, Bianca would have believed exactly what she was probably thinking right now.

Hunter tightened his hold on her and leaned closer. "Do you want me to help you downstairs?"

Oh, no. That wasn't happening. "Hunter, I'll take care of Bianca. You can leave."

Hunter ignored him. "Just say the word, and I'll do whatever you want."

Bianca put her hand on Hunter's cheek. "I know you would. Thanks, but I'll be okay on my own."

On her own? "You're not on your own."

Hunter stared at him with a combination of pain, disappointment, and condemnation. That hurt. The twins had always looked up to him. He wasn't that much older than them, but he was the oldest, and he grew up fast after their dad took off. Shit, this was bad and definitely going to get worse—he hadn't even gotten the guts to look at Bianca yet.

Hunter took the box from her grasp. "Well, you two probably have a lot of talking to do, so I'll just—you know, go, unless you want me to wait downstairs?"

She gave him a shake of the head.

He stared into Bianca's eyes. "Remember what I said. Let him explain. Keep an open mind," he whispered, and then kissed her cheek. "Call me if you need me—anytime."

"I will, and thanks for everything, Hunter. I'm sorry you've been thrown in the middle of this. It was never my intention."

"You want me to beat him up for you? Just say the word."

She let out a rusty laugh that sounded as joyous as a squeaky hinge. "A tempting offer. I'll keep it in mind."

Hunter stood, filled his big chest with enough air to make him look like the Superman balloon in the Macy's Thanksgiving Day Parade, and ran right into Trapper. They were almost exactly the same height, but Hunter outweighed him by a good twenty pounds of pure bulky muscle—most of it probably in his head. Hunter didn't say a word, but then, the threat in his eyes made words unnecessary. He drove the box Trapper should have burned years ago into his chest, bowing it. Then Hunter shoved him and seemed to rethink the strong silent thing and jacked him up against the wall. "You hurt her again, and you won't be fit for dog meat." Hunter's words were softly growled. Calm. Cool. Deadly.

"Do you want to do this now, in front of Bianca?"

"No, that's the only reason you're still in one piece, Brother."

He set Trapper back on his feet and shook his head. "I hear it's hard to grovel with a broken jaw. You've got a hell of a lot of explaining to do. You might want to invest in knee pads."

"Yeah, thanks for the helpful advice."

"Call me. I'll be waiting. If I don't hear from you, I'll be back with reinforcements—I'll bring Mom."

Trapper had a feeling the only reason Bianca was still in the house was because she couldn't get off the chaise by herself.

He took a deep breath and went in. He had no idea what he was going to say or do to make this right, but he wouldn't stop trying until he succeeded. He couldn't lose Bianca.

She didn't look at him; she was busy twisting her fingers in the fringe of the throw lying on the chaise. She wasn't crying. She was dry-eyed and enraged. She looked stoic, but ready to explode.

He never thought he'd see the day he'd miss Bianca's tears, but he did now. She looked like a statue—lifeless and vacant and hard.

He'd lost her.

She didn't need to say it; he saw it.

He could barely breathe.

He was suffocating. It was as if his chest was so full of regret there was no room for air. "It looks as if I owe you an explanation."

"You owe me nothing. I was just trying to pack my things, and I didn't know that your personal items were in there. I wasn't trying to snoop into your life."

"Snoop into my life? You are my life."

She finally looked at him then, and he couldn't have gotten a bigger chill if he was standing in the Arctic Circle naked. "I'm sorry. I know I should have told you about Paige, but it was a long time ago."

"Like I said, you owe me nothing. As a matter of fact,

why don't we just drop it? I really don't want to talk about anything with you. I have a massive headache, and I just want to go to bed."

"Too bad, sweetheart. We're never going to get past this unless we discuss it."

"I don't feel a great need to get past anything."

"You're not even going to hear me out?"

"Not if I'm given a choice, no."

"I'm just asking you to listen."

She looked away. Her whole body was rigid, her face pale.

"Paige and I met at a legal function in New York." He didn't think telling Bianca he'd had Paige out of the dinner and into his bed in less than three hours would help his case any. "We started dating." Yeah, they'd never really dated. They'd started sleeping together, although there wasn't much sleep involved. Before he knew it, she'd moved in. And now, he felt like a liar. He hated lying. He didn't do it.

"People usually date before they get engaged."

"We lived together for a few years, and Paige wanted to get married."

"You didn't?"

"I don't know. I guess I thought it was next, you know?"

"Next?"

"We'd been together for three years. It made sense. We both respected each other's careers and long hours. I wanted to wait to get engaged until we came here for Christmas that year, but Paige was impatient. I knew the family would be upset, so I didn't mention it, thinking we'd announce our engagement when we got home."

"Your family hadn't met her?"

"Paige wasn't much into family get-togethers. When I came home, she went off with her friends or stayed in town and worked. Hunter came to New York once unexpectedly. He met Paige then, but we'd just started…"

"Dating?"

"Not really. We were having sex, and she kind of stayed. I don't think I ever really asked her out. She was putting in her hundred and twenty billable hours a week hoping for a quick partnership, and I was an assistant DA fighting the good fight. Our relationship was convenient."

"Until she got pregnant."

"Paige was working on a big case—the case of a lifetime—she was second chair to a senior partner. I came home one night and found a positive pregnancy test. We'd both been working so much, we hadn't been together like that in a while, and I always used condoms because she couldn't take the pill."

"Can you move it along, Trapper? I'm really not interested in hearing about your sex life."

"Fine. I thought…well, you can imagine what I thought. So I went to her office to surprise her, to celebrate, and I caught her and the senior partner together with their legal briefs down, doing the nasty on the boardroom table."

Bianca hadn't moved other than to twist her fingers in the throw.

"I moved out the next day. I never asked for the ring back—I didn't want the damn thing. I didn't know she was still wearing it until I saw her at the same function where we'd met four years before. I was blindsided when that picture was taken. She'd never told anyone we'd stopped seeing each other. It turned out the senior partner was married and didn't want to claim her or the child until he could get an uncontested divorce. If his wife had known, he would have lost his shirt."

"And the baby?"

He pulled out the paternity test and handed it to her. "Not mine. I never thought it was—the timing wasn't right—but I had to wait until she had the baby and a paternity test to make sure."

"Of course. You always do the right thing. The honorable thing. I'm sure if the child had been yours, you would have done the right thing and married her too."

"I would have made sure she and the baby were taken care of. I would never have married Paige."

"I know you, Trapper. You would have married her, and you would have raised your child." She neatly folded the paternity test and set it back in the box.

"That's it?"

"I don't know, Trapper? Is there more?"

"Bianca, sweetheart, don't you see that Paige has nothing to do with us?"

"How can you say that with a straight face? I know I'm not one to talk—Lord knows, I have more issues than *Vogue*, but now everything—you, me, the babies— makes perfect sense."

"What do you mean? Paige is ancient history. I love you, Bianca. I fell in love with you the second I saw you."

"Trapper, you fell into our relationship the same way you fell into your relationship with Paige."

"I never loved Paige. The way I feel for you is a billion times what I felt for Paige Baker."

"The only difference as I see it is that these children

are yours, although I don't blame you if you want a paternity test."

"Bianca, this has nothing to do with the babies, and everything to do with you and me. I love you, and I know you love me."

"I do love you."

He was ready to jump for joy when he saw the first tear fall. A big fat one, followed by another that she swiped away with an angry, swollen hand. "Thank God." He tried to wrap his arms around her, needing to touch her, but she pushed him away.

"My loving you doesn't matter. I told you every-thing—I told you about Max and my parents. I loved you enough to tell you the truth so you could make an informed decision. I didn't want you to be blindsided by finding old news reports or a secret stash of incrim-inating photos. I burned them years ago." She stopped and fought for breath, her tears streaming down her face, clogging her throat. "But you kept yours, Trapper. You kept the pictures. You kept the ring you gave her. You kept everything, and you never told me." She took a stuttering breath. "You let me find out on my own. God, you let me find out in front of your brother not hours after you accused me of cheating on you. I might be in love with you, Trapper, but I don't believe for a second that what you feel for me has anything to do with love. If you truly loved me, you never would have done this to me."

"I do love you. I made a mistake. I'm not perfect. I was afraid if you found out, you'd think just what you're thinking."

"Thinking that you loved her enough to ask her to

marry you? Thinking that I'm stupid for ever buying into your illusions? You don't love me, Trapper. You never did. You love our children, and I'm just the vessel they're growing in. You've spent the last three months taking care of me for their sake. So, yeah, I think I'm a damn fool. Again."

Bianca gritted her teeth and rubbed her belly—not the way she usually did. This was different, and the way her face looked—she looked as if she were in pain.

Then she groaned.

He knew how Bianca sounded when one of the babies pounced on her kidney or got a foot stuck in her ribs. He'd never heard her sound like this. Every muscle in his entire body froze, and his stomach flipped and tangled with his throat. "Bianca? What's the matter?"

She wiped her face, anger replacing the tears. "My back hurts—it's been bothering me all day. I'm swollen, and fat, and I have a headache like you read about. It's not often I've been accused of cheating and found out the ugly truth about the man I love on the same day. I just want to go to bed."

He took a look at her, a close look. God, her ankles had disappeared, and her hands were really swollen. "How long has your back been bothering you?" He wrapped his arms around her and practically picked her up.

"Since this afternoon."

"Why didn't you say anything?"

"Because I wasn't speaking to you, remember?"

"We're going to the hospital."

"No, we're not. I'm going to bed, and you can go to hell."

"I'm already there, sweetheart."

She grabbed her stomach, doubled over, and roared—it wasn't a little cry; it was a roar.

Oh fuck. The babies. "Breathe, Bianca. I think you're in labor. Breathe, come on, just like in childbirth class."

"It hurts."

"I know, baby. I know."

"No, you don't, you ass."

He pulled out his phone and called the doctor.

Bianca panted like an overheated dog. It felt as if someone had tied her stomach muscles into a knot, lashed it onto the end of a pickup truck, and hit the gas.

"It's Trapper Kincaid. Bianca Ferrari is in labor. She's had back pain since this afternoon. Thirty-three weeks, twins. Yes. Her blood sugar was 162 an hour ago, and she's swelling."

God, it was too early. This wasn't supposed to happen until after April 18. She'd had Braxton Hicks contractions before, this wasn't Braxton Hicks, this one was the real thing.

"Why do you need to talk to Bianca? She's in labor!"

She hit him. "Just give me the damn phone and stop arguing." She took it from him. "Hello? Yes, Bianca Ferrari. I'll be thirty-five next month, on the twenty-fifth. Dull back pain. It comes and goes. How often? I don't know. It comes and goes. We're about five minutes from the hospital. Yes, thank you."

Trapper had his hands stuffed into his jeans pockets and was sweating. She didn't ever remember seeing him sweat. "What did the nurse say?"

"Dr. Weaver is going to meet us at the hospital."

Before she knew it, Trapper had her off her feet and in his arms.

She wanted to kill him. "What the hell do you think you're doing?"

"Taking you to the hospital."

"Put me down. I can walk. You're going to kill us both."

"No."

"Trapper, I have to pee. I've been sitting here listening to you go on and on forever. Now, put me down."

"Fine." He walked into the bathroom, set her on her feet, and waited.

"Leave."

"What if you have another contraction?"

"I'm sure I will—eventually. There's not a whole lot you can do about it. Now get out so I can use the bathroom before I explode."

"I'll be right outside the door."

She watched him leave and did her best to keep from completely freaking out. "Why don't you go downstairs and get my purse and my phone? I'll meet you down there."

"No."

"You sound like a two-year-old."

It took her a minute, but she pulled herself together. Hysterics weren't going to help the babies. She washed her hands, splashed some cold water on her face, and pushed the pain away. Not the physical pain. No, there was nothing she could do about that. She pushed the heartache away—if she didn't, she was sure it would crush her. She stuffed all the pain, the disappointment, and the fear, locked the steel door on that vault, and promised to deal with it later.

When she opened the door, Trapper was right there as promised, but now he was back on the phone.

She waddled past him and started down the stairs. There was no way she'd let him pick her up again. After today, she wished she could just erase the last three months from her memory. She didn't know who Trapper was talking to, nor did she care. All she cared about right now was getting to the hospital and taking care of the babies. God, she couldn't lose the babies too. She'd rather die.

For the second time in his life, Trapper found himself in a hospital waiting room without his hat and holding Bianca's purse. He'd filled out all the paperwork and cleaned out her purse again by the time his family rushed in.

Fisher walked right past the waiting room and threw the doors open into the maternity ward.

Trapper's mom came right up to him and engulfed him in a hug that was enough to bring tears to his eyes. God, he was a fuckin' mess.

"What did the doctors say?"

"Not a damn thing. They took Bianca in and told me to wait. That was a half hour ago."

"Fisher will find out what's going on."

"Mom, Bianca's in labor. I think she was having back labor all afternoon and didn't tell me. I knew I shouldn't have left her. God, if anything happens to her—"

"Stop it, Trapper. Nothing's going to happen to Bianca or those babies. And whatever problems you two might have will be worked out eventually. You have two babies depending on you now."

He only wished he was as sure of that as his mother seemed to be.

Jessie was sitting holding Gramps's hand and biting her bottom lip. Hunter sat on the other side of the room with his arm around Toni, shooting his death glare at Trapper.

Trapper couldn't even blame the guy. This nightmare was entirely his own fault.

Fisher walked in wearing his doctor's face—the serious, things-don't-look-good face.

Trapper was suddenly glad he hadn't eaten.

"Trapper, come on back. Dr. Weaver is almost through with Bianca. We need to talk to you. There are decisions to be made."

"Is Bianca okay?"

Fisher took his arm. "Come on. Weaver's waiting."

Bianca lay in the hospital sweating. The nurses said it was normal, but it wasn't normal for her. None of this was. She was trussed up like a Christmas goose—a fetal monitor went around her belly, a heart monitor was taped to her chest, a permanent blood pressure cuff strangled her arm every few minutes, and an IV beside her dripped a cocktail of medication into her veins.

At least the ringing in her ears was subsiding, and her vision was clearer. That had to be good, right?

Dr. Weaver didn't say much. He just typed things into the computer in her room and didn't look particularly pleased. She wasn't sure if he was upset about her, or about having his evening disturbed.

"I see Trapper is your designated health care agent."

He looked over the top of his glasses, his eyebrows raised in question.

"Yes. But that's only in emergency. Where is Trapper?"

"We asked him to wait outside until we assessed your condition. He's probably breaking down the doors by now. I sent Dr. Kincaid to talk with him and bring him back."

"Fisher's here?"

He looked over his glasses again, as if he were trying to measure her mental acuity. "The whole family is here, even Big Joe Walsh. The nurses said they're quite a crowd. They've commandeered the waiting room." He moved, patted her shoulder, and watched the monitors for a moment, but didn't look as though he was seeing them. He looked miles away, as if wrestling with a decision. "I'll bring Trapper back to see you in a few minutes. You just rest, and let the medicine do its work. You need to stay calm and lie on your left side for as long as you can stand it."

"The babies are okay?"

"We've stopped the labor and are treating them with steroids to help increase their lung function. You need to stay calm and still for another forty-eight hours."

"Why not until April 18? I thought that was the target date."

He gave her shoulder a squeeze. "I think these babies are eager to make an appearance. We'll be lucky if we get a forty-eight-hour reprieve. Rest and relax now, while you can. I'll send Trapper to see you in a few minutes. Call the nurse if you need anything." He handed her the call button. "I'll be here tonight to keep an eye on you."

"You will? Why?" The labor had stopped. "What else is going on?"

"Nothing for you to worry about. Right now, everything looks as if it's under control. Rest, close your eyes, and try to get some sleep."

Nothing for her to worry about? But there was definitely something to worry about. She was a master of body language—that's one of the things that made her a good model. She knew how to stand and move to communicate whatever mood she was told to instill. Dr. Weaver could use a lesson. Whatever he was selling, she wasn't buying.

———

Trapper stared at Fisher wearing his serious doctor expression. He'd never been on the receiving end of a look like that before, and he didn't like it. His heart beat against his ribs like a jackhammer. "I need to see Bianca."

Fisher dragged him through the swinging double doors into the maternity ward. "You will, but first Dr. Weaver wants a word." A very pregnant woman wearing a robe and slippers walked past them like she was doing laps around the ward.

Dr. Weaver stepped out of a room and away from the door. His gaze collided with Trapper's, and his face settled in the exact same expression that Fisher wore. If Trapper had any question as to the seriousness of the situation, he didn't now. This wasn't good. He reached for his hat, but it wasn't there, so he settled for raking his hand through his hair and waited for the bad news. "What's going on?"

Dr. Weaver looked back at the open door and took his

arm and dragged him farther down the hall. "Trapper, we're trying to stop Bianca's labor. I think we've succeeded, but there are complications."

Trapper tried to take a deep breath, but his lungs weren't cooperating.

"Bianca's blood pressure is dangerously high, she's preeclamptic, and her sugar is high. We're trying to regulate her blood pressure and sugar by increasing the dosage of her medications. The labor has stopped for now."

"It can start again?"

"We're hoping to get a few more days if we can get her sugar and blood pressure under control."

"And if you can't?"

"If we can't, we'll do a C-section and deliver the babies. But due to the gestational diabetes, there might be a lung development problem. We're treating the twins with antenatal corticosteroids. It takes a minimum of forty-eight hours to fully benefit a fetus's lungs, but even twenty-four hours would provide some benefit. The longer Bianca can carry the babies, the better off they'll be."

Dr. Weaver's frown grew more brittle. The man was edgy, and he and Fisher were having some kind of silent conversation that Trapper couldn't decipher—other than it was all bad.

"What aren't you telling me?"

Dr. Weaver took a moment to gather his thoughts. "It's a delicate balancing act. The longer Bianca carries the babies, the more stress it is on her system. If we can't get her blood pressure under control, or if it spikes, she could have a stroke or a heart attack."

The cold sweat of fear ran over him, bile burned his throat, his lungs refused to draw breath, and his vision grayed. Trapper leaned against the wall, not sure his legs would hold him any longer. "Take the babies. Take them now."

Fisher put his hand on Trapper's shoulder and squeezed. "Trap, we're not ready to do that yet. We need to give the medication a chance to work."

He looked from Fisher to Dr. Weaver and swallowed the panic threatening to overwhelm him. He wanted to grab the doctor and shake him until he listened, but he needed to keep it together for Bianca. "You don't understand. I can't lose Bianca—she's my whole world."

Chapter 21

BIANCA LAY IN HER BED AND LISTENED TO TRAPPER'S deep, stilted voice rise over the din of the monitors.

She heard the fear in Trapper's words.

She heard the certainty.

She heard the love.

He loved her.

"Doc, I won't have Bianca put in danger. We'll take care of the babies. Those kids are little fighters; I know they are. You do whatever you need to do to keep Bianca healthy. Do you understand me? Bianca comes first."

Oh God, he did love her. He really loved her—not just the babies. He was terrified of losing her. She knew how he felt. She'd been terrified of losing him too. She wasn't now.

"That's not good enough, Doc. I need you to say the words, and I'll sign anything you give me to make sure that's understood."

Trapper's panic rolled over her. He sounded as if he was losing it. God, her heart ached for him, but she wasn't about to let him take the babies yet. No, it was too soon. They needed forty-eight hours, and that's what she was going to give them. *Please, God. Don't let Dr. Weaver listen to Trapper.*

"Bianca comes first," Dr. Weaver repeated. He spoke softly and firmly, obviously trying to calm Trapper down. "Let's just pray it won't come to that—"

"If it does, you take the babies."

She didn't bother trying to stop the tears.

"They need their mama almost as much as I do."

Stroke, heart attack? No wonder Dr. Weaver didn't say anything to her. God, what would happen to the babies?

She had to stay calm. If something happened to her, they'd have Trapper. They'd have the whole Kincaid clan. The babies would be fine.

She wiped the tears from her face, and something warm and soothing enveloped her. A sense of peace, of rightness. The Kincaids would take care of the babies. They wouldn't have it any other way. She couldn't have picked a better, closer, more loving family for her kids if she'd searched the world. No matter what happened to her, she knew the babies would be loved and cared for beyond anything she could have imagined. Even without her, she knew they'd be fine. She took a deep breath and concentrated on relaxing. Just because she knew her babies would be loved beyond measure didn't mean she wasn't going to do all she could to make sure she was there to take care of them and love them too.

"Where is she?" Bianca knew that tone of voice. Trapper was bound and determined. God help her, she slid a hand over her stomach. She needed to talk to him. She needed to tell him she'd be fine. She knew it, just like she knew the babies were going to be fine—she just needed a little more time.

"Bianca?" Trapper came barreling through the door. His hair looked like he'd been running his hands through it. The poor guy, he'd forgotten his hat.

"I'm here, Trapper."

His arms came around her, and everything seemed

right. He stared into her eyes, and his looked red and glassy. He was better at holding back the tears than she was. Her tears had been falling for a while now.

"You're going to be okay." She wasn't sure if he was saying that for her benefit or his. She wished he looked like he believed it. The words "stroke" and "heart attack" reverberated in her mind like a deadly mantra.

"I know. But you have to promise me something."

"Anything."

She held his face in her hands—the face she saw in her dreams, the face she loved, the face she wanted to look at for the rest of her life. "Promise me you'll give the babies the forty-eight hours they need. I'll be fine."

"You don't know that." A tear slid out of the corner of his eye onto her finger, then another, and another. "I can't lose you, Bianca. I can't live without you. Please don't ask me to. I'll do anything you want, but please don't ask me to choose. Don't ask me to let you go. I can't. I won't."

"Trapper, it's okay. Nothing's going to happen to me. I'm not going anywhere. I love you. I'm not going to lose you now. We're all going to be okay. I know we are. You need to believe that. Believe in me. Believe in us. I'm just asking you not to give up."

"I'll never give up on us. That I can promise."

"I guess that will have to do. I'm really tired."

"I know, baby."

"Do me a favor and call Nan. She wants to be here for the babies' birth."

"I'll call her first thing in the morning. I'll have Gramps send a plane."

"Trapper?"

"Yeah?"

"Could you lie down with me and just hold me for a while?"

"Sure." He kissed her, one of those sweet, meaningless pecks that meant the world to her. He took off his boots, skirted the bed, and slid in behind her, wrapping one arm around their babies. "I love you, Bianca."

"I know." She wanted to tell him she loved him too, but she didn't have the energy. Her eyelids seemed to have turned into lead weights.

When Bianca awoke it was still dark. Trapper sat in the chair beside the bed looking like death. "You moved."

"The nurses weren't too happy with me sharing your bed."

"They're just jealous." She stretched and did a little mental inventory of her condition. Her ears weren't ringing—that was good. Everything she could see in the dim light was clear. That was good too. Her back wasn't hurting any more than what was normal before yesterday—another plus. Maybe things were looking up.

"How are you feeling?"

"Thirsty, hot, but good."

"I'll get you some water. Don't move."

"Like I could if I wanted to, they have me practically tied down."

He filled a glass with ice water and held it with the bendy straw so she didn't even have to lift her head. She drained the glass, and then pushed it away. "Trapper, why don't you go home and get some sleep? I'm fine, but you look horrible."

"I'm not leaving you. Ever. If you're here, I'm here. When you go home, I'll go home. Do you want more water?"

She shook her head. "You forgot your hat."

He smiled and pointed behind her. His hat hung off the corner of her headboard. "Karma packed a few things for you and brought my hat over."

"Do you feel better now?"

He actually looked confused. She supposed a grown man, even one as secure as Trapper, would have a problem admitting to wearing his own version of a security blanket.

She pictured her kids walking around the backyard with their dad, the three of them wearing their cowboy hats at the same angle. The image brought tears to her eyes. She just prayed she'd be around to see it. She didn't think she was in any real danger—she felt fine, except for all the swelling. She prayed she wasn't wrong. She finally had everything she'd never dreamed about—everything she wanted with every fiber of her being was within her grasp. God wouldn't be cruel enough to snatch it all away now, would he?

"I feel better now that you're talking to me again. I'm so sorry, sweetheart. This whole thing was my fault. I should never have left you. I should have thrown that box away years ago—"

"No, I'm the one who's sorry. Hunter told me I put you in an untenable situation—I hadn't thought about it, but now, I agree with him."

"You do? Hunter really said that?"

"He did. Actually, he said everything was my fault. I think he might be right." Especially the part about her saying she'd never marry. Could she really blame Trapper for believing her? Hell, she'd believed it herself, or she never would have said it—over and over and over again.

"No." Trapper got that indignant curve to his lips. She knew his every expression and loved them all— even the ones that made her crazy. "None of this was your fault."

"Trapper, do you love me?"

"More than my life."

She stared into his eyes and saw only truth, assuredness, and strength.

"You know I love you. Don't you?"

"Yes." He took her swollen, ugly hand and kissed it. He didn't even seem to notice it looked like a marshmallow with fingers. His hands were shaking and clammy, clammier than hers, and that was saying something. "You're going to be fine. You're not feeling bad, are you?" He stood as stiff as Frankenstein. "I'll go get the doctor—"

"No, Trapper, I'm fine. Calm down."

He sat again, but stayed at the edge of the chair, like he was waiting for something terrible to happen. "What's all this about? You're not the type to throw I love yous around. You're scaring me."

"I'm sorry. I'm fine. Scaring you was not my intention, believe me."

His eyes bored into hers until he finally accepted she was telling the truth.

That kind of pissed her off until she thought more about it. Would she lie to keep the babies safe? In a heartbeat. He knew it, and so did she.

"What exactly was your intention?"

Nan thought she should put on her big maternity panties and propose to Trapper. Until a minute ago, it seemed like a good idea. Now, with him looking at her like he was waiting for her to stroke out or go into labor—not so much. "Never mind. It's nothing. It doesn't matter."

"Bianca, it's four thirty in the morning. Whatever it is you're not saying obviously matters to you, or you wouldn't be talking about it. What is it?"

"Nothing. Just drop it and go to sleep."

"That's not gonna happen, sweetheart. Why don't you just tell me what it is so I'm not sitting here for the rest of the night stewing about it?"

She thought she had the guts to ask or at least mention the *M* word. What a great time for all her intestinal fortitude to go AWOL. She should have thought about how to do this without running blind. She was usually a pretty creative person. She'd never had a problem thinking on her feet, or in this case, her side, but for the life of her, she couldn't come up with one idea on how to nonchalantly mention marriage, a family, their future. This so wasn't going to happen. She'd just drop it. She shook her head and pasted on what she hoped was a serene smile. "Never mind. It's really nothing. Honest."

"With you, sweetheart, it's never nothing. You're a woman; when you say it's nothing, it's something. Something big. Something that's going to bite me in the ass when I least expect it."

"No, it's not. I promise."

"Then you're lying."

"I don't lie. I already told you Hunter said this is all my fault. So if anyone's ass is being bitten, it's mine."

"What does Hunter have to do with this?"

"I'm tired, Trapper.

He pulled out his phone. "I'll just call Hunter and clear this whole thing up so we can both get some sleep."

"You can't!"

"Watch me. I have no problem giving my little brother a hard time—the fact that it's almost five in the morning is just a bonus. Toni won't mind."

"Fine, I'll tell you. Just don't call Hunter. This is embarrassing enough as it is."

"Bianca, you never have to be embarrassed with me." He looked so damn serious.

"Right. Like I believe that."

"Why don't you just tell me what was said?"

"Hunter explained that when you overheard me tell someone that I loved them over the phone that you were jealous. He said that since I don't have a ring on my finger, I was fair game."

"For once my brother was right."

"Trapper, I'm eight months pregnant, or did that escape your notice?"

"What's that got to do with anything?"

"Wow, you men really are insane, aren't you? That's exactly what Hunter said."

"We're not insane; we're correct. Go on."

"I told him that you'd never asked me to marry you and that we haven't even discussed it in months. Hunter said that was my fault. He pointed out that I *may have* mentioned never getting married."

"May have?" Trapper's eyebrow rose so high, it disappeared in his hairline.

She ignored him and just spit the rest out. "And that I never once said, and I quote, 'unless you ask me nicely.' Hunter made some stupid sports analogy I can't remember, but the gist of it was that no man is going to ask a woman to marry her unless he has better than even odds that she'll say yes. He said asking Toni to marry him was the bravest and scariest thing he'd ever done, and she's not as difficult as I am."

"Give the man a gold star. He's got that one right too. So what's the embarrassing part?"

"Nan said if I wanted to marry you, I should ask you. So, there it is. Are you happy?"

"Am I happy about what exactly?"

"See, this is the embarrassing part."

"Sweetheart, it's only embarrassing if you asked me to marry you and I politely declined."

"Are you?"

"Am I what?"

"Declining?"

"You haven't asked me anything to accept or decline."

She blew out a breath and cursed the fact she was practically tied to the bed so she couldn't reach over and strangle him. Maybe she could use the cord attached to the nurse's call button. "You're really enjoying this, aren't you?"

His smile almost cut his face in half. "Oh yeah, I can't think of a better time. There is some satisfaction when the cowboy boot's on the other foot, so to speak. So was there something you wanted to ask me?"

"You know, Hunter did tell me something that was true."

"What's that?"

"He said that just because you're a judge, doesn't make you all that. He said you wear a robe in public—which in his opinion is embarrassing as hell—and he said it was a robe, not a cape. It doesn't make you Superman or even supersmart." She blew out a frustrated breath.

"I'm not like you. You're always so damn sure of yourself. It's irritating."

If anything, his smug smile got broader. "You love that about me."

"Fine. Trapper, will you marry me? Will you be my whole world for the rest of my life? Will you put up with me and love me in spite of my being difficult? Will you be possessive, stubborn, and incorrigible? Will you kiss me every day, and bring me roses every once in a while, and cook all the time—'cause you know I can't. And know this: If you say no, I'm going to have to kill you, because if word ever got out that I asked you to marry me, and you politely declined—"

He kissed her, and not just a peck. It was an all-out oral assault. He sucked the rest of the words right out of her head. He pulled away way too soon and waited a moment for her vision to clear. "Sweetheart, I thought you'd never ask."

"What do you mean Charlene Murphy is missing?" Trapper took his hat off his head and beat his thigh with it. Thank God he'd stepped out of Bianca's room. "I thought this was an assisted living care facility."

"It is, sir, but Charlene has her own house. She's completely independent. The assisted living care area is available to her should she need it, but Charlene doesn't."

"She couldn't have just disappeared. Did she take a shuttle and not return?"

"No, sir. She took her car. I do remember that she asked Alphonso, a staff member, to help her with her bags early yesterday evening."

"This is an emergency, Heather. Did Charlene happen to mention where she was going?"

"Hold on, let me check."

Trapper paced.

"Judge Kincaid. I just spoke to Al. He said she was going to visit her granddaughter. Al is supposed to water her plants until she gets back."

At least Bianca's grandmother was on her way. "Does Mrs. Murphy have a cell phone? If she does, I need that number. And if you could give me the make, model, and year of her car, and the license plate number, I'd appreciate it."

"Certainly, sir. Please hold."

Hunter strode in carrying two teddy bears with their arms wrapped around each other and a bouquet of flowers. Only his brother could walk around with stuffed animals and flowers and still look like a he-man. Hunter screwed his face up in a sneer. "Why aren't you with Bianca?"

Bianca may have forgiven him, but it looked as if Hunter hadn't. Not that he needed forgiveness—not from Hunter at least. Trapper reminded himself that he owed Hunter—after all, if it weren't for his brother's warped sense of right and wrong, he and Bianca wouldn't be engaged. At least, not yet. He'd had the ring for months and had been waiting for the right time to broach the subject. He was more than a little relieved that Bianca had asked him. He covered the speaker on his phone. "I'm doing my best to turn my robe into a fucking cape. Is that okay with you?"

Hunter didn't look the least bit ashamed of getting busted dissing him.

"I'm trying to find Bianca's missing grandmother. It

sounds as if she left Cincinnati right after she got off the phone with Bianca yesterday and is on her way here."

Now Hunter looked a little worried—maybe he remembered exactly what he'd said. Bingo. He just realized it's probably not a good idea to tell your brother's girlfriend he's not too bright.

"I don't know if I should tell Bianca or not. She doesn't need anything else to worry about."

"Judge Kincaid—" The woman came back on the line. "I have that information for you. And as far as anyone knows, Charlene doesn't have a cell phone."

Trapper wrote down the information on Charlene's car and license plate number and wondered how many favors it would cost him to get the chief of police to have the police en route keep an eye out for the old girl? If a cop could flag her down, Gramps could have her on a plane to Boise within a few hours. "I got it. If you hear from her, could you please have her call me at this number? Thanks for your help." He ended the call.

Hunter looked him up and down. "How's Bianca? You look like shit."

"You spend the night sitting in a chair praying the woman you love doesn't stroke out or have a heart attack because she's pregnant with your twins, and we'll talk."

Hunter swallowed hard and paled. Good.

"As for Bianca, she's doing okay. The meds seem to be working, but she's swelling up pretty badly. So, you know, don't say anything, and try not to look shocked."

"She's worse than she was yesterday?"

Trapper only nodded. She looked like the Pillsbury Doughboy with breasts, but he'd die before he said it.

"She's going to get back to normal eventually, right?"

God, he hoped so. He didn't think Bianca would be too happy if she didn't. Thank God there were no mirrors in her room. "Of course she will."

Hunter looked at the door to Bianca's room and then back to him. "Maybe you should bring this in to her and tell her we're all thinking about her."

"Oh no. I'm sure she'd want to see you after all the two of you shared yesterday."

Hunter gave him a weird look, seemed to steel himself, and walked into the room. "How are you doing, beautiful?"

By the time Hunter came out, Trapper had stopped just short of promising to name his firstborn Cyrus, after the chief of police, in order to exact his promise of help in looking for Charlene over her route of travel.

Hunter returned, looking the color of a moldy orange—grayish green. "Everything okay?"

"No, man." He wiped his face with the sleeve of his flannel shirt. "I'm thinking of having a vasectomy."

Trapper laughed. "Get in line. The thought's crossed my mind." A thousand times since yesterday.

"You think this is funny? Look at what you did to that woman."

"Toni might have a problem with the whole vasectomy thing."

"Not after she takes one look at Bianca in her condition. If Toni gets a load of Bianca, I might never have sex again. Hell, I wouldn't be surprised if I end up with performance issues. Bianca could be the poster woman for birth control. God, how is she handling it?"

"Amazingly well. She's convinced she and the babies are fine."

"And you?"

"I'm doing everything I can to keep her calm and happy. I have every police officer between here and Ohio looking for a white 1976 Eldorado convertible driven by a seventy-six-year-old woman I've never set eyes on."

"What is that gonna cost you?"

"I haven't a clue. It's probably best I don't."

"It sucks being you."

"It sucks worse being Bianca."

"Seriously, Trap. Are you okay?"

"I will be in about thirty-six hours. Until then—" His throat closed up, and he forced out a breath and turned around. He'd never been so not okay in his life, and he prayed it didn't get worse.

Hunter had the decency to stare at the ceiling until Trapper could get himself back under control. "Karma wants to see Bianca."

Trapper was about to say "hell no," when Hunter held up his hands. "Don't worry. Mom's already threatened her life, and she's going to come in with her. That girl is twenty-six years old and still needs a keeper."

Didn't he know it? He'd been her keeper for a while now. "I still don't like it, but I can't override mom."

"Yeah, I wasn't asking; I was informing. Maybe you should go home, get a shower, and shave. Mom will stay with Bianca."

"No, I'll just grab a shower in Bianca's room. I'm not leaving her again. I should never have left her yesterday. I knew she was upset—"

"Jesus, Trapper. Stop already. You are not in control of the universe—you never were. There's nothing you could have done to stabilize Bianca's condition. Look at her.

She's over her snit, and she's still—" This time Hunter was the one fighting to keep from embarrassing himself.

Trapper gave Hunter a guy hug. "I know."

Hunter slapped him on the back. "Keep it together, Trap. Get cleaned up, and don't let her see you upset. She doesn't need to worry about you too."

———∿∿∿———

Bianca lay in her room counting down the seconds, minutes, hours…hopefully days. The babies had their normal playtime after breakfast—give the kids a little food, and they're energized. She could see one being a kicker, and the other a soccer goalie. Then one strummed her ribs, and she reconsidered—maybe a harp player. Harpist? Was that what they were called?

"Knock, knock. Can we come in?"

Leave it to Kate Kincaid to be the first to actually ask the question. "Yes, please do."

Kate bustled in with a big bag—the woman didn't just walk, she advanced with purpose. "I brought some things for the babies. They're going to be here before we know it, and we still have to bring the car seats. I packed a bag for you and Trapper too. If there's anything else you need, just let me know."

"Thanks, Kate." Bianca received a good long hug and a kiss on the forehead that had tears plopping out of her eyes faster than she could swallow them back. This was what it felt like to have a mother. She'd never really felt that before.

Kate held on to her and rocked back and forth, and like that, all the tension she didn't even realize she'd been holding disappeared.

"It's almost over, just a little while longer. You're doing great. I'm so proud of you, Bianca."

"I was in labor, and I didn't even know it."

"Ha, that's nothing. I almost had Trapper on the way to the hospital, and I was driving. Stupid me. I was waiting for my husband to return from his excursion. He was two days late—Trapper's dad, not Trapper. Trapper was over a week late, but that's beside the point. The point is, I knew and waited anyway. You're one up on me, kiddo. Back labor is easy to misread. Besides, you and those babies are fine."

Kate had her crying one minute and laughing the next. "Okay, I'll forgive myself."

"You better get used to it. Parenthood is nothing if not a learning experience. I've made every mistake in the book."

"Are you talking about me behind my back again, Mom?" Karma breezed in, her ponytail bobbing behind her. "How are my nieces doing today?"

"One's practicing her kicks—she's going to be a Rockette, or if she's a boy, a kicker. The other I think will be a child prodigy on the harp—right now, she's practicing on my ribs."

"Sounds good. I saw Trapper in the hall. I don't know who I'm more worried about—you or him. He looks like something the cat spit up."

"He sat up all night. I told him to go home and get some sleep, but he refuses to leave."

Kate patted Bianca's hand—the woman was a toucher. It took Bianca awhile to get used to it, but now that she had, it was oddly comforting. "Trapper takes after his grandfather. Joe's been here all night too."

Karma tossed her leg over the arm of the chair. "Gramps got plenty of sleep. The nurses made a bed for him. I guess it's the perks of having a wing of the hospital named after you. I think the nurses are hoping after the babies are born, they'll get a new maternity ward."

Kate shrugged. "Joe wanted to know if you were up for a visit from him, but I can see you need to take a nap. Why don't you rest, and I'll send him back about lunchtime? I'm sure the nurses will send up an extra tray for him. The two of you are on the same diet. That way he'll have to eat it, and I won't have to listen to him complain. Does that sound good to you?"

"Yes, Joe can come visit anytime. I'd love to see him." And Kate was right; she was tired. "Do you think they could get a bed or a couch in here for Trapper? He says he's not leaving until I do. I could be here awhile."

"I'll have Joe take care of it. Don't worry about Trapper. He's worried enough for both of you. Men always have to fix things. They're not very good at letting nature take its course, but he'll be fine. I'm sure he'll be back by the time you wake up."

Bianca was sure of it too.

Chapter 22

TRAPPER FELT LIKE HE HADN'T SLEPT IN DAYS—MAYBE that was because he hadn't. He'd spent the last two nights watching Bianca sleep and toss and turn while he prayed. They were at forty-three hours and counting. The forty-eight-hour mark couldn't come soon enough.

Bianca already had a few spikes in her blood pressure—the nurses ran in and gave her more medication. A couple of times her blood sugar went way too high, but the nurses were right on top of that too. The doctor had been right when he said it was a delicate balancing act. It was like walking a freakin' tightwire in a windstorm without a pole.

The waiting almost killed him. Bianca didn't seem at all worried. She either didn't know the danger she was in, or she honestly believed that woman's intuition of hers. Which, when he thought about it, was probably a good thing. She didn't need to add emotional stress to the physical stress she was already dealing with, which was why he'd kept mum about her grandmother's joyride.

He shook his head and saw Gramps waving him on. "I thought you wanted me to send a plane to pick up Bianca's grandmother."

Trapper took off his hat and beat it against his thigh. "I did, but she's ignoring the cops following her. They have their lights flashing, their sirens going—she's either deaf, blind, or both. I called the dogs off when she hit the mountains. I don't want to scare the old girl. I just want to get her here faster."

"Bianca has been asking for her."

"I know, and I'm running out of excuses. The last thing Bianca needs is something else to worry about."

Trapper tossed a handful of Tums into his mouth and chewed. His stomach felt as if he drank a fifth of battery acid.

Gramps looked him up and down, and then gave him his you're-pushin'-for-a-lecture look. "When was the last time you ate, boy?"

"Not again. I'll tell you the same thing I tell everyone. I'm not hungry."

Gramps grabbed his arm. "Come on. We're going down to the cafeteria, and you are going to eat. The last thing Bianca needs is you passing out due to lack of food."

Trapper shook his head and looked back toward Bianca's room. "I don't want to leave her."

"Do the girl a favor, and give her a break. You hovering over her the way you do has to be getting on her last nerve."

"I don't hover."

"Right. You're as jumpy as a hooker at a nun convention."

"Have it your way. You always do." Trapper set his hat back on his head.

"Not always."

Trapper hadn't left the maternity ward since he'd walked in the night before last. The sooner he dealt with his grandfather, the sooner he could get back to Bianca. He followed Gramps to the first-floor cafeteria and through the line.

Gramps stuck a burger and fries on his tray.

"I told you, I'm not hungry."

"You'll eat."

He went to the condiment station, filled up on ketchup and fry sauce, and joined Gramps at the table by the window.

Gramps stared at him. Oh, here it comes—the lecture. Which was it going to be? Then he realized he didn't care. He was too damn tired and stressed to venture a guess, and from the look on his grandfather's face, he'd know soon enough.

"Trapper, if I had my way, you'd have already married Bianca. When are you planning to seal the deal and make an honest woman of her? After the babies are born?"

Trapper just raised his eyebrow before taking a bite of his burger. He chewed, swallowed, and checked his watch before dipping a bunch of fries in sauce. "How do you know I haven't already sealed the deal?"

"If you had, Bianca wouldn't be laying there in a hospital bed, unmarried still. She'd at least have an engagement ring on her finger."

"If she had a ring on her finger, they'd have ended up cutting the damn thing off already. Have you seen Bianca's hands lately?"

"You know what I'm talkin' about, boy."

Trapper had just about enough. "Gramps, I'm thirty-five. I'm not a boy."

"You're a damn sight younger than me. You'll always be a boy in my eyes. I just wish you'd get off your ass and get that little filly tied down already."

"Bianca's a modern woman. I had to make it look like it was her idea." Just then, blue and red lights lit up

the room through the window. Trapper stood to get a
better look over the hedges. A white old car, decidedly
antique with back fins, circled the parking lot with no
less than half the Boise Police Department trailing at
about two miles an hour.

The car took a pass by the window, but he couldn't
make out who was driving. It looked like a kid on a
joyride. Only a baseball cap was visible just above the
dash. He was probably going slowly because he couldn't
reach the pedals.

The boat—it was that long—made a five-point turn
into a handicap parking spot, lurching back and forth
until it came to a full stop. Not bad for a kid.

"What do you think's going on?"

Everyone in the cafeteria lined the windows, wearing
matching expressions of shock and awe.

"I don't know."

The police jumped out of their cruisers, guns drawn,
and surrounded the car.

"Come out with your hands up," an officer yelled into
a bullhorn.

The door swung open. It wasn't just a door; it was
a long, heavy door with red interior. One ruby red
slipper hit the pavement, followed by the other, and
a figure in a red crushed velvet jogging suit stepped
out of the car, hands held high, jewels sparkling in
the sunlight.

The driver turned, and Trapper got his first good
look. "Oh shit! Come on, Gramps. We gotta go. I think
that's Bianca's grandmother, Charlene Murphy."

Gramps smiled, his eyes sparkling almost as brilliantly as Nan's bejeweled fingers. "The woman

certainly knows how to make an entrance. I haven't seen this much police action since Nixon came to visit. It must be a slow week for the men in blue."

Trapper grabbed Gramps's arm and dragged him out of the cafeteria. If it were Bianca's grandmother, he'd never live it down.

———— ⁓⁓ ————

Bianca looked at all the Kincaid women sitting around her room. The place was so full, the nurses had to bring in more chairs. Kate sat on the one Trapper usually occupied, and Karma was on the far side of the room and had been on and off her phone during the entire visit, furiously writing on a pad of paper.

"What is Karma doing?"

Toni sat on the foot of the bed. "She's taking bets. She's turned into a regular bookie."

"She's betting on the babies?"

"Oh yeah, time of birth, gender, height, and weight."

Jessie leaned in from the chair she straddled. "There's even a bet on whether or not Trapper passes out."

"Is there anything Karma won't bet on?"

Toni and Jessie looked at each other and then back at her. "No," they said in stereo.

Kate stood. "Karma Lynn Kincaid, put that damn phone away. I've had it with all the betting you and the boys are doing. This is not the time or—" She looked out the window. The sound of sirens filled the room. "What the heck is going on out there?"

All Bianca could see were flashing lights. "What is it?"

Everyone but her moved to the window.

Kate let out a laugh. "There are seven police cars following a huge white car going about five miles an hour in the parking lot. It's like a slow-motion car chase."

Bianca had a very bad feeling about this. "Could someone help me up?"

No one moved away from the window so she rolled herself out of bed—not an easy thing to do considering her girth. She felt like a beached whale. She tried to stick her swollen feet into a pair of Trapper's old slippers, grabbed the IV pole, held up the other monitor cords, and waddled toward the window to get a better look. She held on to the sill with shaking hands and spotted the car surrounded by police—the thing was a boat—the same boat her grandmother drove. The boat she'd dubbed the HMS *Charlene*. "Oh my God. That's my grandmother's car they're surrounding."

Nan's car made a five-point turn into a handicap-parking place, nearly hitting a police officer. "That's it. I'm taking her license away as soon as she gets up here—if they don't shoot her first."

Then she heard a cop on a bullhorn telling her grandmother to get out of the car with her hands up. "Oh, God! They can't be serious, can they?"

Kate moved beside her. "Don't worry. Look— Trapper's down there. See him in his hat?"

Yeah, Trapper was in the thick of things. She just hoped Nan didn't go after him too.

"The police will listen to him. I'm sure he'll get everything under control." Kate moved beside her. "Come on. Let's get you back to bed."

"Okay." She took a step, and then there was a splash. "Oh God." She looked down and was standing in a puddle. The babies moved, and more splashing ensued. "Um, I think my water just broke."

Karma, Toni, and Jessie all gasped and stared and took big steps away, as if she'd just urinated. Kate was the only one who didn't look shocked. "Toni, Jessie—you go get the nurses. Tell them Bianca's water just broke. Karma, you go downstairs and get Trapper and Bianca's grandmother. Whatever you do, please don't give the police officers any reason to shoot you. Trapper has enough to worry about without you getting in the way or stirring up trouble."

When no one moved, Kate just shook her head. "*Now!* Move it!"

Wow, that got them going. Everyone skirted the ever-growing puddle and ran. Bianca was happy to see them leave.

"Kate—" Her future mother-in-law looked as if she dealt with this kind of thing every day of her life. Thank God. "If you're worried, why did you send Karma down there?"

"I know Karma. There's no way I'd be able to keep her away from the scene down there—a warning was the best I could do."

That made sense.

Kate's arm tightened around her. "Are you having contractions?"

"No, not yet. At least, I don't think so. My back is killing me though."

"Okay, I'm going to get you a fresh gown. We need to change you out of those wet things."

Bianca looked at her feet. "Trapper's slippers are toast."

Kate laughed. "That's okay. He never did wear them anyway."

She felt tears sting her eyes. "I know, but they were the only shoes that fit me."

—◦◦◦—

Trapper made eye contact with every one of the seven police officers surrounding what he thought was Bianca's grandmother's car. When he scanned the license plate, he was sure. Fabulous. The only good thing was he knew every one of the officers standing there.

The leader was Officer By-The-Book, and he'd had a nightstick stuck firmly up his ass since he'd entered the police academy in the early 1980s. He hiked up his pants. The man had a major case of Dunlop's disease— his belly *done lopped* over his belt buckle—and strode to him. "Judge Kincaid, you need to step away from the vehicle."

"Officer Jones, is it? Yeah, well, you need to call your chief of police, Cyrus Stanhope, and tell him my future grandmother-in-law just arrived in Boise. You and six other officers are scaring the crap out of her." The big man paled. Good, what the hell was he thinking following a little old lady like that? "I'd really appreciate it if you'd let me take her upstairs to see her granddaughter, my fiancée, who is about to deliver our twins any minute."

"Trapper!" He turned at the sound of his name and saw Karma flying toward him. "Trapper, the babies are coming! Bianca just exploded!" Karma made an explosion motion with her hands.

"What?"

"It was like a gusher!"

"Her water broke?"

"I guess. They're taking her into the OR. She saw the whole thing, Trap." She pointed to the windows.

Fuck.

"She knew that was her grandmother, and the next thing I know, it's like someone dropped a full trough of water between her feet."

"Oh, God! Okay." He turned and spotted a flash of red behind a wall of blue. "Charlene, Mrs. Murphy?"

A small woman pushed her way through the police officers and looked up at him. "Are you Trapper Kincaid?"

"Yes, ma'am. Please come with me. Bianca just went into labor. I need to get you upstairs."

"What about all these cops?"

"It's taken care of." His gaze flew from the gray-haired woman who came up mid-chest to Officer Jones. "Isn't that right, Jones?"

"Yes, sir, Judge Kincaid. That's right. It's all taken care of."

Trapper took Charlene's arm and nodded at the law. "Thank you. Please give my regards to Cy, and tell him I'll call him later."

He did his best to slow his steps for Bianca's grandmother's sake, but he had to take off. Gramps and Karma stared at Charlene. "Ma'am, this is my grandfather, Joe Walsh, and my sister, Karma. They'll take you upstairs. I have to get up there. I've got to… I'm sorry, ma'am."

Charlene waved him away, and he took off running.

He took the steps three at a time, figuring that waiting for the elevator would likely kill him. He slapped through the double doors of the maternity ward without slowing down and skidded to a halt in front of the nurse's station. "Where's Bianca?"

One of the nurses shook her head. "Go put your hat in her room for safekeeping, and I'll take you down to get you gowned and gloved. I suspect they had to start without you, Dad."

"She's gonna kill me."

The nurse just walked alongside him. "She heard all about the ruckus outside. I'm sure she'll think you're a regular Prince Charming as long as her grandmother doesn't end up behind bars."

He tossed his hat in her room, not bothering to look where it landed. "Okay, where is she?"

"Don't worry. Your mother's with her. Just take a breath, Judge. The last thing Bianca needs is you running in there like your hair's on fire."

Right. Like he could breathe at a time like this. "I just need to—"

"Get gowned and gloved." She pushed him through some doors and smiled at the women in the room. "Here he is—you know the drill."

He had to scrub up, his hair was put in some stupid-looking hat, a mask was put over his face, and he had a blue paper gown. Hell, even his boots were covered.

The one nurse looked him over. "Are you ready to go in there?"

Shit, he didn't think he'd ever be ready.

"Just focus on her face, and you should be okay. I'll stay with you until you get in the chair. Let me go and get your mother. She's been taking care of Bianca since you were running a little late."

"Okay." It came out sounding more like a croak. Great. He really regretted that hamburger his grandfather forced down his throat. *Please God don't let me be sick.*

His mother came out and hugged him. "She's doing fine. They just did the epidural."

"Thanks for going in with her, Mom."

"She'll be happy to see you. Good luck." His mom gave him a look he'd never seen. She looked as if she was about to cry.

"She's okay?"

His mom just nodded, as if she couldn't speak.

The nurse gave him a shove toward the door. "She's about to be a grandmother, Judge. She's just a little choked up. Now, in you go."

He hadn't been prepared for all the bright lights. It was like high noon on a cloudless July day.

He hadn't been prepared to see Bianca lying there with a sheet over her, and some kind of drape in front of her belly.

He hadn't been prepared for all the people or the way the place looked like an operating room.

The nurse behind him gave him another shove. He was really getting sick to death of that.

"There's a seat right next to Bianca's head for you. I suggest you sit down before you fall down. You're not looking too steady on your feet."

He saw Bianca's face—she was the only one without a mask. He wanted to kiss her, but that might be pushing it. "How are you doing, sweetheart?"

"I'm okay now that you're here. Is my grandmother all right?"

"She's fine. I left her with Gramps and Karma. She's waiting with the rest of the family. Mom will see she's set for the night. Let's just concentrate on you, okay?"

Dr. Weaver came in and stepped beside Bianca. "So, it looks like we're going to have a few babies this evening."

"I shouldn't have gotten out of bed—"

He gave her hand a pat. "Bianca, you lasted longer than I expected. You and the babies are going to be fine. I just thought I'd chat with you about having your tubes tied while we're in there. I strongly recommend it. Another pregnancy isn't advisable. With your age, your proclivity for gestational diabetes—"

Trapper swallowed hard. He felt nothing but relief. He wouldn't want Bianca to go through another pregnancy ever again. Hell, he'd already planned to talk to her about it.

Bianca looked at him, and tears streamed down her face. "Trapper?"

"Sweetheart, you and the babies are all the family I'll ever need. I never want you put in danger again. If we want more kids, we can adopt. Okay? As long as I have you, I'll be more than happy."

"You're sure?"

"I'm positive."

The doctor looked from Trapper to her and back. "Are we decided?"

Trapper took her hand in his. "Is it okay, Bianca?" He held his breath.

Bianca looked at the doctor again. "Are you certain this would happen again?"

"I'm ninety-five percent certain. Bianca, believe me when I say that we were very lucky this time."

"Okay, then." Her hand tightened on Trapper's. "Tie my tubes."

Trapper wasn't the only one who let out a relieved

breath. He could swear if he removed Dr. Weaver's mask, he'd find a smile.

Dr. Weaver clapped his gloved hands. "Okay, people. It looks like it's time to have a few babies! Bianca, Trapper, you've met Dr. Stephens and Dr. Luntz—they're here to assist."

Trapper must have nodded. But he wasn't sure all he could do was concentrate on Bianca's face and not look at the mirrors they had everywhere—it was like watching a game at a bar filled with big screens—there was no way not to look. God, he was so thankful he'd never have to do this again for as long as he lived.

Dr. Weaver nodded to someone, and they lowered the drape. "Okay, Bianca, lots of pressure on your tummy now."

One of the doctors stood on a stool and actually pressed on Bianca's distended belly.

The grip Bianca had on his hand tightened, and the next thing he knew a little baby's head popped out, resting in Dr. Weaver's hand. A nurse suctioned the mouth and nose even before Dr. Weaver pulled the baby the rest of the way out.

"It's a girl." The doctor handed the baby to a waiting nurse. The other doctor clamped the umbilical cord in two places and cut it, handing the baby to a waiting doctor.

"Charlie," Bianca whispered. "Charlie's the oldest."

A second later, he heard it. It started out as a cry and ended with a wail. God, she sounded pissed. Pissed and healthy and squirming.

"Charlie's the kicker."

They took Charlie away.

Dr. Weaver's eyes crinkled in what must be one hell

of a smile. "She looks fine. They're just going to check her out, clean her up, weigh her, and make sure she's breathing well."

Everyone started talking at once. He heard six pounds one ounce, perfect little girl, look at all that pretty blonde hair, curls, and something about a good APGAR score.

The doctor was still pressing against Bianca's stomach.

Dr. Weaver nodded to someone. "Okay, we're ready for baby number two." A half a minute later, Katie was delivered.

Trapper only caught a glimpse of her, but she looked smaller. He waited. Held his breath. Then he heard it. A cry—a little cry. Not loud like Charlie's, but it was there. They took longer to suction Katie's mouth and nose, and she didn't like it at all. He watched her squirm, her arms flailing. His Katie was fighting the tube they had in her mouth. She had spirit.

Dr. Weaver looked up from the baby. "She's doing well, Bianca. She's smaller than the first, but still a good size. She's breathing on her own."

"She's fine, sweetheart." Trapper wrapped an arm around Bianca's head and listened.

Five pounds two ounces, same blonde hair, same curls, same perfection, not as large but a good size, APGAR was lower. She was okay though.

A nurse carried his daughter over to him. "Here you go, Dad. Here's your first little girl. Keep her wrapped up. You can take my word for it—all her fingers and toes are accounted for, but we need to keep her nice and warm now."

"Okay."

The nurse handed over the smallest baby Trapper had ever seen—well, okay, Katie was smaller.

"Hey, Charlie. Look at you." He blinked back tears as he held his little girl so Bianca could see her. "She's gorgeous, just like her momma." Then he looked into his daughter's eyes and couldn't believe how perfect she was. He remembered seeing Karma and the twins after they were born. They were all red, and their heads were cone-shaped. Charlie was a perfect pink bundle. They had a little pink hat on her head, but it was nice and round and fit perfectly in the palm of his hand. "God, she's so small."

Bianca couldn't do much moving around, but she placed a hand on Charlie's little body. "She didn't feel that small."

Dr. Weaver cleared his throat. "We're going to start stitching you up now, Bianca."

"So it's done? You did the tubal?"

"Yes."

Tears Trapper knew weren't happy ones escaped and rolled down Bianca's cheeks. "Hey, look at what we've got. I'm the luckiest man alive."

"Are you ready for number two, Dad?"

"Oh, yeah. Come here, Katie."

"We're just going to take—"

Bianca smiled. "Charlene Ann, but we call her Charlie."

"Charlie Kincaid—nice name. We're going to take little Charlie into the nursery while you're finishing up here and in recovery. The doctor wants to give both babies a thorough once-over."

"Trapper, go with Charlie and Katie."

He cradled Katie in his arms. Her face screwed up in a pout that started as a whimper and ended as a cry.

He was incredibly happy to hear it. "I don't want to leave you."

Bianca put her hand on Katie's little squirming body. She did not like having her arms inside the blanket. "Go with the babies. I'm fine."

Trapper looked up at Dr. Weaver. "Bianca's okay? Her blood pressure—everything. She's doing well?"

"Bianca's doing beautifully. All three of your girls are doing better than I could have hoped for."

"Thank you, Doc." He got up, holding Katie close to his chest, and did his best not to look at the incision. He tugged his mask down and kissed Bianca. "I love you, sweetheart."

"I love you too. Take good care of our girls. Don't leave them, okay?"

"I promise. I'll be with them the whole time."

A nurse took Katie from him, and another pulled his mask back up. He watched as the nurses put the babies in little incubators, took one more look at Bianca, and then followed the nurses and babies into the nursery and to the waiting doctors.

Chapter 23

KARMA PACED THE WAITING ROOM. GOD, SHE ACHED all over. As soon as she saw Bianca's water break, she swore she was getting her period—which was weird because it wasn't due for another week and a half. She grabbed a cup of coffee and downed four Motrin.

"Karma Lynn." Her mother's voice rang out across the waiting room. "If you don't stop pacing, I might just have to duct tape you to a chair."

"Mom, it's been an hour. How long does it take to deliver two little babies?"

"As long as it takes."

For all her huffing, her mom looked just as worried as Karma felt. She just did her worrying sitting down.

As much as Karma hated to admit it, she was as worried about Bianca as she was about the babies. Maybe more so. She'd never seen a woman look worse. If anything happened to Bianca, she wasn't sure what Trapper would do—he was over the moon for her. She'd never seen anyone fall so far so fast. She'd never seen her big, can-handle-anything-he-man brother look so scared before—not even when Gramps had his heart attack. That alone was enough to scare Karma.

Bianca had really grown on her over the last few months. She wasn't at all the witch she liked everyone to think she was, and Karma didn't think that just because Bianca was having her nieces either.

She ignored her mother's glare and took another turn around the room while she sent up a quick prayer that she was right about Bianca having girls. If not, she was going to lose a shit-ton of money.

After seeing her friends, her brothers, and cousin fall in and out of love over the years, she was glad that she was immune to that kind of thing. Hell, at twenty-six, she'd never been in love. All her friends had. Granted, Mary Claire had only been in love once, but she'd never fallen out of love with Jack, so Karma had to count it. Her friend, Trish, had been in love at least three times, but her love never seemed to take. Still, Trish kept looking for "the one." All of Karma's brothers and her cousin Ben were in love, and even with the heartache that came along with it, they happily took to love and marriage. She was happy for them. She just didn't see it ever happening to her. No, she was too busy to deal with a man full-time. Between the bar and Three French Hens—the store she owned a share of—she didn't have time to deal with romance. Not if she wanted to make her dreams of franchising Humpin' Hannah's a reality. Besides, she'd never met a man she didn't want to wave good-bye to when she was finished with him. She just hoped that once Trapper talked Bianca into marrying him, Gramps wouldn't set his sights on getting her hitched. That would definitely be a problem. She'd hate to break her grandfather's heart, but there was no way any man was going to drag her down the aisle.

Dr. Weaver stepped into the waiting room, and Karma had to stop short to avoid an unintended tackle. The doctor had his mask hanging from around his neck and wore a big smile. "Bianca wanted to make sure I told you that she and the babies are all fine. She's in recovery, and the babies are in the nursery. Everyone is doing well."

Karma jumped up and down on the balls of her feet. "Are they girls or boys?"

"Girls, one was six pounds two ounces, the other weighed in at five pounds one ounce. They're breathing on their own and doing fine. Trapper and their doctors are with them now. You should be able to get a look at them through the glass in the nursery."

"You said girls, right, Doc? I'm not hearing things?"

"Two girls. I checked them myself."

"Oh, thank God. We've finally got the boys outnumbered! Thank you, Bianca!"

The doctor laughed. "You do know the sex of the babies is determined by the father, don't you?"

Karma waved him away. "It's not as if they can just dial M for male, Doc. You don't seem to understand. I have three brothers and one male cousin. These are the first Kincaid females born since…well, since me. Now the girls outnumber the boys! It's a great day to be a Kincaid."

Bianca's grandmother pushed by Karma and looked up at the doctor. "May I see Bianca?"

"Sure, you're her grandmother I assume? I heard you caused quite a stir earlier."

She placed her hand on the doctor's arm. "Young man, I've been causing trouble longer than you've been alive. Hasn't stopped me yet."

Dr. Weaver let out a laugh. "I can see that." He gave her a wink. "I'll have one of the nurses take you back to see Bianca in recovery. I think she'll rest better knowing that you're here and not behind bars. As for the rest of you, go ahead and see the babies while they're in the nursery. As soon as Bianca gets into her room, I expect they'll be moved in with her. Why don't you plan on visiting Bianca tomorrow?" He stopped and looked for someone. "Kate?" His eyes landed on his target. "Bianca asked for you earlier. If you'd like to go into recovery with her grandmother, I'm sure Bianca would appreciate seeing you."

Karma was surprised that her mother looked so shocked—it was obvious Bianca needed a mother. It was a good thing Karma didn't mind sharing hers— she was getting tired of being the only problem child in the family.

Her mom's eyes got all shiny again. "Yes, I'd love to." Karma didn't get the whole mushy crying thing all the women in her family were prone to. She was so not a crier. She slid around the doctor and headed to the nursery, trailed by her brothers and their wives.

Karma turned the corner, looked through the glass, and there was Trapper, her big brother, all suited up in blue, sitting in a rocking chair and holding two little pink bundles of love. Her nieces. One was waving her little arms. The nurse kept trying to tuck her hands back into the blanket they wrapped around her, like a little mummy, but the kid was determined to be free. She looked so much smaller than her sister, but, damn, she had moxie.

Karma stood between her brothers and their wives. Hunter and Fisher wrapped their arms around her, and she was bombarded with familial love. She felt tears stinging behind her eyes and blinked them. So okay, maybe she did cry every once in a great while—not that she'd ever admit it. She snuck a glance at Fisher, and his eyes looked a little glassy. Same with Hunter, so she didn't feel that bad. Gramps tapped on the window, looking like the proudest peacock around, and handed out Cubans to anyone who passed by.

Fisher squeezed her shoulder. "The nieces were born on April Fool's Day. That's going to be easy to remember."

She looked at the littlest Kincaid and felt a connection she'd never experienced before. Not that she didn't feel something for the other…but there was something about that little girl that pulled on Karma's heartstrings.

Ben and Gina ran up. Ben stopped behind her. "What'd we miss?"

"They're girls. You owe me a bundle."

The three guys all looked at one another, and Ben pulled out his wallet. "We're finally outnumbered, guys."

Gramps laughed. "There's a way to fix that. You just need to keep plantin' those seeds, and we'll catch up right quick."

Gina, Ben's wife, scooted in front of Karma and put her hand up to the glass. "I remember my little brother was small like that."

Karma wrapped her arm around Gina. "You know, I was thinking about your brother earlier. I have some time off. I thought I'd check out a baseball game or two. I'd be happy to feel Angel Anderson out."

Gina tore her eyes away from Trapper and the babies, and her golden gaze hit Karma. "I thought Trapper was going to handle it."

"He was. But he's got his hands full now. Let me go down and check things out. I'll be discreet."

Ben laughed. "You're anything but discreet, Karma.

As a matter of fact, I think that's the first time anyone has used your name and the word 'discreet' in a sentence together. Ever."

She put her hands on her hips and stared up at her cousin. "Benji, when it comes right down to it, I'm your best bet. Who else do you know is part of the family but can't be connected to you in any way, shape, or form? Who else do you know is devious enough to get the skinny on Angel Anderson?"

Gina looked at Ben and laughed. "I know I'm going to regret this, but I can't think of anyone as devious as Karma."

"Jessie can get me tickets to the season opener. Hey, maybe I can talk Andrew into introducing us. He doesn't know anything about it yet, does he?"

"No, we haven't mentioned it. I don't think Jessie would have either. But we'd better ask just to make sure."

"Good. I'll check with Jessie, and if we're right, I'll call Andrew and see if he's up for a road trip. But if he's not, that's fine too. I've never had a difficult time meeting men."

Ben gave her one of his you're-like-a-little-sister-to-me looks. "That's what I'm afraid of. Your brothers are going to kill me."

She looked over and saw both Fisher and Hunter with their wives, fawning over the twins and whispering in their wives ears. It looked like they'd be pleasantly occupied for a while. She gave them a year at most before they started popping out little Kincaids. Oh, yeah, she saw a lot more betting in her future.

———

Trapper sat on the bed with his arm around Bianca and wondered how everyone in the family could fit into one hospital room—it was literally overflowing with people.

James, the twins' self-proclaimed godfather, perched himself on the arm of Karma's chair and held Katie like a pro. It was obvious he had nine nieces and nephews he was close to.

Jessie—the amateur of the group—held Charlie under the watchful gaze of Fisher, as if she were holding a ticking time bomb.

Trapper took one look at his sisters-in-law and wished his brothers luck. It looked as if the youngest set of twins had sent both Jessie's and Toni's biological clocks into alarm mode. Better his brothers than him.

Gramps was crammed on the torture device the hospital called a couch between the silver-haired Charlene and Jessie.

Hunter still wore the green tinge he'd sported for the last three days and held up the wall while he watched Toni coo at Charlie over Jessie's shoulder.

Ben leaned against the windowsill and held Gina in front of him, whispering something in her ear. The way his hand kept straying to Gina's stomach made Trapper wonder if they were keeping a secret or making a plan. Either way, Gramps would be happy with the outcome.

Gramps rose with more agility than any octogenarian should have. But Trapper didn't know why he was surprised. There weren't many eighty-somethings who still skied with two artificial hips no less. The man said if he were going out, he'd go out with his boots on, whether they be ski or cowboy, made no difference to him. Gramps cleared his throat. "I think it's time we all take off and give Bianca and the babies a break. They're going to be home tonight, so you all can see them tomorrow at their house." He held his hand out for Charlene, who rose with as much grace as any short woman could. Her feet had barely hit the floor when she sat on the couch.

Charlene pushed her way through the throng, already comfortable enough with the group to sweep Charlie right out of Jessie's arms. She snuggled Charlie close on the way to Bianca and reached up to kiss Bianca's cheek before handing over the baby. "Kate and I brought you clothes to wear home and even a new pair of slippers that should fit. The boys have already put the car seats in Trapper's behemoth of an SUV. I swear I'd need a ladder to get into that truck."

"Thanks, Nan."

"Dinner will be waiting for you when you get home so you won't have to worry about a thing."

Bianca ran her hand over Charlie's curly blonde hair. "Trapper does all the cooking—I never have to worry about that. As long as I stay out of the kitchen, he's happy."

Trapper didn't bother to hide his laugh. "She's got that right."

Gramps stole Katie from James and buzzed her forehead before settling her in Trapper's arms. "You and Bianca have some talkin' to do, if you know what I'm sayin', son."

"I hear you loud and clear, Gramps."

"Good, then we'll leave you to it."

There were hugs and kisses all around. His mom took a stack of photos and laid them on the rolling table at the foot of the bed. "I went through all the baby pictures last

night and brought newborn pictures of each of you kids.
I thought it would be fun for you to compare them to
Katie and Charlie. Charlene even thought to bring a few
of Bianca." She rested her hand on Bianca's shoulder.
"You were adorable, by the way."

"Thanks, Mom."

Trapper did a double take. When had Bianca started
calling his mother "Mom"?

Bianca reached over and gave his mom a one-armed
hug and a kiss on the cheek.

From the pleased and teary-eyed expression covering his mother's face, he figured she was thrilled with
the change.

Karma stopped to fawn one more time over Katie—
the two seemed to have bonded—which frankly, made
Trapper more than a little nervous. "I'll see you when
you get home. Auntie Karma has a special surprise for
you both."

Trapper cringed. "What did you do?"

"Don't be such a downer, Trapper. I promise, you and
Bianca will love it. I'll show you when you get home."

When Trapper gave her another look, she blew her
hair out of her eyes and smiled. "Mom and Charlene
approved, so you have nothing to worry about."

"With you, Karma, there's always something to
worry about."

Ben moved Karma out of the way, probably for her
own protection, and handed him the keys to the Sequoia.
"The car seats just click into the bases. I left the seats
over by the door for you, Trap."

"Great, thanks."

"Gramps even had them checked out by the cops

trailing Charlene's boat. He thought they should do something productive."

"I thought Bianca took her license away," he whispered.

Ben shook his head. "She said she'd have to pry it out of her cold, dead hand."

"The cops are still following her?"

"Yeah, but she let Gramps drive. He just gave them a wave, and they didn't pull him over. I think he has a serious case of car envy." He leaned closer. "Or maybe it's the girl with the hot car he's interested in. She's packin' a hemi under the hood, so it's hard to tell. They've been spending a lot of time together." He waggled his eyebrows. "I feel like a freakin' chaperone when we're at the house."

"Dude, I really didn't need to hear that. But I guess it's good to know Gramps has still got it."

"It might be good to know, but I can tell you, seeing it is altogether another matter." Ben looked at the twins and let out a wistful sigh. "You're a lucky man, Trapper."

"You're looking' pretty lucky yourself. Anything you want to tell me?"

"Nope, not yet." But that didn't stop Ben from grinning the same grin Trapper had been wearing for the last five months.

Trapper raised his eyebrows and watched Ben usher everyone out of the room. "Alone at last." He pulled Bianca closer and kissed her temple. "It feels as if it's been days since I've had you to myself. Let me just put the girls down, and we can make up for lost time."

Bianca handed over Charlie, and he got the twins settled just the way they liked it—together. He'd learned early on that everyone in their little family slept better in pairs. Trapper wondered if he should even bother putting the second crib together—he doubted they'd use it. Before heading back, he closed the door, hoping for privacy. He needed at least a few minutes wrapped around Bianca—it had been days. When he turned, he found her on her feet staring at the babies all snuggled together in the crib. So much for his plan. He settled for stepping behind her and wrapping his arms around her waist. She was still swollen, but even that was getting better. "How are you feeling?"

"Blessed."

"Yeah, that pretty much sums it up. The three of you are healthy and perfect and so beautiful." He kissed her neck. "I still can't believe you're mine."

Bianca turned to him and smiled that smile she had reserved just for him. "I love you."

"I have a little something for you. I got it months ago—before we left New York in fact, but I wasn't sure you'd want it."

"And you think I'll want it now?"

"Since you proposed to me, I'm pretty sure you will. When I bought it, I wasn't nearly as confident."

"Then why did you buy it?"

"It was the day I found you. I left the hospital and was walking up Fifth Avenue toward your apartment. I had just gotten off the phone after telling Mom about the babies. I stopped in front of this shop, looked in the window, and I saw this ring. It reminded me of you. It was a ring I could picture you wearing for the rest of your life, so I went in and bought it."

"Just like that?"

He shrugged and sent up a little prayer that she'd like it. He held out the red box with the gold leaf.

"You just happened to stop in front of Cartier?"

He shrugged. "I didn't realize it at the time. I just saw this—" He opened the box, held his breath, and watched her face. The center diamond sparkled like her eyes; the diamond-studded platinum band formed a heart that cradled a smaller diamond on either side of the center stone.

"You saw this and thought of me?" She still hadn't stopped staring at it.

"I did. Do you like it?"

"It's…it's so beautiful."

He released the breath he'd been holding. "Yeah, that's what I thought the first time I saw you, and the first time I saw the ring."

"I love it." Then she looked at her hand, and tears started flowing. "But my fingers are still so swollen."

"I thought of that too, so I got you something else."

He pulled a chain out of his shirt pocket. "I wanted you to be able to wear it. And I know it's kind of a tradition to get the mother of your children a gift." He held up a chain with two diamonds set individually. "Did you know that diamonds are April's birthstone?"

"Yes, my birthday is in April."

"I know that."

"I love diamonds."

"That's a good thing." She was getting quite the collection. "Until the swelling goes down, I thought we could put your engagement ring on here." He slid the ring onto the chain and set it between the diamonds. "Turn around, and I'll put it on for you."

She caught the ring and held it close to her heart before turning to face him. "I love them. I love you. Thank you."

"You do realize I had been planning to propose to you. I was just waiting for the right time."

Her smile told him she wasn't sure she believed him. "Of course you were. I have proof." She held up her ring and stared at it for a few seconds.

He pulled her close like he'd wanted to all day and kissed her until they were both breathing heavy.

She slid out of his arms. "I just hope I can get back into a size six in six weeks."

"You want to get married in six weeks?"

"Do you want to wait?"

"Hell, no. I'd marry you today if I could. I don't care if you're a size six or sixteen. I just want you happy and healthy."

"I am both. So, okay, six weeks—no matter my size." But the look on her face told him she'd be a size six no matter what. Women. Damn, now he had three of them. Life was sure going to be interesting.

He stepped back and hit the table, almost dropping the pictures his mom had left. He saved them from ending up on the floor.

He checked out the first one. It was of Bianca—he knew this because it was the only one professionally done. "Wow, look at you. Were you always this beautiful? Did you ever hit an awkward age?"

"I don't know. I guess when I lost my teeth—but my mother refused to have any pictures taken of me during that time. I was already modeling by then. I think I started before I was about a year old."

He held her picture up and looked at the babies.

"Charlie and Katie look nothing like me."

He didn't see much of a resemblance either.

"Who is this?" Bianca took the next picture and looked at the back. "It's you. You were so chubby. God, you were cute."

His head looked as big as his shoulders. He was a ten-pound baby. Looking at that picture gave him a whole new appreciation for his mother.

Bianca's gaze went from his picture to the babies. "They don't look like you either. You were bald."

"Until I was almost two."

"Oh, look at the twins. I can't tell which is which."

He flipped the picture over. "Hunter is on the left." They were bald too. "The only baby I remember having hair was Karma." It was just a vague memory of Karma with her hair tied on top of her head like Pebbles in the *Flintstones* cartoon.

Bianca shuffled through the photos and stopped. Looked at the babies and then back at the picture. She handed the picture to him.

He stared. The feeling of dread and shock crept up his throat. "It's incredible." He'd never seen anything like it.

"They have the same curly blonde hair. The same nose. The same chin. Even their lips. They look exactly like—"

He backed toward the bed and sat. He didn't need to see a mirror to know he wore a look of horror.

Bianca took one look at him and laughed so hard she hugged herself, almost doubling over. "Oh God, don't make me laugh. It hurts."

"It's like there are three of them."

"I see that. I certainly hope you're up for the job."

He ignored Bianca's laughter. He didn't really need

to look, but he did anyway. He flipped the picture over and read the name written in his mother's handwriting. "Oh my God. It's Karma."

In case you missed them, read on for excerpts from the first two books in the Wild Thing series by Robin Kaye:

Wild Thing

Call Me Wild

From *Wild Thing*

TONI RUSSO STOOD ON THE PORCH OF THE SAWTOOTH Inn ignoring the mountains cutting the bright blue sky, concentrating instead on Hunter Kincaid's very confused, very green eyes. She recognized him from the photos on the River Runners's website. They didn't do him justice, probably because there was no way to transmit the pheromones rolling off the man onto an image.

Hunter stared at her the whole way from his old Land Cruiser to the porch. He stopped, tipped his baseball cap back, and then put his hands on his hips. "You're not who I expected to see."

Well, no shit. "Yeah, I guess you'll have to learn to live with the disappointment. I know I have."

"Toni?" A look of relief flashed across his face, then a smile ticked up the right side of his mouth as he made a slow perusal of her from head to feet and back again.

She waited, knowing it would take awhile. Ever since she'd landed in Boise, she'd experienced the same thing. No one quite knew what to make of her. Holding her clipboard to her chest, she wondered if it would have been better to have spent her time in Boise shopping for less interesting clothes. She mentally shook her head and knew it would never have worked. You could put her in a sack, and she'd do something to stand out. She'd long since given up trying to rein herself in. As Catherine Aird said, "If you can't be a good example, then you'll just have to serve as a horrible warning." So far, it had worked for her.

Blowing her bangs out of her eyes, Toni checked her outfit. The short, red plaid kilt wasn't too offensive. She pulled her clipboard away to see she had on her *Stay Away* T-shirt. Maybe he had something against the collage of pistols, brass knuckles, knives, and bullets. But really, he didn't look like a pacifist, not that she wasn't—it was a T-shirt for goodness sake, not a personal manifesto. The kitty-face Mary Janes and red skull-and-crossbones knee-socks were a bit busy. Okay, Hunter's thirty seconds were up. She fingered the D-ring on the studded collar around her neck and cleared her throat. "Do you mind?"

Hunter took a sip of whatever was in the travel cup he held. "Not at all—just wondering if you were going for that naughty-schoolgirl-fantasy look."

"No, I was going for my not-quite-sure-what-to-wear-for-a-meeting-with-Davy-Crockett look. How's it working for you?"

Hunter's mouth worked its way into a full smile. Great teeth. She had a thing for nice teeth, and yeah, his mouth was full of them.

"Really well, thanks. Over the phone, it sounded as if you wouldn't be caught dead out here. When Bianca came to scout for photo shoot locations, she said something about you having a phobia. What changed your mind?"

Toni took in the rustic porch wrapping around the log cabin lodge and decided to sit on a rocking chair. There was nothing else to sit on except the steps, and they needed a good sweeping. "You asked Bianca about me?"

Hunter leaned against the rough-hewn post holding up the corner of the porch. "I didn't know it was a federal offense."

"Bianca was involved in negotiating a big deal so she sent me." Toni placed her clipboard on her lap and clicked her pen a few times in rapid succession. "I had no choice."

Hunter's big hiking boots filled her line of sight. Her gaze wandered up to where neatly rolled, rag-wool socks met hard, tanned calf muscle with just the right splattering of leg hair—not so much you'd be tempted to take a brush to it, and not so little you'd wonder if he routinely waxed. He wore khaki shorts low around the hips, his green River Runners T-shirt pulled tight against his chest and abs. She'd seen him without a shirt thanks to the picture on the website, so she knew if she poked him it would feel like poking a brick wall. She'd bet dollars to doughnuts he didn't get that hard body in a gym.

When her eyes hit his stubbled chin, she encountered another full-toothed grin. Damn, she hadn't meant to be so obvious.

The slap of an old-fashioned screen door broke the tension. "Sorry." James, Bianca's right-hand man, appeared with two cups of coffee. He handed Toni hers. "That's decaf. Maybe you'll be able to sleep tonight."

Not likely. The woods seemed to inch closer and closer to the lodge. God only knew what roamed out there. She took a sip of bad coffee as James, an ex-model and now her partner in managing the series of shoots, shook Hunter's offered hand. James's dark hair glittered with silver at the temples, his bright blue eyes were full of intelligence and humor, and his build was still trim and muscular, but not like Hunter's. Hunter's muscles were brought about by his life's work, James's by a trainer, weight machines, and a strict diet.

"James, this is Hunter Kincaid. Hunter, James Ness."

"Hunter, good to see you again. Do you want coffee?"

"No, thanks, I brought my own." Hunter's handshake turned into a guy hug, which was weird considering James's sexual preference was in direct opposition to the one Hunter oozed.

Toni caught James's eye with a raised brow. A quick shake of his head confirmed Hunter was, in fact, straight. She'd forgotten James had accompanied Bianca on the scouting trip. The guys had obviously bonded.

Hunter set his travel cup on the table and sat. She finally saw what was written on the side of the cup: "The Way to a Fisherman's Heart is Through His Fly," along with a picture of what looked like an insect with a hook up its butt. Nice.

"I was surprised to find Toni here," Hunter said as he eased back on the chair.

James let out a laugh that grated on her nerves. "No more than she, I presume. Bianca didn't give her much notice. Or should I call it warning? Still, Toni can run the show with one hand cuffed behind her back. We won't have a problem."

"I wasn't worried." Hunter watched her over the rim of his cup as he sipped his coffee, no decaf for him. He slept like a baby every night, no matter how late he drank coffee, but he wouldn't mind spending a few sleepless nights with a beautiful woman.

He'd wondered what Toni looked like since the first day she'd called River Runners in January. Her deep, husky, raspingly sexy voice brought to mind an unbidden picture of a young, blonde, long-legged Kathleen Turner. The New York accent was all wrong, but that do-me voice was right on. Man, was he ever way off base. He found himself eye to eye with the polar opposite of the woman he'd pictured. Toni wore her jet black, shoulder-length hair in pigtails. Instead of making her look like a schoolgirl, it made him wonder what kind of underwear she wore, if she was into bondage, or if she just dug the whole collar-and-cuff thing for fashion's sake, and it had him searching all exposed skin for ink. When he didn't see any, he thought about putting himself in the position to do a full body search.

Checking his dive watch, Hunter looked around for the models he'd promised his brothers they'd be working with when they signed on as guides. That was an ingenious idea if he did say so himself. By bringing Trapper and Fisher along, he not only got free guides and someone to distract Bianca, who, on their week-long outing, had been determined to share a sleeping bag with him, but supplied a physician and legal help if necessary. Since his brothers had plenty of vacation time racked up, they jumped at the chance to spend a week escorting ten models through the mountains and down the Middle Fork of the Salmon River in the Sawtooth Recreation Area. Hunter could have gotten his brothers to pay for the privilege, but he hadn't pushed it since Bianca Ferrari, the owner of Action Models, had paid top dollar for his services. "My guides, Trapper and Fisher, will be here any minute for the barbecue and to meet your group."

Toni flipped through the pages stuck in her

skull-and-crossbones stenciled clipboard, which, if he wasn't mistaken, was shaped like a coffin. The clasp was a bat forged from what looked like pewter with onyx stones for eyes. "I've called a 9:00 a.m. meeting tomorrow, and then the models can spend the rest of the day getting acclimated."

Hunter stopped staring at the clipboard and shrugged, trying not to envision what that bat would look like tattooed on Toni's lower back, its wings spanning her small waist. "We can take a short rafting trip and have a picnic down by my cabin. Bianca had planned a shoot there. There's a nice beach with plenty of space for sunbathing and a regulation sand volleyball court. It'll be an easy trip and will give your group a chance to have a lesson on the rafts."

James nodded. "That sounds great. I'll make arrangements to have a lunch packed for everyone. It's gorgeous, Toni. You're going to love it."

Toni paled, which was hard to do since the girl without makeup was pale enough to qualify for a vampire casting call. She was definitely a candidate for skin cancer. Hunter made a mental note to make sure she wore plenty of sunscreen—he'd be happy to help with the hard to reach spots.

She shook her twin ponytails as her lips drew into a deep frown. "I'm sure you'll have fun. I'm going to stick close to my cabin. I brought plenty of reading material."

Hunter crossed his arms. "You really need the lesson on the raft, and the only way to do that is to get you on the river."

Still shaking her head, Toni backed away. Not a good sign.

"If you want to get out of the sun and hang out in my cabin and read, you're more than welcome to. Put your book in a Ziploc, and bring it along."

Toni held her clipboard tight against her chest. "I won't be joining you."

Hunter moved toward her like he would a spooked horse. "You're not going to supervise the photo shoots?"

"Of course I will. That's my job."

It took him a moment to compute what she'd said since she'd spoken so fast. He tried his most encouraging smile. "Then you'll want to come tomorrow. If not, you're not going to be able to do at least two of the shoots Bianca planned."

Toni stared at James as if she expected him to jump in and save her.

Hunter watched the silent argument going on between them. When no words were spoken, he cleared his throat. "It's perfectly safe. Everyone wears PFDs and even lightweight helmets. We teach you everything you need to know in case you fall in. We show you how to get back into the raft, how to paddle, and what to do if we get stuck. We'll be running down a lazy part of the river tomorrow. I promise there will be no class-five rapids."

When James did nothing more than shrug, she tossed her clipboard on the table and turned on Hunter with both hands on her hips. "What the hell is a PFD?"

"A personal flotation device."

"And why would I need a helmet?"

"The helmet protects you in the rare instance you should fall and hit your head on a rock in the river."

Toni blinked twice and looked as if she needed to sit down and put her head between her legs.

"Are you okay?"

She didn't answer. She just stood there, wide-eyed, looking as if she wasn't breathing. Really not good.

The purr of Trapper's Sequoia broke the silence. The engine died as doors opened and shut.

Hunter looked for help from James who suddenly found his shoes very interesting. Great.

When boots hit the steps, Hunter turned. "Trapper and Fisher, this is James Ness. He's working with Toni Russo, the manager of Action Models in New York." Hunter turned back toward Toni only to find she'd disappeared, coffin clipboard and all.

From *Call Me Wild*

JESSIE'S EYES DARTED FROM ONE NAKED MAN TO THE next. As a sports reporter, she'd done her share of major league locker room interviews over the years, but today it was as if every player knew something she didn't. She couldn't remember when she'd seen more balls—and not the kind you hit with bats, unless you were a jealous husband or wife.

Jessie squared her shoulders and pressed the record button on her iPhone—just for audio—she certainly wasn't going to film this nightmare.

Tonight the men on the team showed as much skin as possible. She hadn't had that problem since she was a cub reporter they thought they could shock easily. Every now and then, she had to teach a rookie a painful lesson, but for the most part, the guys were polite and kept their towels in place. Until today.

Wiping her suddenly clammy hand on her Ally McBeal skirt, at almost six feet tall, Jessie had no problem looking most men in the eye. She zeroed in on the shortstop. "Carter, is that you?" She'd never liked the obnoxious man and figured he was as good a victim as any. Jessie dropped her gaze to his package for a few beats and pointed to his junk hanging unencumbered and proud—well, it had been until a second ago. Now it looked even smaller, having evidently wilted under her scrutiny.

An uncomfortable silence filled the room—at least it was uncomfortable for Carter. His face turned a putrid shade of red, a few shades deeper than his carrot-colored hair, and then his smile crumbled like a winning streak after a team photo on the cover of *Sports Illustrated*.

Jessie kept her focus on Carter. "For a moment there I thought I'd walked in on a peewee baseball team. My mistake."

The team laughed, and when her gaze slid over each player, she found they'd rediscovered their manners and their towels, or at the very least, their jockeys.

Nakedness didn't bother Jessie; lack of respect did. After quieting the team's laughter, she got down to business. She did her interviews and left, wading through the throngs of fans on the way to her Eighth Avenue office.

In the elevator, Jessie wondered what caused the scene in the team's locker room. Maybe it was a full moon? A nudist baseball player's convention? She wasn't sure, but she knew something was wrong. It was as if they were humoring her. The reporter in her sensed a juicy story. She'd do some snooping around after she filed her column.

The newsroom always felt different this time of night. Most of the staff was long gone, and a quiet settled over the usually insane place. There were no clacking keyboards, no raucous conversation, no slamming of the editor's door. Jessie dumped her messenger bag on her desk, tossed an old Starbucks cup into the trash, and tried to ignore the itchy feeling crawling up the back of her neck. Something was off.

Looking through her game notes, she checked her stats. Her memory had never failed her before, but she wasn't about to chance screwing up. The readers of her column and blog knew the stats almost as well as she did, which was saying something. She played the interviews she'd recorded, still trying to ignore that niggling feeling, and wrote her story, leaving out the part where the team lost their shorts, jockstraps, and manners, and filed it well before her deadline.

Spinning her chair toward the window, she stared out over Eighth Avenue. She supposed she could go home, but thanks to the coffee and the win, she was too hyped to sleep. She picked up her phone and called her best friend Andrew in LA.

"Hey, sugar," his deep voice came through the phone. "What's up?"

Jessie leaned back in her chair. "Good, you're alone."

"How do you know?"

"You never call me sugar when you have a girlfriend around."

"You caught me. Nothin' personal, but most women don't believe my best friend is female and that at least one of us is not secretly in love with the other. I've found it easier not to mention you are."

"Not mention I'm what?"

"A woman."

"You're kidding." Jessie twisted in her chair until her back cracked. For once she was glad she didn't have a social life. No dating, no explanations. Then again, no dating, no boyfriend. No boyfriend, no sex. Yeah, that last one was a real bitch. Jessie didn't miss having boyfriends, she did, however, miss sex. A lot.

Andrew continued. "They assume you're a guy, so if I were to call you sugar, they'd wonder if I was bi."

"I'll bet. I guess that's one of the downsides of dating."

"Sugar, all you see are the downsides." Andrew cleared his throat. "What are you doing? I thought you'd be writing your column. I caught the end of the game."

Thank God he changed the subject. Smart man. Jessie twirled around in her chair. "It's filed."

"Okay, so cross off writer's block. What's the problem?"

"What do you mean?"

"Don't give me that. Something's wrong. What is it?"

Jessie shook her head, "Probably nothing. I'm just overreacting." She should be used to Andrew's hyper-sensitive, highly accurate, best friend ESP.

Andrew remained quiet, which made her nervous.

"Fine, I went into the locker room for interviews, and every last player lost his shorts. They were playing a trick or a game, and I was the only one not in on it."

"And what'd you do?"

"I told Carter that I thought I'd walked into a peewee team's locker room. It'll take him a few weeks to heal from the wound to his manhood. For such a big prick, who knew his would be so little?"

"You're skating on thin ice, Jess."

"Enough about me. What's up with you? How's work?"

"It's a soap opera, but it pays the bills."

Jessie spun her chair around and clicked on her email, sifting through the trash while she and Andrew spoke. She still couldn't believe her best friend since freshman year at Columbia was writing for a soap opera, even if the money was damn good. Whatever happened to his dreams of writing for film? "Have you been working on your screenplay?"

"Have you been working on your novel? See Jess, two can play that game."

"Hey, I'm living the dream. I'm a sports reporter for the *Times*—I've already achieved my goal. You gave up on yours."

"I didn't give up. I have a day job so I don't have to live in my car while writing my screenplay. I'm an artist, just not a starving one."

Andrew talked about how hard it was to get into the film business. She knew from experience it would take awhile for him to go through his litany of excuses. Instead of wasting her time, she did what every woman was capable of; she multitasked and went through her hundred or so emails. At least by doing that she had a prayer of finding something original and or new, maybe even exciting.

She scrolled through the usual junk—drugs to enhance the size of her nonexistent penis, an ad for dates with naked women. She wondered if it was her androgynous name that brought all this crap to her email box or if everyone got it. She deleted it all without reading, while saying her "uh-huhs."

Jessie flagged the emails from fans of her column and blog, moving them to her file to be answered—an early morning task she did over coffee. She opened an email from her boss, and for the second time that day, wondered if she'd entered an alternate reality.

She pushed suddenly sweaty bangs off her face with a shaking hand and looked around the deserted office. Had she been *Punk'd*? "Oh God."

Andrew stopped kvetching mid-word. "Are you even listening to me?"

She blinked at her computer, and it was still there—an electronic pink slip.

She swallowed hard. "I think I just got downsized." This couldn't be happening to her. She worked all her life for this position—her dream job. She loved it, she was great at it, and now, they were taking it all away.

"What do you mean?"

"Look for yourself." She hit send. "I'm forwarding you an email from my boss." It should have been highlighted in pink. She hadn't heard about any more layoffs. There was no warning. No sign anything was up. Was she the last one to know about her pink slip?

Jessie checked the time stamp. Noon. Her editor must have assigned another reporter to cover the game. No wonder the guys in the locker room had been naked. They obviously hadn't expected her.

She rubbed her stomach. If she'd had some warning, she would never have eaten that second hot dog at the stadium. Gray spots danced on a transparent veil hanging over her computer screen, and she swallowed back the saliva gathering in her mouth—the usual preamble to violent illness. She pulled her trash can out from under her desk just to be safe.

"Oh shit, sugar. I'm so sorry."

"I just signed a two-year lease on my apartment last week." She pressed the heels of her palms against her eyes to keep from crying. "I can't afford my apartment without a paycheck."

"Don't worry. We'll work this out."

Who'd have thought? A pink slip didn't need to be pink to pull the Astroturf right out from under her feet.

—⁓—

Fisher Kincaid gazed across Starbucks, over the top of his *Idaho Statesman* newspaper, at the woman sitting behind her MacBook Air, staring at a blank Word document, and chewing on the cardboard lip of her venti cup. This was the second time he'd seen her today. Since it was barely 7:00 a.m., he hadn't slept with her, and she wasn't a patient, that was notable—even for a city as small as Boise.

"Checkin' out the new customer, Fisher?" Laura, a barista with the voice of an angel and the body of a porn star, handed him his daily refill, which meant it was almost time to leave to make rounds at the hospital.

"I took a run earlier and followed her for five miles." He didn't mention that he'd barely kept up with her.

Laura raised her perfectly plucked eyebrow.

"What was I supposed to do?" Fisher's hands went up—coffee cup and all. "She was in front of me and turned at my usual place by the park."

"Five miles, huh? So that's how you keep in shape." Laura ran a hand down the button band of his shirt, stopping just above his belt buckle, and making her way slowly back up his chest.

Ah, to be twenty again. Those days were long gone, and so were nights with anyone like Laura. She turned her back on him and was already belting out a Lady Gaga tune and hamming it up for the regulars. She spun around, grabbed his free hand, and lifted it high before dancing under it. He set down his coffee and dipped her until her ponytail touched the floor, receiving a round of applause from the crowd.

Fisher pulled Laura up and released her. He nodded toward the woman with the amazing ass and even more impressive stamina he'd followed just that morning. "What's the deal with her?"

"Not sure." Laura wiped the counter, looking at Mac-chick chewing on her cup.

The woman was nervous—the kind of nerves that couldn't be blamed on coffee, even if she'd downed a few venti quads. Her eyes darted around the small store in a sweep of the area, not meeting anyone's gaze, but missing nothing.

Pacific Northwesterners never had a problem looking strangers in the eye. Obviously, the woman wasn't from around here. With her self-imposed isolation and the way she frowned at the copy of the *Times* she'd bought off the rack, Fisher pegged her for a tourist from the east coast.

He hadn't seen her type a word on that computer since he walked in and recognized her, taking in her blank face and her blank screen. He'd said hello to the morning regulars, talked golf with his buddy Dana, and fishing with Alan, as they joked with the baristas and each other. All the while he'd had the distinct feeling he was being watched.

"What's her name?" Fisher asked Laura. If anyone there knew, it would be Laura. She had a great memory for names and drinks.

"Jessica. The two of you have a drink in common, but she likes her venti Americano with sugar-free vanilla instead of a half cup of sugar, and she doesn't bring in her cup for the discount."

"I don't do it for the discount; I just hate cold coffee."

He threw his arm around her shoulder. "And I love the way you always heat up my cup—it keeps my coffee hot longer."

Laura tilted her head toward him. "Too bad the only person getting hotter than your coffee is me. Yeah, hot, bothered, just sayin'."

Fisher stepped away as he watched Jessica open the *Times* to the sports page and scowl. Not many women he knew went right to the sports without first checking out the front page and the lifestyle section. Hell, most women he knew never made it to the sports page at all. That's why he hadn't had to buy a paper in ages. He usually found it littering a table just waiting for the next guy to read.

Steph, the manager, sauntered out from the back of the store, "Hey, Fisher. What are you still doing here? You're running late today."

He checked his watch. Damn, she was right. Heading toward the door, he waved good-bye to the baristas, gave Steph a wink, and walked straight into Jessica. His arms went around her as her body slammed into his. He instinctively tightened his hold, drawing her close, doing his best to keep them from falling, as he struggled to catch his balance without spilling his coffee all over her.

Her solid muscles vibrated with what seemed like barely contained indignation. She was tall, just a few inches shorter than him, and at six feet three inches, it was unusual for him to be eye-to-eye with a beautiful woman. She was lean with sharp angles, sinewy muscles, and what looked like keen intelligence, once you got past the pissed-off, icy glare. Even her expressions were hard. The only things soft about her were the breasts pillowed against his chest.

Her deep brown eyes were shot with specks of gold and blasted insults loud enough to be heard without speaking.

"I'm sorry." Fisher did his best to steady her, moving his hand to her small waist. No hint of softness there either.

She jerked away as if he'd zapped her with a defibrillator.

"Easy, I was just trying to make sure you were steady on your feet."

She grabbed a handful of her long chestnut hair and tossed it over her shoulder. It was not the usual look-at-me hair flip. No, hers was pure exasperation, not a come-on, which was a damn shame even *with* her prickly attitude. "I thought this was a coffee shop, not a dance club."

Fisher did his best to squelch his urge to smile. "Coffee's a requirement, dancing is optional." He took a deep breath and caught her scent. It was somehow familiar, but unknown, arousing without being overbearing, light and a little dark at the same time. Captivating.

"Obviously not for me." Jessie had spent the last half hour watching this guy and wondering what the odds were of running into the man again after he'd followed her on her morning run. It had damned near killed her to outpace him.

His untamed white-blond hair curled over his collar and looked as if it had been gelled and slicked back in a vain attempt to rein in the wild curls—at least temporarily. His bright green eyes were clear and crisp as the high mountain lake she and Andrew used to hike to. He was at least six three, and ripped in all the right places. He looked like a surfer doing a really bad job of impersonating a professor.

In the half hour she'd been at Starbucks, she'd watched him schmooze every female barista and customer, and most of the males too. Oh yeah, she knew his type. He was the guy who spends half his time working on his tan and the other bleaching his teeth, all the while living in his mother's basement.

Jessie gave him the Bronx stare, the one that deflated a professional athlete's ego faster than you could say Goodyear Blimp, only to be met by a grin—a dimple bracketing one side of his mouth and a Tic Tac commercial smile. Crap, the guy must be thick too.

"If you're uncomfortable dancing here we can go to Humpin' Hannah's or Shorty's."

Jessie struggled to keep from rolling her eyes. "Not interested, but thanks anyway." She was surprised to see his smile widen.

"Okay, then. I guess I'll see you around."

"Not if I see you first."

He shot her a wink before he turned toward the door. His smile hadn't dimmed one little bit. Yeah, he was definitely not a member of Mensa. Maybe he had processing problems. He'd figure out that he'd been turned down sometime in the middle of next week.

Acknowledgments

I'd love to tell you I wrote this book all on my own, after all, part of the writer's mystique is the solitary life we live. Well, for me at least, the solitary part is a load of bunk. For me, it takes a village to make a book. Here are some of the people who have helped me:

I'm lucky to have the love and support of my incredible family. My husband, Stephen, my children, Tony, Anna, and Isabelle, who are my favorite people to hang out with. Alex Henderson and Jessye and Dylan Green, whom I love like my own kids. All of them make me laugh, amaze me with their intelligence and generosity, and make me proud every day.

My parents, Richard Williams and Ann Feiler, and my stepfather, George Feiler, who always encouraged me, and continue to do so.

My wonderful critique partners Laura Becraft and Deborah Villegas. They shortened my sentences, corrected my grammar, and put commas where they needed to be. They listened to me whine when my muse took a vacation, gave me great ideas when I was stuck, and answered that all-important question: Does this suck? They helped me plot, loved my characters almost as much as I did, and challenged me to be a better writer. They are my friends, my confidantes, and my bullshit meters.

I owe a debt of gratitude to their families, who so

graciously let me borrow them during my deadline crunch. So, to Robert, Joe, Elisabeth, and Ben Becraft, and Ruben, Alexander, Donovan, and Cristian Villegas, you have my thanks and eternal gratitude.

I'd also like to thank my writing friends who are always there when I need a fresh eye or a sounding board—Grace Burrowes, Hope Ramsay, Susan Donovan, Mary Freeman, R. R. Smythe, Margie Lawson, Michael Hauge, and Christie Craig.

My dear friends, which include Laura Becraft, Deborah Villegas, Amy Greene, Anne Burger, and Ginger Francis—who have given me more love, laughter, and support than I ever knew existed. I'm so blessed.

I wrote most of this book at the Mt. Airy, Maryland, Starbucks, and I have to thank all my baristas for keeping me in laughter and coffee while I camped out in their store. I also need to thank my fellow customers who have become wonderful friends: Cory, Melissa, Liz, Barbara, Mike, Teresa, Jerry, Anne, and Joni.

As always, I want to thank my incredible agent, Kevan Lyon, for all she does, and my team at Sourcebooks—the cover artists for the beautiful job they did, and my editor, Deb Werksman, for all her insight, direction, and enthusiasm.

About the Author

Robin Kaye is a professional writer and winner of the Romance Writers of America Golden Heart award for her first novel, *Romeo, Romeo*. Her romantic comedies feature sexy, nurturing heroes and feisty, independent heroines. She lives with her husband and three children in Mt. Airy, Maryland.